THE COMPLETE
ACCOMPLICE

STEVE AYLETT

THE COMPLETE
ACCOMPLICE

STEVE AYLETT

ONLY AN ALLIGATOR
THE VELOCITY GOSPEL
DUMMYLAND
KARLOFF'S CIRCUS

THE COMPLETE ACCOMPLICE

REVISED ACCOMPLICE SERIES, COLLECTED, 2010
AUTHOR'S PREFACE COPYRIGHT 2010
INTRODUCTION COPYRIGHT 2010

ISBN: 978-0-9565677-0-3

scargardenmedia@yahoo.co.uk

INTRODUCTION

For me, there is only one outstanding living English absurdist, in the great tradition of Sterne, Firbank, Richardson or William Burroughs, and that's Steve Aylett. He sees the world in those same strangely consistent terms and needless to say doesn't take its pretensions and ambitions hugely seriously. Some of Aylett's funniest work can be found in these wonderful Accomplice novels which are at last back in print, demonstrating his magnificent talent, his extraordinary imagination and precise, original prose.

When I came across Aylett's work ten years or more ago I was genuinely disappointed, filled with regret that I no longer had a magazine in which to publish and publicise him and his work. It isn't every day I have this feeling. Too often the books I see are what I generally call 'xeroxes' - effectively copies of copies of copies of other people's novels. It doesn't matter which genre the writers have chosen, whether western, romance, science fiction or 'literary', their books offer a thoroughgoing sense of *déjà vu*. Their characters, stories and backgrounds have a familiarity about them which is matched by their over-familiar prose styles. Not so with Aylett, whose freshness and originality I welcomed with delight and considerable relief. His talent continues to exhilarate me and I look forward to his work as I anticipate few others. The Accomplice sequence, in particular, holds a special place in my affections.

In these novels Aylett is at his ebullient, inventive best, his talent concentrated and expansive at the same time. If that seems contradictory it's because I'm talking about his prose on one hand and his ideas on the other. It was a joy for me to come upon a writer with a style so distinctive and whose ideas are so exuberantly fresh. I found him a joy and set about buttonholing the world and telling it to read him. This was how I felt when I first read *The Eccentricities of Cardinal Pirelli* or *Titus Groan*, the difference being that, unlike Firbank or Peake, when I read them, Aylett was near the beginning of his career and I could (and do) look forward to many more books by him.

Everything about Aylett was fresh. Even the map at the beginning of the first Accomplice book *Only An Alligator* promised something different. From the Awkward Forest down to the Juice Museum everything about it spoke of an author who had abandoned genre altogether, having parodied and lampooned hardboiled detective stories and science fiction hilariously in earlier work like *Slaughtermatic* and *Atom*. My kind of author, in fact, who, after showing what he could do with genre and won his authority, produced work which, like Ballard's or Peake's, was immediately identifiable as that of an idiosyncratic, highly individual writer who took almost nothing seriously except his craft. He had become, if you like, his own genre.

I suppose if Accomplice resembles any genre at all it is closer to the horror story, since the city has humans above and demons below and the two interact, but it is like no horror story you have ever read before and unlikely to appeal to the average *Buffy* or *Elm Street* fan. Although the demons and their deeds are hugely inventive and often pretty grisly, their effect is essentially comic rather than terrifying, the creation of a genuinely fresh imagination as are Aylett's characters – Barny, Sweeney, Gregor and the rest, all of whom would be eligible to join Maurice Richardson's Surrealist Sporting Club (cf *The Exploits of Engelbrecht*) or perhaps hang out with Pere Ubu or even some of the great Boris Vian's characters from *I Spit on Your Graves* or *Heartsnatcher.*

Probably Vian, that master of French absurdism, who read science fiction and noir detective novels, played the jazz trumpet and died of a heart attack when watching a movie of one of his books, is the closest comparison we can make, for Aylett has a similarly sardonic view, an unwillingness to compromise at any level, a steady trust in his own strange vision of our world (if it is our world) and its inhabitants, a sardonic inability to force that vision into any mold other than the one he has invented for himself.

Aylett is alone amongst the published writers of his generation in maintaining a steady integrity, refusing compromise and earning the respect of his readers through his persistent consistency, his refusal to meet anyone halfway. He is the kind of writer who, having earned that respect, will continue steadily to gather readers through his career. Those readers, if they are anything like me, will use their enjoyment of books like the Accomplice sequence to determine who they are likely to get on with, just as readers of my generation used the older writers I've mentioned here to decide if they would get on with new acquaintances. That readership is never going to run into massive figures because his books are the very opposite of the crass best sellers we so frequently see in the lists. But it is a discerning, slow-growing readership which, once it has read and enjoyed Aylett, is never going to desert him. I hope I'm addressing that kind of reader here. If I am, I can assure you that you're going to enjoy the ride and that you have much, much more to look forward to. You might find you'll want to do what I usually do, which is to finish the sequence and go straight back to the beginning to read them over again. But whether you're a regular Aylett fan or a new one, I guarantee you'll find nothing quite like this anywhere else in contemporary fiction. Enjoy!

Michael Moorcock
Lost Pines, Texas
February 2010

PREFACE

Converge upon the truth any faster than the growth of a lime tree and people may suspect you actually want to know. At school I had trouble with geometry - parts of my body angled off into a dimension invisible from there. Recently I saw one of my childhood arms emerging from the corner of a brownstone building, very briefly.

Amid the deciduous tiki and filigreed exotica of an already-changed climate, Accomplice is a hallucinatory narrative gizmo of a town which, like the actions of its inhabitants, is both tangibly limited and seemingly without economy. It works by the souping together of the incredibly light, the meaningful and the extreme to make a surface as apparently random as reality. Its protagonists are different from my other characters in that they are a group of friends living life just as they find it. They're reactive or indifferent and rarely initiate or incite any correction. Their top-of-the-line lethargy, oblivious flaunting and effortless affront are of less consequence than those occasions when birds abandon the assigned songs and begin chirping at random.

Barny is a rare innocent, unpoliticized and shielded only by translucent and guttering luck. Around him operates a codified console of slobs, dolls, zombies, dogs, fruit, effigies, roots, hedge saints and jesters, while dark infraction alchemists rewrite mass emotion with all the barefaced slanting of treaty language. Unlike real life, most Accomplicers are aware of and ridiculously articulate about their own delusions, but like real life, they don't change.

There persists a notion that humanity will learn lessons as a result of the upcoming collapses and that human denial has a limit (a notion mentally sustainable only because it doesn't). In fact the best we find at land's end is a society where the considered life plan is still a choice of which exalted con-game to fall for. Demons who are merely throwing scares into the bone-idle come to realise that human beings, especially *en masse*, are worse by far than any demon. The devil is a crowd.

Steve Aylett, 2008

ONLY AN ALLIGATOR

"Woken by searchlights in a soaked field,
I began to wish I had never met the mime."

- Ben Rictus
My Crunchy Past

1

THE IDIOT

Enthusiasm and coherence don't always go together

Maybe it was the mascara in the spaniel's eyes, or just dumb luck. Either way Barny was playing blithely with fire. As they passed the scary glare of the creepchannel entrance the dog began laughing so hard the mascara was blotching with tears and Barny knelt to check it out. Behind him, sour light needled from the creepchannel mouth like a drench of ice and vinegar.

The dog Help had always been a strange one. He could shuffle all his fur down to one end of his body, sit upright in a chair like a human, whistle after women, and attack anyone who started singing in a sprightly manner. He'd clamp his jaws and hold on, looking up at you silent and rueful of this unwanted intimacy. His ears turned blue and flowed like water. The butter-wouldn't-melt mischief of his species had reached its pinnacle with Help. So it was no great surprise to Barny when he slipped his leash and did a runner into the stewing vortex.

Kicking through emeralds, Barny ascended the little slope, passed a beached and tilted grandfather clock and entered the demonic transit system. Of course he was instantly assailed by searing pain, stickled spinelight and corrosive etheric bile, but he was thinking about his dad's birthday. Pa Juno had been complaining about some undulant psychic parasite in his shack. Classic poltergeist activity and everyone was sure it was the ghost of his hair come back to mock him. Pa didn't go for that but Barny thought if he could help snare it using a Spitain Box or something, domestic order could be restored. Barny wasn't one to push out his belly and claim it was a stormfront - that kind of public mischief he left to Prancer Diego. Barny knew trouble was already in the mix, and had said so to Edgy one time. They'd been browsing in the Shop of a Thousand Spiders and Barny picked up a Vanta grid, which closed on his hand and forced a volley of curses from his gob. It was amid this volley that he conveyed the notion of trouble being in the mix. Edgy tore the shirt off a passing customer and offered it to Barny as a bandage, at which the customer barrelled into them with both fists in front of him like diesel buffers. A while later Barny and Edgy were shambling down the street like shattered puppets, but still Edgy was a happy man, gustily breathing the warm Accomplice air. 'Head securities, Bubba,' he said. 'That's the bottom line. Adopt a head. It's a stellar choice. Mine's right there on the register.'

Barny glanced at Edgy's head, thinking it looked like a hairy knife. 'Do you mean your ideas?'

'No - the head, Bubba, the head, the meat. You give a trade description of your head with its age and condition and it all goes into the index, which everyone ignores. Only a madman would check the prices. I can't believe anyone knows about it but me. Ah, what a beautiful day Bubba.' He squinted up at the trees. 'I doubled my money the first six weeks. And I spent the whole of that six weeks crying, and rubbing my face.'

'What's good about that?'

'I told you, I *doubled* my money. You can still make a bundle in this town if you keep your cheeks and so on in good condition.'

But as ever in trying to help a friend Edgy had made a sacrifice - what with the damage to his nasal septum from the enraged customer, his entire head was now devalued. So Edgy was still ensconced at the Bata Motel, hanging on to his room by pretending to be a ghost. And it seemed to Barny that with this sort of stuff occurring without provocation, trouble needn't be sought out. All he wanted was to care for the winged and stepping animals of the earth, and be happy.

Barny's distraction ended when, slipping in tubeway sputum, he couldn't get his hands out of his pockets fast enough to break his fall - he slammed his skull on the creepchannel's icy floor. *Pain can't be wounded*, as Violaine said, and here it blended with the howling atmosphere.

But as Barny's eyes focused, he saw padding across the frost a pair of beautiful white feet - there was a girl, ducking under spite icicles and looking back once as Barny sat up. Where had he seen her before? She climbed into a phosphene blot which showed intermittent flayed shavings of a hallway, cupboards, filigree. Barny looked around him at the pulsing vessels of the subway wall, which were encrusted with blown clocks, lawyers and other detritus. The blot had faded like a bruise by the time he stood.

Up ahead was a sunken car, poison drumming its roof. Turns in the tunnels showed frying glimpses of exit domains. Rigging and rind swayed from the ceiling. Barny picked up a steel head bucket and thought of taking it home as a feedbox for the leopard. That little cutie had swiped him hard in the chest the other day, bless him.

But he dropped it when a tumble of bugs caught his attention.

They were rolling out of a valve, glittering down the wall and across the tunnel floor, where they pooled around a chest-of-drawers in the shadows. Drawing closer in the yellow light, Barny found an eye amid the flow, blinking. Below this was a rail of teeth. Stepping back, he detected the form of some kind of crocodilian caught in the melted pizza cheese of the channel wall. How long had this poor snapper been here? Barny tore aside the thick webbing, scalding his hands. 'You're sick,' he said, getting a good look at the reptile, and took it around the middle, dragging it off the shelf. Nerve-wire stretched behind it, snapping. 'You're a crazy gator,' whispered Barny, setting it down. 'An eight-footer. Wait till the guys at the office get a loada you.' The gator thrashed sluggishly as he secured the leash, but seemed to be coming around.

When Barny emerged from the creepchannel all begrimed with gore and apocalypse dust, seaweed hanging from his ears, the predator was slowly regaining its curiosity. The dog Help was capering round a nearby tree. Barny was one pest up on the deal. What a find!

'Is a thing most fully itself in the darkness or the light?'

In a vaulted cave the size of an aircraft hangar, Sweeney strummed his white gills thoughtfully. His fiddling imperial exoskeleton was bound by tender gut to a giant hull seat from which he was released when digestion allowed. A network of coaxial plasm cables fanned from the throne to phantom bandwidths. Sweeney thought about umbilical soda and painted bones and revisionists cooked in their shells as he gazed about him at the wall-gallery of lank, rag-like faces and the immense walls riddled with channel vents like withered wasp-cells. Nerve storms crackled in the altitudes of the roofing. 'I say: why add to something that's fine to begin with.'

The cook approached down a fatty ramp. Sweeney noted without optimism that he was spattered with green paint and carrying something angular on a giant dish. The cook placed it on a side table. When Sweeney blinked, little jaws flashed together instead of eyelids. 'What the hell do you call this?'

'I call it "Replacement Alligator of Boxes, in Green", for Your Majesty's pleasure.'

'Well there's little enough pleasure to be had here, it's made of boxes, man, boxes. What's this? "Wheaties." And none in there. What's the meaning of it all?'

'I feel it symbolises the power of casual disregard. A cool man is different from a cool day. For a start, he's smaller. Then there's the matter of acceptance -'

The cook's eyes boiled and sputed. His gurgling face fell like a hangnail as shrike branches rushed upward, splitting him like sliced bread. Then he exploded with cackling anatomies which shot legs and fiddled his pieces away into the corners. Sweeney was already calling down the Ruby Aspict, a bloody jewel which lowered through thunder. Veins and heart-rind made spirals in its slow rotation. 'Show me what happened to the gator,' he said thoughtfully. The crimson compound eye flooded the cavern with arterial light as Dietrich Hammerwire entered. 'What do you make of this?' Sweeney asked him.

Dietrich raised his wet anvil head. In the Aspict deeps a figure picked through an upper creepchannel. 'Not much meat on him.'

'Nothing was triggered, Dietrich - no alarm shrikes, no nerve snares - look at him.'

They regarded the moon-faced moron calling 'Help!' in an inquiring, sing-song voice. 'Old shaman's trick, that cry. Distress camouflage.'

'Yes, no real fear in it.' Sweeney sat back and clattered a mandible down his ribs like a stick down a picket fence. 'Well this fellow entered the channel and improved the shining hour by stealing my lunch. You know how bland souls are these days, I'm having to marinate them in the nerve nets for days to give them any flavour at all. They haven't even the imagination to be horrified half the time.'

'We should involve their legs a lot more. People don't like their legs interfered with.'

'You and your legs. Seriously, I was looking forward to it - that particular channel had the ambitions of a million paralegals flash-frozen into a stain in the walls, you can just taste it can't you, a reptile caramelised in that nightmare? Well, let's get our thief a name shall we.'

Barny's name chimed from the guts of the Aspict.

Sweeney knew he needn't fear this Barny Juno. He had a specific vision of the man, or beast, he should fear. It had been foretold by good old Bingo Violaine years ago. Sweeney had been eating the philosopher's brain from his head and as the lower functions collapsed Violaine had begun yammering loudly through a heavy nosebleed. Dietrich was there and he and Sweeney often joked about Violaine's predictions, until they started coming true. This was the problem with tilling through someone's synaptic soup - the soul's a thread through the head and under threat it'll squirm into itself like a burning hair strand, ending as an untraceable atom without ego, breath or danger. Nobody else's business anyway. The solvent stench of old resentments will distract while you pack up and shoot into the drywall. Violaine survived in this form - he's telling you so.

'There we are,' said Sweeney, ratchetting his shoulders in a shrug. 'This Barny fellow, you'll have to pop above and eat the cob-webbed cherries of his heart, I suppose. Bring the reptile here and do a sort of spangly tumbling act when you arrive, for m'pleasure.'

'Me? Not Trubshaw?' Dietrich ventured, thinking of the chaos above. 'Or Kermit?'

'Skittermite's stuck in a drain and Trubshaw's a monster.'

'That's what I mean,' protested Dietrich. 'I know he is.'

'You're the fiend for the job Dietrich, and you're starting to annoy. So get out - and take the hanging loops of your venom delivery system with you.'

2

DEAD LETTERS

To smoke a cigar while being tortured is the ultimate gesture

Sweating like a bastard, Gregor jogged heavily up the wooden ramp, pressed himself against the front door and whispered Barny's name. The door opened and Barny stood there, next to the lion. The animal was doing the very snaggle-toothed motion of his mouth and head which had inflicted so much turmoil on Gregor's pants since its rescue from Karloff's Circus a while ago. 'We're in for a storm,' said Barny almost inaudibly amid the chatter of monkeys. He began laughing in the delight of his activities. 'I'm rearing cochineal beetles on prickly pear cactus to produce the red dye used in campari. Edgy's idea.' The aspirin eyes of lizards winked in the swirling dark behind him. 'Cash cow. And the geckos love 'em.'

A rotund pebble of a man, Gregor whimpered a little, then pointed to what he believed were the external facts but which were actually those ensconced behind his eyes. 'Barny. You can't keep this lion here.'

'Doesn't it have integrity then.'

'Integrity? The point is it's a mammal and I know you understand that. There's just no telling. Look *out* you bastard.'

'Calm down Gregor - rest on its head now.'

'No fear.'

'Eh?'

'I said I'm damned if I'll "rest on its head" as you claim. Are you stupid? *Mad*?'

'Don't follow you, Round One.'

'Don't call me that. Oh, I'm in *hell*.'

'There, there.'

'Get away from me.'

'I was just putting my arm round you.'

'Like hell you were. I just don't know what to say about you standing there in front of the lion and all.'

'So what. In his mouth a body tastes much the same as it would in yours.'

Gregor didn't know whether to ram or run. As a distraction from his woes he found that Barny held his own hazards.

'Pop round the back, Gregor, there's something that'll interest you.'

'He'll drag me apart,' Gregor added as Barny closed the door on the lion, and they walked around the side of the house.

'Just waiting for Golden Sid then I'm off. What you doing here anyway?'

'Nothing really, got a little problem,' Gregor muttered. 'I thought if I went for an early run, people would see me and think I was a healthy man who knew what he was doing.'

'We can go in to work together then,' said Barny as they entered the half of the perspex hothouse which had once been the home of a green iguana called Mister Spiderman. This web-throated lovely had gone to heaven and Barny had buried him in a ceremony which caused outrage among the local doll men and powderheads. 'I'm damned,' Barny had said, 'if I'm going to fire Mister Spiderman out of a cannon.' Protesters had turned up at the funeral and Barny's picture ended up in the paper because his trousers fell down as he read the eulogy.

'There he is,' he said now, gesturing to the reptile on the terrarium floor. The gator turned half around, hissed at Gregor, and closed its mouth with a wet slap. 'The food rips as he shuts his gob. Look at him, sleek as a Maserati. I'm gunna need bigger reptile lights for this charmer.'

'Barny? How can you think this is normal?'

'I don't know, was I wrong? If I'm wrong I stand corrected I suppose, ha ha.' Barny crouched to attach a leash to the reptile. 'Anyway, think of it as a dinosaur. They're great value, Gregor. What did Violaine say - "Everything is an advantage to the indiscriminate".'

'It's nothing like a dinosaur,' Gregor groaned. 'I wish it was.'

'Everyone loves dinosaurs,' said Barny, not hearing him.

'Not like me. I *love* them.'

'We all do, Gregor.'

'You're not listening, Barny, this is the problem I mentioned earlier. I really - you know - *really* love them. I mean, tented trousers and all.'

'What?' Barny straightened up.

'You know.'

'Tented trousers you said.' Barny stared at him a while. 'And you're casting asparagus at *me*? Dinosaurs? You'll achieve a reputation you bastard. I don't understand. D'you even care if they're male or female?'

Gregor hung his head, gloomily abashed. 'Not really.'

'They're *dinosaurs*, Gregor. Look, I don't want to continue with this, it's planting a pain behind my face. See a doctor or something, you see? Here's Golden Sid at last. Don't say any more.'

A man like a startled ant in buff overalls, Golden Sid went the gangplank route around the house, flinching at every screech and wall-bang from within. A lot of the houses around here were built on stilts due to the floods of snot which roared down the street from the chef school. 'Hey, Sid,' Gregor muttered as they passed, and Sid gave a weak smile, pathetically grateful for any encounter which did not end in violence. Pop-eyed and bespectacled, he tarried on the yard platform until Barny, Gregor and the alligator had shuffled away into the street, then he leant against the door, breathing deep as before a dive, eyes closed.

He threw open the door and entered, already screaming.

As the gator wallowed across the hot tarmac, Gregor chatted absently about tomorrow's ballgame but he was clearly distracted. The day was humid and fertile, masonry flaking amid hard plants and salty air. A Gubba Man stood on a corner, a black nebula of ants glistering its face. Stray rib spirals stood here and there, the result of stray boneseed spores.

Passing through the centre of town, Barny and Gregor led the gator across the main square. Here was a statue of Bingo Violaine on the site of the bandstand where the philosopher died, inconveniently clawed underground by a white devil. An inscription on the plinth read: TRY TO ACCEPT THAT INTELLIGENCE IS ABOARD. Other folk on their way to work never gave it a glance but Barny liked sometimes to climb the figure and swing on its punching arm. From here he could see the distant bone wall, the swamplands, turquoise glimpses of ocean. The ashes of a tailor gusted from a darkened patch near the steps of the mayoral palace, the shadow of last night's reveries.

All this roofed a blind underworld of poison light which nobody recalled until they blundered in. The creepchannel network was side-on to sight, a bandwidth away, sick and aglow. Demons blurred through it like subway trains going elsewhere. The sundrenched land above was small fry.

Down an alley and through a side door - Barny, Gregor and the gator descended iron steps to the sorting office. It was a low-ceilinged basement, slick with condensation. From above, a delivery chute fed the long black tongue of the sorting table, which bisected the chamber and could not be ignored. One dirty lightbulb hung into this wedge-shaped cell, picking out a few bony chairs. Shelves of plate fungus held impoverished ornaments to the wall, withered attempts to make the place more homey. The ornaments, too, were made of fungus and the only way to personalise them was to dope the spores with cells from the workers' bodies. It was similar to the boneseed principle used in Accomplice architecture. But the figurines produced were of such intensely subconscious significance to one and all that they became yet another subject to evade. On the opposite wall a flat fungus like a massive starfish spread from corner to corner, pullulating at the centre. When I say that this was the drinks dispenser, you will understand the state of despairing extremity persisting in that place.

When Barny's co-workers clapped eyes on the reptile it was like he'd hefted in an outsize flounder and whapped it across their faces. They stood in gratifyingly varied stances of appalled incomprehension and to Barny's loving eyes their opinions unfurled like flowers.

'It's moving.'

'Doomed - I'm scared I'm -'

'The weirdest since the landcrab.'

'Look - he's saying it's his friend.'

'No stopping him.'

'Like he doesn't have a choice.'

'I can't believe he doesn't know.'

'Got a crazy man on our little hands.'

'It's real. I've just understood.'

'Keep him talking and I'll throw the lid.'

'Village idiot with snarling trumpcard.'

'I'll have the roast beef platter.'

'Repeatedly fails in the harmless department.'

BB Henrietta squinted back and forth from Barny to the reptile. 'You don't give up, do you? This fucking animal?'

'You need to take a nap, Bubba,' said Edgy, standing like a ragged exclamation mark. 'We'll take care of this little problem.'

'I found him in a loada slime,' said Barny, looking proud. 'I'm a lucky bum, I know it.'

'I'll throw the lid now,' whispered Fang, and tried flinging a hubcap at Barny, but the boxing gloves he wore hindered the procedure and it clanged straight at the floor near the stone steps. Fang looked gloomy, and sat down at the sorting table.

'A reptile can be powerful-hostile to your passerby, Bubba.'

'I told him already,' said Gregor, lumbering in with a pile of timber. 'But I'm starting to get used to it. And you can bet the Blaze'll get off on the monster.'

Barny hadn't thought of his girlfriend's response. She'd think he was reckless and love it. He felt another door slam on clear understanding.

'It's low to the ground, Bubba.'

'I know, like a drop-head. They're slower and less aggressive than crocs.'

'Bless. And the tail's sorta squared off, Bubba, top and sides. Almost looks mechanical.'

'The tail's perfect, of course. It downright makes me want to cry.'

'All right,' said BB Henrietta, holding up her hands. 'You guys can stand there crying about the shape of that animal's tail as long as you like. I have a job to do.'

'Mister Spiderman was a herbivore - I'll need to sort a diet for Mister Newton here. And I'm making a diagram of his head.'

'Good for you, a diagram,' said Gregor, opening the furnace.

'I foresee no ordinary diagram, Round One. It'll show the charm of the skull and inner nostril circumstances for everyone to understand. You see, the head's flat like a pike. The gator has one of the longest brains in nature.'

'Longest,' said Edgy. 'Did you say "Mister Newton" before?'

'I said so because that's the creature's full name.' Barny tethered the reptile and sat at the sorting table. 'Boy, I've done it now. And I couldn't have without Help.'

'Oh, you mean mascara boy.'

'Mascara?' asked Henrietta, toying with a package.

'Barny's dog wears mascara.'

'How could you do that, Bubba?'

'He doesn't - he says the dog applies it.'

'How?'

'Nobody knows. He's never seen it happen. Who understands the ways of dogs. It's possible Help's some kind of celebrity in the dog world, and has to keep up appearances at all times. Maybe he's a male prostitute. Or perhaps he just likes to look good at all times.'

'He doesn't look good to me.'

'Of course not, BB. But he feels good about himself, and that's what's important. Hey Barny that reminds me - I spoke to my friend who works at the publishers, they're after someone to do a book about dog experiences. I told them to all intents and purposes you are one.'

Past bestsellers from Feeble Champ Books had been an account of fanatical ear-varnishing, *Nothing Sacred*, and a study of man/rhino love, *Never Again*.

'I don't know how to write a book, Edgy,' Barny said.

'I'll ghost it for you.'

'Really?'

'What's not to ghost? I could even add some personal touches - I've had a few dog experiences of my own you know.' Edgy smirked scampishly. 'They're thinking of calling it *My Dog Friends*. There could be a rich oil painting on the cover of me smiling with my arm round the shoulders of an alsatian, something like that.'

'Why'd they want a picture of you?' asked Gregor, sitting down.

Edgy muttered to Barny, and took him aside for a word.

'Listen Barny,' he whispered. 'Here's the main business. The Round One's got a problem. With dinosaurs.'

'He was telling me about it, I didn't know what to say.'

'We can help him.'

'I don't think so. Not this time.'

'He's besotted. He needs to purge it away, express himself by consummating these feelings. I went to Doctor Perfect and pretended to have Gregor's symptoms, okay? He said I was crazy, a bastard, sick, a threat to society. He actually said I reminded him of himself when he was younger. Then he kicked me, over and over and over again, calling me a poison. He said he, er ... "relinquished all responsibility", that was it. Told me to go out and just do whatever I had to do.'

'With a dinosaur? Where?'

'Well, there's the museum.'

'The Juice Museum?'

'No, Bubba, the normal museum, the dry one with the bones. I've seen them in there, big girls too. Hadrosaurs.'

'But they're skeletons, I don't understand. They're *dinosaurs*, Edgy.'

'You bet. I might even have a go at one myself.'

'But that's -'

'Necrophilia I know, but can you see a *live* Tyrannosaur around here Bubba?' He glanced back at Gregor sitting under the bulb, and continued in hushed tones. 'It's lucky Gregor can distinguish between a T-Rex and a gator or we'd maybe have the sickest ever paternity suit on our nervy hands my friend. We need him on form for the game tomorrow. So you, me and Gregor are busting into the museum tonight.'

Barny was about to protest when a tumble of objects crashed down the chute - the stuff already radiated dread and anxiety into the office. Looking down, Gregor seemed about to cry.

It just kept coming, every day. Miscellaneous objects wrapped in paper and card. Magazines. Notes and forms full of writing. But none of it related to anyone here in the basement. Nothing was mentioned but strangers and their obscure affairs. Why were these objects turning up? What did it all mean? And what, above all, was expected of them here?

They had devised a number of means of disposal. Some they burned as they covered their faces with rags. Other stuff they tried to eat. The big objects they sculpted into an angular sentinel in a conical hat, which they pelted with cans until everyone became embarrassed and fell silent. Fang would stuff it all in a car boot and drive it over a cliff. Gregor had taken to baking the things in a high-tech ceramics kiln. He would remove the ingredients before the process was complete and form this mush into a poultice for his arse. Near the cabinet was an 'open corner', a stale etheric fold gaping into seemingly bottomless space - this blot of shadow they called the Drop and it was invaluable, swallowing just about all the stuff they could dump there. But throughout they suspected there was something more specific and important they should be doing with it all, and sometimes, in private, they wept with the build-up of sheer, unspoken stress. At other times one of the group would go into a hysterical screaming jag at the unstoppable flow of material sliding down the chute from above. But they never openly communicated their deepest doubts. Inadequacy, depression and fear of discovery grained the gloomy air.

'Well,' said Edgy, unbuttoning his Hawaiian shirt and fetching the scarrification gear. 'Let's get to work.'

When the Captain entered an hour later, the office had sunk to a level of savage superstition. Edgy was blowing a bone whistle and hanging back from a rawhide cord skewered to the tenting flesh of his chest. Gregor was bent in worship before a papier mache effigy of a normal fella and Barny had begun screaming in a demented way, frightening himself with his intensity. Fang was cooking pasta, an ominous look on his face. Gregor stood to attention with a hysterical giggling which tumbled over into wrenching sobs - he tore aside and hid his face against the wet wall. 'The boys are sorry, Captain,' said BB Henrietta, who was sat at the table wearing a useless wooden helmet. 'They're upset about ... the election. Fang's been told he can't vote because he's all dead and going to slurry.'

In the daylight hours Fang refused to behave like a scary revenant and found it hurtful when certain people still didn't accept him.

'We're all excited about the election, lads,' stated the Captain, frowning. Bloodshot eyes were turning from their inner torment to focus slowly upon him. Gregor had sunk down the wall and clung there like a workhouse orphan. 'But I answer to Mr Gibbon. There are quotas to be filled in this important time and that's what you know. Are those bats?' The Captain framed this as a question though he could see the bats quite clearly near the ceiling. By parsing the data this way he planned to draw the workers out of what appeared to be a back-alley suicide pact and into an informal but constructive dialogue. Though the Captain too was completely in the dark as to the purpose of the office, he was no fool. It took expert management to employ a zombie wearing boxing gloves and get away with it.

'I'm part time here,' said Barny, shuffling forward a little.

'That's right, er, Barny. These bats, boys, now I'm as liberal as the next man of course ...'

'I'm part time here,' Barny choked, grimacing as he approached.

'Yes, yes you are. Now come on, lads - bats I mean now.'

'*I'm part time here!*' Barny shrieked, throwing himself into the Captain's arms and hanging limp, emitting raw sobs like a castaway.

The Captain threw him off. 'Can't you see I don't give a damn about that? I'd prefer to know how these bats got in here. What have you guys been up to?'

'We need them for company, Captain.'

'Well for the sake of all that's pure you can't have a conversation with those mothers can you.'

'We kiss them Captain,' Fang volunteered. 'It gets awful lonely down here.'

'Is that why those wooden chairs are drawn up to the corners?'

'For standing on. Then we purse our lips and kiss those little beauties on their snouts.'

'They enjoy it,' said Gregor. 'They start quivering all over.'

'And staring,' added Fang. 'As if they can't believe their luck.'

'Captain,' sighed Edgy dreamily, squinting slowly aside from his tilted suspension. Dark blood coated his chest. 'Me and the Round One need a half-day tomorrow.'

'For the local semi I suppose,' nodded the Captain, a little uncomfortable. 'Alright. Give 'em hell.'

'You're a good man,' Edgy rasped, and then the skin of his chest broke, allowing him to fall to the concrete floor in a state of total exhaustion.

'I don't need to tell you how to do your jobs,' the Captain stated firmly, ignoring the sudden attentive looks the statement provoked, 'but it's come to my attention that -'

And turning on his heels, he trotted up the stairs and slammed out.

'I wish he wouldn't do that,' muttered Fang. But there was a flood of feeling in the room when they realised that the alligator, sitting utterly still near the shredder, had gone unnoticed and forgotten until the doorslam sent it into a surprised frenzy of thrashing, hissing and quite frank and open biting of three staff members, each of whom screamed at the top of their lungs that there was no saviour local enough to take away this agony.

The leopard sprang upward, swiping, and snagged Sid's trouser leg. The big cat hung a moment, its screech phasing like a race hog, and fell back into the kitchen. Golden Sid clambered on to the rain-lashed roof and dropped the hatch closed, his shredded clothes flying with water. Sobbing and babbling, he stumbled on the teeming slope as a burst of lightning freaked the sky. Something banged on to the roof behind him and he squinted around at a form feathered with shadows, folding into itself and stepping forward. Wings tucked behind a metallic bone soldier hung with surgical tubing. 'Mind if we have a natter,' said the stone beak which prowed from the head's hanging varicose tangle. Sid could tell with a doomed acceptance that this was the sort of over-familiar ghoul who'd think nothing of stabbing you with its chin. On his knees, he watched it approach - a lattice of biological junk barely contained by clawed ribs which blurred and stretched through the rain on his glasses. Then the creature's sternum opened like a wet rose and threw something at him.

Dietrich shook the storm from his plasmic hair and watched the roiling trees as Sid twitched, a nerve cable strung from the centre of his forehead.

3

BONER

The stumbling idiot may evade the traps

Barny and Plantin Edge sauntered through the dark museum, their steps and the slap-shuffle of the gator reverberating down the hallways. Gregor had run ahead to the Cretaceous section.

Rows of cases contained bones as fragile as antique combs.

'Boy, these critters are really thin.'

'They're skeletons Barny, remember? I can't believe you brought the gator here.'

'Don't you think it'll be an education for the lad, seeing his ancestors all done up in scaffolding and so on.'

'Would you be educated? What if your dad was here, all dried out?'

'He'd ask me what the hell I was doing.'

'And what would you learn?'

'Nothing, I admit. You know, my father's got a problem with his hair. It's haunting him.'

'Why, what's the problem.'

'I told you, his hair is haunting him. You know a bit about this stuff Edgy, can you help me pick up an exorcism trap at the Shop tomorrow?'

'I'll tell you what, Bubba,' said Edgy with a touch of reverence, stopping everything. They'd turned a corner to confront the frozen snarl of a stuffed sabre-tooth tiger on a pedestal. 'Maybe there's a lesson here after all.'

'Like what.'

'Stress, Bubba. Remember they always say it's caused by the old "fight or flight" response, which in primitive times was meant to save cavemen from the tigers? But today it's got no outlet, causing ill-health. And that's where you come in, my friend.'

'How.'

'By re-introducing the tiger factor. People round here can't walk the street without the very real terror you'll take one of the big cats for a stroll again. Remember when the lion attacked Dot Spacey at the gas station? He actually laughed at first. And he couldn't molest the vehicles for a whole month afterward. People need a little danger.' They wandered past the skeleton of one of the legendary Steinway Spiders, a ribbed piano with bony legs. 'So they seek it out. You know the Patently Damaging Sports Club? That's the kinda thing I'm talking about. Dangerous activities like, uh … driving a car at top speed while being knifed by a crazy midget. Or slamming your face against a concrete abutment while gulping some kind of venom. Wow, Bubba. I'd give anything to join. But it's exclusive membership, all very shady, you know. You have to wait to be approached by a member who reckons you're the right stuff.'

'I heard Neville Peth's a member. He drove a sort of burning trolley van across a traffic island.'

'Neville Peth? Guess which course of exhaustion he favours.'

'I don't know.'

'He's a financial adviser. Office across from Spacey's station.' In fact Neville Peth was a specialist in dove insurance - Accomplice citizens were regularly injured or killed by small groups of doves. 'You see, Barny? All walks of life. Well, I guess I might let him happen to see what a clumsy risk-taker I can be, eh?'

They stood before a stand bearing a grey pineapple of hard dust. 'What's this?' asked Barny.

'Drylord seed, for court cases. Don't touch it.'

'I've never seen one,' Barny muttered, and tapped it lightly. It released a spuff of dandruff.

'See, Bubba?' Edgy smirked. 'You would have missed that little glory if you'd gone to your parents' tonight. You should get out, see more of the world.' A piercing klaxon alarm exploded through the establishment and Edgy grabbed his arm. 'We're done for. We'll be explaining it all to a judge - *this* one, probably.' He pointed at the egg. 'Run, you idiot.'

'What about Gregor?' asked Barny as they ran, the reptile in their arms like a rolled carpet.

'The Round One can sprint away from anything - it's his special gift.'

The demon perched on the family home like a designer label. Dietrich had learned precious little from the quailing unfortunate on Barny's roof. Normally the shock of fear pushed everything salient from the victim in a gutburst, but this poor guy seemed to have been deliberately conditioned into such a pitch of terror already, the facts emerged in a dribble. Even this sample was mostly incoherent, though Dietrich had established that Barny was due to visit his folks here in the swamp tonight. The only other dreg to come through concerned a rumour. Some jokers in the town had been going on about Barny looking after 'eight hundred eels' in his garden. Apparently they were so insistent about it they even had Barny convinced, in his weaker moments. Eight hundred eels in his garden. And none of this was true. Dietrich looked out across the swamp - an object tangy and steaming like something spilt on a kitchen floor - and knew once again why he disdained the world of man.

The shack was a shabby porched affair but the gutters were sturdy - Dietrich hung upside-down and peered in the window at an illumined tableau of marital exasperation. With his demon eyes he could see something silver in the air, flowing like a watersnake - the couple seemed unaware of it. In the corner was a canary cage in which a squeaky perch was swinging. On the perch was a moth. The woman cast frequent fond glances at this.

They were sat in concrete rocking chairs. The old man smoked a pipe into which he pushed a few crackling bugs. The old woman read a newspaper called *The Blank Stare*. Their conversation, as related to the demon Sweeney at a later date, went like this:

Mrs: Says here the Mayor's out kissing babies.

Mr: He been caught?

Mrs: I mean door-to-door in the ancient style.

Mr: Saw the Mayor with a baby once. Held it like a rifle. Took me right back.

Mrs: In the land of the blind the one-eyed man fears the snakes.

Mr: Before long he'll be outta there lugging a case tied shut with an extension cord.

Mrs: No, he'll pull some stunt at the Parade like he always does. And he's planning to drone on about statues this time. Why don't we go to the Garden as a family anymore?

Mr: Last week we went. You kept going on about the girl statues.

Mrs: They were everywhere, including that Blaze woman. Someone should take a hammer to her dummy.

Mr: That's statucide, Ethel. 'All remote the formal buildings of punishment', eh? She's not worth it.

Mrs: She'll strip him to a skeleton and shoot him through a hoop.

Mr: Well, she hasn't moved in at least. Last time I was there I spent a good hour getting clobbered by the hose-like face of an aardvark.

Mrs: He's not happy unless he's sitting around with the winged and stepping animals of the earth.

Mr: Anything goes with that guy.

Mrs: What are you getting so steamed up about? He's your son, you should be thrilled to bits he doesn't lick his own eyes like a gecko.

Mr: Fine, I'm going to fish.

Mrs: Go fish then.

Mr: Ah, there's nothing fierce enough to be worth the catching.

Mrs: In the world?

Mr: The swamp, Ethel, the swamp, have you looked lately? Even the wrens are slimy round here. On the porch the other night - heard the motorized buzz of a horseshoe crab. *That's* how low we've sunk in the world.

Mrs: 'Ideal thoughts teach us what we needn't expect.'

Mr: And so what if he can't lick his own eyes? You rather your son lick the eyes of a stranger? Aren't you *haunted* by that idea?

Mrs: We both know perfectly well what haunts *you*, Julius.

Mr: Fine, I'm going to fish.

Mrs: Go fish then.

Mr: Ah, there's nothing fierce enough to be worth the catching.

Mrs: In the world?

It went on like this for hours and Dietrich Hammerwire began to feel that the centuries he'd spent in the hellish catacombs were a lovely, lucky dream. He'd been led into the most fiendish, mindless of blind alleys – and Barny never showed.

Edgy spat aside on to the bleak forehead of a crow. Rearranging his crotch, he hunkered on the mound.

'They still there, Palatino?' sneered GI Bill.

Edgy had always claimed his balls detached and flew away at night, returning at dawn all begrimed with moss and lemongrass. Gregor once said Edgy went on about this to keep his women alert. 'Alert?' Edgy had snorted, looking distastefully at Gregor. 'You've got a lot to learn about women.'

'You'll pay for tearin' my shirt that time, Palatino,' called GI Bill, whose face signalled a detour from the species.

'Quit flappin' your gills, doughboy. Let it go.'

Not much chance of that. GI Bill put on his clothes each morning without taking any off the previous night, so that he bloated out over the weeks until the moment the authorities forcibly undressed the bastard. Today he was the size of a bouncy castle and the shirt was at the heart of it. 'You shouldn't oughtn't to have done it, Pal.'

'So regret me. Hey Bubba, where's the Round One?'

Down the far end of the field, Barny swung the guppy stick absently. 'I'm worried about the leopard,' he called. 'He's moody.'

'Moody leopard or not, keep your face on the game,' Edgy shouted. 'We're missing our leaver, where *is* the bastard?'

'Maybe behind bars, skimming cards into a hat.'

'What's wrong with the leopard,' yelled Edgy.

'Something spooked him,' Barny hollered. 'Sid too.' Barny related how Golden Sid had woven his screams into an aural tapestry in which some bleak envoy landed on the roof and was limbering up for a freakish procedure when Sid snapped with the strain. And apparently it was pissing down the entire time.

GI Bill and his team looked on in disgust. 'Can we get on with this?' Bill demanded, hefting a battered leather bag which knocked and jounced in his hands. Inside was a grade-A veggie ball with a sick mind of its own, capable of flying by its own steam and spurting unnecessary slime at one and all. On release, the name of the game was to avoid this gilled abomination at all costs. Dodgers, screamers, hitters and leavers made up the team, and upon every player in a team being accosted, that team lost. Everyone was here but Gregor. And their dodger, the mechanic Mike Abblatia, had a bad back that was swelling.

'You think Gregor's still in the dino era?' Edgy bellowed.

'That's enough,' said GI Bill with finality, and opened the bag.

'It's like Bingo said,' Edgy remarked jauntily as they entered the Cretaceous section, 'the great man carries a number of auxiliary morals of his own devising.'

'Why is Gregor a great man,' Barny asked, leading the gator. Since it pulled a U-ey and snapped Fang on the noggin, Barny had been dressing it in a flowery skirt and hat for reasons which are still a mystery. Theorists have claimed that he hoped these pastoral glories would percolate into the long brain of the reptile and serve as a balm to its savage instincts. In my capacity as a free-range spirit I can select which mind or object to inhabit at any one time and I'm sorry to say at that moment I was laughing it up in the whipping antennae of a tsetse fly. I was amused to see that the insect's knee was like the spring joint of a beanpod, but as to this skirt and hat business I'm a washout.

'By not showing up he won us the game. He's a champion, Bubba.'

'I thought he got stuck here last night,' said Barny, frowning. 'Isn't it why we're here, Plantin?'

'Oh, Barny boy.' Edgy lit a slim cigar. 'Sporting genius is a funny thing.'

'Alright, well I'll look at the Iguanadon over there, it's giving me the thumbs-up.'

'Wait a minute Bubba.' Edgy pointed at a horned bone tank with classic plates and a skull the size of an engine block. 'Gregor's always had an eye for the ladies. This here Triceratops could see off the formidable Gorgosaurus with that armoured crest and disastrous horns. Take a look underneath, there's a thing like a mechanics' pit down there.'

'He's not down there,' Barny called, peering under, and stood to admire the proud face and beak. 'Look at that, Mister Newton. This Tops is like an alligator snapping turtle - bite like a giant hole punch.'

At this point the accountant Neville Peth entered, spectacles glinting, holding a lunchbox. Startled, Edgy pitched his cigar aside, yelling 'And that's exactly what I'm starting to do - because I'm an adrenalin junky, Bubba.'

'Eh?'

Edgy was forcing his head into the dinosaur's gob, shouting. 'That's right - look at me placing everything I need at risk between the hazardous sharps of this - *Chhhhhrrriiiisst*!' And he tore his head out again, staggering back.

Disappointed, Neville Peth turned and walked out.

'What's your Uncle Edgy doing now?' Barny asked the gator indulgently.

Edgy was jittering. 'I found the Round One, Bubba. That sick bastard's hiding in the skull of this monster. He musta crawled up through the neck cavity. He's stuck in there folded up like a boy.'

Barny sprang into action without thought for himself or anyone else.

In the eaves of the museum, Dietrich pinned himself open like a lab bat. He heard the approach of a gaggle of kids. Now was the moment to drop - and he saw this scene below: Barny Juno gesticulating at his scarecrow friend, scarecrow man hoisting up the reptile and waltzing awkwardly with it while screaming, and Juno taking a fire axe from the wall. As the crowd of kids entered and their terrified attention was claimed by the bad man dancing, Juno split a fossilized skull, which released a blathering, blob-faced tar baby. Its features were inlaid with teeth and softboiled eyes, and it seemed overcome with emotion, hugging Juno as its creator.

In the acid night of Sweeney's throne room Dietrich substantiated his florid account by waving a copy of *The Blank Stare* which bore the headline LARD-ARSE BORN FROM FOSSIL.

After the initial clang as he deployed his ears, Sweeney remained silent until the tale was told. Then he pursed his lips thoughtfully. This was preferable to Sweeney in a good mood as he had a spiral smile which operated like a Chinese finger trap, inescapable up to your shoulder.

'I seem to know the minutiae of your failures, why is that?'

'Because you are with me in spirit, Your Majesty.'

'Yes but here's a man, some drawling layabout, I ask you to kill him in a broad, general way, and what happens?'

'Disaster, Your Majesty.'

'Well disaster's putting it a bit strong but here I am enthroned in a veined hull and so on, see what I mean? Out you go, and come back with a frankly dreary story about a shamanic chancer. I mean, be ominous at least. What about the reptile?'

'He's patched it up.'

'Knowledge?'

'He hasn't asked it anything.'

'Is he a moron?'

'His attention seems to be elsewhere.'

The huge white beetle considered this. 'No, it's controlled folly. The man's a sorcerer. Think about it, half of what you gleaned from that screaming tosser on the roof was mere fancy, a planted lie. Even he probably didn't realise it. And when you go to the assigned destination you're treated to a stream of top-of-the-line drivel from what were probably two unemployed actors doing him a favour. It all led you to a museum - there's a message in that. Raising the past, starting with the gator.'

'I thought dinosaurs became birds. Remember what Violaine said about creation? "If you're going to make something light, be sure it contains the important parts of something heavy."'

'Don't quote that bastard to me - wasn't he in here prophesying doom on all cylinders while I ate his head like a herb? *God* Almighty!'

'Doom perhaps but not by Juno's hand, remember. Anyway no-one gave a damn about Violaine till you crashed up through that bandstand and clawed him down in a spray of blood and enzymes. The crowd had actually been throwing pieces of flint till you did that,Your Majesty. Now he's everyone's favourite brainsaver. It worries me to hear you talk that way.'

'Well, never mind Violaine for now. This fool, this lethal idiot you describe - he created a prime pig servant, at a public venue, before your eyes. What's he telling you? You aim to kill him and at that instant he raises life from death. He's laughing in our baked faces. No, we need a different strategy. Accomplice is bound in, knowing only itself. Pop 'em a rumour and it pinballs to a blur. The truth soon becomes an unattended sideshow. Morality? They wear the notion like a wig. We'll use the community against him, Dietrich. It's a long game but I like that sort of thing.'

'By your command.'

Dietrich took a face from the ancient gallery.

4

TRANSMISSION

Authority insists misery is an education

The ornate blood clock was weighted into motion, two doors of red gold flipping open - from each a glossy figurine propelled into jerky battle, signalling the hour with a clash of swords. On the balcony above, the Mayor bellied out like a figurehead. He took a dim view of the town square - across which a lone figure drew a large sea chest - and returned inside. He called from his desk for the next dupe to be ushered in.

It turned out to be a towering, slack-faced man in a woollen hat and coat which seemed a needless extravagance in the day's wet heat. The man sat down in a studied way, as though the act were a foreign custom.

'Mr ... Hammer is it? Mayor Rudloe. I suppose it's about the Parade?'

'I know nothing of any Parade. I've been sent with a proposition for you.' He looked aside at the balcony window. Clouds like a scattered jigsaw. 'Your little world here. It's icing on top and dead inside.'

'Well holy smokes man, we try. Denial's our middle name here in Accomplice. We positively flaunt our denial.' The Mayor broke off to throw a paperweight at a large floor lobster near the desk. These huge house insects, physical manifestations of corruption, infested the mayoral palace. 'And keep our moral fibre under armed guard. You know the tower across town? Like a lighthouse? It's housed there. Length of muscle, stretched between two pegs. I've seen it of course, as Mayor. Quite a sight. Twanged on the hour. I'd have it here if I could, but ... tradition, you know.'

'You're in the manipulation business. I respect that. My master's taught me the current manner of things in this place. Said I'd need a special shirt and so on. When you speak to me, you speak to him.'

'Why do I want to, Mr Hammer? What are you offering?'

'I could put a cobweb on your PR wound, Mr Mayor. From me to you. You have an opposite in contest for power?'

'No-one special - doomed Eddie Gallo is all.'

'Doomed Eddie Gallo.'

'Don't worry, the blossoming cancer of modesty blots any talents he may have, thank goodness. Armchair ideals. Kind. Feeble. Walks with his mouth. Stay away. Whereas my next platform'll be statues, probably. Hell of a statue problem in this town. And then there's what I call my "vacuum proposals". A Gubba Man on every corner. Stores that bite over your head. Work and get worse. Swerving's a no-no.'

'When driving?'

'Or walking. Think about it. Then there's guilt designation and so on. Yes, I expect another resounding mandate for my personal wealth.'

'And it's true people still bow to these institutions?'

'"The dead branch still draws water."'

The man didn't seem impressed by the Mayor's knowledge of

Violaine philosophy and got down to business all the faster. 'My master can defeat more enemies for your meat dollar, Mr Mayor. He has knowledge of the perfect spanner in the works with which to crowbar your crowd. There's a man named Barny Juno whom you can quite easily portray as a threat to society.'

'Why would I do that?'

'Least importantly, because he is. He owns a stolen reptile which has and will injure the innocent. The reptile was stolen from my master and I'll require its return. More importantly for you, Juno's the perfect target, a scapegoat for the ills of the area.'

'Well now that I know all this, why do I need you or your boss?'

'Endorsement, for one. Endless resources for another. He's what you'd call a demon. In fact, *the* demon.'

'You're saying that were I to meet this gentleman, I'd call him "the demon".'

'Yes.'

'And this is the man who wants to publicly endorse my campaign.'

'Suitably disguised, of course. As a goat-herd, say. Or a large, turmoiling maggot. A winner with the kids.'

'Maggot.' The Mayor steepled his hands in thought, then gave a little gasp of exasperation. 'Mr Hammer, I'm not sure you understand the ... principles on which a political campaign is run. If this demon -'

'- *The* demon.'

'... er, *the* demon you refer to were to endorse me as his man for office, he, she or it would have to appear undisguised, otherwise what would be the point?'

'Well, he's very similar to a maggot, but far more chitin. He's very pale, a kind of pale insect, if you like. But as strong as an ox, I assure you.'

'How is this all relevant?'

'Well, if the public at large were to clock him as he is, I'm not sure they could take the stress. Though he does go completely black occasionally, when he's in a mood. That might win some votes.'

'A poster campaign showing a jet black insect endorsing my candidacy.'

'He'll leave most of his carapace behind. He has to, anyway, when he comes above. Oh, and I should mention he can only emerge into your world when his bowels allow.'

'Thank you, Mr Hammer, for dropping by. I'm always happy to speak to members of my constituency on matters which concern them. Don't let the door shatter your brittle arse on the way out.'

The man stood. 'You're making a disastrous mistake, Mr Mayor.'

'It won't be my first disastrous mistake. Nor my last. Good day.'

When the man was gone, the Mayor buzzed for his campaign manager, the lawyer Max Gaffer. 'What do you know about a man called Barny Juno?' he asked Gaffer as the lawyer seated himself.

Gaffer added statute to his water and spoke as it dissolved. 'I think he's the one who held an illegal funeral and then tugged his trousers down. Bit simple-minded. They say he keeps eight hundred eels in his garden.'

'Has any of this been substantiated?'

'Everyone knows it. Jumping counters and pissing on arable land. Skimming manhole covers at old women. Some people are just basically rotten.'

'A simple "No" would have sufficed. What else?'

'Lives in that lopsided wooden thing on stilts. Near the chef school.'

'Looks like a giant chicken coop?'

'More like a gormless young man with your downfall on his mind.' Gaffer drained the glass. 'In the Coum district. Shacked up with about ninety animals. Or maybe a hundred. Around fifty percent of them dangerous.'

'If there's a hundred, that'd make fifty of them dangerous, right?'

'I'm having a hard time following what you're trying to tell me, Mayor. Try pushing your lips out more.'

'I'm pushing my lips way beyond the boundary of good taste already - it's up to you to make it work for you. And where's Erno? That mute bastard's meant to sweep the building for floor lobsters first thing in the morning. I had to interrupt a serious meeting just now to stop one - look at that.' The Mayor pointed at the splat of exploded meat and shell on the carpet.

'Your office: your subconscious. So what was the meeting.'

'Chap swanned in here getting all bonier-than-thou. Wanted to back us. Claimed he had the red ear of the devil. Said Juno was a campaign handle. Pitched a poster campaign. This from a guy whose head was basically an elephant skull with a trumpet for a nose.'

'Really?'

'Well I imagine so. He was wearing some kind of mask.'

'Beware dreams born of paper, Mayor. You've got the Conglomerate to think of. And I've got underwear to buy.'

'You paints your wagon, you takes your choice. Remind me. What is it which, after a passage of time, leads us to question whether our colleagues are malicious or just stupid?'

'Their wisely ignored advice.'

'That's right.'

'So are you counting the mask man a friend of yours?'

A shop with its own weather, the Thousand Spiders was a place of gut-turning symmetries and the slap of palpable etheric manipulation. In fact it was impossible to tell whether you really wanted to buy what you bought there. Barny, Edgy and Gregor moved between betsy lamps, puffwell traaasers, Spitain boxes, gas radios, galore sticks, vesta powder, canned stone, titan blades, carnival skins, scarcar spares, tree teeth, blackout cakes, cigars and dynamine mirrors. 'What's the big deal?' Gregor was saying irritably, looking at a punnet of pain spores. 'Of course I didn't want to be stuck there the whole night. I'd like to see *you* try.'

'Oh I get it,' said Edgy. 'Wham bam and you're outta there. Don't you value the closeness afterward? Aren't you interested in what's inside someone's head?'

'Closeness? There was a dead rat in there. How much closer could I get? I was the biggest thing inside her head. *Me.*'

'The ego on the guy. Eh Bubba?'

'I don't know, Edgy.' Barny was examining a small tin pyramid. 'Should I get one of these?'

'I'll tell you, me and Gort aren't afraid of affection. What about you and Red Alert? You snuggle up afterwards, right Bubba?'

'Well to tell you the truth Edgy, Magenta's sort of difficult to relax with.' In fact she made him feel like a bomb disposal expert. Just because he kept a few snakes and what have you, Magenta had pegged him as a roaring boy right off the bat and was furiously resistant to the barrage of contrary evidence. This extended mismatch was wearing him down but he was too placid to break it off. What a mess. He was less and less willing to lay amid this duplicitous construction. 'She's a real sparkplug.'

'For example.'

'Well, even her windchimes play nosebleed techno. Says it helps her sleep. She's so strong and vivid, Plantin, what can I say. She is beautiful.'

'She'll bring out the worst in you Bubba. You ready to learn that?'

'Yeah,' Gregor pitched in. 'Then bury you with a heart-shaped shovel.'

'Well at least he doesn't sleep with animals who've already been buried for a million years, dinosaur boy. I had to dance with a reptile to distract the community from what you did. I'll never forget the terror of that moment. Its scales were like dark jewels. I was in tears, Round One. *Tears.*'

'Can we change the subject please?' Gregor shouted. They all looked aside at the proprietor, an utterly rigid goat which, like all goats, dared one and all to believe it was made of timber. Dust was in her fur and darkness at her hooves. She hadn't moved.

'Put down the Spitain, Bubba. It isn't good for what we have in mind. We need a Vanta grid like the one you were looking at that time GI Bill attacked us out of the blue.'

'Why again do you honestly believe you know so much about this stuff?' Gregor demanded.

'Beltane Carom's a friend of mine, and he's the real thing. In fact he calls this place a Mickey Mouse operation.'

'Well that fills us all with confidence - eh Barny?'

'I don't know, Round One. So why can't I use a box for the job, Edgy?'

'A Spitain works a certain way, Bubba. Hooks into the overlap of two warring entities, using the point of distraction as a weakness. Silent equivalents are born in the box which draw in the real thing like an anchor. So they're inside fighting like scorpions in a bottle. That's what keeps them in there.'

'What about a betsy?'

'Listen, a modern betsy lamp's basically just a palladium cathode in ectoplasmic suspension. It's like using a lava lamp as a head-stone.'

'You know I can see auras, Edgy,' said Gregor in a contained sort of way. 'And yours is a bullshit borealis.'

Edgy picked up a thing like a collapsible kitchen trivet. 'That's the snare for the job, Bubba. Hey that reminds me, I'm gunna need some extra muscle stealing a funeral cannon from the church later on.'

'Why,' squeaked Gregor, 'the *hell* do you need a church cannon?'

'Because Neville Peth's a member of the Patently Damaging Sports Club and he was distinctly unimpressed by my risk-taking in the museum the other night - thanks to you and your depravities, Round One. So anyway I'm planning to put on a little display for him and I need the cannon. And Barny, you owe me for taking the dog book off your hands.'

'I didn't ask for that, it's nothing to do with me.'

'Well listen I've already made some progress on it. I'm organising the whole thing under chapter headings. Dogs With Eager Faces, Dogs Who Are Warm to the Touch, Vertically Bounding Dogs, Dogs as Big as Me, Dogs in Cardigans, Enigmatic Dogs, Dogs Who Know My Name, Dogs Who Grudgingly Obey, Dogs of Neon, Dogs in a Pond, Dogs Who Gaze Into Infinity, Spent Dogs and like that.'

'Is this the book with the oil painting of you and the alsatian?' Gregor asked.

'Yeah but the publishers, they're re-thinking the title. They're considering something along the lines of *My Dog Hell*. It's a marketing ploy. So Bubba, what about stealing the cannon?'

'I can't tonight, I'm seeing the Blaze. Ask Fang, he's a big man.'

'He's a *bog* man.'

Barny turfed through some weirdware. 'Think I should get something for the Blaze?'

'Everything comes with a reason not to do it,' muttered Gregor, examining a hex barb.

'Maybe you should pay more attention to those reasons, Round One,' Edgy murmured. 'You know GI Bill wants to kill you for what you pulled at the ballgame?'

'Kill me. He said that?'

'Well he used the word "destroy" but a man like that says more with his gestures. There were chopping motions, and he strangled the air. I think he'll maybe leave some remains.'

Barny selected a small gas radio. 'Can one of you take this up to the counter?'

'Don't tell me you're afraid of the goat. The little boy takes care of the punters.'

Through the sour, icy breeze from the darkling wormhole at the rear of the stock room, waddled the kid Barny called 'Spooky Staring Boy'.

'I always forget there's a creeper exit back there,' Gregor muttered to himself.

'It's the boy I'm scared of,' whispered Barny, ducking. 'He never says anything as I pay. He stares at me.'

The kid would serve in silence and, at the last minute, murmur something which gave everyone the heeby-jeebies. This time they got as far as the door when, behind them, they heard the flat voice say: 'To pull up the soil and find blood.'

The way he welcomed the demon into his home, it was clear doomed Eddie Gallo was a mild man who persevered. To Dietrich's eyes he was little more than a cardigan with lips. On the wall were antlered potatoes. The demon laid out the campaign notion and the candidate made coffee. 'Siddown Mr Hammer. I hope five hundred rich tea biscuits aren't too many for you.'

'Thank you.'

'I see you've a copy of *The Stare*. Yes, Juno's attack on that useless fossil was pretty goofy if I say so myself.' He chuckled. 'Mind out for the piece of living death on the carpet there Mr Hammer. Now. I know Barny Juno. I stood up for him in court that time he pulled his pants down at the funeral. He's a nice man. Turns out I was stood in the dock stark bollock naked. These days frankly I don't dress unless I have to announce something to the town. And since I'm not an elected official and never have been, it almost never happens. Except I suppose in the courtroom, and I forgot that time. Everyone seemed to understand.'

'I see. I see. So. What's your electoral gameplan?'

'Well, there are some barely mobile sloths on the flyover. I'd like to raise people's awareness of their attitudes.'

'These are the animals that block the road and explode when people get near them?'

'Yes, they basically prevent travel in that direction. Then after making a few damaging admissions I'll probably base everything around a general slogan. "A smile makes people wonder", something like that. It always goes that way. You know, I could give you a special balm for them saggy jowls, Mr Hammer.'

'Don't you think Barny Juno's been waiting for a way to show his gratitude? For your appearance in court? He'd love to give you a leg-up to the mayoral office. And my master can fund the entire sick jamboree. Remember what Violaine said about the fruitful thing?'

'"The fruitful thing is true."' Doomed Eddie Gallo took a thoughtful snap from a biscuit. 'And Juno really wants to help me? He agrees to this? I suppose this is how it's done, isn't it? When can you start?'

Hammerwire stood, raised an arm and unfurled one white claw toward the centre of town. 'Now.'

It's impossible to actually excel at table manners - you conform to the pattern and extend no further, without expressiveness. Barny was ignorant of this - he only knew there was more oil on the table than in the vomit of a whale. 'It's everywhere,' he protested, looking at his hands.

'It's meant to be that way,' said Magenta Blaze. 'You're joking, right? It's vinaigrette for the salad.'

'This meal should be given a decent burial Madge, look at it.'

'You're hilarious.'

'I'm not,' Barny protested, 'I'm serious - we've been served a meal that's basically sports turf. Look at it - it's arbitrary. What do they teach in that chef school?'

'Give it to the gator,' Magenta laughed, her big red mouth eclipsing her face. The reptile was under the table, sated with steak. The management of the Ultimatum Restaurant thought long skirts on the tables gave the place a sense of mystery, refusing to acknowledge that such a sense was supplied by the food.

'I got something for you,' said Barny wearily, producing the present.

'What is it? Stone make-up?' She unwrapped the gas radio, a natural gadget extruded from demon-blown amber which transmitted metallic whistling from the upper pain spectrum. 'Well. Wow.'

'Listen, Madge,' said Barny, as a strange mariachi band strolled up and began assailing their table. Magenta held the radio to her ear. 'I know you want to believe I'm some kind of wild man or something. And maybe I let you believe it at first. But the fact is, I don't really mean anyone any harm and never have. I'm a very boring person. No threat to anyone. I just want to care for the winged and stepping animals of the earth, and be happy. So I think maybe we should just forget the whole thing.'

The band finished with a cry, throwing their sombreros at the ceiling.

'Did you say something, zeppelin?' said Magenta, taking the radio from her ear and squinting forward.

'Yes, Christ Almighty, I was saying I wouldn't harm a fly. Not the big ones anyway.'

Blaze laughed. 'Tell it to the trolls, baby. And pay the band.'

'Alright I'll pay 'em.' Barny reached into his pants pocket for change and at that moment the gator launched out of its hiding place and clamped through the lead guitar in an explosion of twanging splinters. The guitarist screamed as if it were part of his body - which is the sign of a good musician.

'Let's go,' said Barny and went to snuff the candle flame between his fingers. Soaked in oil, his hand caught fire with a sound like a jet ignition. He ran shrieking like a girl, setting fires around the establishment and finally punching his fist into a trifle.

It's a sad fact that most of their dates ended with them gazing out on a smashed landscape of slow flames, harking to the call and response of fire hydrants. The radio was the weirdest gift he'd ever given her. All she could hear on it was a metallic voice saying 'Now' over and over.

As they led the reptile from the burning restaurant, the creature seemed to give a snapping yawn. The night walls, freaked with orange light, were plastered with campaign posters. Blaze was stumbling with laughter. 'When you said you'd pay the band, then reached down and set the gator on 'em? Then lit all those fires? You are the *man*, Bubba!'

'Magenta, you don't understand.'

The posters they were passing bore the image of a scorched, fanged mantis with eyes like golf balls. Slogans varied from I SUP-

PORT DOOMED EDDIE GALLO IN HIS FIGHT AGAINST HAZ-ARDOUS BARNY, through the quirky 800 EELS? 800 TOO MANY to the merely suggestive BARNY JUNO MUST BE 'DISPOSED OF' SOON. But these were topped out by the absolutist BARNY IS THE MOST DANGEROUS MAN IN THE WORLD. Magenta Blaze stood in front of this one as if it were unassailable holy writ.

Even Barny was able to detect the factor common to them all. They had all appeared sometime in the last hour.

It's amazing how a couple of thousand hostile posters in a two mile area can mess with a person's progress. A baying mob's the thing to prevent a man from making plans and thinking of the future. The following day as Barny walked under a sky of cardiac blue, he drew the attention of a few sightseers who had been drinking official bile and gazing up at the Tower of Nowt. It was rumoured you could glimpse the moral fibre if you peered from a certain spot and this had become a site for stands selling hazardous snacks embossed with a worthless, treasured insignia. Barny's blank face was all the proof they needed. Their mouths advanced like car grills through street steam. And as Barny stood with the lightest curious frown, they inflated their lungs and banged out a volley of accusations at the region of his head: Sideburns on his legs. Overcast with hunger. Wears translucent pants. Secretly eats kebabs. Inflammation of the soul. Ignition socket instead of a knob. Summoned pig servant. Stood in fire, war typhoons shrieking from his ears. Nails behatted chicken heads to doors. Caused a house blast which shattered the exit ramp. Cast squirming package into the lake. Combs his spine with a wire brush. Wears a fish-head on his nose. Likeable as a chimp in an opera cloak. Risky as a dog in a chopper. Eight hundred eels. Dirty care and sax clubs. Alcohol twists his words. End of the sixpack, end of the world. Cheap with burning. Exhausted and wanton. Kidneys of stone. Flyaway sanity. Death grin. Code suit. Bollard hat, and so on.

As squalls of fresh slander were gathering, Barny made a mistake. Spotting a Gubba Man standing a short way off, he went over. These flesh statues were completely inanimate until someone approached them for help - then they would grab the poor sap and hold him in place with an iron grip. Some people starved to death in their clutches; some went mad. Others, prevented from escaping their pursuers, were left tilting bloody and deceased from the strong arm of the Gubba. Nobody really knew if the things were alive or contained anything more sentient than a one-way reflex mechanism. It was Barny's alarm and confusion which propelled him toward this vegetable sentry, and as the thick hand closed on his upper arm, he realised he'd got himself snared. Flooded with panic, he knew what it must feel like for the winged and stepping animals of the earth when they were cornered by chinless wonders. He scrabbled frantically at his restraint as the mob advanced.

Barny was spun to the ground. Feeling spaced out, he saw that the Gubba man's arm was still attached to his own. The crowd were screaming as the Gubba stood like a stone image, lacking a limb. Brought by Sid to meet Barny, the gator had flexed at the sentry, biting it through at the shoulder. The stump showed no detail, white as double cream.

People wandered frowning and puck-lipped out of bars. Neighbours aimed handheld cats at the commotion. No matter how long it went on, nobody could ever get used to the electoral process.

5

MIDNIGHT, UNSUCCESSFUL

Any fool can last long enough to command respect

There was a little fuse chapel near the courthouse seeding lot. It was like a garage, the big door opening on to a short symbolic runway. A mid-sized black sternchaser faced away from the altar. Edgy and Gregor walked around the cannon, shining torches. Gregor was restless. 'Why do we spend our lives breaking into places at night?'

'That's a matter for the authorities, Round One. Right now we've got a job to do.'

'Shouldn't we be wearing some sort of black clobber for this?'

'I'm okay. Remember what old Bingo said? "Beauty, like nature, is unapologetic." I mean it.'

'White pants and a Hawaiian shirt? What's wrong with you?'

'Take a look at this altar, Round One.' Edgy ran the flash over streamer rolls, astrolabes, ready reckoners and target badges.

'It stinks in here.'

'Gunpowder. They call it "the lint of a joyous life". Get the bung and the hardhat, in the corner there.'

'Aren't these cannon places meant to be some kind of frenzied riot?'

'That's the Powderhouse, the main fuse cathedral. This here's just a funeral unit. See this? Velocity Gospel, open at the rites. "Look out now, look out, look out, I'm lighting the fuse. There's gunna be one hell of a bang. Run, run." These guys crack me up.' Edgy went to check out the cannon.

Gregor frowned down at the heavy volume. '"Look at him/her go. Quick, say bye." Are these people serious?'

'They couldn't be more serious,' said Edgy, kneeling to examine the cannon wheels. He pulled out the blocks, tossing them aside. 'The uncertainty of ascension, wiped out in a single initiative. Put 'em into orbit. And they really laugh it up - I saw a segment about it on the Douglas Bar Show. They say the average fusehead writhes his body and contorts his face one hundred and fifty three times a night. It's a bacchanalia round there at the Powderhouse - flaming torches, silver body paint, tumbling midgets, grapes. They go the whole hog. Help me with this, Round One.'

They shoved at the cannon, pushing it incrementally out of the chapel and toward the goods truck they'd borrowed from Mike Abblatia.

An hour later they were across the street from Neville Peth's house in a quiet cul-de-sac. All the house lights were out. Gregor stood on the flatbed next to the cannon, which was pointed at Neville's front window. Head and shoulders projecting from the cannon mouth, Edgy strapped on the hardhat, grinned and gave Gregor the thumbs-up.

'Why couldn't Barny do this?' Gregor asked wearily.

'He's busy, it's his dad's birthday. So let's spark up this bad boy.'

Gregor lit the fuse and Edgy yelled toward Peth's house. 'Hey, Neville, check it out!' Almost instantly the cannon discharged, balking backward through the truck cab. Gregor was on the ground, totally deaf, the look of disinterest frozen on his face.

Lights were beginning to flick on in houses. Wearing pajamas, Neville Peth appeared in his doorway, peering toward the burning truck. After a little while he went back inside. The lights went off.

Gregor scrabbled up and climbed on to the flaming flatbed. Whisping with smoke, the cannon mouth was empty.

Through Accomplice passed a train which had no insides and was as full and solid as a stone. Fog and cobwebs billowed over the grey walls and nothing came out of the filled-in funnel. The driver was a statue obliterated in wall-to-wall marble. The train was born out of suffocation, went from nowhere to nowhere and appeared only at night. Barny didn't realise it was supposed to be scary and travelled on the roof when visiting his parents.

Springing off just after Jericho Bridge, he rolled through the mire and thumped to a stop against a rotten log. After staggering through the soupy swamp for an hour, he stepped through the warped door of the shack.

'Well, look who it isn't.'

'Happy birthday, father. Hello mother.' Barny kissed the top of his mother's head. 'Hello Ramone.' Barny opened the birdcage and kissed the moth in similar fashion. It was inured to this routine and lowered its head to receive the benediction.

'Did you bring a paper?' Ma Juno asked from her concrete chair. 'This one's ten days old.'

'I don't think anything of interest has happened, mother.'

'No paper? You know we rely on visitors out here. Julius, what kind of a son did you raise?'

'He's your son, Ethel.'

'Here's your present, father. And many happy returns.'

Pa Juno tore off the wrap and shop wadding, revealing the Vanta grid. 'A trivet? For holding a saucepan?'

'It's a snare for catching ghosts, father.'

Pa Juno looked wary and evasive. 'So? Why give it to me?'

'Everyone knows your hairline's extended beyond your body, father - what were you going to do?'

'My long-standing policy is to ignore all creepy phenomena and, if anyone mentions it, to quietly make the sort of face you'd see on the side of a church. Let 'em interpret it any way they want.'

'He just wants to pretend he's not as bald,' muttered Ma Juno, 'as a stone.'

'Maybe I've chosen to tuck my hair under my headskin to keep it dry in the summer storms. Did you ever consider that? I'm going to fish - and I don't care if it kills me.'

'Go fish then.'

'Ah, there's nothing fierce enough to be worth the catching.'

A chill stream of ghost-smoke flowed across the rear wall, blasting ornaments off the mantel. Barny's father stared pointedly the other way.

'Let's set it up then eh father?'

'You make this gizmo yourself? You using your welding skills?'

'Why would your son ever weld anything?'

'We sent him to welding school didn't we? You never know when you're gonna need to weld two things together. Any number of social situations could arise. And he's your son.'

'I bought it, father.'

'Shop of a Cool Thousand?'

'A Thousand Spiders, father.'

'There - your son's been dabbling in the dark arts after all, Ethel. Didn't I say he'd hit the headlines for crimes against nature?'

'A good father should give his son a chance, Julius. You know we need etheric insulation. We can't be here inhaling ghosts. Sharp on the throat. "Mankind is meat - nature's in league with the stones."'

'So Edgy says it works like flypaper,' Barny continued, placing the grid at the centre of the floor. 'You know that stuff in the tub, in the Shop? Golem fat or whatever it's called. Ecto stuff for building creatures. And EH Hunt, who carries that huge chest around for some reason? Gregor says he was in the Shop, Hunt was, and he was laughing about something or other, and so much his false teeth flupped out into the vat and a travertine demon started growing there - the mix had to be incinerated but Hunt was made to pay anyway.'

'You're the worst storyteller I ever heard,' said Ma Juno. 'No son of mine could relate the facts so badly. And no newspaper!'

'Well, so Edgy told me this works a bit like that, but he says as an anchoring tool. It weaves this membrane between the spokes, which is a really thin flesh bed doped with charged ecto stuff. So the ghost gets drawn to it and stuck? Then you can put it on like a crown, father, and hey presto.'

The forces were activated by placing the grid on a clammy pasta base, which Barny had brought in some foil. Within a few moments a misty cobweb developed across the little 2D cage. Then a few fibres appeared, whisping like fungal spores. Black hair was sprouting, a puppet's moptop. Something semi-visible was pouring into the grid.

'What's this?' asked Ma Juno. She was looking at some scrunched padding from Barny's gift. It was a piece of newspaper which she was flattening out. 'Lard-arse born from fossil? "Barny Juno took the biscuit yesterday by sprouting a living potato man from the skull of an ancient monster. When asked to comment, he said 'I don't understand.'" Your father was right. Crimes against nature. What did you do, create some kind of pig servant?'

'It's not a pig servant, it's Gregor. He got trapped in the fossil.'

'Ethel, look at this - my hair's back.' There was a great pool of hair filling the room out, writhing like snakes, reaching for the walls. Ma Juno started screeching. Chairs and side-tables were shoved by the flow. The hair pool became white at the heart, then stopped growing. The grid buzzed and spat like a frying hive. The room was full. 'It's all the hair I ever had in my *life*.'

Pa Juno skipped through the hair sea and picked up the grid, hauling the hair after like a wedding veil, and placed it on his head. The hair was alive, tentacular, roiling in thick ropes. Pa Juno laughed a gummy laugh, an overblown gorgon, a side-lamp freaking his shadow.

Barny backed into the dark wall, gripping his fear, and a whisper hissed through his head. *I've created a monster.*

6

NOTHING IS REVEALED

Beneath tree birds, cats rise like watchtowers

Mayor Rudloe had ordered Erno to set up a Raj-style carpet fan in the big office and now there it was, slowly swinging with a dozen or so floor lobsters clinging to it. 'What is this,' said the Mayor, 'an amusement park for these animals? Shake 'em off, you silent bastard.'

Erno, drawing slow on the rope, looked at him mournfully.

Max Gaffer shot into the room with a copy of *The Stare*. 'Looka this, Mayor.'

'I'm working up a speech for Parade day. It's all about my jaws, and how the hinges work. It's dynamite.'

'Mayor, listen to this. "BARNY JUNO'S PIG SERVANT STEALS FROM CHURCH. A vat-grown mutant potato creature hatched by Barny Juno from the skull of a massive corpse has stolen a sacred cannon from a fuse chapel and set fire to it in the suburbs. Opposition mayoral candidate doomed Eddie Gallo, whose campaign is centred around the condemnation of Juno, baffled the media by commenting: 'I know Barny Juno. I like him a lot. He takes care of animals in his funny house. I'm sure his pig servant had the best of intentions.' Rod Jayrod, Fusemaster of the Cannon Sect, stated: 'This is not the first deliberate sacrilege perpetrated by this man against cannonic scripture. The bastard planted a dead lizard one time, then while he was pretending to cry, he showed his arse to the whole world. That was a day for eyelids.' Barny Juno, who also uses the alias Juniper, is known to own an eight foot alligator which means business and will kill us all." Then there's a picture from the lizard funeral - looka that.'

'*Get* that thing away from me! How did this happen? If every man were as static as doomed Eddie Gallo nothing in the world would worry me. I ever tell you the first time I saw him? He was wandering in traffic with a maple branch. How did a man like that recognise this Juno trump card?'

'He makes it look so easy.'

'He's probably having a good laugh about it right now. Anyway, an alligator? Any animal that blinks sideways has gotta have some strange notions, if you know what I mean. If it, say, grips a fella with them teeth and makes him perish in a messy sort of way, screams and what have you? What about it?'

Max Gaffer smirked. 'I can see his cavalier leading of a reptile around town could be a disaster for the Accomplice community.'

'You'd cordon off the rain, wouldn't you?'

'It's not enough to believe in ourselves, Mayor - we gotta curse everyone else.'

'That why I'm going out kissing babies?'

'I think we should hold back on the doorstepping, Mayor. The old bag's suing about her fish.'

'That guppy was ceramic! She put it in my hands like an infant!'

'Well she was upset in any case, and the stills of her bent sobbing over the pieces are quite appallingly damaging. You standing there awkward, uncomprehending and all? I tried to buy her off but the crazy bird wanted to handle my underwear. She's a tough nut to crack.'

'You're sure about the underwear? She said this?'

'Well, I got a sense of it.'

'So once again you wreck everything through your belief that everyone's preoccupied with your underwear.'

'You want I should send the Brigade in?'

'Boy, yours is a lofty profession Max. Lucky for men like me. However far we ascend in office, we never reach those heights where the law dwells.' A floor lobster fell on to the desk and both men recoiled. One whiplike antenna nearly had the Mayor's eye out. '*Christ* almighty! Erno, have you heard a bloody word I've said? Put these megabugs in the furnace!'

Erno stopped tugging the pulley and grudgingly got a broom, knocking the giant insects off the fan.

'I want a mailshot,' the Mayor continued. 'The mask man kept going on about the gator. Focus on it in the fliers. "Fatal to you, fatal to me", like that. And I think it may be valuable - offer a reward which we won't give. A mass mailing. Every household in Accomplice. We'll tell them I'm the man to act against the antisocial element or at least look at it for a long time - personally. If the reptile's a dud we sell it to Karloff's Circus. I want them in the mail today. There's nothing to stop us.'

*

In the stale half-light of the sorting office, BB Henrietta considered giving the walls a haircut. Toads surfaced smiling in the watercooler. Sags Dumbar looked glum and doubtful.

In the past everyone had feared Dumbar because his head was actually a chrysalis for another animal. In recent times his face had been almost transparent and they could see something bustle and shift behind it. Finally he'd stopped short in the middle of a conversation and opened his mouth, from which a bunch of fiddling spider legs fanned. Everything else followed and he was speechless and shaking, the only one without a scream to offer as the dog-sized bug quivered into a corner and stayed there to dry off. But he was a steady worker.

The huge bug was kept in a lobster cage in the back of the basement and only Barny was preoccupied enough to approach and feed it some giblets now and again. So why they should be bothered by an alligator is anyone's guess.

'Why do the papers keep calling me a pig servant?' asked Gregor, climbing up from his room in the little sub-basement. It was grim accommodation but maybe he was better off than Fang, who as one of the living dead was obliged to go and bury himself in the marshes and keep his gob shut.

'You can be anything you want to be, fatboy,' Edgy assured him.

Barny had told them how public hostility had manifested itself in the swerving noses of passers-by, whispers, multi-legged attacks and so on. But everyone was more interested in Edgy's adventure.

'I guess when the cannon went off,' Edgy explained, 'I decided at some subconscious level to respond with a kind of flying-through-the-air-and-screaming gambit, sideways through the sky, higher than I'd planned.'

'What then?' asked Barny.

'Well I followed that up with a simple landing gambit.'

'You continued with the screaming?'

'For the moment. Of course I tailed that off eventually and found myself lying facedown in spongy sand and utter darkness. My whole nerve rig was firing. The place was thick with clams. Huge tidal silences, Bubba. Leaking rock pools. Fossil bombs. At midnight, I might add. And you know who I saw there? The Announcement Horse. He was perched there like Napoleon, gazing out. He made a few cracks about me.'

'Cracks?'

'Ah, you know how he is - said I was doomed etc. Burnt paper over my bones, a window made of light, jellyface colleagues with all

the backbone of pizza. What else ... stuff about the community generally, phone-faced killers, several brawls of no great consequence, a
few moonlit riots, beware the chair, one man two names, sores of
beauty. Said only a puzzle with defined edges can be solved. What a
card.'

'Yeah, he's a funny guy.'

'And made completely of metal, I know that now for sure. I'm
telling you Bubba, it's a long while since I visited the old baffling
ocean. We should all go a lot more.'

BB Henrietta pitched in. 'That guy Hunt goes on about it so
much, why bother?'

'BB, remember what old Bingo said? "Joy is whatever you
approach individually, without duty, coercion or clouded mind."
That's what happened to me on the beach, people. But at top speed.'
Edgy described little bony triangular shells and how the succulent
roots fanned out, whipping velveteen husks and polished pupils
about. They had seemed so weird with their limbs out, a sappy predator for the warm mud, gradually revealed.

'You're not converting to Velocity are you?'

'Oh not me. Or the doll house neither. None of it's real to me. And
why would something that's everywhere need a window?'

'Yeah I saw on Douglas Bar how all kinds of people used to have
god harassing them, giving them advice,' said Fang. 'They couldn't
shut it up.'

'Oh I heard the voice of god once,' Edgy told him. 'Yeah, I was at
a buffet, you know? And I was going for the chicken, and this voice
from above said, "Take the ham." So that's what I did.'

'Take the ham. And that's the only time god ever chose to give you
advice.'

'Correct. I can only conclude that in every other area of my life
I've been right on the money.'

'So what did Mike Abblatia say about the truck.'

'Nothing. He'll forgive anything. The man's unnatural. Anyway, I'll
have to impress Neville Peth some other way - he's a cool customer.'

'Alright I've heard enough,' said BB Henrietta, returning to her
work. She was squashing a package of brittle-sounding stuff as
small as possible, to throw into the bushes later. The slightest jog of
the sorting table sprayed salty tears everywhere.

At that moment an explosion of boxes banged down the chute,
tailgaiting eachother on to the conveyor - forty of them. The silence
afterward was broken by a fatalistic groan from BB Henrietta, who
lugged one of the boxes over. Someone had to make a start. Slitting
it open, she removed a paper pocket, which she tore to reveal a print-

ed leaflet which said that Barny's alligator was unpredictable. 'All these boxes? What are they doing here?'

Fang, his face a dried, dented fruit, touched the package gingerly. 'Alright. I'll tell you what we're gonna do. In the Drop, all of them. There's no room for half-measures.'

'No, there's too much stuff,' Gregor snapped, gripping Fang's arm - it drifted away in his hands, water and some black fluid trickling from the shoulder stump. Dropping the limb, Gregor backed up and shrieked in a demented sort of way, his face twisting like a corkscrew.

'There's no *time*,' shouted Edgy. 'It's three o'clock already. Into the Drop.' He speared a bundle and pitched it into the strange maw.

But Gregor's protest was well founded. Apparently bottomless as a skeleton, the Drop made terrifying noises if more than one ton of stuff was dumped at a time. The boxes reached this threshold in a few minutes and the Drop maw started bellowing like a mammoth. Gregor rushed to the furnace and stuffed three boxes in there, clogging the door and tamping the pressure. Blasted by recoil and stumbling with flailing arms, he seemed to the others a dark troll toiling against the ferocious oven. Hot coals spat and rolled to the floor and flame rampaged over furniture like the branding fire of shame. The crew were wading through charred mysteries, every step a deposit for death by worry and wasted time. Ashes drifted past the clockface. 'We can change, can't we?' said Fang, not really believing it. 'Step, step, all smiles. Bam we're in a new location, springing.' And he choked suddenly on his own words, folding down into sobs. Coughing in a fog of swirling cinders, Barny blasted Dumbar's bubbling face with a fire hydrant.

Edgy was saying 'For god's sake stretch my nose to the door and damn the expense!' when the Captain descended carrying a hazardous freight of disinterest.

'Now then lads,' he said, regarding the unliveable hell of smoke and embers, 'simmer down. Some things don't escape me. Barny. It's come to my attention. How shall I put it. It's come to my attention that you have some kind of public feud going on with the devil.'

'Doesn't everyone?' asked Edgy mildly, and tossed a suave grin at the others.

'Or an apparition along similar nerve-jangling lines. It's on posters all over town, saying it's backing doomed Eddie Gallo in his campaign against your hot-damn depravity.'

'One day you'll understand me better,' said Barny, squinting through the foul air with bloodshot eyes.

'Well that's as may be, but gee whiz I cannot allow my employees to be menaced by a bleak demon, fire hosing out its nose and so on. And as for an angry mob. Unacceptable. So I'm going to have to let you go, Barny.'

'What?' Edgy spluttered. 'You can't do it. He's got eight hundred eels to take care of - as everybody knows.'

'I'll have the roast beef platter,' said Sags Dumbar - the only thing he ever said. His placental head lolled on to his shoulder.

'And get me a shrimp cocktail,' Barny piped brightly.

'Wake up, Bubba, he's firing you.'

'Firing me ...' Barny's slow bewilderment was perfectly apparent.

'Someone set him up,' said Edgy.

'You have enemies?' the Captain asked Barny.

'He's got thousands. Ask around. Bubba here's hit the jackpot as far as nemesi are concerned. He's unspeakably offensive. Tell him, Bubba.'

'A person can only have one nemesis,' stated the Captain weari-ly. 'That's the nature of a nemesis. And in regard to *your* conduct in this matter, Gregor. We all know you as a bloated fool who tries and tries. I confess until I read the headlines today I didn't realise you were Barny's pig servant - now I see that by golly you've never been fully responsible for your own actions. Church theft and vandalism reflects badly upon this industry and I answer to Mr Gibbon. However, I'm told you have a legitimate statue in the Garden and so I intend to intercede on your behalf. It's known that a simple exor-cism procedure followed by counselling can make an ectomorphic mutant like yourself a passably productive member of society. Here's Doctor Perfect's number, call him today. Give a good account of your-self in public and after some passage of time we'll review the situa-tion. One chance, Gregor. Behave.'

'Ectomorphic mutant?' Gregor gasped.

'And as for the rest of you -' snapped the Captain, and trotted up the stairs, slamming out.

'I wish he wouldn't do that,' muttered Fang.

'Out of the frying pan and straight to video eh Round One?' said BB Henrietta.

Edgy watched Barny with concern.

'Don't worry about the Captain,' said Fang, draping his arm around Barny's shoulder and walking away. 'Pound for pound he's more of a ponce than anyone.'

A half hour later, Barny wandered dazed from the office and stood in the street like a fool newly made.

High above him hovered the demon Dietrich, like a coat thrown into the sky.

7

PANTOMIME HORSE

Never use your eyeball as a paint roller

Laughing as the lion licked eight layers of skin from his face, Barny shoved him away and got a steak out of the oven. 'Body temp,' he said, prodding it with a thermometer, and flapped the bloody meat toward the cat. He gestured at his gruesome generator. 'Thank god the place is powered on dung. But what about food and supplies? I need reptile lights for Mister Newton, mice for the snakes, raisins for the mice, fruit for the chimps, gore for Mister Braintree here. I can't set him loose on the community like Karloff used to. Can I?'

Edgy rested on the lion's head. 'You need to find a new course of exhaustion, Bubba. I'll coach you. Del needs a tong man at the Foundry. Anyway he looks as if he does. He's badly burnt. And we know Stampede have got at least one vacancy for the old door-to-door.'

Edgy said this because when Barny got back from being fired he found the alligator in the course of eating an alleged Stampede Products salesman. Golden Sid clung screaming from a light fitting as the gator thrashed the furniture to pieces and the visitor's screams merged with his own. Barny noticed a target badge on the stranger's chest as the reptile chugged him back. Phoning the Powderhouse he got only laughter and a heavy beat on the line. Barny would never understand that the salesman was in fact an assassin sent by the Powderhouse in retribution for the Mister Spiderman funeral. Ironically the man had been hyping damnation curtains, which were traditionally hung to signal to the neighbourhood that everything was going to hell inside.

Barny looked gloomy. 'Just when I get the gator settled in enough for Golden Sid to handle twice a week, it looks like I'm going to be here anyway. At least he won't need paying.'

'Do you get the full meaning yet re the gator? You see, your gator? Inscrutable. Enigmatic. It's got a way of posing totally still, not a flicker. That'll freak anyone out. Then it suddenly jolts into action. People have got a right to scream, Bubba. Can't you understand you're the only person in the world who thinks that monster needs protecting?'

'Isn't that the definition of love?'

'What?'

'Its legs are really quite delicate.'

'What? So?'

'So it's slow. Slower than a croc.'

'Listen to me, you've gotta do something about it. Everyone obviously hates it and they'll start to hate you. I've seen it happen.'

'How can they not adore it? It's got a head like a pike, you've seen its head.'

'*Yes* I've seen the head. But people judge by broad, general appearances and this gator of yours has the appearance of being a giant, toothsome reptile with the potential to throw a tantrum no matter what you say. Remember Joe Fuel?'

Edgy reminded Barny of the Prancer-organised campaign among the Accomplice community to stare, point and whisper regarding Joe Fuel's facial area, adding enigmatic phrases such as 'Not enough money to see to it?' over a period of years until Joe Fuel came to a gritty acceptance of what he was finally convinced were the most inconvenient cheeks in the world.

'So what?' asked Barny. 'What's that got to do with Mister Newton?'

'Appearances, Bubba. We'll dress it up as something else. A judge. A failure. A portacabin. A little lamb. A ladle. A monster of some kind. The possibilities are, yes, limitless aren't they? See what I'm saying?'

'Or a gimble.'

'What's a gimble?'

'I don't know,' Barny confessed.

'Well, that's a good place to start. The important thing is to be inconspicuous. "Until inactivity is recognised as an expression of willpower, people will disregard it", that's what old Bingo said. These people are afraid you'll damage the moral fibre.'

'Why? I've never seen it. The only time I stood near the door of the Tower I had a really dodgy time with the guard guy Murdster.'

'What did he do?'

'Stepped forward and forward, hands raised and rounded like claws, and held my neck tightly, his teeth like a car radiator. I realised after a while that he meant to kill.'

In the acid night of Sweeney's cave, the demon looked through undulating blood at Barny's moonlike face as words echoed. 'I realised after a while that he meant to kill.'

'Look at those wide, vacant eyes,' said Sweeney. 'This is a man without the inconvenience of caution. I was correct in thinking he was only hex-protected against direct assault. The strange, ramped design of the house appears to incorporate several unfamiliar geomantic hypergrams.'

Using a dog's ribcage to comb the arterial tubing of his head, Dietrich glanced up at the Ruby Aspict. 'The scarecrow man in the bright shirt, the one who rests upon the lion's head. His name is Plantin Edge. He flirts with danger. This activity seems to serve as an entertainment for Juno.'

'A jester? Apprentice? Or a protector?'

'He boasts that his balls detach and fly away at night.'

'An apprentice then. A novice still impressed with parlour tricks. And what are these you've brought me? Headstones for moths?'

'Rich tea biscuits, Your Majesty. Some form of "gift" forced upon me by doomed Eddie Gallo.'

'Five hundred of the buggers. You seem to have made an impression on the upper world, Dietrich, but don't let it go to your slick head. I won't have another desertion.'

Dietrich was making a wounded reference to the demon Gettysburg, who had defected to the upper world after popping out for some cigarettes.

'Something's happening.' Dietrich's rock fissure eyes squinted at the Aspict - its rotation had begun to accelerate. 'I can feel corpse shoes creaking in chill hallways.'

'It's got a hook in them,' said the huge white beetle, leaning as far as his armoured throne allowed. 'Onrushing like a shark tag. Now we'll see some action.'

It seemed things were moving quickly. Baffled by the non-delivery of his leaflets, the Mayor had begun a specifically anti-alligator poster campaign. Barny and Edgy set upon an iffy course of camouflage. At first Barny thought it would suffice to add some length to the snout and a couple of false externally visible lower teeth, thus disguising the alligator as a crocodile. Staring pop-eyed at the carnivore, the inhabitants of a kebab shop ran screaming exactly as if it were an alligator. Barny ran after them with a colour-coded jaw diagram. 'The teeth you bastards, the teeth!' The incident was held up as proof, if any were needed, of Barny's precocious evil.

The grey-green rocky monster seemed to work well as an old log until a cat tried to climb inside. As a sleeping tramp under a battered coat it regularly broke character to snap at charitable strangers in a thrash of incisors and hectic dust. Its appearance as a giant furled leaf was baffling to EH Hunt and they had to explain it to him just as if he were a child. His bafflement reached such a tortuous extreme he was blatantly relieved when it turned out to be a mere reptile. The rills on its back suggested to Edgy a rigid stage prop representing seawaves, so they painted the gator blue and stood pulling it awkwardly back and forth behind the actors in a production of Violaine's *Exhaustion Babe*. The audience were baffled, not least because the play was set in an urban wasteland and contained no reference to the sea. The entire effort was a waste of time.

Turning from these scenes in the Aspict, the demon Dietrich felt a tiny worm squirm in the wet clawhammer of his head. Was Barny Juno no more than an unbelievable moron?

Barny was trudging subdued through the square as Prancer Diego, founder of the high-speed run-up point-blank insult, stood yelling some towering truth to one and all. 'Hold up, Bubba,' Prancer shouted, and came over.

Barny liked Prancer in a cautious way. The prankster shuddered and grinned a lot and blew industry-standard magnets out of his nose. When reversed baseball caps came back into fashion for a while he wore the bill forwards and had his head surgically reversed. He even questioned the bells of despair.

'Oh, hi Dago,' said Barny.

'That monster of yours doesn't have much to recommend it, Juniper. Why not gut the thing and pump it up, make it a balloon? No? Well, don't say I never gave sound advice in times of peril.'

'I dunno Dago, everyone seems to hate me in an unfocused sort of way,' said Barny. 'Got me fired. I can't see why the gator can't participate in this community. They're always claiming that's the goal.'

'Charm can work when culture negatives other tricks. Watch this.' And Diego approached a small bright-eyed dog, which looked up at him eager. 'Use me, use me!' he shouted at the mammal, which reacted by yapping loud, skittering sideways. He strolled back to Barny, grinning with pride and high spirits. 'So you see? I'm correct.'

'You're a nice man, Dago,' said Barny. 'But you're not very good with the winged and stepping animals of the earth.'

'Everyone yelps when they've got a principle, Juniper, uncertain if it's a thorn or a medal.'

'I've got no idea what you're talking about.'

8

KING VERBAL

A patron is like a loving devil

Despite his protestations of harmlessness Barny had a tendency to eat small, struggling trolls when nervous. BB Henrietta sometimes shook him by the shoulders but apart from this he received no organised support toward kicking the habit. In fact her shaking him by the shoulders made him giggle like a child and he liked it. Barny carried a small troll in his briefcase as he entered the boneseed factory and ran through his answers in his head. Edgy had coached him with ruthless efficiency, grabbing him by the face and stretching his cheeks out in a desperate sort of way. Toward the end Edgy had shouted 'Take it or leave it!' three times and begun sobbing with anger. Barny chased the alphabet with cloak flying, and resolved he was ready. King Verbal guided him into a plush office with gales of good humour. Radiating brisk, boundless energy, he directed Barny to a seat.

'Barny Juno. Thrilled to bits you came in. I will not, cannot believe, that a beekeeper's mask is necessary at an interview of this kind.'

'I opted for the formal.'

Verbal sat in a soft lurch chair. 'You'll find we're quite relaxed here Mr Juno. Coffee?'

'Bring it now.'

'Pop the mask off and put it here. That's right. Yes, I've looked at your application. I've had that honour and I must say your CV's an abomination.'

'Thanks. My friend Sags Dumbar's got a transparent head.'

'Really? Really. Well you saw my partner, King Fletch, through the broken door just now. King Perchant has a massive hernia and won't be joining us. He's the money man. My chief concern these days is quality control. It's a key issue with me. Efficiency has moved on immeasurably since the skeleton coast disaster. Look me in the eye and tell me you don't know about *that*. Sure you do, who doesn't? And as the founder of the boneseed process I was a key player in the mayhem that followed.' Verbal steepled his hands and looked aglow. 'I used to be a doctor. Along came some ill bastard and my medical career hit the fan. In this universe, lungs are in a tiny minority. Minerals are where it's at Barny, get my drift?'

'Yes, ma'am.'

Verbal chuckled benignly. 'Alright Barny, but when you get to my age you'll be regaling one and all with stories of your own achievements, and just looking at you I can sense your potential. You've got a big life ahead of you boy. So humour me a little further. See that map of Accomplice? The whole west side was open country back then. One day I was churning toxins with a handle when one of my many enemies attacked from behind, falling in after a brief struggle. I looked down into the tumult - I'd like to say his bones were reacting with the mix in a useful way, but frankly he was just floating there. However, that was the start of my life venture. Hardhat research, a trip to ancient trinkets and erosion, I waded in heavy. My big dream of an automatic building material able to spread from seed. Five years later my first boneseed complex was spreading like frost on a window, completely out of control as it turned out and clogging the entire west horizon. Boy, there's a day I won't forget in a hurry. Terror, screaming, people getting caught in the flow and bonding in forever. Seventeen hours it took. I remember one in particular when a towerlike confusion of ribs locked upward into stairs, oh, no-one could deny we'd arrived. As you can tell, I'm secretly proud of Accomplice's botched geology. The chaos of the coast is classic, behold. But in business nothing stands still. We've developed the shortlife mix which you've seen in the courthouse and other buildings. We're working with colour compounds for brighter striation, bird calcium for finer design - stand back and watch me dream of a brighter future. Yes sir there's a party in my arse and everyone's invited. And this is my challenge to you, Barny. How far can you obsess? What's your dream?'

'I want to care for the winged and stepping animals of the earth, and be happy.'

'Ah don't we all - that's a cop-out answer. I mean your fiercest dream Barny, something that grabs your gizzard and chokes it like a swan.'

Barny recalled Edgy's teachings, and recited: 'I want to be tormented by duty, Mr Verbal. Until I weep.'

'Well, strictly speaking, Barny, we don't like our employees to be tormented to that degree. But I admire your spirit. How was it in your last office? Good atmosphere?'

'Together we watched rats eat the clock. Decorated invisible bees with ribbons. Dust everywhere. I have marmosets.'

'Is that so. Well you've seen the scope and grandeur of our operation, Barny. No floor lobsters on us, we see to it. We live by the first rule of business: garbage at crippling prices. As a Boneseed employee you'll run the gamut. Learn ugliness and groundless respect. Notorious pint initiation. A minimum of five hours a day in the bird room with bandaged shoulders. Despair the live-long year.'

Barny flipped the catch on his briefcase.

'So here's the bottom line Barny. Why do I need you? What sets you apart from the mass of people?'

'A shrapnel scar on my spine the colour of banana talks to me at night, filling the room with whispers.'

Verbal frowned a moment. 'Well by god that's the best answer I ever heard. I want to hire you Barny - I know you must have other offers. If they insist, the only possible course is to shrivel and twirl, acting strange till they leave you alone. Kick those bastards into touch. You're made for life. Golden address and foreign guests, you'll never look back you rascal.'

'Caviar is murder.'

'Beg pardon? What's with the troll?'

'I can't put a stop to it.'

'Barny. Barny don't be doing that -'

Barny bit into the troll's belly, tearing out the blue guts.

Verbal bridled. 'Hey Juno a young man's personal chaos is terrible and bad I'll grant you - but that's a *troll* you're eating there. A *real troll*. I mean consider the science, look at me. Tell me you're hungry for challenge, boy, I can see it in your eyes ...'

A dream seemed to settle over Barny's sated face. 'I bite and bite them Mr Verbal.'

Verbal closed up, becoming grim. 'Don't mess with me Barny. I elbowed a chimp to get this far and I won't let you wreck it now.'

Of all life's instants, being ejected from a job interview one backward step at a time, each step provoked by a punch upside the face from the interviewer, is one tailor made for grim reflection. Barny squandered this opportunity. The above scenario was repeated with only minor variations at a dozen offices that day, until the gored and purpling Barny approached the Shop of a Thousand Spiders. One half minute late for the interview, he found the door barred against him in the dimming light, Spooky Staring Boy standing utterly still beyond the threshold.

His last stop was Del's Fright Foundry, a psychodimensional vortex from which the gruff barrelman Del would drag horrific artifacts directly on to the street. Totally useless, these arcane masses would sit steaming in the public byway until the populace dared urge him to get them out of sight. 'Who said I need an assistant?'

'Edgy. He said you were getting badly burnt.'

'Do I *look* badly burnt?'

'Yes.'

'Come into the garage.'

Del had a garageful of massive insect skeletons which he'd brought through from another realm. Grey crablike things the size of cows. Great serrated saw-wavers. Buggy-whip antennae. Whiskered shells. Called it the Dark Armoury, and so it was.

You could all-too-easily picture these mothers ratchetting and alive - it was something to do with the dozens of legs and confounding detail. Played jumpy tricks on the eye. One bug, an armoured beast the size of a Volkswagon and which Del had christened 'Trouble', was exactly like one of those supermagnified carpetbugs from the wonders of science. Its roof was thin dry flaky leather. Del said there was next to no meat inside and that the brute lifted as light as an inflatable chair.

Upon introduction to these beasts, the scenario Barny feared was that one day Del would return to find that the position of one of the exhibits had subtly changed. Del confirmed that this was a regular occurrence. Barny had visions of the creatures slamming into each other like dodgem cars the moment they were alone.

'If you work for me,' said Del, 'it will be your job to stay in here overnight and observe.'

'Well I'm sorry we couldn't do business Del.'

They walked back out to the foundry mouth. Del picked up the massive tongs and plunged them into the flurrying vortex. 'Ask the sorcerer Beltane about those stupid posters.'

'He scares me.'

'You scare us all, lunatic. With your goddamn placidity.' This last was drowned out by gurgling birthcries as a snagged neck emerged black from the static.

9

TAKE A DEEP BREATH

Only a bastard tries to cauterize a wound with an account of his own past injuries

Fear the doctor who snorts in breeches and lives in a dungeon.

'Blame me for everything,' he whispered to himself in the scabby cavern of his surgery. Dirt fell from the bulbswing roof as the stone train roared overhead. 'We have only the turnip of conformity to fend off our demons. No wonder. And nobody hears my name. From here I can blame everybody. Monsters visit me here, banging me on the back and saying I've done well. Call me a "rascal" and expect me to respond. Why can't I be left alone to hammer these grail fragments to the wood backing? Freedom is tasteless, tell everyone.'

The marriage fanfare announced his entry into the toilet. 'By god, give me a nation and I'll stare blankly at you, whoever you claim to represent. Bloody my hands with your pre-structured farm notions? Crop rotation? Just bake me something and get out of here.'

'Doctor Perfect?'

The Doctor halted abruptly, realising he had been talking aloud. He emerged from the toilet, wiping his hands. 'Conscious of the floor are we?'

Doctor Perfect's brain was external, perching on his head like a gran's hairstyle. The brain was in a visibly bad state, yellow infections beating like a heart amid dockleaf veins and a peppering of skull lint. No-one ever dared mention it.

Gregor approached his betterment like a clown talking through a taut door chain. Confronted with this shambling grotesque, he stood fidgeting and picking at own his aura. 'I didn't know you did head work, Dr Perfect.'

'Why shouldn't I?' snapped the doctor. 'What kind of question is that? Just sit yourself on the smashed Daimler there. We'll tongue the planet in your skull. Or you'll end up exploding naked into the streets, screaming and demented, semolina dripping from your beard.'

'I don't have a beard,' Gregor quailed, laying back on the banging roof of the crushed car.

'Trust me – you will. You know, the Captain's sticking his corded neck out for you. Front page news - PIG SERVANT STEALS FROM CHURCH. You must be terribly proud. You've got a head like a scallop bulb, you know that?'

'Yes.'

'Well that's a start. Health is part boredom and part repair.' Doctor Perfect sat on an upturned trashcan. 'I want to make it clear at the outset that I resent golem cases and I resent you. Between you and me this flimsy headcharge you call a life strategy is propelling you like billy-o toward your downfall in flames and trouble, explosions banging open right next to your ear. Not to mention the appalling expense. You were created by a co-worker a few days ago using a dinosaur head as a template, correct?'

'No.'

'Let me be the judge of that, laddie. Exomorphs can even be made by accident. You know Hunt? The guy who drags that chest every-where -'

'I know, he dropped his false teeth in the vat.'

'You've heard that one?'

'I was there.'

'No, this was months ago.'

'I'm nobody's pig servant!' Gregor spat in strangled exasperation.

'That's the spirit. But the flesh is weak. Get any exercise?'

Gregor muttered something about a morning sprint combined with the punching of blurred strangers. He looked without much interest at the Doctor's desk. Cobweb decanter, stiff raven and ancient wax puddle. There were several mannikins propped in the shadows. 'What's with all the dummies?'

'Oh, I have an interest in the statue problem round here. I'm not even sure it's a *problem* at all. I'm thinking of stealing a Gubba man and seeing what's inside.'

'Barny broke one the other day - there's nothing inside but solid milk.'

'Oh, I doubt very much that he did,' said the Doctor with a patro-nising smile. 'Ever heard of statue therapy, laddie? No? Might be just the thing for you. It's a matter of identity and esteem, you see. You go to Scardummy Garden. Find your statue. Pamper that abomina-tion. Give it some nice threads. Decency anticipates investigation, but it's a start.'

Gregor whimpered with impatience. 'I can't ponce around in the Garden, it creeps me out. I don't have time, I have responsibilities. GI Bill says he'll destroy me for stealing the ballgame.'

'I doubt he used the word "destroy". GI Bill's a butterball with a smattering of motor skills, nothing more. But I accept that stupidi-ty's crown presses upon you with its duties and obligations. Elderly folk to care for?'

'No. They used to live in the Swamp of Eternal Enmity/ Degradation. Got sold some tin siding that gave the shack too much weight. It sank without trace.'

'How convenient. Without trace you say? And you still deny you're a pig servant. You're a sly bastard, eh?'

'Listen, I was in the dinosaur skull because I wanted to purge my lust. The guard came in. I had to hide. That's all.'

'Fascinating. I happen to know it was your gaunt associate Mr Edge who suffered that repellent complaint.' The doctor's laugh was harsh. 'You know what Bingo Violaine would have said about you, laddie? "The need to convince is unique to plain men." And if you were in the head, where was the brain?' Doctor Perfect demanded, leaning forward so that his own skull tackle threatened to tip into Gregor's face like a jelly. 'There's two ways we can do this, laddie - the easy way, or the hard way. I've decided that we're going to do it the hard way. So just say whatever comes into your head.'

'What'll you do?'

'I'll do the same. This friend of yours - Barny. You seem to idolise him.'

'Not really. He eats baby trolls, after all. When he's nervous.'

'Trolls are just mimic vegetation. At the purely physical level they're a sort of fungus. Tell me in your own words, what's the look of an elephant.'

'An ant.'

'The same?'

'Bigger and deformed.'

'Same noise?'

'Magnified.'

'To the power of?'

'A million.'

'What do you see in this inkblot?'

'A brain.'

'And this?'

'A brain.'

'And this?'

'A brain.'

'And this?'

'A brain.'

'And this?'

'A brain.'

'And this? A brain I'll bet, eh laddie?'

'Yes, yes a brain, how can I think of anything else with that suppurating lump of slime sat on your head like a rotting frog?'

'What?'

'Your *brain*, doctor, your *brain* - let me outta here!' Gregor sat up and shoved at his inquisitor. Stumbling backward, the doctor began shrieking incoherently - his brain had toppled from his head and hung between his shoulderblades, connected by a few taut arteries. He whirled around the dungeon, grasping backward like a harpy trying to zip herself up. The screams were outraged, wounded, inhuman. Gregor ran as fast as his arms and legs could take him.

Doomed Eddie Gallo sat smiling, the room a sunless forest of drying underwear. He looked up vaguely. 'Mr Edgy. How are you?'

'Enjoyment keeps me huge, doomed Eddie Gallo, you know me.'

'Yes I do. Siddown. I met that girl of yours - Amy. She was out there snogging a flower. I asked her its name and she said she didn't know. You young people today, eh?'

Edgy chuckled affably, admiring the room's adornments. 'You sure are the last word in underwear, doomed Eddie Gallo.'

'Think so?' The candidate radiated a shy pride.

'But be careful. Public biological steaming is considered a weakness in politics. The Mayor does his laundry behind bronze doors three foot thick. That's sort of what I need to chat about.'

'Lard cake?'

'No, thank you. So listen, what's with you and Barny?'

'Barny. Oh, he's great - a star.'

'You like him, right? So why put up thousands of posters all over town saying he's a bastard?'

'Oh, that was old Mr Hammer, some chap who wandered in here. Said he had a fishy master of some kind who'd back the whole nine yards, make me a present of it. Sure you won't have some lard?'

'What did Hammer look like?'

'Tall. Heavy coat. Clearly a stranger to the climate round here. Had a big, stretched nose. No eyes at all. Below that, jowls. Took only five hundred biscuits in return. It's alright, Barny agrees to the whole thing.'

'Where'd you get that pretty idea?'

'Hammer said so.'

'D'you believe everything you're told, doomed Eddie Gallo?'

'Why not? What did that Villain say? "An original hides his confusion."'

'Violaine. And it's "Confusion hides its origins". This campaign of yours has got Barny canned from the sorting office and pounced-on by one and all. An old woman punched the front of his face near Snorter's. You've got to change your policy.'

'I don't mind. I'd no intention of causing distress. As a matter of fact I'm not sorry to change. I'd prefer something sunnier anyway. I saw a dog the other day - something about dogs, perhaps?'

'Dogs are good for nearly anything.'

'Think so? Whatever it is, it'll need to involve some sort of row or disagreement. That's how it works, apparently.'

'Dogs stare. Pant. Fight in the street.'

'Really?'

'It means less than nothing to them. I'm writing a book about it. It'll make my fortune, why not?'

'A book, with pictures? What's it called?'

'I think there'll be one picture, an oil painting. But they keep re-thinking the title. They've changed it now to *Savaged Beyond Repair*.'

'I'll look out for that.'

'You've got my vote, doomed Eddie Gallo.'

Mayor Rudloe welcomed a young *Blank Stare* reporter into his office. 'Sorry to bring you all the way up here - I'm up to my fleshy face in vital paperwork as you can see. And here you are, full of bones and spirit. Well done.'

'Thank you Mr Mayor.' The journalist sat and flipped open a note-book.

'Well, you can be proud, coming out into the field - journalists are the butter in society's backside - pardon the terminology but I'm another one who likes to tell it like it is, you and me alike. I wish I was in a real position of power, such as yourself - I'm just a servant of the people, what do I know? I'm just a man. "Cures are still hostage to nature," as our great philosopher said. I'm at your dis-posal.'

The journalist related unconfirmed reports that a group of pro-testors had stood outside Barny Juno's house, wringing their hands so hard they wore down like soap. 'Apparently they all left with tiny hands.'

'This sort of thing doesn't surprise me in the least. The man known as Barny Juno is walking streets for which he is manifestly unqualified. He's unpalatable, devious, given to fits of rage, his man-ner wild and truculent and, yes, he's quite the waste of time. You might say he's the mutant in society's boiler room.'

'Have you met Juno?'

Rudloe laughed without a shred of meaning. 'I have reports that he gads about with an actual zombie. It wears sparring gloves, if you can believe it.'

'Do you believe it?'

'I believe whatever is necessary for the continued wellbeing of this community. Another of his friends is a man with a transparent head, filled with cloudy water. Now I ask you, is that any way to run a set of blameless associations. It seems that if anything holds still long enough, he'll befriend it. The man's drunk on his own power. Thriving like a bastard while the sun sets on us all.'

'Why don't you send in the militia before he wigs out completely? Do you have some serious reservations?'

The Mayor leaned back and demonstrated that he could puff his cheeks out with the best of them. 'That's a large subject. There is no precedent for such an action. Meaning, we've never set the militia upon this particular man before. But they are maintaining a state of constant readiness and I've made it perfectly clear that I will not hesitate to devise a sacramental penalty to the satisfaction of jeer and justice, subject to procedure. This knife will not forever sleep in my head. And it is my considered opinion that, for whatever fantastic reason, Juno is spoiling for censure. I offer no apology for my hard line on this matter. This community has a great many strengths and I will not see it dishonoured.'

'What do you see as those strengths?'

'I'm glad you asked. Two words. Two life-changing little words, my friend. Frisky skylarking. When I stand on my balcony and gaze down I see a people who are spirited, folksy and with no elite.' The Mayor set his jaw like the sternest of statesmen. 'I find it sad that one bad apple chooses to stretch and dye his earlobes for the sole purpose of instilling sick apprehension in the onlooker. And I make no bones about it - insolence and ostentation, biting at random, all the really back-breaking work of social outrage, these spell disaster for our community. And that's just a baffling fragment of my policy in that area.'

The reporter wound up with the usual question regarding rumours of an infestation of floor lobsters in the mayoral palace.

'Well now how could that be? Floor lobsters are the result of a corrupt environment.' The Mayor made a heavy stamping motion under the desk, smashing a scuttling carapace and covering the sound with a blustering cough. He shook hands again with the journalist while guiding him to the door.

When the journalist had left, Mayor Rudloe sank back into his own face. 'That'll put fish in his custard.'

'I ate all the headstones you brought,' Sweeney gurgled, the glass mask of his chestplate filling with bile. 'None of which will be of much use again.' The convolute emperor of white shell and gizzard shifted in his arterial chair. 'Worked wonders on the digestive tract.' He spread his ribs like a flashcoat, revealing intestines and a mothball heart.

Dietrich raised his black ice skull from the padlock embryos he'd been puzzling over. 'Frustration's fathom gold to us. Are you sure you want to go up there? You'll have to downsize a little.'

'The man's almost incoherently mellow. Harrowingly honest. I'll unravel the conundrum of his guts.' Sweeney's own guts were pullulating, umbilical colours shining like china and framed by buck ribs which closed again like the jaws of a shark. As he sealed and hardened over, Sweeney's yellow eyes were distant, focused on inner processes.

'You're sure he's your enemy?'

'Does a stream flow on the seabed?' Sweeney replied, and clouted Dietrich's nose with a vague gesture. He pushed down on the arms of the shell throne, his hydraulic gullet dumping black ink in a damburst. 'Well it's iffy, you're right. But the wheels of hell turn slow. Shift gears occasionally.' At the join, spinal resin stretched, snapping, leaving rounds of shell like a king prawn hull. Sweeney straightened up, dangling semi-liquid and gushing bloodwater. 'Vast future, I squash you in the nursery.'

Sliding his shadow along, so thick it was almost a voice, he became a silhouette before blue alcohol flames.

He squinted to perceive a horizon churning with targets. Though too small for even a demon's eyes, I withdrew through miles of rock into utter safety.

1O

HOUSE TORNADO

All life wears a surface for your glance, like you're doing now

Barny had a brief natter with Feral Beryl, a useless old hag who lived in the swamp, knew nothing of interest and wanted to be left alone. The notion that she was wise persisted through the gobsmacked embarrassment of her inquisitors and their subsequent falsification of the wisdom received. No-one liked to admit they'd just been screamed at and kicked savagely in the balls.

When Barny arrived at his parents' shack he was still gasping from the Beryl attack and, leaning into the moth cage to kiss Ramone hello, sucked the silvery creature into his mouth.

'You brought a paper?' Ma Juno barked from her concrete chair.

Barny swallowed reflexively. 'Er ... no mother.' He slammed the moth cage and became brisk. 'I see the hair's still attached and thriving, father. Let's go on to the porch and check it out.'

'What?' Pa Juno was bewildered as Barny hauled him by the arm.

'Go, Julius,' cackled Ma Juno. 'He's your son, not mine.'

Swamp glue crawled past the porch. The darkness zipped with

springloaded gobs and blurring stings.

Pa Juno's plasmate hair was palpitating slowly, aglow like a fluorescent kraken. He spoke in a low, confidential tone. 'I think I understand why you wanted to get out of there.'

'Oh?' Barny choked.

'Saw the paper. BARNY JUNO RELEASES CROC IN PACKED THEATRE. Hid it from your mother, on the floor of the moth cage. Another headline like that'd break her heart. I'd like to know what exactly you hoped to achieve when you did a thing like that.'

'I've got a problem with the Horned One, father.'

'Why you coughing, you got a cold? You on drugs?'

'Something in my throat. So what do you think I should do?'

'If she's that horny, stick with her. You think you know fear?' Pa Juno glanced cautiously in through the stained window. 'That woman married me to within an inch of my life. A vacuum kills guarantees, boy. A maggot turns into a butterfly, a lover turns into a maggot.'

Barny had already heard about his parents' early relationship. At the wedding they exchanged rings with such venom the priest let out a small cry.

'And you damn well better mark my words because I know this - it's like cooking someone from frozen, it takes a while. That's how it is when you know the complicated pain of marriage ...'

Stunned with boredom, Barny watched the light and shadow cast on torn wood by his father's undulating locks.

'Remember what I always told you?'

'Never eat grapes.'

'Not that, boy.'

'Hold the hen and I'll do the rest.'

'No.'

'Broken glass at street corners is vitamin C.'

'No, I told you happiness functions best in bed. So hang on to Magenta Blaze. Know what I pray of a morning? That god should leave me alone, if he can. That, Joe, is my brief opinion.'

'Well my name's not Joe, but I see what you mean.'

Ma Juno exploded from the house shrieking 'Gone - Ramone is gone, oh my papery boy' or something like that and Barny knew the jig was up. 'Look what your son put in his place.' She held up the newspaper with the croc headline and her face roared off in all directions.

'I never released a croc - and anyway it was an alligator. Its legs are delicate.'

'Oh they're delicate are they,' sobbed his mother as Pa Juno held her, scowling at Barny. 'Well what about the thin, silvery wings of

Ramone. My tiny quivering fluff-faced child. He was more of a son than you'll ever be.'

'And you're no son of mine,' said Pa Juno.

The shaman Beltane Carom glanced at the poster of the jet black demon, its filed teeth and fungal white eyes. 'I know of a fiend designed along those lines. Articulated. Bayonet ears. Sweeney.'

Edgy was stood in Carom's yard, a tile court worked into neat geometries. The walled sanctuary was scattered with barnacle leaves. 'What would it want with Bubba? It's levering the election - you seen the paper here?' Edgy slapped *The Blank Stare.* 'Drunk with power, says the Mayor. Barny's never been drunk with anything.'

Carom was a mild, soft-spoken man, not given to drama. He gave the thing proper consideration. 'Sweeney sits at the hub of a billion creepchannels - a lot on his plate. Maybe Juno's got something this demon wants. Or Juno took something from him. You know when you take the heart, or the spine? Or whatever of a demon? The motorcord fluid's a fine natural weedkiller. There's a defector demon living here in Accomplice but I don't think he's involved. Juno's into animals, right?'

'The winged and stepping animals of the earth, right, he lives for them.'

'Maybe Sweeney covets one of those. He's a soul eater. Marinates them delicately in the creepchannel nets. Considers modern souls are too bland without it.'

'Barny's not a channel racer. Hasn't got the hardware, them fancy motors with the nerve chassis. Doesn't interest him.'

'Folk wander in by accident. Most people suspect the existence of these adjacent realms as one nostril suspects the existence of the other.' Carom gazed at a little sun balancing on a leaf, though there was no sun in the sky. 'Or maybe something about Barny sticks in the demon's craw zone or gullet area.'

'I don't get it.'

'When a monster passes, we take it for another whose favourable opinion we must seek. Barny doesn't because he's unaware of that stuff. Not dumb, just totally preoccupied.'

'I know what you mean. I saw him carrying a church bell made of jelly one time. He dropped it and started crying. Eight squirrels and eleven birds came down out of the trees and sat on his shoulders. It looked like they were whispering comfort into his ears.'

'I wouldn't like to have nineteen animals on *my* shoulders.' Carom absently shuffled a stack of meat cards as big as a loaf of bread. 'I was there when Mister Spiderman's funeral blew up in

Barny's face. Mayhem of a very particular type does seem to accrete around the guy.'

'Okay well I'm meeting the gang up the Anti, wanna come?'

Carom begged off, saying he had to explore his dark side.

'I'm supposed to do something for the Plunder Parade,' said BB Henrietta, smoking a cigar. Most of the crew were in the Anti Room, a club accidentally bonegrown from a drifting spore. The walls were rippled and ribbed, slimy white, sporadically flushing and pumping with fluorescent smears. Sometimes cinderblocks were lowered quickly from the ceiling on tarry rope, injuring or otherwise inconveniencing the revellers before being drawn up again.

'So?' asked Edgy.

'I don't wanna.'

'What about the amateur dramatics etcetera? That production you did of *I Love Strutting* a few months ago was a riot. People were screaming with laughter. I pissed myself.'

'People were screaming *because* you pissed yourself. That's what caused the riot. Even *you* weren't laughing. I just don't feel like standing on a float dressed as a cake or whatever, I'd rather watch.'

'Amy'll be disappointed, I think she's writing something.'

'Oh god. What?'

'A recital or something. I think it's about eyelids.'

'Eyelids.'

'So? Yes, eyelids. Anything wrong with that? Give her some support.'

'She's *your* girlfriend, Edgy, it's your place to support her goddamn eyelids.'

'But the Parade's traditional.'

'So's death and decay.'

Fang, cutting a sorry figure in stripes of duct tape, was staring at oblivion in a corner and didn't comment.

'I'll watch,' BB continued. 'From the Tower.'

'The guard guy Murdster won't let anyone up there. Some kinda trouble with the moral fibre a few years back.'

'I know all about it.'

'You don't know.'

'Oh I know the story on the fibre. Made of ham.'

'No.'

'And a dog got it.'

'Dogs don't eat ham.'

'They sure as hell don't eat moral fibre, Scarecrow. You see ads for dogfood saying "with added moral fibre"?'

Gregor came back from the bathroom and sat down. 'So I went to the shrink. Left him shrieking, with his entire brain hanging right down on some nerves. Says I should go pamper my statue. I might even do it.'

'Really?'

'I can take or leave it. I suppose I'm just clutching at straws. Where's Barny?'

'Gone to see Feral Beryl. I guess if anyone knows what's going on, it's her.' Edgy downed his drink. 'That Bubba, he's got a head on him like a baby dog.'

BB Henrietta frowned. 'You mean a puppy?'

'Head like a puppy, that's right. And it's getting younger and glossier by the minute.'

'That's not what it says in *The Stare*. According to that he's drunk with power.'

'According to the Mayor,' grunted Edgy with disgust. 'Enough of the yammer. I'm dancing.'

'Why don't you just stab us in the heart,' said Gregor.

BB honked with laughter.

Edgy got up, walking off as music began flushing the capillaries in the wall. Edgy had created a dance called the Last Straw. Mankind, plodding and perishable, would never be equal to this flailing freak-out. Passing fungal tables and rib-caged lightbulbs, alternately staggering under some killing weight and sloshing back and forth in an exhausted way, he reached the floor and began a set of murky and obscure manoeuvres. He seemed at first to be climbing against a landslide. Soon he was arc-welding a large copper melon. Then he pumped one arm as though mashing the face of a monk against a rippled glass partition. Now he was trying to stuff an octopus into an overhead luggage rack. Next came something like a frantic yank at an emergency cord - the invisible cord came away in his hand, wrapping round him like a snake. Then he began windmilling his arms in shockingly arbitrary vortices, volleying barely audible shouts above the music. Finally his body exploded into the tantrum of his career, a mazurka which, appended to his human qualities, rendered him temporarily into a more perilous species.

Like snowflakes, no two fistfights are the same. When a strange raver approached Edgy - one togged up like some giant white mantis, all slick and fluted - Edgy was pitching a fit which seemed the hairtrigger release of a lifetime's rage. Amid strobe-glimpses of zombies having a tough time, hectic bone dust and benthic wall channels, the stranger's pelt of sickly yellow leather was glistening open to show a black lattice-work of nerve barbs. Tormented by loose-jointed convulsions and releasing sporadic yelps, Edgy whirled loose, kicking him with an arm that wasn't good for much else. A set of mantrap teeth spun into the shadows.

Opening his eyes a short time later, Edgy was becoming dimly aware that he had struck someone - but his attention was caught by Neville Peth and his wife, who was as primly pretty as a paper doily. They were sat in a booth and seemed out of place here, evidently slumming. But Edgy's performance had them agape. What a godsend!

'That guy shouldn't have got in my way!' Edgy shouted, spotlit and tussling with his own stomach. 'I'm harebrained and reckless, I don't mind saying. A beacon for trouble! I could even join a club for hazardous activities!' He stanced wide, beckoning the masses. 'Come on! I'll take you all on! I don't care what danger I'm inviting!'

Disgusted, Neville Peth and his wife shuffled out of the booth and skittered away toward the exit.

'I love the glories of danger!' Edgy called after them as they slammed out. He looked back to find himself surrounded by growling adversaries.

Ropes of gore hanging from his broken mouth, Sweeney flung himself down a side alley. In one wall was a mundane door over which he had superimposed a gore gate. He stepped into this now and was folded down to a pain bandwidth where he hung in the chiming cold. Dietrich floated up to him, bile corpuscles bouncing off his breastplate. 'I told you, he's a nutter.'

1 1

MUSETTE

A single punch can be directed toward a waiter and your own advantage

Barny was fortunate in having a couple of back-up father figures. The first was Mr Peterson, who sat forever poolside with a drink the same colour as his tan. Peterson owned a few hydro farms and basked in this and other facts. He had a fat, friendly smile and a right hand made of coloured glass. Barny drove a car for him once when a friend of Mr Peterson had to run from a noisy building. Mr

Peterson appreciated this kindness so much that he listened to Barny's problems now and again, though whatever the problem was, Mr Peterson put it down to women. Barny found a broken cabbage near a rusty generator one time and Mr Peterson said the problem was with women.

'This your idea of a dark night of the soul, Barny?' Mr Peterson asked now. 'A few housecalls? Tea?'

'Got any biscuits?'

'Drink this - it'll put hair on your grave. So what's happening in the random world?'

'I seem to be having some kind of problem with the devil, Mr Peterson.'

'No, Barny. Your only problem is with women. It's like you to blame it all on some vengeful mutant. Eh? What are we dealing with here? Fuzzy thinking, Barny, you being the worst offender. I mean here you are, a young guy, with okay looks and a cock as big as all outdoors. You could have any girl you wanted. And you got the real, dyed-in-the-wool, water-on-the-snaredrum unoriginality to hang around with someone like the Blaze, just for the looks of her. Insulting to her too, if you want the raw truth of it. And I know how it is, there's certain images make an ache in a sensitive man. Like Bardot hugging that baby seal. Wouldn't you like to just jump in there. So what if she was blond. So was Bardot and it served her well.' Mr Peterson gestured across the pool to the allotment, where Mrs Peterson was crouching amid transparent, pullulating globes. 'She's in my blood and my understanding. I don't know anymore what she looks like to other people. I'd want that for you, Bubba.'

'Is your wife growing jellyfish, Mr Peterson?'

'Never you mind. I don't wanna get into the whole thing with you here, but go with a girl where you have to be faking it and you'll strip your gears. An honest relationship's as satisfying as drawing in biro on a banana.'

'Good then?'

'God Almighty, Bubba. I'm saying faking doesn't take, except as a terrible sickness. I remember one time, a beautiful girl asked me if I could ride a horse. I said I could, of course I could ride a horse. In fact I was racking my brains to remember what a horse *was*. She wanted to take me riding.'

'Did you fall off the horse, Mr Peterson?'

'No, I was fine actually. Damnedest thing. I thought I'd fold like a cloth hat.'

Barny looked at the slow surface of the water.

'So, er, what shall I do about this devil problem, Mr Peterson.'

'Ah there you go Bubba, getting all agitated. Alright, here it is, something I read once, I always remembered it. From me to you. "Age is not care, starvation is not understatement, thoughts are not invocations." Eh? What, too rich for your blood? Just talking to you's exhausting, you know that? God Almighty. Okay, get this simple setup into your skull, Bubba. Men love women. Women can't handle how much men love them. Men get confused. There you have it. Now leave me alone, I'm eating a sandwich here.'

The other paternal fallback ran the Juice Museum, a repository of ignored stories, rejected wisdom and forgotten capers, based in a derelict stone watchtower near the sea. It was in the nature of the Juice Museum that it went almost totally unacknowledged by the populace.

Mr Low, an old man with a face as furry as a dust ventilator, was stocktaking when Barny arrived. If Barny was after tea he'd come to the right place - Low drank more than was required to kill him, and hallucinated. His tea genie appeared to him in the deeps of evening, chattering about sand slues and starched delicate bombers, shredded linen draping through them like ghosts. Barny made deliberate noise as he entered the small storeroom. It was a place of instrument chairs, escaped filigree, police trees and clock lanterns - plenty of stuff to clatter. 'Eh? Juniper my boy, I'm sorting a bunch of Maraffi sketches. Anything else of the kind. Map of the demi-maze.' Low pointed to an involuted diagram which trailed into vague waves at one end. 'Tally sticks,' he said, picking up and discarding some notched wood. 'Heart dust in a smoked bottle, seashells gone to sleep in offices, glass eyes chipped in a playground, a dead baby as a result of language, the sound of an illusion ageing, a dozen tumour gods, and this box here. Wood is time tided.' He opened the small wooden box and his face glowed with the fluttering light. 'The resin-scented dark of a fir forest, eyelash afternoons of flybuzz, trams smelling of thunderstorms.' He shut the box and tossed it aside.

'I need your advice Mr Low.'

Low sat on a chair as fragile as himself, breathing hard. 'Ah. Your problem with the Mayor and so on, I saw the paper, you're drunk with power now, it seems.' He trotted his tongue on the roof of his mouth. 'You're a decision grafted onto confusion, Juniper. No solution. Ill-matched, oil and water. But you'll serve, you see? It's an old trick but folk forget so as to be fooled over and entertained. Denial on all fronts. Weather wasn't always like this, you know that? This heat. Tropical storms. People forget it rained painfully cold back a way. Started with the loss of nature. Love concrete and the moon's dirt, you see? Measurement razors the sky, wintering history. New songs eat at the nets and stone lips pocket the truth. Look at this.'

Low reached into a tea crate and dragged out a plate of hammered tin. 'Kelman's Deadly Sombrero - hazardous titanium headgear worn by Jack Kelman, a stoker long deceased. Here's an otherwise unremarkable man, never sought liberty, dated no stars, went away unknown - but left this in testament.' He rummaged again, bringing out more arcane salvage. 'Flower's Joyce Belt. A True Polychrome Lad. The Barefaced Cheek. The Skeleton of Manila's Mustache.'

'Who's Manila?'

'I don't entirely know. And these sea-stained books here exist despite the entrenched scepticism of the official line - *Cable's Diary*. Got a book on the Glass Alphabet with pictograms and all. Learnt some.' He chirped strangely, then continued. '*Doll Apocrypha*. And here are the *Violaine Prophecies*.'

'Violaine's not forgotten, Mr Low - he's a what-do-you-call-it, a brainsaver. For when people go a long time without thinking but want to say something anyway.'

'But few people know about the *Prophecies*. He said this stuff while a demon was eating his brain. Listen to this: "Where the word goes, evil follows." Not up to his usual standard is it? And what have we got here, the *Silvane Letters*.'

'The Silvane what?'

A dark-haired girl appeared in the doorway. 'The Wesley Kern Gun, father.' She was holding something which looked like a twist of bleached beachwood.

'You've met Chloe, Juniper.' Mr Low stood to take the relic. 'This belongs downstairs,' he said, and shuffled out. The girl came over and sat on a table, looking at Barny with eyes as black as concord grapes.

Barny had last glimpsed her against the bitter bile-light of the creepchannel. He wasn't sure he'd ever seen her here. Barny was again completely hypnotised by her bare white feet. He wanted to kneel and lick upward until his face was buried in her fur. 'What's your favourite accident?' she asked suddenly.

'Oh ... um, flying bar of iron.'

'End to end?'

'Yes, from a building site to a passerby.'

'Me too.' She looked at him like a bead-eyed wombat. 'Are you alright? Worried about the animals?'

Barny was watching how each sentence strummed the sinews of her throat. 'Golden Sid's at the house,' he said absently.

'Golden Sid?'

'Yeah. He's a class act. And I've put dark glasses on the gator.' He told her about the mob which had been picketing his house until the lion, chased by hunger, exploded through a window and galloped down the gangplank, feasting someone to the ground. 'As luck would have it it was just a tailor.'

She looked as if she cut her own hair. Barny thought the dreams underneath would be the warmest and safest in the world - that's how bad it had gotten already. She was talking about something and swinging her legs back and forth. Somehow because she was barefoot she was completely naked to him. 'Like the little triggers inside an insect,' she was saying. Her mouth was so big it almost flipped her head in half.

'Uh?'

'Wesley Kern.'

Barny stood up like a robot. 'Well, it's been good, but I've got to go and help Sid now with the leopard, who's a bit moody since I had a meat gargoyle clinging to the roof over there. I hope to see you again madam.'

Walking out with the awkwardness of a rod-puppet, he felt like a man leaving a bank with a gold bar in his pants.

Becoming a little desperate, Barny went to consult the Church of Automata re his problems. He didn't know much about doll worship and had it pictured as a listening head on a larynx, tilting a little with each statement, shit-scary. He rapped at a door made of solid diamond and, seeing it nudge open, began to relate his tale. But the head poking from the doorcrack was a worn china skull inset with smoked glass eyes. Barny started screaming, a Doll Engineer swept out and, instantly apprised of the situation, tore the belt from Barny's pants for the purpose of thrashing the living daylights out of him.

Hammering at the door of the Powderhouse a short time later, Barny was greeted by a Fusehead with party streamers hanging from his ears. Beltless, Barny's pants descended. The affronted priest slammed the door in his face and opened it again to beam at the damage.

A while later Barny was sifting for scraps in a trashcan out back of the chef school. He needed meat for the animals but all he could find was pasta. Noises from inside - the back door was ajar - Barny peered through.

The instructor Quandia Lucent, who also ran the Ultimatum Restaurant, was strutting up and down before the initiates. 'Perfection including tip,' he was saying. 'Behold.'

And he opened the double doors of a garishly painted cabinet.

Inside hung a seahorse the size of a child, its ragged gills quivering like lettuce. The initiates gasped, kneeling. 'There is detestable dinner made,' said the seahorse in an eery, quailing voice, 'eventually someone must retrieve it. Thus, we thrive.'

'We thrive,' the initiates repeated.

'Try explaining tyranny,' the seahorse sibilated, 'without using the word "pasta". These fools can't get enough of it. If a genie gave them three wishes, they would select pasta for all three.'

'Recite the creed,' snapped Quandia Lucent.

'Garbage,' called the initiates. 'At crippling prices.'

The gang were at Snorters cafe. Edgy had not remained unaffected by his encounter with the eight-foot mantis, and was telling Barny about it. Only one of his legs had been broken in the later brawl and he felt like a lucky man. 'Punched something, apparently. Rhymes with "demon".'

'Was it a demon?'

'Yes. Purporting to be a normal fella.'

'That dance of yours is a heck of a deal.'

'It wasn't purporting to be normal,' stated BB Henrietta for the record. 'It was like the thing in the posters, but white.'

'I swallowed Ramone,' said Barny. 'My mother thinks I stole him and set him loose on the community.'

'That's tough, Bubba,' said Edgy. 'How about you replace it with a cigarette butt.'

'I think they'll notice the difference,' BB Henrietta pointed out to Edgy as though speaking to a child. 'You do know there's a difference, right?'

'Well not everyone has my razor-sharp perceptions, baby. I have to be that way, the life I live in the Motel. In fact the sensations in my extremities are seven times more intense than those of the average man. With their richness and distinction, I could sell my leg perceptions alone for a mint.'

'Extra strong?'

'That's what I've been telling you.'

Gregor chipped in, stirring his coffee. 'Maybe Bubba should say he tracked the moth down, then buy another one, show it to 'em.'

Barny intercepted this. 'No, they'll know right away - you think moths are uniform, featureless, then look at one close up and it's got the face of Walter Matthau.'

'You wish,' snorted BB Henrietta.

'So what are you doing for the Parade finally, little missy?' Edgy asked. 'What do I tell Ms Gort?'

'Tell her what you like, I'm not doing it.'

'Okay, just play merry hell with everything. Things being how they are, she'll just have to do a reading. And God help us all.'

'What's so bad about the poetry?' asked Barny.

'She's got theories, Bubba. Says it should come naturally, blend with nature. So when people hear her read it they should respond like nothing's happened.'

'So what is it, pastoral stuff? Flowers?'

'No, it's terrible. I don't understand what the hell's going on. She's got this thing called "I Freeze and Smash the Velvet". I hear it, I feel like I'm reversing down a skyride. She's wanting me to get her published by Feeble Champ Books, like I've got any influence.'

'How's the dog book going?' asked Gregor.

'Really well, Round One. I've done a few more chapters: Casino Dogs, Dogs in a Warm Breeze, Dogs Who Change Directions, Dogs Who Sin Against Me, Dogs With Blurred Legs, Tramlike Dogs Who Shuffle, er ... Dogs With Weepy Eyes, Tapdancing Dogs, Dogs Who Know But Don't Say, Dogs Who Enlist, Dogs With More Than Five Ears, Dogs Who Freeze Solid and er ... oh yeah, Labradors. But Feeble Champ went and changed the title again.'

'To what.'

'*When Dogs Seize Control*. They don't know what the hell they're doing. And the marketing plan's conspicuous by its absence. So I've decided to kind of advertise it myself at the Parade. Me and some dogs, with a sign about the book. It'll go down a blast.'

'What about the cover,' Gregor said. 'The oil painting. You with your arm round the dalmatian's shoulder.'

'Alsatian,' Edgy corrected. 'Anyway they seem to have forgotten about it. They want a photograph of a dog, now, walking along a path. It's insanity. But never mind all that.' Edgy adopted a wily, confidential tone. 'Because while everyone else has been out eating moths I've been consulting an authority on matters demonic about Barny's situation. Answer me this, Bubba. The gator, where did you find it?'

'In some slime in a creepchannel wall.'

'Well there you go, the worst I suspected. You're not a creep racer, that kind of commute takes nerves of steel, Bubba, steel.'

'Fang goes through sometimes.'

'Bubba, how can I ever make you understand - Fang's dead. He's a really old dead guy walking around. Why do you think he drinks embalming fluid? Sleeps in a peat bog? His head's black and swollen like a bowling ball.'

Barny chuckled to himself. 'He's great isn't he?'

'Yes he is.'

'He's a tough hombre.'

'But listen Bubba, this creep entrance, where was it?'

'Well you know how it is, you never know where they are until you're near and you remember, so there it is suddenly, and afterwards you don't remember again.'

'Because it's semi-etheric, right? Like how you forget a dream. But you know the general area?'

'I remember I was walking Help in the Furfur district, around the scrub near the skeleton coast road.'

'Case closed. That reptile's been doped with knowhow from the creepchannel,' Edgy concluded. 'Maybe it's even smart and that's why it hasn't bitten the hell out of you. The demon wants his bone back. Say it with me, people.'

'I've never understood the Announcement Horse,' muttered Gregor vaguely, gazing into space. 'What's he meant to be, a robot? Another statue, made of metal? Does he eat hay like a normal horse? What's the deal, has anyone ever asked him?'

'Doctor Perfect says it's just armour filled with heavy smoke,' said BB Henrietta.

'Has anyone heard a thing I've said?' barked Edgy.

'I was behind the chef school,' Barny began to confide haltingly. 'Earlier on. And I overheard the chefs taking ... taking orders from-from a giant seahorse in a painted cabinet. Talking all about pasta. Oh Edgy it scared me.'

'Of course it's scary, it's inescapable.'

Edgy stopped, gasping.

'Pasta. That's it.'

He clattered his bone crutches into place, and tilted out of the cafe.

12

THE SCAR GARDEN

A man without error is a geographical impossibility

Barny showed up at the Mayoral palace and was taken to Rudloe's office. Max Gaffer's eyeball abacus bust and went everywhere. 'Very foolhardy, Juno,' said the Mayor, standing. 'You come in here tracking mud all over my campaign. Oh, you don't need to tell me. You want I should hold off, go easy on you. I need hardly remind you each of that gator's teeth is a snag in my plans.' The Mayor turned to Max Gaffer. 'Eh?'

'Outstanding, sir.'

The Mayor was getting into the stride. 'Carnivore on a short fuse? I don't think so. Thrashing? Not in this town. We deal with the Steinway Spiders don't we? I intend to spearhead speculation as to your irrefutable guilt in this matter.'

Barny sat down amiably. He didn't seem in a hurry to respond.

Uncertain, the Mayor seated himself also. 'Alright, I've heard enough. You know, in my darker moments I rue the fates for making me mayor of a place so obscure it's where ants go to die. People frying eggs on their cars all goddamn day. I feel exhausted just talking about it. This position involves more than just pointing a crusher at some tame flunky, you know. Which reminds me.' He picked up the phone. 'Erno - get these clattering vermin squared away will you?'

Erno came in with a metal hook and started swiping at the floor - Barny realised there were three huge corruption bugs on the carpet. Not for the first time, Barny wondered whether these creatures were related in any way to the thing that had birthed from Dumbar's head. The number of legs differed, alas.

'You see, Juno, it's like this. You can't go wrong spending money on death and murder. A lot of people have noticed it through the years. But besides the appalling expense, why squander the goodwill of the electorate immediately? All we need is deceit, an enemy, and negligence. Phrase horrors like an invitation and you'll get a crowd. Ask Sidebar Billy over there. Even the pessimist believes he'll finally acquire others' respect amid rubble. Of course by that time I'll be dead and swelling the strawberries. Eh Max?'

'Outstanding, sir.'

'So crawling in here trying to bargain, Juno, you're walking on dangerous water. Between you and me the Conglomerate have got it all tied up anyway. You're mining your own road. Give it up.'

'I'm not sure what you mean by all that, Mr Mayor, but I'm pleased to meet you.'

'So what do you want.'

'I'm looking for a job.'

'A job.'

'Yeah as a doorman, a bodyguard, anything you like.'

'A job.'

'Beggars can't be choosers, ma'am.'

'I don't believe it,' the Mayor groped. 'I don't ... tell me why the hell I should give you any kind of a job here.'

'I think shoes should be sold in big jars. Like gherkins.'

The Mayor leaned forward, enunciating carefully. 'Do you understand that I'm basing my campaign on a demonisation of you and your supposed depravities?'

'Eh?'

'I don't believe it, you're a fantastic moron. Hey, what's with the troll? Oh my god. Oh, mother of mercy. Max, are you seeing this too?'

'Outstanding, sir.'

'In my whole life I've never ...' The Mayor fell silent as, crossing some inner threshold, his rage boiled into focus. He swelled with malice. 'Get out. That's right: out.'

Barny stood calmly, smiled in bewilderment at all present, and left. As the door wafted shut behind him he heard the Mayor snarl something about waking the Brigade.

'Agree,' thought BB Henrietta, 'and he'll believe he's thinking.' She had a mop of blond hair like the seedhead of a dandelion and failed to inform the relevant authorities. She approached the Tower of Nowt and banged loud at the door.

Murdster the Sentinel opened up, glowering.

'You make that look so easy,' grinned BB Henrietta.

A beefy man with a boilerplate forehead, Murdster seemed always in a foul and vengeful mood. When mixed with his surprise at BB's temerity, this resulted in something resembling contemplation. 'I'm locked in my safety.'

'You certainly are.'

'Tradition doesn't play.'

'But that's so sad.' BB adjusted her head angle, tipping it carefully aside.

'Snort and people retune their ears.'

'I know what you mean.' A slumping nod.

'Ears won't live forever - anyway they're like erasers.'

BB's giggling skills were badly marred by cigar use but she had a go.

'They call me "stone face".'

'That's horrible and it's not true.'

'Sober yet all aflame, the new sinners time their generosity.'

'Oh I agree.'

'You want something from me.'

'Bargain Basement Henrietta. And I see there's no fooling you, Mr Murdster sir.'

*

It's difficult for a man made of a single muscle to look shifty - this was to the slab-bodied GI Bill's advantage. Still smarting from his recent defeat in the ballpark when Gregor had failed to show, he lurked after Barny and Gregor as they approached Scardummy Garden. The Garden was an ornate precinct containing statues of everyone in Accomplice - it was traditional to visit and decorate your statue with fancy clobber. Some never bothered, letting theirs over-grow with ivy. The statues changed over time and crumbled when the person died. A citizen could kill another by smashing the other's statue, but their own would shatter simultaneously, killing them by the karmic principle of statucide.

The weedy paths into this green-and-clean vista were fringed with radio discards, slash water, blown-out watches and jawflowers. Long logs lay shedding copper scales and red shreds. 'Let's deck the dummies and get out of here,' said Gregor wearily as they entered the huge standing landscape.

'I thought you were here on doctor's advice.'

'I don't know, he doesn't seem to have a good word to say for me. Maybe I can just tell him my dreams or something. They're the one thing about me that's definitely unbeatable. Last night I dreamt I picked off the shell of a waitress. Inside was a wallet.'

'And in the wallet?'

'Cannoli.'

Colonnade gusts skittered leaves as Barny and Gregor strolled under a dome of dry plaster. Through the other side and pretty soon they were among statues, some plain and white, others dressed and made up, still others mottled and overgrown. The keglike statue of Gregor stood backed against a bush as though cornered by an advancing mob. It was half swallowed by a tide of weeds and lichen had cowled its head. Gregor started tearing feebly at the weeds, a look of distaste on his face.

GI Bill leaned behind a whiskered stimson tree and listened to their blather.

'You make me nervous when you're quiet,' said Gregor.

'I think I'm going to hide out for a while. Edgy says the gator's valuable and unpopular. I think Mister Newton is a reptilian gentleman. The food rips as he shuts his gob.'

Gregor bitterly threw clumps of grass aside. 'Why do you keep telling me that - you think I don't know? It rips it rips, are you satisfied?'

'Golden Sid's a man among men. Behind those wire spectacles are his eyes and part of his head, that's for sure. But when it comes to getting him to speak in a normal voice, well, all you can say is he's a bastard to convince. You're going to have to help out in the evenings.'

Gregor straightened up. 'Eh? I'm not going in there with your god-damn monsters. I'll be reduced to a hundred treat bones for a dog. Remember what Violaine said? "Whether tears do good depends upon the philosophy of the onlooker." Those bastards won't hesitate for a second.'

'Why so tense, Round One? Don't you like animals at all?'

'I don't know, I mean, they don't speak. Why don't they speak? Are they proud? We're meant to *guess*?'

'They talk. Sometimes. I'm ready to listen. I'm ready, so should you be. *Are* you?'

'Am I ready to listen to animals talking, is that what you're asking me?'

'Yes.'

'Do I *look* like I'm ready?'

'But we're blessed by the winged and stepping animals of the earth. And cows. Don't you feel blessed by cows, Gregor?'

'*No* I don't feel blessed by cows. They stare at me. Like they're expecting something. Or like I've committed some crime and they know all about it. Plus when you walk through a field of cows, you don't know when one's going to decide to come up and indulge in some unwanted intimacy.'

'Are we talking about the same animal?'

'Yes a cow a cow, the big thing with the horns.'

'No, that's the devil, Gregor.'

Dumb but never idle, GI Bill slunk away with the greatest freight of knowledge his head would ever carry.

In fact Erno wasn't mute but nobody listened to him. He'd said the Raj fan was a bad idea. Now he was up a ladder dismantling the thing. He decided the main support strut with the hidden micro-phone could stay for the moment. Below him the Mayor completed a phone call. 'The fee is agreed. Ten for the dog, eighty for this myste-rious business with the gliding penguin.' As the Mayor slammed the receiver a thug barrelled into the room, Max Gaffer in pursuit.

'I got information about Juno!' shouted the guy.

'The spanner in the ointment,' said the Mayor, waving the lawyer back. 'What about him?'

'He's in the Scar Garden now! Says the gator's a gentleman! It's valuable! He's planning to disappear!'

'Now or never eh? You deserve as real a medal as we can manufacture from snot, whoever you are. God bless you sir, off you go.'

'Don't I get pay?'

'Let me be the judge of that. That's more than adequate from you.'

When GI Bill was gone, the Mayor stood. 'Shake my hand, Max. I'm a bastard.'

How can you recognise the sound of a sergeant and not learn the language of dogs? The dialects are almost identical. And the truth was, when the Sarge spoke the hounds came running.

The troops were stored in reverb space, a vault of repetition sealed from the thinking world. Shockwaves of smugness rocked out as the vault was unbolted. Within minutes of being thawed the Sarge was at a crusted mirror, shaving with an axe-head. Limbering up behind him was a crack team of utter bastards, pumped right up on unexamined rhetoric and ready for anything. Finished, he turned to his deputy, who brandished a dish.

'Snail, sarge?'

'Don't mind if I do. What are they?'

'Snails sarge.'

'Snails. Don't mind if I do.'

'Get your face round that then.'

'What is it.'

'A snail, sarge.'

'Snail. Alright then. Eat it do I?'

'Eat it sarge, that's right.'

'What is it.'

'Snail - a snail, sarge.'

'Snail.'

'A snail, sarge. See? It's a snail.'

'Snail is it. Well now.'

'Snail.'

'Snail, eh. Well, don't mind if I do.'

'Good on yuh.'

'Right.'

'You eatin' it then?'

'Eh?'

'You eatin' that?'

'What is it.'

Before the deputy could reply, Max Gaffer came down with their orders and a look which said his underwear was forever beyond their reach.

Neville Peth looked up at a rapping sound and saw a ragged man on a cleaner's scaffold suspended outside the office window. The man, whose leg was in a cast, gestured frantically and seemed to be spooning pasta shells into his mouth. The man gave an exaggerated grimace, bucking as though sunk with venom.

Then the man seemed to be distracted, looking away. He quickly pulleyed the platform down and disappeared out of sight.

Neville Peth rose and went to the window, gazing down - a Brigade squad were stamping by below, followed by a ragtag pack of dogs. The thin man hobbled across the street to the gas station and stole a truck, peeling out and passing the troops. Neville Peth raised his eyebrows, found himself unequal to the effort and quickly lowered them again.

'Bubba, is that you?' Magenta Blaze appeared nearby. 'And the Worried One. Is that your statue? I always thought it was a boulder.'

'I've seen worse statues,' said Barny, trying to be kind.

Magenta squinted at Gregor's statue as though at a bug. 'Than *this*?'

They went and watched Magenta decking her statue a while. She was plucking lashes from her vertebrae and slathering the face with stone makeup. 'So what you been up to, Bubba?' she asked, casual. 'Too preoccupied by your run-ins with the dark forces and being a social pariah to see your little Madge?'

Barny was transfixed with guilt.

'Couldn't even send me a letter?'

'A what?'

At that moment a truck exploded through a hedge, a busted statue on its hood. Edgy hung limp from the cab and gasped 'I stole another truck from Mike Abblatia. Remember what Violaine said: "Don't expect sincerity from a man unless the tide's coming in on him." I think he meant that trust goes unnoticed until it's broken. Like so much else. Laws, nature, my leg.'

'What the hell are you talking about?' Gregor snapped.

'The troops are coming,' Edgy explained, and passed out.

Upon examination, the statue on the hood turned out to be GI Bill's. Its leg had smashed in the impact. At the same instant Edgy's leg, just beginning to set, had shattered again.

The Brigade arrived at Scardummy Garden and the Sarge ordered a containment. 'I don't want the perimeter penetrated - the joke is, drills unrestrained can do it easy.' He shouted through a trumpet. 'Surrender or we celebrate.'

The deputy rushed up. 'No-one here Sarge - just the statues.'

'Nature ramble due to lack of assailants,' the Sarge ordered. 'I want acorns, fallen bark and rotting stag beetles here in one quarter hour. Go go go go.'

Soon a heap of detail lay in the clearing. The haul was dappled, rich and varied. 'No sign of registration Sarge. No serial numbers.'

'This one doesn't work, Sarge,' said a cadet, trying to push an acorn into his forehead.

'What are you doing, boy? What's this - a rotten inner tube Perkins? Put it back.'

'Is this a groundnut, Sarge?'

'Yes it is, Ripper. They ripen underground and are used in confectionary and as a source for peanut oil. The presence of this alongside the acorns highlights the idiosyncratic mix of tropical and deciduous flora in the region. What you got there Gibbs, some moss?' A sudden caterwauling started up, growing louder. 'What the hell's that now?'

'It's them dogs again, Sarge. They're attracted by your voice.'

Twenty dogs bounded into the clearing, ripping through the nature pile in an explosion of twigs and leaves - the troops fell back in distress and disappointment. Perkins knelt sobbing and clutching a fern.

13

LIVING IN HARMONY

Don't unravel them - your ears are meant to be that way

Mr Low said of course Barny could stay in the Juice Museum a while, and welcomed the gator like a long lost brother. Chloe said nothing of the beard of drool Barny had been wearing when he last departed, and busied herself settling the gator in. There was a massive dead lamp in the watchtower's belfry, as mysterious to Barny as the moral fibre. Mr Low took him up there to look out over the baffling ocean but said it was no place to hide. 'Not from the forces that are ranged against *you*,' said Low cheerfully. He led him down the main spiral staircase, descending lower than the levels Barny recognised. They were soon underground, walking sloped subterranean passages. 'A place like this needs shadows. For things to fall into -

and crawl out of. Secrets soak up the abyss, some.' They passed caves of forgotten wings, pyramids of misinterpreted enterprise, boxes overflowing with fossil keys and the spent hair of beauties.

'Here,' said Low, stopping in a catacomb corner wedged with filing cabinets, 'are the biological archives.' He retrieved a stack of parchments and flicked through in a flash of anatomical shadows, an arm of nerves, a head of blades, wingspread diagrams pinned with annotation. 'Demons. They can appear as fast cracks driving through walls, plans and mourners. They'll have your shoulders cramped with meetings, reduce your thinking to the market, import conclusions. Or they can flaunt their biology. Some are living wounds. Some are solid beef. Some are raw and slack, unclassifiable, some mere mechanisms. See these things like the underside of a crab? Disguise themselves as free tickets to a gig, then unfurl at night, scuttle in the mouth, and bang. Some are almost transparent like pearls, and appear at the window. Some are havoc angels, some are slaves, some are infective defectors. Some will mischief your life into despair.' He continued to browse through the ancient papers, where sawtooth skulls and latticed ribs had been numbered and named by some cursed scholar. 'Skittermite,' said Mr Low, allowing Barny a mere glimpse of a deltoid head before turning the page. 'And your friend Sweeney - *demonid scarab gargantua*. Necrotic flesh laced with infernodyne veins. Craves human salt. A soul's like the average vitamin, Juniper - the body can't manufacture it.'

'So what do I do, Mr Low?'

'Well. Could have done a lot worse than have a silver-eyed demon rasp doom in your ear. And this fellow couldn't begin to fathom how its innards are laid out. Console yourself with that, eh?'

After a few days drinking human spine milk direct as through a straw, Sweeney replaced his jaw by visiting an etheric forge into which he tossed a priest, a timid triangle player and the priest's beloved Jag. A surge of rage drew the lava into needles, crusting the hole and cooling it into black metal. He ate a few bottom-dwelling phantoms and deemed it a sterling job.

Dietrich strode down the ramp, admiring a new bracelet made of a cat's ribcage. 'How's the gob, Your Majesty.'

Sweeney's mouth spat out a fireball. 'Bloating rotbodies tip in the surf and all's well. I found the greater part of our activity a lark and these new choppers'll paint the town red next time.'

'The Aspict's still having trouble getting anything on Juno. He's completely screened somehow. But I think there's someone I can talk to above.'

Sweeney was distracted, admiring his reflection in a mirror. 'Oh?'

'Someone familiar with the community. Tap his head and free the necessary.'

'Alright,' Sweeney sighed. 'And if you see a car, wad oatmeal in the tailpipe. We might as well stupefy a few drivers.'

The mirror was full of chains.

GI Bill levered himself toward Barny's house, hollering his intentions to Gregor. The faintest hint of a thought process tinted the white emulsion of his words. He included 'stole the ballgame' and 'kill', ending his sentences with 'I sure will'. He was baffled at his recent injury. It felt like an invisible truck had piled into him, smashing his leg. Now he used his crutches to batter at Barny's door.

After the failure of the statue therapy, Doctor Perfect had advised Gregor to openly express his feelings to one and all, but Gregor was now bound into a network of ropes and pulleys he had rigged up to keep safe above the big cats. Edgy had warned him therapists were laughably out of touch with the exigencies of real life. Haggard and feverish, his clothes torn and a spider monkey on his face, Gregor looked across at the beaten body of Golden Sid, which hung lank in a snarl of ropes like a netted seal. 'Sid!' he hissed, trying to wake the man while not disturbing any more animals. The leopard prowled back and forth below, tormented with hunger. The snaggled stairwells and galleries were out of reach, spinning. 'Remember what Violaine said: "Sleep is but the -"'

A loud hammering at the door woke both Sid and the lion, amid a caterwauling of dogs, chimps and exotic birds. A chameleon fell unnoticed from the wall. Sid began screaming, tears spitting from his eyes with the force of blowdarts.

'Sid,' Gregor snuffled through the chimp's belly, 'we can use this distraction. Get a swing going on the ropes, you can reach the window.'

A brown wave of monkeys tumbled up the walls toward them, springing across and subjecting the two unfortunates to the worst kinds of inconvenience. One swiped Golden Sid's specs and placed them on its own face, springing away. Sid seemed equally bug-eyed without them. Gregor swung several times toward him, finally snagging his rope bundle and clinging on. 'Isn't it time you put all this behind you?' he hissed at the sobbing man. The door below splintered open, the subsequent commotion of pouncing predators and deadly injury disturbing a cloud of birds which swarmed upward at Gregor and Sid. 'I'm hit!' screamed Gregor. Letting go of Sid, he swung in a wide arc toward the opposite window and exploded through it.

GI Bill slammed from the house, hobbling down the gangplank as the door banged again behind him, a big animal pounding close. He turned in time for the lion to swipe him hard upside the face. Then a leopard skittered fast across the lion's back and the two went into a rolling frenzy, blurring dust. GI Bill began dragging himself away from this caterwauling violence, and came face to face with a small spaniel, which bit him on the nose and then seemed to laugh. Getting to the phone box over the road, he drew the door closed and called Spacey's gas station. As he waited for someone to pick up, he watched the dog sitting sentry outside. It looked like it was wearing eyeshadow.

Five minutes later, Mike Abblatia arrived in a tow truck to find a lion and a leopard stalking the street. GI Bill leapt from a tree and landed on the truck roof, dragging Mike out and stealing the vehicle.

Erno set up the stepladder and gave the mike a few last minutes. The Mayor was telling the effigy tale again. In his many months as a whipped cur, Erno had heard it a dozen times.

'... Exhausted and panting, my eye alighted on a tiny red stone amid the ground's grit and gravel. Reaching down to pick it up, I found on closer examination that it was a microscopic effigy of myself, carved out of flint and painted dull red. At that moment I knew I'd grow up to become a fat overlord. And here I am.'

'I've heard it a hundred times, Mayor,' sighed Max Gaffer.

'So regret me. I'm thrilled to bits, I must say.' The Mayor went on to the balcony and gripped the rail, breathing lustily and gazing out at the square. 'Even hell hounds look cute from up here. High balconies don't go around demanding action do they?'

'You're thinking about the Parade.'

'Looking forward to it, Max. Which is my best side, d'you think?'

Max Gaffer made a rambling, convoluted remark about the Mayor's Picasso morality, by which his morals were crowded on to one side of his face. 'But it doesn't matter,' he added. 'These voters and their wacko, ravaged heads are all for you.'

'I think you're right. With the powerhouse wonders of my cunning? So what if you and your echoing goons couldn't find Juno? He's about as fierce as a sardine. Now that he's served his purpose it's better for us he's out of the limelight. Keep them squared away.'

'"When you fake a threat you grant options to trouble."'

The Mayor came in from the balcony. 'If needs be we'll sort him later. We've got a full roster of Parade float applications and your forms have gone down a treat. People despaired of the staggering crosshatched career section. Understanding it's the work of ten men. I commend you.'

'Thank you sir. I laughed a lot.'

'And the new bond plan's a winner. Coin of the dark realm. It'll all work according to my inspiration.' The Mayor perched on the corner of his desk, chuffed and casual. 'Ah, Max, power's a funny thing. Thrombosis money and gamey combustion. A stranger blowing worms from his nose and saying we have his support. Forty pints of plasma always on hand. Thumbs touching brains without a diagram. Transport moving the bare necessities. Wrinkled mouths tearing at children. Flames wrecking the bales of hats. Hunchbacks ordering pizza. Bilge spurting out of necks. Bees fill the cake, wine jackets the senses, bird faces disintegrate against the darkness and drawling layabouts rattle at the handles. Laughter as my ashes blow back in your blank face. Summer days.'

'You lost me there Mayor, but thanks for sharing it anyway.'

The Mayor spotted a floor lobster which had appeared during his reminiscences. Frisky and playful, he picked it up in both hands and tossed it at Erno. 'Missed one, Erno,' he chortled.

Erno calmly climbed the stepladder and began removing the fan crossbar and hidden mike. During his labours Erno had come to three conclusions about revenge: it was humble in its toil, it aped more traditional hobbies, it was symmetrical when viewed over time. The recordings were his farewell message to servitude, the fart upon which he would jet into the sunset. He too was looking forward to Parade day.

When Mike had been sitting in the tree for a while and the two big cats were nesting contentedly below him, he happened to look over at the ramshackle Juno house. Through an upper window, he saw a man braced in some kind of rope-and-pulley system. Above this, sitting on the roof, was the man they called the Round One, swinging his chubby legs back and forth like a kid's. The three men smiled and waved vaguely at each other, nodding.

Night was falling. The cicadas began to call.

Flickering his way around the wind, Dietrich folded himself and dropped through the night like a dead bird. He banged on to a rough backroad, straightened up and shook the veined downpour of his head. Approaching on the road was a demon with da Vinci wings and eyes of broadband static. It strolled like an oldtime gentleman pacing his estate. Its head was a bladed mace which the demon had made a little effort to disguise with a torn woollen hood.

'Gettysburg, my brother in poison,' Dietrich announced. 'Mind if we walk and have a quick natter?'

'By all means,' said Gettysburg, unsurprised.

It was a strange night. They walked in silence for a while through the scent of apples, a warm southern breeze hissing the whiskered trees.

'How's Kermit?'

'Oh, that one. Apparently he's stuck in a pipe.'

'Good old Kermit. And Rakeman?'

'Top o' the line demons, every one.' Dietrich paused, uncertain. 'So what do you do? Sell indian relics by the road?'

'I get by. With the blind man in the observatory. I'm an assistant. I get a bed over the streetnoise, held from the window by a length of floor.'

'He doesn't see a meat demon embedded with tin.'

'Sees whatever he wants. The root of an object isn't necessarily the part to watch, as I found to my cost once when a waiter belted me.'

'A man ought to corrupt his neighbours, at least.'

'I'm not a man.'

'Yeah well you chose to live as one. So, a demon then - that should be worse shouldn't it? I can't help being appalled. You're feeding the mask.'

'Uh-huh. Well my conscience is as clean as an operating room, old friend.'

'Conscience. That's you, Getty. Alright, dive into the waters of majority, see if you get clean.'

'Majority? You misunderstand everything. I have the precious gift of patience. Time means nothing to me.'

'That isn't patience. It's disregard.'

'You're wrong. I disregard only fashion.'

'So I see. Is that really a balaclava.'

'Yes. It's rented.'

'So this is what my master's up against,' Dietrich remarked dryly. 'A rented balaclava. Dare I tell him such fearful news.'

A warm rain began to fall. Gettysburg knelt and picked up a traumilus shell. 'So what's up.'

'Someone's thieved from His Majesty. Some meaty lizard that's absorbed a full load off the nets. Not human, just a snack. But etherically the thief's a bit tricky.'

'I saw the posters. He must have been angry when that picture was taken. "Propaganda's a poor union of gesture and delusion."'

'Nice. It's so simple-minded up here isn't it. I find these 3D buffoons such easy meat. The day's sworn and boring.'

'On the contrary, Dieter. I believe you find it chaotic beyond endurance. Politics. The impossibility of disgrace. Compared to all this you're a lightweight.'

'I can't feel compassion for flattened cats in the street like carpet samples.'

'You don't mean that remark. It's glued on.'

'With rusted blood I suppose.'

'Don't.'

'So the defection thing. What's the racket in putting your minutes here?'

'I learn stuff.'

'Example.'

'Well,' said Gettysburg thoughtfully. 'Light mixes with the wind. Gulls ride at personal risk. Dreams cling to criminal wombs. Nobody slips sitting. The direction of flatfish is impossible to anticipate. Honesty tastes bitterly of roses. A broken fountain blows aside a spray to blacken paths. Wounds open shockingly fast. When a man is unhappy, cupboards crowd him and cabs pass by. Likewise when a man is happy, cupboards crowd him and cabs pass by. Teeth and celery don't mix. Gardens lay dripping by the river side. Rubies on a lean man are wasted. Memories, overweight, are the pits.'

'You've gone flesh-simple.'

Rain was swarming through the trees. Gettysburg breathed deep, his head glittering like a depth charge. 'This stuff's more interesting than the cold treasure of the void, or your flames and dark wage. Dumb people cast an honest shadow, at least. Hooligan night's innocent in its old-fashioned simplicity - even within the plastic shell of celebration they've their own reasons for enjoyment. See for yourself in a few days. Everyone busts out in consolation and gum display. A parade - it might interest you.'

'Everyone?'

'Oh.' Remembering something, Gettysburg extruded a pocket of pullular skin from his flesh coat and retrieved something. 'I got those fags, by the way.' He proffered the cigarettes to Dietrich.

The hammerhead demon was distracted, ignoring the cigarettes. 'I'll see you Getty,' he said finally, and deployed his wings, ascending like a cannonball.

Three trucks stolen, marvelled Mike Abblatia. *Ah well, forgive and forget.*

The only one of the three men still awake, Mike saw the two big cats get suddenly spooked and dart away inside the dark house. His back was killing him. He was about to climb down when he saw two weird, giant guys standing near the tree, having a discussion and ignoring the rain. One had a head like a hammer, tubular hair which hung like soaked macaroni and a body of eroded armour. The other had a head like a spike glove and a ground-skimming coat of white leather. As he gestured, the spikehead's eyes flashed in the night like dashboard lights. They seemed to reach an impasse, and spike offered hammer a cigarette. Hammerhead unfurled a massive super-structure from his shoulders and flew upward, banging through the tree's furthest branches in a spat of leaves.

The spikehead seemed to think for a moment and then tapped out a cigarette for himself, lighting it by dabbing it into his eye. He stood there in the rain enjoying it, the blue smoke wraithing thin around him until, as Abblatia watched, he vanished as miraculous as a headache.

The spare bed was on the small granular shore of a subterranean sea. A jet black expanse of water was rippled by a breeze from the distant cave mouth, a low opening which showed a sliver of the night sky. Barny's bed was a few feet from the tide, the bedside table wedged against the grotto wall. He had fallen asleep counting bats in the dark ceiling, and when he roused an ambient light was wobbling around as though a shine of liquid and shadows were generated underwater. The slice of sky was lightening and the cavern had turned real marine, a pure green gold.

'Look simultaneously at the horizon and the detail in coins,' said Chloe Low, padding down from the passage. 'There's a test of perspective.'

'What's that - Violaine?' Barny asked, sitting up.

'No, it's father.'

'Where is he?'

'He's sat upstairs looking to his left. His tea genie's visiting. Come with me, I've got something to show you.'

'It's not a rotted turtle or something is it?'

She led him up the gradient of a tunnel panelled with polished oak. He watched her walk, wanting to thank every inch. They reached a level plateau. It was a gloomy hallway of cupboards and filigree. At one end was a painting with a bronze title plate set into the frame: *The sea is railed with teeth, the authority of nations.* Barny scrutinised the portrayal. Holes in the great swell of the ocean, yellow and blue boats in a havoc of water, passengers howling and moral, wearing bonnets. Chloe pulled at the painting and it swung outward like a cupboard door. On the rock wall behind it scrambled a phosphene blot of sickly light.

'Last time, you saw this from the other side,' she said, 'in the creepchannel. One time before that you wandered down here by accident and saw me coming out this side, and I had to bust you over the head with a drugged club so you wouldn't remember.' She looked at him and saw that he didn't get it. 'Okay: everything here has some kind of story or knowledge connected with it. The name of the game. But why not get the story direct? The creepchannel's one big etheric infection. It's tangled like spaghetti. In fact some of it actually is made of pasta. Like illness, it's a way of learning the worst.'

She showed him the soft underskin of her arm and drew a coaxial nerve cable from a pink scar.

'Once I'm in, I plug this into the creepchannel wall. I've seen stuff you wouldn't believe this way. Peacock fountain lands, copper gardens of girls laughing, awe-white souls, temple hangings cradling the dead, stone banquets left in scatters, voyages to invade swept away, golden victims, garment tides, unknown noble crews, bitter militaries, rubble families, sweat and rumours - all that. And old stuff called snow, white ice floating down like dust. I sometimes bring objects back too.'

'Like Del's Fright Foundry.'

'He just reaches in and gets musty old ornaments. If you look at the Foundry from the other side, it's a storage closet.'

'Do you drive one of those creep cars, like Karloff Velocet?'

'I go to learn, not to travel. I have to be really touching all the stuff there.' She hid the hole behind the picture and hid her eyes behind her fringe. 'And it gets me off.' She sucked on the end of the nerve cable, fed it into her wound, and tugged down her sleeve. 'That's where I got the *Violaine Prophecies*, but I didn't tell father that. He needs things to be stumbled on, picked up at random, like the Kern gun. That's his prize exhibit.'

'I don't know who that is.'

They walked up the winding galleries toward the upper building. 'We're too young to remember. Kern was a hero, now he's dug under dirt and denial. Innovative resentment made him sample the moral fibre. What he discovered led him to build the gun and fire at the Mayoral palace from the Tower of Nowt. They set the troops on him.'

'How'd he respond?'

'With some kind of capture, dying and funeral gambit.'

'Followed by a decomposition gambit?'

'Yes. He didn't die by the troops though. He was sentenced to death. While he was waiting for the bright hour he was attacked and killed by a flock of doves which fluttered through the barred window into his cell. They say he was the first Accomplice citizen to die that way. In his will he left the skeleton of a man wearing an iron cross, and a dog which barked when the weather was humid. I wish I could have met him.'

'Where have you put Mister Newton?'

'Your gator's comfortable, upstairs. Listen, Father thinks we can find an exhibit which'll help you with your problem. Take a gander at this.' She went into a storage room and sat next to a tea chest full of snot dust. 'There's a load of objects packed in here. Lucky dip.'

Barny rummaged and fished out a jewel-encrusted dog collar. Chloe took it from him. 'Okay. The collar belonged to Harley Quinn the architect. This guy built tower blocks out of dessert sponge so they'd dissolve before anyone could complain. He'd deny everything. The only person who didn't complain was Nana Rem, a designer in his office, who was in love with him. Her father owned *The Blank Stare* newspaper and hated Harley. Harley's was a delicate livelihood but the artwank crowd admired him, their appointment books squabbling like sparrows. A part of his head had been praised and relaxation became a real threat. He started trying to impress - forgot the mischief. Inspired by the night train, he built the ultimate council block - made of solid concrete, wall to wall, no doors or windows, no gaps inside for people to inhabit. Just a huge solid block. Nana's father helped in the construction of a by-the-numbers social outcry, fine lady swoon-progress halted by a chair and so on. Harley caught a fever and bagged a delirium vision of the world's crimes. These he plastered on to the outer wall of a gigantic dome and slated them over. Invited people to inspect the names under the tiles, but the public are so timorous Barny. They really believe in that one in a million chance - what if they peeled one up to reveal themselves? The dome was blown to pieces by the Mayor's office and Harley crashed with it. Rumour coils stiffened around him. Under stony scholars he kept mum, his face packed with people. Finally he tried ducking out to get his priorities, but Nana's father wouldn't leave him alone. Harley went to the local shaman - the old one, before Beltane Carom - who advised him to store his soul in plain sight. Harley chose one of a thousand dalmatians in a dogpound, and the shaman installed him.'

'Dogs get everywhere,' Barny remarked pensively.

'Yes they do. So rumours of a soul procedure abounded but Nana Rem didn't know where he'd gone, and grieved. Nana's father followed up a joke story about a dalmatian which had a blob on its coat in the exact shape of Harley's face, convinced that this was Harley himself. He bought the dog and used it as a mascot for the paper, mistreating it on the sly. In fact the dog, which finally sprang up and bit a hole in his face, was the wrong one - Nana could sense as much and went to the pound, finding the real Harley and bringing him home. She bought him this jewelled collar, and he lived the rest of his life happily, as her dog.'

'As her dog,' repeated Barny in a trance. Then he shook himself. 'How the hell does any of this legendary shit help me?'

'Give yourself up to the heavy machine of interpretation. It's the best way of hiding, and they'll do all the work for you. Let's go see the gator.'

They went up, entering the round master bedroom. It was the coziest chamber in the lamp tower. In a kingsize bed lay the reptile, wearing a frilly bonnet.

14

THE PLUNDER PARADE

Politeness lasts like a flower, then curls, darkens and returns to itself

Mayor Rudloe ceremoniously donned his garland of tumours. 'We are scheduled to jubilate, Mr Gaffer.'

He cast open the balcony doors and stepped out. The crowd below was an irritating dissonance, a sea floating with trash. The Mayor bellied up to the microphone and began his address. 'It is with a heavy heart that I gaze upon your slack faces, upturned and vacant as ever. I've done precious little on your behalf while in office, except to receive the red levy and designate guilts to you all. I feel it the greatest honour to ease myself upon your industry. But someone asked me a question the other day, as I walked the streets of our community like a normal man. He was a citizen with bloodshot eyes and duds off a lorry. And his question was this: "Does the human muscular system differ from that of other creatures." Let me place your minds, such as they are, at rest. Muscle fibres differ from species to species of animal and also between parts of the same animal. There's the distinction between voluntary and involuntary muscles, and in structure and activity between striated muscle and smooth muscle. It seems basically that there's a great deal of variation on every level. So let us not pretend that all is ideal and pleasant. We have a bad statue problem in this town. The Steinway Spiders are of no small consequence. And we all know that the swamps are a hotbed of horseshoe crabs and illegal brain farming. I pledge to do whatever it takes to scour your inky hearts of desire. Bring me your huddled masses and I'll adopt a look of fierce consideration.

'But do not let alarm roast us black. Some say Accomplice is blocked in - I say it's cherished within walls of wonder. The baffling ocean to the south, the skeleton coast to the west, endless swampland to the east, and to the north a deadly chasm with a stumped, mined flyover. If those aren't tourist attractions I ask you what is. And when the rest of the world chooses to contact us, we'll be waiting for them, limbs akimbo. This pretence at a symphony of purpose is a real black eye for the scoffers. Vibrant buffoons unite!

'I, Mayor Rudloe, safekeeper of the moral fibre, raise a momentary choice prayer to enterprise, and inform you at this time that there exists a golden opportunity for every man jack of you. I can suspend and relax my lower jaw by mental determination, at any time. The upper jaw is completely fixed. But it doesn't have to move for the purposes I have in mind. A brief demonstration.'

And Rudloe silently moved his lower jaw up and down like that of a ventriloquist's dummy.

'That's just a sample. Don't want to give too much away at this stage of the game, eh? The point is it has a thousand and one applications. I can begin marketing in two years with the right kind of backing early on. And that's where you come in. If each and every citizen purchases twenty registered jaw bonds, stamped and authorised, then beautiful in progress we will journey toward tether's end.

'So buck up. We are claiming this festivity is more precious than it is - which lights up our eyes with love. When all the while it's as good as stealing from you. Light up with simplicity, all! Inhale from flasks! Move many limbs at once! Madness onrushing! We celebrate!'

The torpid sermon would enjoy fame as a sedative. But now it was time to hear from doomed Eddie Gallo. As was traditional on Parade day, the opposition mayoral candidate gave his speech sandwiched within a giant hamburger made of toughened steel and razor wire. Only his head hung free - thankfully, perhaps, since he was naked. His new slogan was 'Badgers Can't Decide'. It was months before anyone discovered what it had meant - something to do with them having both black and white stripes. 'They also change directions sometimes when shuffling around,' he would explain later still. 'For that they have my sympathy.'

But today this was still obscure. In all innocence he'd bought a philosophy meant only for display. This was one of his few opportunities to display it. Level with the faces of the crowd, he was strained but cheerful. 'Hello. The day's quite hot, isn't it? Um, gravity - I'm thinking aloud here - gravity re-arranges certain things. I have no reason to doubt that melting scarcely makes any difference, really. Who is to say we may not perform some easy operations drunken. Or in the blue gem jelly of sedative sleep. Running killer bee farms is a thing I never tried, because I heard it was too much like hard work. Bees are all sentiment, aren't they?'

Grimacing slightly as he shifted within his limits, he settled down again, breathing heavily.

'To the words of our Mayor - to that I say, the hands for his arms are held by bone, and with him as with everyone, er, well, shovel the wrong way and spuds ... spuds resist. Melons are noses, visiting eden, bulging - and grinning inside. I'm bewildered, d'you think that'll count against me? The same situation happens during negotiation. Well. A plank is a possession. Be happy. Let's hear no chit-chat about -'

'That's just grand,' the Mayor interrupted, applauding crisply, flushed with spite and good spirits. 'He had a great deal to say didn't he. And now this year's appointed poet, with an airy thought for us all.'

Amy Gort stood on a scaffold podium in the square and leaned to the mike. 'Here's a poem called "My boyfriend claims his balls fly away at night".'

Scholar, gunner, cresting accuser
lost flock of birds
all this
in my fucking face

Alarmed, the Mayor frantically blustered into his microphone: 'Time to spit on your hands and take up the axe of jollity, everyone - let the Parade begin!'

The yearly Plunder Parade was held in honour of the thief Zeuxis Dyabell, who stole everything in the universe and, when hunted down by the mob and told to empty his pockets, turfed out every object imaginable. This creation myth was celebrated with floats bearing whatever the celebrants chose. The arbitrariness of the tradition resulted in some of the most hair-raising spectacles in the Accomplice calendar. As the crowd fused into emergency colours and the floats set off around the town, all was garish, ranging right across the visible spectrum of cack-handed trash. The gigantic shattered overcoat moved like nothing on earth, pumping stains into the air. A chipped life gallows shouldered along in glacial inevitability. A disembodied belly bulged down the street, dripping semolina and cod oil. Here rolled an open tank of dank water in which a non-swimmer perched yelling on a quivering unicycle. Waving to the crowd, King Verbal stood on a metamorphosing float of skeletal chaos, crystalline calcium exerting in all directions. A vicious knife fight occurred on a kind of wheeled raft, all seven combatants yelling continually that this should not be construed as endorsing the concept of violence. A man dressed as a hen stood on a frail float of woefully thin ham. Pulpy gourds and melons hung from a comical Steinway replica painted all the colours of the dead and studded with arrows. Doctor Perfect sat upon a giant rolling throne, crowned with his own rotted brain. Professionals giving a silent demonstration of 'deciding' began to convulse, dark spew fanning from their mouths. Microlady danced upon a hypodermic needle, her rolling platform fronted by a surgical magnifying screen. Fang rode smiling upon a painted wagon, his head running like a candy apple, and cast strips of his own flesh into the crowd. Like every other year, Dot Spacey juddered headfirst upon a titanic petrol cap. The master chef Quandia Lucent sat high in a saddle lashed to a giant pasta shell which trolled down the street like an anaemic beetle. Mimes lay completely immobile in a large wheeled deathbed. Magenta Blaze rode spreadeagled and gleeful on a rocket-sized tube of lipstick. One-day avatars flared into bonfires. GI Bill had fitted tank-tracks to a toilet and rumbled forward on this, waving a piece of radish and shouting something inaudible above the applause - what he had in mind was anyone's guess. An unmanned transparent inflatable blob was later said by Mr Peterson to be 'one o' them floating waterbugs o' the eye'. Biophantine butchers acted wooden scenes from Accomplice history on a float of laminated confidence. Dressed in doublet and hose they portrayed the tortuously mannered meeting of Bingo Violaine and the Clown of the North.

'How long has this handbag existed.'

'Precisely ten hours.'

'The man who made it was an expert.'

'Make your report this dignified always and we shall proceed well.'

Many in the crowd would later claim they had seen a cheerful Mike Abblatia hovering seated above the ground, his float having been stolen.

And amid and around it all were prancing processions of blood-soaked waiters in boneseed masks which grew by the second, pushing out crests and antlers. Bastards on stilts tangled with mooring lines, toppling slow and beautiful, cloaks flowing. Farmers strode tricked out in clothes made of stained clay, bulrush antennae clashing together. A classic pagan green man went pale and started banging his heart with his fist. Twenty-three weeping sportsmen hugged each other, confessing their love. Inexplicable tableaux were enacted left right and centre.

Edgy carried out the plan to advertise his book by padlocking himself into a trundling mobile cage with a dozen dogs. These animals had become instantly affronted at their captivity and took it out in snarling rage, biting the hell out of Edgy and each other in a whirling display of savagery. Edgy had prepared a banner detailing the book and its contents but at the last minute the title was changed to *I am a Failure*, and Edgy had frantically replaced the banner with this phrase scrawled on a piece of timber. There was nothing to indicate that this screaming, bloody, wretched captive was advertising an upcoming book.

After several days spent fending off a puma with a pair of nasal clippers Gregor stood utterly silent on a bare float, his clothes and flesh torn and patched with alley garbage. His face was blackened and swollen. In the crowd the Captain shook his head, disappointed.

The Mayor was represented by a massive silent replica of his own head, the lower jaw moving slowly up and down like a visor. Inside at the wheel, Erno geared up for his mighty moment.

BB Henrietta glanced as they entered the upper chamber and saw two pegs on a pedestal, between which was spread a strip of clinically pink meat. But she wasn't interested in the moral fibre. She went to the window, peering down at the passing procession.

'The life of a window includes the horizon and the wall,' rumbled Murdster the Sentinel, tending to arcane controls on the pedestal's fender.

'They certainly do,' muttered BB. 'I mean, it does.'

The floats passed, crass and methodical. There was a deep pan pizza, a blacktie pike, a tubeless sports tyre. Once again the Church of Automata had snubbed the proceedings, while the Powderhouse was represented by a living pyramid of damaged personalities.

'The rain put moss in this house,' declared Murdster behind her, 'things began to get lumpy. I allow myself so few visitors here. I'm innocent of all delights but one.'

'Well now that shouldn't be,' said BB in a distracted way, then piped up. 'Hey Mr Murdster sir, do you know there's some sort of carnival or celebration going on down there? I had no idea - how lucky to be up here and get such a great view.'

'The Parade. It has a funerary grace.'

'Does it ever.'

'I anticipate all the more the peace concussion.'

'Oh I agree. I agree.'

Passing below was a red velvet float upon which a fierce-looking devil was guarded by a scruffy woollen ape with a pitchfork.

'Tradition is barbaric and formidable. Notions spoken on a rail. Bold music and toy voices. Flags like slabs. Empty-handed jesters bulwark our eyes against the circle of father death.'

'Sounds like a plan.'

'I am a repairman surrounded by jokes,' said Murdster, his voice thick and glutinous. 'My rusted truculence clattering about this bell-tower. But I'll shut the window on the holocaust of leaves. We gate-crash the fates together. Come, Bargain Basement Henrietta - I'll make you admit an unattractive virtue.'

'Eh?' BB turned around and first emitted a caw of laughter, then understood what she was seeing. Murdster, his face ghastly as a wal-nut, neck thorns flushed to bud with his exertions, was bent to the moral fibre and licking it with a tongue which resembled a hen's liver. Sweat glistened his corrugated forehead. He straightened up, raven-ing and a-shudder as he glared at her, his face congested with lust. BB volleyed a scream, the horizon spinning.

Dressed as an ape, Barny stood attendance beside the gator. It had been a simple matter to tog it up as the devil. Propped upright with scaffolding, garbed in red mask and horns, concealed wheels and a scarlet cape, it was a marvel of camouflage. The cherry on the cake was the use of Sweeney's salvaged teeth to hide the reptile's own. 'All I lack now is a sandwich,' thought Barny, wheezing with laughter.

Right about then BB Henrietta flopped out of an upper window in the Tower of Nowt, hanging rag-limp over the sill. This seemed to disturb the gator - it heaved a sudden thrash. Barny was caught between concern for BB and the stirring carnivore and yelled for help, pointing up at the Tower. The gator pumped its legs frantically, scooting off the float and into the crowd. Upright and with cloak aflow, it sped through them on its hidden wheels, teeth snapping. Many of the spectators felt their strongest emotion of the day. Once assured they were alive and intact after the evil one's passing, the onlookers turned to its hairy cohort with gobs of outrage.

Barny immediately opted for a basic running and panting gambit.

With the Parade well under way, Erno threw the switch. As the jaw on the massive Mayoral head continued to move ponderously up and down, the Mayor's voice began to echo out: 'Offer a reward which we won't give. People despaired of the staggering crosshatched career section. A stranger blowing worms from his nose and saying we have his support. The new bond plan's coin of the dark realm. People frying eggs on their cars all goddamn day. Laughter as my ashes blow back in your blank face.' Giggling like a kid, Erno peered out through the mouth to see the effect his work was having on the crowd, only to find that the crowd was gone, a last few spectators rushing off to the left.

Erno ejected himself from an ear of the mobile head as it motored along. Other floats had been abandoned askew or left to trundle through fences. There was something going on in the area of the Square. Seething with baffled frustration, he stalked off in that direction.

The Captain hopped up on to Gregor's spartan float. His expression was clenched and grim. 'Gregor, I gave you a chance - I distinctly remember it - regarding your rambunctious public conduct. I even recommended medical assistance. And yet here I find you've rejected every social custom after all. Look around you - by golly man you've ruined the Parade.'

Gregor turned slightly toward him, his eyes bloodshot. It was not clear that he perceived the Captain at all. Certainly he offered no apology for his poor condition.

'Well?' the Captain demanded, embarrassed. 'For all that's sustainable, man, are you determined to stand there like a statue?'

Gregor's face seemed to crack with some extremity of grief, and he fell limply backward from the float as some commotion exploded past. When the Captain looked, he saw Gregor riding upon the back of the devil himself, pursued by an ape and a turbulent, screaming populace.

Perched on the Tower roof, Dietrich watched the crowd. Pre-arranged vigorous antics forgotten, they were entirely occupied with baying and stepping ever forward. Despite all the excitement he saw faces not aglow with mischief but sealed closed as though with plastic glue. Were these the cheeky funsters Gettysburg admired? They wanted a way to express their resentment, not some theoretical joy. And they just got it. Barny, holding a fake pitchfork, caught up with his pig servant and gave it a few inaudible orders, then grabbed the disguised reptile by the cloak and guided it toward the mayoral palace.

Dietrich stood and fanned his wings. As he prepared to launch off, a woman hanging half out of a Tower window awoke from a stupor, saw him and screamed, falling from the window into a passing tank of dank water in which a non-swimmer perched yelling on a quivering unicycle.

An angled tumble of roofs and he was in the Mayor's office, shuttering his wings and examining the decor anew. The non-pliant pictures on the wall were indicative of a cornered philosophy. The Mayor, smoking a cigar, stirred bewildered, blinking at the intruder and wondering at his sudden entrance. One curtain flapped like a fish.

'Yer nemesis is at the door.'

'Eh now? What's this?'

'Barny Juno comes to barter and bargain. He has with him his pig servant and an alligator dressed as the devil. Bored dupes pursue him.'

The Mayor stood. 'You were here before. Representing yourself as some sort of man. Thought you'd swing by and stick your distorted oar in again eh? Max!'

'You'll want to give an enemy to the people, but I'll take the small matter of Juno and the reptile off your hands.'

'That creature's highly valuable,' the Mayor stated tersely.

'Oh? Where did you catch that idea?'

'A little birdy told me. A birdy with no neck, thick arms and a gill-ball shirt.'

Dietrich frowned. 'You're sure this was a *birdy*?'

Max Gaffer entered and stopped short, looking at the demon. The Mayor chucked an alert look at him. 'Throats to the wall, Max.'

A marble staircase echoed. An ape and the shambling, worse-for-wear pig servant entered, panting, followed by the gator, which thrashed in on all fours, caped but with its supports trailing. It opened its mouth in a long silent display of fangdom, finally slapping it closed and looking enigmatic. Barny tore off his gorilla mask, gasping for air.

Dietrich looked into Juno with his demon eyes. While the others here were matted with spiny rotwork and muddy toxins, and the Mayor was even now extruding another floor lobster through a tangle of etheric bile cables, Barny was a mere scaffold of running bone and nerve fire. He was a man entirely without suspicion. It was like looking at the simplest of animals. Love attached him to the gator like rich filamentous bunting.

'People are chasing us,' Barny cried. 'Help us, Mr Mayor.'

15

DEATH TO WHOEVER

We may change; we may change a victim

The Mayor browsed lies before replying. Mouthing outside were the outraged; time to climb into a skip and make the best of it? The anvil-headed demon, all sneer ducts and mantis joinery, grinned wickedly. The minutes themselves would answer if the Mayor left it much longer. The century flower of his conscience still a tightfisted bud, he opted for a volley of offended bluster. 'I remain calm in the face of all provocation. But this goes beyond my visual register. Shelter? Protection? The head of a man and the body of an ape? A fork in one hand and a set of false teeth in the other? Pig servant? And that reptile in a cape and horns? What ... what's ... ? Do you comprehend that this monster and its blunt snout and thrashing motions are completely lethal and I've been damn near growing tusks trying to tell everyone about it?'

'Mister Newton wanted to -'

'Who?'

'- see the Parade. The gator.'

'Did you bar the door?'

'Of course.'

'It'll take them a good ten minutes to get through. Where's Erno? Look at these bloody floor lobsters. It's demolition of duty. Let him arrive on a stretcher or not at all.'

'Change of subject, Mayor?' asked the demon sardonically.

'Nothing of the sort. Er, Max, how's your underwear doing?'

'Eh?'

'I made an offer, Mayor,' the demon remarked, leaning slack and casual against a bookcase. 'My master. I can see him now, tearing brain from brainpan like a jellyfish from a rock. Your nose is a meal in itself.'

The Mayor swanned it, smooth and groundless. 'With respect, Mr Hammer or whatever your name is, I'm reluctant to get into further dealings with demons. Remember that "Adopt a Horned One" campaign a few years ago, Max? Punishing paperwork. Black and yellow ectoplasm on the chairs. Treating the floor lobsters like kittens. God help us.' The scheme had been popular among the well-to-do and a formal signing ceremony had taken place. Upon signature a dozen shrill, spicy freaks actually showed up. These crimson slurry princes made short work of their patrons, closing serrated jaws on heads and bursting eyes like berries. The Mayor had had to dispose of eight bodies by fire. He turned quickly to Barny. 'Here's the bottom line, Juno - what do you want?'

'Well, I could use a fully-antlered adult caribou if you've got one.'

The Mayor sighed with grievous disappointment, glanced at the demon and slowly drew himself up, to mutter with salvaged pride: 'Very well sir. Certainly, come over and intervene, by all means.' He gave Barny a look of distaste. 'We're all friends here.'

'Then here's my suggestion,' stated the demon. 'Dress some convenient lackey in that cape and devilwear. Chase him out on the balcony with the pitchfork and pretend to thwart him in the glare of the public. They're morons to a man, heads searing with detergent. This is politics. Words of certainty alter their course. Death cools the blood.'

The Mayor gave an urgent hiss. 'Max? The smart move?'

'Yes, stage a valiant exploit,' nodded Max Gaffer thoughtfully. 'Outstanding.'

'Good, then let's tog up the pig servant,' announced the Mayor.

Gregor roused very slightly.

'Gregor,' Barny whispered. 'They want to dress you like the devil.'

'It was only a matter of time,' Gregor sighed with a smile.

At that moment Erno entered, panting.

'Erno - thank god for the servants' entrance. He'll make a better evil one, eh?'

Erno stopped, looking at the assembled figures. Worry hung on the wall above his head. Max plucked the cape and horned eye-mask from the gator and danced up to Erno, throwing the cape across his shoulders. The Mayor took the pitchfork from Barny.

'You'll serve, my quiet boy,' the Mayor chuckled. He swerved the stunned, gaping Erno toward the balcony door, and paused. 'I hear popular panic, and I love it.' Then he strode out, pushing Erno ahead of him.

The crowd roared when they saw the horned demon backing onto the balcony. 'You've the strutting arrogance to interfere with our bucolic celebration eh horn boy?' the Mayor bugled, sweeping into view. 'You and your Aztec nostrils. Yes, you. I'm not making this up. I'm ruddy furious and here's the visual proof.'

He struck forward with the pitchfork and Erno grasped the shaft - a precarious tussle ensued. 'Help,' Erno said wanly, but nobody heard him.

'Repulsive oversight, bump to a halt here,' proclaimed the Mayor and shoved forward with the fork. Tipping over the rail, Erno fell with a dismal bleat, landing on the poetry platform with his mask askew.

The cloak hung snagged on the balcony rail. Mayor Rudloe sensed the grind-stoppage of synapses amid the onlookers. Erno was recognised. Conversation stirred.

A face poked through the curtains. 'They think you planned the entire thing,' said Max Gaffer in a husky whisper. 'Make light of the situation.'

'Doesn't matter,' the Mayor called out, shrilly casual. 'Power's purified by the death of smallfry. Yes, good old Erno - we all knew him. A real fighter, that one. Sixty of his mouth screams slammed up at his attacker. The landlord of life has draped the towel on his pump. And I love you all.'

All I need now, thought the Mayor, *is a heart attack or seizure. The sympathy would come pouring down as though from a tipped vat.*

But before anything of the kind could occur, the mayoral float burst through a fence and trundled across the square, its jaw working slowly, projecting the Mayor's voice: 'You can't go wrong spending money on death and murder. Lucky for men like me. However far we ascend in office, we never reach those heights where the law dwells. Phrase horrors like an invitation and you'll get a crowd. Shake my hand, Max. I'm a bastard. I'll insult everyone necessary and do little else for now. Juno - do you understand that I'm basing my campaign on a demonisation of you and your supposed depravities? I rue the fates for making me mayor of a place so obscure it's where ants go to die. I'll break you, Erno.'

The giant artificial head was making its way toward the palace through the parting populace.

'That's ... not my voice,' shrieked the Mayor. 'I loved that man.' He pointed down at Erno's body. 'He was like a son to me.'

The giant head crashed to a halt against the poetry lectern, its jaws opening and closing on Erno's body while booming the words: 'That'll put fish in his custard. Erno, you silent bastard. I knew I'd grow up to become a fat overlord. All we need is deceit, an enemy, and negligence. Shake my hand, Max. There's nothing to stop us.'

'I'll never understand political strategy,' said doomed Eddie Gallo from his steel encasement.

'All right!' yelled the Mayor with scornful superiority. 'I admit my heart's a howling wasteland! Thrive you all in misgivings and misery! Cretinous wretches! Credulous *bloaters*! You'll even vote for me yet! Damn you all!' And he flung himself inside as the crowd erupted.

'Way to go, sir,' said Max Gaffer archly, stuffing a few necessaries into a bag. 'Fires will bond this moment to our memory.'

The demon gave a sharp laugh. 'It's the starving dog that leads us to the body,' he said, speaking unfolded and triumphant at last. His leather wings batted open, darkening the room. 'Time to see the blade sever the looking-glass, Juno. We're leaving. I'll go easy on the animal if you come along quietly.' And he raised an open claw toward Barny.

Throughout the preceding events Barny had been wondering about the reptile's health. It was really too big for Mister Spiderman's old terrarium and all this excitement was disturbing. He wondered if he should release it in the swamp. His father was always saying there was nothing very fierce or challenging out there.

So when the weird guy reached out and said he'd get them out of here, he automatically grasped the claw, forgetting he was holding Sweeney's jaws in that hand. Then the demon was screaming, black liquid spurting from a stumped wrist - his claw lay on the carpet. Two floor lobsters began to show interest in it.

'And there's your answer,' came a voice from behind him, and there was a tall guy looking more dead than he had a right to, shrinking his wings. He had flickering eyes the colour of nothing and wore a white vinyl coat. 'What was your method, Dietrich? Sneer to establish teeth, cast a sharp shadow, angle your noggin? And bloodshot eyes - that's the cardinal rule. Don't you get bored with it all?'

'You're another demon,' snapped the panicked Mayor, rifling his desk drawers for a weapon. 'Think you're fooling anyone with that derby hat?'

'No? Well, I had a balaclava but it was only rented. I had to return it.' The pale demon removed the hat, revealing a skull like a bladed mace. 'Mr Rudloe - we've never met exactly. Gettysburg's the name. The people will be in this room in two minutes. Some will clobber you with fragments of timber. Others will drag you down the stairs by the right leg. Whether any of this will effect your votes, what do you reckon. They demand only satisfaction. Nice flowers in that vase, by the way.'

'Getty,' snarled Dietrich. 'This is entrapment.'

'You think I'll accept a thing just because some wag of a demon drew my attention to it?' the Mayor shouted. 'Max, these wingnuts think I give a damn.'

'You speak on the dotted line, Mr Rudloe,' said Gettysburg, a beehive behind his eyes. 'And your man there's full of dust and chilled tar.'

'Saying this sort of thing to them's like throwing a carpet under a bird,' gasped Dietrich, bent over his cradled arm. 'Like it matters.'

'It does matter,' said Gettysburg. 'I live here.'

'Accomplice's trophy demon.'

'So regret me.'

Behind Gettysburg a crimson stain bloomed quickly on the door, bulging into meat which made the doorway an oblong clot. A gap flumed open at the centre, fast cold air flying from it.

'Barny Juno. I know a shortcut. The four of us are leaving.' Gettysburg patted Gregor on the head, took his hand and walked toward the gore door, looking to Barny to follow. Barny led the gator through the block of meat and a gush of bloodwater swept the room away.

Dietrich threw himself after them.

16

GOING THROUGH HELL

Never arrive at a funeral by parachute

Nothing in Gregor's career as a coward had prepared him for the events in that room. The two towering demons had made everyone else into children. Now he seemed to be roving the byways of reason. Looking back, he saw the Mayor's office rocketing away, its final circumstances branded on to his retina. Seconds after the demon Gettysburg dragged them through the gore door, the enraged citizenry seemed to have burst through the underlying one, so that they appeared to be trampling away from this hellish tunnel. Dietrich had thrown himself forward and GI Bill, tripping on a litter of floor lobsters, barrelled into him, embedding his solid head in the demon's stomach. The Mayor and his lawyer were set upon by the cacophonous masses. 'Don't touch the underwear!' screamed Max.

'Your underwear is not the matter at hand!' the Mayor managed to thunder. Three children made a spirited attack upon his leg and began to drag him away. The Mayor attempted to bargain. 'My leg maintains that it must live in my house!'

And then Gregor looked ahead, rushing weirdness hammering past him. It was a ride through schemes, the blurwalls ringing with scionic squeals.

Then they were stood on a companionway over horror, Gettysburg pointing like a tourist. Deep detail in big time. Structures infinite. Tortured miles flavoured with accidents. 'Mere corpses don't make them proud. Oak can mature about a body. Nothingness is a waltz, vacuums twitching.' They were coasting past galaxies of criticism and society, black breath blasting through them. Body fat was cooked into tears. 'Apocalypse. Stink-millions swelling and throwing sparks.' A billion migrating dunces crossed a chaos of unvoiced assumptions. 'Dark matter sometimes breeds in silence. Children here meet the floor without mattering, lost magnificently in nursery forges.' Bladeshadow shivers of locusts turned heads in regard, piling hivesights into rooves, mandibles feeding. 'Revenant market. Head trauma unit. Sweeney's torturers. They're obsessed with beauty.' A couple of poor fiends attempted to eat fruit in difficult circumstances.

Gettysburg made his three charges peek out of a vent in the sickstone wall of a cavern, looking miles down at a parasite the size of a whale. The white arachnoid was braced at the bullseye of an etheric nerve sea, electricity exploding between the cables. 'Sweeney.'

Bubblewrapped in Gettysburg's protection, they drifted along a narrow ledge. 'You'll like this.' Below were a load of ruins piled in a corner. 'Violaine Prophecies.' He pointed at some blather engraved on a sulphate slab:

'Beware the Beast Man, simple and true.
He'll kick the living shit out of you.'

They were moving through darkness, walking now. Dim clutter and junk was stacked here. Gregor read off labels. 'Skull sand. Mole pearls. Umbilia.'

All but the demon were shivering, frozen. They pushed through a door into another collection of lethal novelties. Looking to the left, Gregor saw a rigid goat standing behind a counter. They were in the Shop of a Thousand Spiders. Night had fallen. Gregor remembered the darkling creep exit at the rear of the store, then began almost at once to forget it.

Barny seemed more scared now than ever. Even the demon Gettysburg seemed suddenly cautious. Spooky Staring Boy was somewhere on the premises.

They crept toward the door, jumpy and almost free. Gregor just wanted to be sleeping in his burrow under the office. The night looked fresh and healthy. Barny put his hand to the handle.

'The throat was shocked before lines cut little rubies,' said a voice behind them. They turned to see the small figure staring blandly at them. 'And the grave digests in plump welcome.'

*

Edgy lay in the Aquarium Hospital, his symptoms exposed to the world. In beds to either side of him lay Gregor and BB Henrietta. BB lay stiff as a plank, staring into the sky. The three spoke very little. Edgy was wrapped almost entirely in bandages and wished he was allowed to recuperate back at the motel - he could easily incorporate the look into his ghost scam.

Barny was visible a long way off, navigating the glass corridors. With him was the gator, loping its short legs forward with a slap. And finally here he was, beaming at the three.

'I brought grapes,' he said, dumping a bag on to a side table. The gator dragged its tail past a glass medical stand which crashed to the floor, bursting a plasma packet. 'And grubshoots. Guaranteed to dart up the walls and snap at any bugs around here, then rot to grey in the corners.'

'He brought the gator,' mumbled Gregor, and pulled the invisible covers over his head.

'Get that monster away from me,' shouted BB, 'you *lunatic*!'

'It's perfectly legit,' said Barny.

'That's not the point, Bubba, oh tell him Edgy, *tell* him in a way he'll understand!'

The Captain entered, dapper as always in his white uniform. 'How's the staff?'

'Mine's worked better,' said Gregor.

'Before you say anything, ma'am,' Barny told the Captain, 'I've decided to say goodbye to Mister Newton here. People aren't good for him.'

'Well by golly in light of the traditional revelations about Mayor Rudloe at this time of year, I think I can set aside his allegations about you. And I just had a chat with Doctor Perfect - it seems I owe you an apology, Gregor. He says he advised you to hot-damn express your feelings directly to one and all and this you sensibly did. But I came here primarily to see Mr Plantin Edge.'

'Me. What have I done.'

'I witnessed your little display in the cage full of dogs. I must say I've never seen a more reckless and stupid act in my life.'

'Well listen,' groaned Edgy from a ragged hole in his bandages. 'Who's to say the dogs, at least, didn't enjoy it.'

'It was a mad, brash act, and on the strength of that I'd like to give you the glad hand and invite you to join the Patently Damaging Sports Club.'

'Eh? You?'

'Oh yes. I've been a member for some years. Threw myself arse-first into a barrel of rattlers. Rather amateur really - you'll learn, as I did.'

'But I've been trying to get myself invited by Neville Peth. He doesn't seem to think I'm worthy.'

'Neville Peth isn't in the Club. He sells insurance, for pity's sake. And I'll tell you another thing.' The Captain turned and strode out.

'I wish he wouldn't do that,' said Gregor.

Sweeney sat in a pall of noxious steam. 'Look. I'm bonded again in this bloody network hull. I only sat down for a moment. There must be a better way of keeping a grip on things.'

Preoccupied with the rope darkness of his stomach, Dietrich did not reply. A mess of wing blood, ink and steel, he stumbled down the slope.

'Where's Juno? The gator? Dead at least?' Sweeney fidgeted in his throne, shrike cables flubbering slow around him. 'Even that Bingo bastard said regarding human character, to simplify is to insult, to kill is to simplify absolutely. Straightforward enough.'

'Not dead, Your Majesty. I suspect ... the Prophecy -'

'What's *that*?' Sweeney pointed at Dietrich's right arm, which now terminated with a sort of bone mantrap.

'Your ... old jaw, Your Majesty. Floor lobsters ate the claw. I had to use what I had. It's bloody chaos up there. Those ... *people*. They're not *civilised*. Getty's insane to love them. Look at my stomach.'

Boiling with rage, Sweeney flushed the colour of black glass. 'Gettysburg? You've been consorting with that turncoat?'

Dietrich didn't know what to say.

'And no Juno? Get out of here!'

Dietrich turned and blundered from the cavern.

Sweeney stared about at the empty cavern. 'Dare I send anyone for cigarettes?'

And he wept chains which dangled clinking from his face, tenting the skin.

Barny took the gator to the swamp, releasing it into mile upon mile of twisting waterways and mangrove islands. Determined that the reptile should be forgotten, he took one of the creature's teeth and gave it to Chloe Low in the Juice Museum. Before filing it among the other exhibits she held it in her hand and closed her eyes. 'It says: "I bite for you, I chew for you, but taste nothing. Teeth are citizens of the body." Hmm, it's like that sometimes. I'll put it with the gun, shall I?'

Then they sat on a rock by the baffling ocean and smelt the salt of the moon. Shadows ate the valley, dead men dappled in the morgue and the cold middle of a church got even colder.

But there's more.

ACCOMPLICE 2

THE
VELOCITY
GOSPEL

"John's head exploded during cremation
and everyone heard it but pretended otherwise.
There'll always be an England."

- E.Gamete
Punching the Sarge

When someone tells you life's a dream, you can bet they're about to inconvenience you very badly. I was watching when Barny Juno stole a small midday snack from the forces of evil, thus setting in motion a series of adventures which still amuse and appall people with time on their hands. It pulled monsters into the world like meat from a shellfish, all white to the sun. Why didn't I interfere? Just before my death I did nip in with a prophecy regarding the demon who was eating my head at the time. But backbone needs a body. Since I abandoned the daily business of human anatomy I've spied from an etheric sideband, cosy and floating. Accomplice was a tropic of slack-jawed nutters. Justice as rare as a jelly fossil. And Barny couldn't concentrate on the evil at hand. Mind elsewhere and nothing furtive. A manchild whose life had slipped into a casual fairy tale, as the heated air fluttered like a ghost.

1

NEVER TALK TO STRANGERS

A story is ready when it falls out of your face

A massive hot ruby hung steaming in space a country mile beneath Accomplice. Its heart a turning red rind, it added colour to the skull-studded extravaganza of air pain and spinelight in that neck of the world. Lounging in a veined halfshell, a white mantid ghoul with complicated mouthparts had a famous time distributing nightmares and inconvenience through a network of thick coaxial nerve cables. Sweeney's egg eyes and huge blown head like the skull of a whale - this was the first face a fool would see after getting his arse caught in the drum of a player piano.

Branched glimpses of electricity banged across the walls and floor of the titanic cavern. 'Night is never terminal,' Sweeney sighed, turning his attention to the boulder-sized gemstone. 'Where is the man Barny Juno.'

'He is among a crowd of people.'
'What's he doing.'
'He searches for a snake ...'

The old blood clock counterweighted into motion and two mechanical knights propelled on to a narrow platform. As the blue and yellow figures clashed swords, Mayor Rudloe stepped on to the balcony above and regarded the broth of humanity which had gathered in the sun-white town square. Most of them were staring up at the palace like gooney-birds. The Mayor ballooned out, speaking. 'I have asked you to infest this square in order to impart warning of a dire threat to our community. I've been passing myself off as the big authority round here for years. You granted me that honour at breakneck speed, all almond-eyed and eager. You turn in unison like pinstripe fish and I bless you for it. Maintaining m'stranglehold here's the only exercise my brachioradial muscles ever get. Boy, is it ever sweet. But as Accomplice's single organ of government and frankly the only man with any ideas around here, I must talk to you regarding certain bastards who would defame our imploded society. They call themselves the Followers of Cyril. A ravening rabble lacking the gratitude which most of us take for granted, they are workshy and pensive - and probably, if they've got any sense, armed to the teeth. Strictly speaking this is baseless but I love it. Revolution - how the cured thing dooms the rest of us. They're playing merry hell with everything and this half-arsed development couldn't have come at a better time. There's a red deficit - isn't it a pity? The mechanised knights below, ever toiling in their faithful service, require an extra bloody tribute to keep them clashing. I wept lard this morning as I thought of how vexing and costly it will be for you. Then I carved the lard into the shape of a raven. So you see how I put you people first? Nothing is wasted. I save on expense by shrugging with only one shoulder. Get a loada this - heyup.'

Down among the socket-faced masses Barny Juno and the gangling Plantin Edge were discussing corpse praline and radio cartoons in an absent sort of way. Barny looked moon-faced and wondering through the crowd and occasionally crouched amid their shuffling legs. Plantin Edge was wearing a sheet and eating popcorn in the Accomplice heat. 'So you went to the Garden with Madge yesterday Bubba?'

Barny looked uncomfortable. 'I had to borrow a book from someone. I've been boning up on moths. I reckon the one I ate was a geometrid. Maybe Fang could find a replacement for me - he's a bug man.'

'He's a *bog* man. And you borrowed a book eh? I get it. From that little fringed musette at the Juice Museum.'

Barny sighed dismally. 'We pranced weak with joy through some of the big flowers they've got round there. She's ... limber. Bendy. Fang says I've only got one tongue and I might as well use it.'

'So what's the problem?'

'Magenta Blaze. She's convinced I'm an interesting man and won't let go of my leg.'

'You're sure you want Chloe Low at the Juice?'

'I agree with all of her heart, Edgy. I can't explain it.'

Edgy crammed popcorn and thought. 'Get around to Beltane Carom. He'll give you some arcane and surefire method of dumping the Blaze.'

'At least he's not one of those gurus who thinks he's funny. They're the pits.'

'Yeah, and everyone's too respectful to tell them? No, he's a shaman, Bubba, a master. He's giving me some advice about Amy. You know she wants me to help her publish that terrible poetry of hers, like I've got any influence on old Crash Test Nureyev over the publishers? The wand jockey listened to the problem and set me straight. His nose was pullulating the whole time.'

'So what did he say?'

Edgy frowned in recollection. 'The object of many dimensions is to make all things ignorable by a simple manoeuvre.'

'What does that mean? Is this stupid sheet part of it?'

'No, I was halfway through a haunting at the motel when I heard about this little shindig. Well I had to come along Bubba. You remember last time? That massive galvanised tin head eating the populace? The bite radius on the thing, boy oh boy. For all his faults the Mayor knows how to put on a show.'

'Why's he going on about his shoulder?' Barny muttered, preoccupied with peering amid the crowd.

'Could it be otherwise? Misdirection, Bubba. Look at him. Too sure to look shifty. Unencumbered by memory of his mistakes, the man's cheeks are completely out of control.'

Barny glanced up. 'His bones are coming through his mouth.'

'Those are his teeth. They live to serve him.'

'I don't understand what he's talking about.'

'You're not supposed to. What did old Bingo Violaine say? "Deflate a gasbag at your peril."'

'Right now I'm just worried about Misses Kennedy. This is no place for a puff adder, Edgy. Really big vipers need shelter and care. She's excited now but she'll get anxious later. I caught her tanning in the sandwich maker and she must have thought I was angry and ran away. Put a centre parting in the lawn by the roundabout. Maybe she's nervous about the contest. She's around here somewhere, maybe under some cycads.'

'She'll be fine. Hey Barny, can I go hang with the leopard with you? I think I could handle it, you know, if he took a swipe at me with his paw.'

'Well Edgy, treat him with respect. His ears might be velvet but he has mood swings that'll make your chin stand on end.'

'You're the best friend the winged and stepping animals of the earth could have, Bubba, but you should chill out. Take some popcorn. It always reminds me of little skulls or something.'

'You know if they were real and had some meat on them, they might tempt Misses Kennedy. Are you sure it's just popcorn?'

Edgy sifted through the carton. 'It's a needle in a haystack.' He emptied the carton on to the ground. 'There - if there's a skull we know who'll find it eh? Lateral thinking.'

'I never would have thought of that,' Barny nodded in frank admiration. Edgy had a sharp mind in that tall, tufted head of his.

Barny squatted amid the forest of legs and squeaked a beckoning call to the serpent.

'Hey, you know who I can see, Bubba?' Edgy called down to him, and squinted over the assembly. A keg-shaped man with a head like a potato stared up at the mayoral palace in rapt attention. 'It's Gregor. Yeah he's right at the front of the crowd. It looks like he's really into it. Hey, Round One!'

The cry registered dimly on the Mayor's consciousness and, thinking it referred to him, he discarded it. 'We have yet to see the Followers of Cyril in the full bloom of atrocity,' he was saying. 'I don't pretend to understand their contempt. I'll not deceive you, I regard new systems of humour with suspicion. Accomplice is a community unto itself. Be vigilant. At a time of social emergency it's crucial to abstain from riots as irksome to me as their necessity is to you. It is written here in our Constitution' - and the Mayor dabbled his fingers in a tray of water - 'that money's an opinion we daren't lose. However, the good news is, I can help you. First I declare a state of constant readiness. I will decide in due course that the levy must be increased to counter the baleful crisis. At that time I will set upon a policy greatly at odds with your wellbeing, squashing your faces as though against a rippled pane of glass. This will be followed by a root and branch review, a clamour of ear-grinding excuses and, finally, the really back-breaking work of denying everything. One or two timid witnesses will drift down a river and deal out into the sea. Then I'll give a big horselaugh. We haven't a moment to lose. I foresee a land positively blistering with safety. One of green television fields and beaches shut with tides. Pearls barricade the advancement steps and cranks watch summer from the porch. Working hands down, you shroud the dying in laughter. Exhaustions brow the night. Rejoice. These lofty notions are food and drink to you aimless wonders. You're supported, you're safe, you're happy -'

'You're okay!' yelled Barny, raising the venomous adder above the crowd. The assembly exploded outward like the primal bang. Screams wheeled and intersected as hundreds legged it and Edgy's sheet was torn away in the commotion.

Before the Mayor was fully aware of events, he was gazing down at an almost deserted town square. Only three people remained - the man with the deadly viper, a naked man who stood like a used match, and a spudlike creature who stared silently up with a look of gluey need. This last one, the Mayor realised with alarm, was playing pocket billiards. The other two seemed to understand this at the same moment and, rushing forward, bundled the round man away.

The clock knights, swords locked in silence, finally disengaged and swerved backwards, doors of red gold flipping closed upon them.

'Business as usual above,' Sweeney ruminated, turning from the Ruby. 'But see how Juno and the scarecrow ran to the aid of their piglike friend, the creature they call the Round One. A weak link?'

'Juno's kept aloft and unreachable,' said Dietrich the Hammer, entering the cavern astride a scuttling legal cadaver, 'on the thermals of his own ignorance.' He drew to a stop, all membrane wings and stained armour.

Sweeney clacked his shoehorn tongue. 'I've a mind to send Skittermite above.'

Dietrich twitched his tomahawk head to peer at the emperor grub. 'Kermit?' he spat.

'He's been punching below his weight for a while now. Not still stuck in that pipe I suppose?'

'No, but if he hadn't the wherewithal to avoid the simplest drain, how could he navigate Accomplice? It's chaotic beyond endurance up there – just because those bastards are completely covered in skin they think they can deny their insides.'

The sheer architectural extravagance of demonic biology was mostly open to inspection, infernodyne veins and pulsing bile yolk fully visible through wide-flung ribs.

'You want to go back, after Juno's sucker-punch?' Sweeney leered like a burning snowman. 'One of the best tunes and you've changed it. You didn't used to think he was worth the candle. Pegged him as a simpleton.'

'So he is - a man "simple and true", like the prophecy of your downfall, Your Majesty.'

'Please don't complicate such a simple matter. Fetch the imp.'

Skittermite was tossing shoes into the smelter when Dietrich came for him. Victim blood still draining from his gills, he scurried after the bigger fiend like a charbroiled monkey, all pickbones and shoulderblades. From his wedge-shaped head projected two thin prongs, useful only for toasting mallows.

Sweeney turned as they entered. Magnesium glares lit the heat-blasted cowling of his skull. 'Pay close attention, flydart.'

Skittermite deployed his ears, flapping them like sparrow wings. Dietrich stood by with a twitching face.

'You and your telescopic canines are going above to Accomplice. Barny Juno needs aggravating unto death. He's hex-protected so nix on the claw-work, we need to operate through the social grind. Luckily there's a political push on the go and mugs will be out in force. Concentrate on the man with the body of a potato, this barrel-being they call the Round One. He's got a medical bracelet that says "Just throw me away". I believe he's the vulnerable point in Juno's entourage. So get some scars, prove you're not too new for the job. Need any of these?' Sweeney indicated a wall of human faces which he called his 'personality pelts'.

'Please no your Majesty thank you,' Skittermite sibilated.

'Good, well: left and right, space is limitless - manipulation therefore is limitless. Dietrich here seems to think they dislike being tackled by the legs - you might try that.'

'Thank you. By your command.' Skittermite dipped his wedge-shaped head.

'Off you go then.'

Skittermite darted up a slope as though launched from a spring-winder, chittering his joy.

Dietrich sullenly picked the eye from his mount - it squirmed in his hand like a fizzing Tylenol. As a paravamp demon his own eyes registered all one-and-a-half thousand shades of black but he could not understand the worth of Accomplice.

'You've been grinding your head about the place,' stated Sweeney, 'since Gettysburg went renegade. You misplace blame. Getty was a good seed, that's all, and good riddance.'

Dietrich looked at the ivory king insect in wonder. It was rare for Sweeney to mention the defector's name. The demon Gettysburg had started his conscientious objecting covertly by inventing the rule that to be invoked, his name must be repeated 86,400 times. Most people got bored or fell asleep before hitting the number and this gave him years to kick back and hang in the fiery deeps. The invocation procedure was clearly useless in an emergency and Sweeney queried it, but Gettysburg insisted that it was sly and evil since it led to people using his name casually and without regard. He claimed that the unsuspecting would one day cumulatively hit the magic number and find themselves confronted by the mirror-eyed shrike. His excuses for mellow behaviour became lamer by the decade. Finally he went out for cigarettes and never returned.

'I've walked the floors of oceans,' Dietrich explained, 'and passed finer society.'

'Look closer. I've known their world, leather to feathers. I even witnessed the grim, fateful appearance of the first herb. Mankind mines a stratum of the obvious so thick it occupies their lifetime. And more good news - every inch of flesh is carvable.'

The Mayor walked in off the balcony and picked among the floor lobsters toward his darkwood desk. These large armoured roaches, physical evidence of spiritual corruption, had monopolised the floor space since the cleaner died. Rudloe kicked one gingerly and it curled up like an ammonite. It also resembled, the Mayor reflected vaguely, a cat that was quite at home. 'I expected more merriment,' he said, sitting down.

'Well sir, pocket billiards,' remarked the lawyer Max Gaffer. 'What could be more merry.'

'I looked away for a split second and the populace was reduced to a child-faced moron with a venomous snake, a rather gormless, uninspired flasher and a round man utterly absorbed with his own balls. Everyone else had done a runner.'

'In record time.'

'That's no consolation, I'm afraid. Who was the one with the death-adder? Have I met him?'

'Barny Juno. He's the guy who held a funeral for a lizard and dropped his trousers during the eulogy. Came in here dressed as an ape. Flies around on a swan.'

'This is all one man?'

'He's a notorious mooncalf, Mayor. A spooky simpleton. Doesn't know enough to stop. Irritates everyone, up to and including our lord the devil himself.'

'You seen him on the swan?'

'Swans are very graceful.'

'So that's a no. Wait a second, this the guy I demonised a while back? Well there's your proof, Max. Inventing a nebulous enemy's the rage. We'll never have Cyril barging in here in a monkey suit, as the bastard doesn't exist.'

'Outstanding, sir.' The lawyer, whose yellow eyes and fishbone hairstyle unnerved the living, conceded that the Cyril mirage was a sound tactic. The Mayor had been in a weakened position since going out on a limb with his 'I am a Beautiful Woman' campaign. Almost everyone agreed he had overstepped the mark, and those who had expressed hearty support became abashed and furtive. The new trap was spare and inexpensive. 'Just keep 'em blaming.'

'Well, I've planted the seed. Get old Turbot to write us another speech, turning up the heat. Behind thick manoeuvres I'll reduce my efforts. The scrap cost can be disregarded. The promises? Forgot into our pockets again. As Violaine said, "timing is the knowledge that society may have been more ready in the past than in the present". Even the waking collective attributes tyranny to the assigned villain.'

The Mayor struck a match on the armour of a passing bug and lit a cigar. The big wheel always came around.

2

FOGHORN MOTHER

A camel cannot be impressed

Barny worked part-time at the Sorting Office, a pressure chamber of swarming embers and anxiety. His co-workers, Edgy and Gregor included, amused themselves with muted but erudite comparisons of snot colouration. Never-admitted ignorance as to the nature of the job filled everyone with stressful dread and morbid evasion. In fact the stress was of such consistent and dependable quality that a clown cartel once attempted to harvest it via quick-blooming nerve pumps fed through the damp walls. When finally a test subject sampled the harvest, his face exploded and showered the onlookers with flaming tar.

Today Barny entered the basement to find that though the morning had thus far passed without bloodshed, their hale supervisor, the Captain, had swung by to find Gregor living it up to the exclusion of all else. The Captain's expression was as clenched and grim as he could muster in the damp heat of the day. 'Jeepers creepers boys, couldn't you keep a friendly eye on this guy? Gregor baby, we all thought you'd made a clean start of it until you decided to astound everyone with your behaviour in the square. From what I heard, you yelled something, tore off your clothes and started waving a demonically oversized whanger about the place. By golly, man - staring directly into the Mayor's eyes the whole time? Aren't you remotely satisfied by your work here?'

'Not the Mayor.'

'Eh?'

'I wasn't looking at the Mayor and ... let's just leave it at that.'

Something drew the Captain's eyes to a corner of the gloomy basement. Gregor had used a load of the baffling papers and packages which poured daily into the office to create a full-sized papier-mache effigy of one of the town clock knights. 'Holy mackerel. On probation from your past and here I find you've been out lusting after concrete figurines after all. By jiminy can't a week pass without me having to fire one of you fellas? Come on.'

'You're firing me?' Gregor mumbled. 'Shouldn't I be praised for trying to get it out of my system?'

'Gregor, your motives are as obscure as a spider's face and much as I love you and wish you well, nothing'll ever escape a system so warped and twisted as I see you displaying here. You know I answer to Mr Gibbon. I wonder why I waited this long. And more importantly -'

And the Captain skipped up the stairs, slamming out.

'I wish he wouldn't do that,' said Edgy.

'Well, for some fantastic reason he's gone weird in the head and fired me,' Gregor laughed uneasily, looking worried at the others. 'Eh? It's probably illegal, right?'

'No he's got you bang to rights,' said BB Henrietta.

Edgy was jittery and startled, looking at Gregor with newly troubled eyes. 'Hey it never occurred to any of us you were looking at those mechanical knights, Round One. And I thought you built this thing in the corner just to get rid of some paper stuff. You'll get a cornerstone order for this. It's way worse than when you forced yourself on those dinosaur remains.'

'How can you like something that was never alive?' asked Barny with genuine curiosity. 'It's like them creepy Church of Automata people.'

Gregor made a disconsolate sound. There was general, appalled agreement that he had gone too far. Though known to one and all as a man who inhabited a species for which he was manifestly unqualified, he had caught everyone off-guard with this lust for a juddering trophy. 'I only like the blue one,' he protested, and immediately knew he'd said the worst.

'Can you hear yourself?'

Backs were turning, including that of Fang, a zombie whose spine-knurls were horribly visible and quite compelling.

'So I've got to move out of the maintenance cupboard?' Gregor asked wanly.

Nobody replied. Gregor released a small whimper.

Skittermite buzzed out of the creepchannel on a gristle bike, slewing to a stop in a spray of blown watches. Hunkering down to eat the engine, he pondered the hot, ripe land about him. A scarlet countryside, earth crammed with tea, funerals ... He was finally going to the show. Some saw Accomplice as a skull, a domain bound by bone and notion. To Skitter it seemed a fertile arena. Angel refineries stood like gravestones and rotten hearts were piled in the sabotage yard. Electric with mischief and anticipation, he resolved to acquit himself well. His plan was to understand the way of things here, blend in and imitate. Then the horror.

That night Gregor slept in a tough leather sack slung from a tree branch. Once again he'd eaten his luck like a tie spooned up with the morning cereal.

Gravel flew against the bag - he unzipped and looked into the night. The pale face of Barny Juno looked up at him, whispering urgently. 'Gregor - sorry about this morning. I don't know why I went along with it. Take some advice and don't tell anyone I told you.'

'What advice?'

'Maybe that Church of Automata will know what to do about them mechanical dummies, if you convince them your problems are creepy enough. And you can stay at my place. This tree's for losers.'

'Ladderland? I'm not staying in that overgrown barn of yours - the lion'll drag me apart and the howler monkeys'll piss on my cadaver.'

'I'm reading about silverbacked apes,' hissed Barny. 'Those mothers monitor the location and activity of the gorillas in their group, decide when and where the group will move, and settle arguments among the females.'

'Have you got anything relevant to add? No? Then don't bother me any more.'

A few minutes later more gravel splashed against the bag - Gregor looked down to see the wiry form of Edgy. 'Gregor - sorry about this morning. I don't know why I went along with it. Take some advice and don't tell anyone I told you.'

'What is it?'

'Go to Stampede Door to Door and tell them I sent you - they'll give you a job. As for all the other stuff, try to rise above it by spurting pints of saliva at your more sedate adversaries. Puzzle all with a new chin. It's a stellar choice. That way they'll remember you.'

'That's exactly what I don't want.'

'Why?' whispered Edgy.

'Well they'll either barge me with honours or single me out for derision, won't they? Either way my nerves'll be shot. Anyway I'm already looking for a job. Talked to Kenny Reactor at the gillball nursery – but he told me he could hear the vegetables crying out against me. He said if I didn't leave straight away, they'd start launching all premature.'

'A gut farmer? That's not the course of exhaustion for you, Round One. Go to the Stampede like I said. Goodnight.'

Edgy left and Gregor settled down. Soon another spray of gravel hit the bag and Gregor peered down blearily to see a thing which was basically a couple of walking elbows and a gob like a staple gun. This bony predator gaped a wound full of needles and chittered. 'Gregor - sorry about this morning. I don't know why I went along with it. Take some advice and don't tell anyone I told you -'

Gregor exploded from the tree, terror blasting from his mouth as he hit the ground running. The wedge-headed stranger seemed to implore behind him as he belted into the night. Gregor took it upon himself to scream as he tripped on an abandoned stove. When the hell would his expression be that of a normal man?

The following morning Barny visited the shaman Beltane Carom as Edgy had advised in the Square. Barny liked the shaman's mild manners and calm way of life. He had once seen Carom push an iron key into the surface of a flowing stream and pull up a transparent lid, reaching in to retrieve a choc ice.

Barny met him in a walled courtyard in which the flagstones were configured to a weightless pattern. The yard had its own sky and a corner pond of green shadow. Carom placed his nerve lute aside and asked what Barny had in mind.

'I need to break it off with Magenta Blaze. She's crazy and loud and I want to be with someone else I met. I can't overlap. What do I do?'

'If you continue with a broken chair, do you snub the truth or accept it?'

Barny shook his head slowly and sadly. 'I just don't know what you're talking about, ma'am.'

'Unfortunate - but true, at least. It's only some facts that a name will stick to - others are too slippery, fast or fierce. Let's see what the cards say.' Beltane produced a deck of blackstrap cards, irregular slabs of threaded meat and woven gristle. Each stacking order created one of twenty-seven different organs. 'To have and to hold, to cut out and keep. Let's see.' He began placing cards and reading their meanings. 'Seven cards. Fornix. "Slaves enter the box, all cities are at an end." Sarcomere. "Smoking a squirrel, I backed into the shed." The first-person statements address the matter of socially transgressive mirth, gold in the water. Buccinator. "He turns the sign against their questions."'

The cards lay like dry steaks, muted whorls and nephritic blemishes unreadable to Barny's eyes.

'Jejunum. "Through a dossier his decency runs like the thwarting shadow of a synagogue." Hypodermis. "By all means moan tonight." Trapezius. "My whisper outraged the debutante." Concha. "No-one else is laughing." There you have it.'

'So what does it all mean?'

'Well, sometimes the truth's right there for you Barny. Like the obvious fact that knees and potatoes are the same thing.'

'What for?'

'Emergencies maybe, that's not the point. This woman, Magenta Blaze, she's not listening - you can push through that self-involvement with something called the Power Shout.'

'Power Shout. How's it done?'

'When the time comes, you'll know. At the very least you'll frighten the life out of her.'

'That's all there is to it?'

'Well, freedom's funny. It looks green but it tastes red.' He began tossing the cards into the pond, where they were snapped down by sudden fish. 'What fury teaches is a candid superstructure to hold happiness. Was there something else you wanted to talk about, Barny? Something deeper?'

'I've put up Misses Kennedy for this year's Deadly Snake Competition. But I don't want her to be nervous or become ill. Everyone reckons she's in line for the Hold It In the Middle and Flinch But Don't Let Go When It Flexes Unpredictably rosette. Anyway so Golden Sid, who takes care of the animals when I'm at work? He's the judge. But Balaclava Lewis, with his black mamba Tamale, he says there's partiality there, so for the moment Sid isn't allowed to work with me until after the contest. People sure are suspicious.'

'Right. So, er ... is there anything else, Bubba, something troubling you, maybe about the family or some such?'

'There's the moth thing, yeah my parents kept a moth in a canary cage, called it Ramone. I ate it by accident and it went to heaven. They think I deliberately let it go to fly away. Why would I do that? Now I want to replace it without them knowing but I can't find the sort of geometrid moth I need.'

'The trickster, what's his name, he has a moth of that variety, which he keeps in his navel.'

'Yeah, you're sure?'

'He cavorts in the Square sometimes - seek him there. If he's not there he'll be behind the snout distillery. And don't take no for an answer.'

Barny was chuffed. 'Thank you, ma'am. You've been a real help.'

Barny couldn't find Prancer Diego in the Square so he went through the snout distillery toward his room. The distillery was a front for a flower store, which fronted a bar full of angry failures, which was in turn the front for a sauna. Behind this were the sequential fronts of a print shop, a karate school, a giant mouth, a movie theatre and a bowling alley. This all fronted a spartan room which had no back wall and was totally exposed to the air - anyone walking the street behind it could see Prancer undressing for bed or sitting bolt upright in a wooden chair, semolina dripping from his ears.

When Barny arrived, Prancer was trying to step with both legs at once and straining with hilarity at his experiment. In this sort of useless activity Prancer was unmatched. He'd dig a shallow hole, do a headstand in it and claim he was wearing the entire world as a hat. He annoyed everyone by wearing nicotine patches on his eyes, talking almost perfectly through his nostrils and doing the Heimlich manoeuvre on people who were perfectly fine. In queuing to end his life at least a thousand people were turned away. When someone gave him the white feather of cowardice he used it to smudge his aura. His skull already made him a human, why did he have to learn the behaviour?

'Oho Bubba,' Prancer hailed him. 'Sorry I'm late. A towering flume of winged demons spurted from a manhole, delaying me.'

'What?'

'A word to the wise, Juniper. When you dislike a comment, chew the nose from the speaker. That way any of your more well-meaning friends may withdraw. And I heard about Gregor's stunt with his whanger. I'd like to shake his hand.'

'Rather you than me, Dago.'

'Reveal a gasp-causing body slain in sobs by a repressed monk. Works every time.'

Barny sighed quietly. 'I suppose it's asking too much to expect a normal sentence from that gob of yours?'

Prancer dodged and ducked as though under attack, all in silence and peaceful circumstance.

'Er, anyway I need the moth in your belly button, Dago. And no stupid games, it's important.'

Prancer's avian head nodded sagely. 'One day breath will be enough. But only by stealth. Cyril doesn't exist and so to save our lovely Mayor the indignity of being branded a liar, we must create this being from air. You and your buddies could really help me out. At a sedate pace.'

And Prancer suddenly wigged out real bad, grabbing Barny by the shirt and rushing him through the bowling alley, the movie theatre, the giant mouth and the karate school until, exploding into the printshop, he produced a bullhorn from nowhere and bellowed through it while priming the machinery. His manner was wild and truculent. 'Society. Bleed but don't make a scene. Mouths tuned to one story and useless leg advice. Some button-head destiny selected from a list, maybe a little friend to point at the chicken dream as immobile creatures report their glued thoughts. Depend on bills, swallow corpses, greet business, die. This forehead of yours responds with fashion merely, fool's gold and fossilfruit.' Prancer tore off his own shirt, stancing heroically. 'Authority - let us do it the supreme honour of incessant disregard. The idea that we should somehow develop a good attitude is to be humoured, fantastical though it is! A stern code of tolerance may yet result from this exercise alone! Chainsmoke menus! Grow out of your size and get respect! Tomorrow I'll celebrate - today here's your neck to grab. I defy the idlers to sleep me out!'

Prancer wheeled aside, flinging himself on to the print machine. He hoist down the spearlike axis of the bare drumholder so that it side-pierced his chest, burrowing through the flesh and nosing out of the other side.

Barny wished he was back amid the natural ferocity of his animals. 'Please, Dago, you're scaring me,' he shouted above the escalating rev of the machine.

'A society with the face of a priest!' Prancer laughed as the drum shaft began to turn, breaking the skin of his chest and rolling his flesh downward like a scroll.

'Dago, you must be really ill,' Barny quailed as the claws of Prancer's ribcage became visible. The air scalded with electrostatic screeching and the stench of bergamot. Prancer lay laughing amid the roar of the machinery. The flesh peeled down, revealing his maverick guts like a bloody oyster. Barny saw the whiskered face of the moth emerge from Prancer's navel, a rat abandoning the sinking ship. He snatched the bug into his palm before the belly's eviscera-tion was completed. *I'm a good son after all*, Barny thought, rushing from the terrible room.

That evening in the Swamp of Eternal Enmity/Degradation, Barny watched his parents' shack from the waist-deep concealment of the oozing bog. When the lamps went out, he pushed through the rank smell of leather leaves and waterweeds toward the stained wood of the shack.

Here the swamp was not the most perilous undertow. His rois-tering but serpent-headed father had chosen to indefinitely postpone acknowledgement of the facts, including that of Barny's genetic rela-tionship to himself. Barny's mother had chosen to do the same - according to each he was the work of the other.

Barny doorcreaked into the shack, where his parents sat asleep in their concrete chairs. The room was illuminated by the dim phos-phorescence of Pa Juno's octopal hair, the ghostly glow of which was muted in sleep. The canary cage stood in the far corner, a black mourning cloak covering the cage itself. Barny crept silently over, tipped the fluttering moth carefully from a matchbox and reached it into the cage - it fitted by feel between the bars. Then he turned and instantly stepped on a rope of his father's hair, blasting the house with light and screaming.

'What the hell is your son doing creeping around here?' shouted Pa Juno, squinting through the false fog of marriage.

'Ask him - he's your son.'

'Er, look at this,' Barny improvised, spinning back to the cage and flourishing the cloak away. 'It's a miracle.'

On the floor of the cage a fruit bat was flapping one wingtip like blown paper and making small glottal noises, its foxlike face wet-eyed and shutting down.

'What have you done?' shrieked Barny's mother.

'He must have fed it something dry,' hollered Pa Juno.

'Something that wasn't fruit,' whooped Ma Juno. 'After taking our beautiful Ramone from us.'

Barny pointed back at the cage. 'I put this one in his place didn't I?'

'Did you hear that?' shrieked Ma Juno.

'He'll do the same to us, give him half the chance. Can't you keep your son under control?'

Ma Juno pressed her tear-wet face against the cage bars, grilling her grief. 'I have no son.'

3

GUNPOWDER TEA

Hoaxers try harder

Gregor, too, had been making progress. Mention of Edgy's name had indeed swung a job at Stampede Products and he was asked to start right away, since another employee had met an 'untimely end', or so the interviewer said with raised eyebrows and the sort of rueful tone which implied that Gregor should easily guess the details.

Gregor steamed in. On the first day a hundred doorsteps were enlivened by his desperation. Stampede's ephemera was aimed at couchbound morons for whom a nervous shudder was exercise. Along with horror-wipe boots for the modern world they sold Live Pants, the pants which grow with your philosophy; Damage Tonic, guaranteed to leave you twisted and broken as though after some ill-advised venture; the Toilet Heart, a heart which lay beating in the toilet; the Mice Device, which you placed next to a mouse for thoughtful comparison; Eggs, a new concept in noses; the Doggone Diagram, a floorplan of somebody else's house which led to mis-navigation through the home; Armageddon Goodies, some bones; and the Impulse Buy, a beautifully-packaged object which nobody could ever describe or remember.

Gregor's pitch began well due to his looking bulby and distorted through door peepholes and then looking exactly the same when people opened the door. Potential customers laughed a lot and assumed he was a joke telegram. Gregor would chuckle along with them and launch into his spiel. 'If you were an animal, sir, which animal would you be?'

'Eh? Well I am an animal. I'm a human.'

'I mean if you weren't human, what would you be?'

'You think I'm not human?'

'It's just a game.'

'Not to me it isn't. I'm damn proud.'

'And so you should be. As Bingo Violaine said, "Duty enhances the handsome man, is an added burden to the unloved." May I come in? There we are. May I ask sir, do you exercise?'

'I puff, I puff, it's the same as jogging. And every two weeks I have a kind of hernia.'

'No need with these. Dangerous copper pants. They conduct electricity. You'll be convulsing, jumping all over. You'll break blood vessels in your head.'

'Is that good?'

'I can guess how it would be,' Gregor nodded, smiling slyly as though at a shared, scampish secret.

The client usually responded with a sudden facial grimace which could mean almost anything, then the seizing of Gregor by the throat. Whenever something like this happened and Gregor asked what the fella was doing, the reply would be 'Something I should have done a long time ago' or occasionally 'What anyone would do'. It got to the point where Gregor would pipe 'Don't tell me' and chant the remark before them.

His favourite product was the Stampede Socket Truss. The prolonged haranguing which accompanied it was a masterpiece of what marketeers call the 'assumptive'. 'The Stampede Socket Truss is able to accomplish what no other eye-truss can.'

'What?'

'I'm glad you asked me. Stampede have designed the Socket Truss to lift and separate the eyes without tugging them out of the sockets. No more cracks from the mother-in-law about you having eyes too close together like a drooling pervert. No more people yelling at, yes, *you* sir in the street calling you an inbred cracker waterbrain with a forehead a small boy could use for stuntboarding. Shall I put you down for fifty trusses or the full hundred?'

At this point the client would eject him in a sudden frenzy of discrimination. The only person who expressed any interest in the socket truss was Max Gaffer, who believed it was an article of underwear. When the lawyer realised his mistake and went to close the door on him, Gregor insisted too late that it could be used for that as well. Copious use of the word 'myriad' and 'uses' in his bellowed spiel failed to unseal the door. He forgot to even mention the Live Pants.

Toward the end of the day he rang at a door which opened to reveal a small wedge-headed dingbat with knitting-needle antennae and dense pin teeth. All jaw and claw and gleeful prancing, it chittered instant interest in the Levity Closet and the Death Challenge Kettle. It was the same demon that had appeared to him under the tree the other night. Gregor tore himself away from the sure sale and ran as fast as his arms and legs could take him.

Gregor felt deflated. Following Barny's advice re the Church of Automata, he visited the Grand Dollimo at their pipe-filigreed factory and claimed he was at the end of his tether. The Dollimo, sitting behind a hydraulic desk, steepled his gloved hands. He was masked in a business suit, bowler and smoked-glass face. 'You echo with dominoes,' he decided, 'all those clinking dogmas. You need merely choose one and the noise ends. I could help you. Death must battle all the more for the practical man. Fit your fancies to my twisted will this instant. Without a doubt, you will gain the joy of feeling specific.'

'Sounds perfect,' blurted Gregor without comprehension.

'Come this way - I'll give you but a glimpse of the dummyworks, accountable to no-one.'

'This crane has a lifting power of three hundred tons,' shouted the Dollimo above the roar of dynamos in the turbine hall. 'Ahead is a thousand horsepower drive platform. Face gripping is a relatively simple mechanism.'

'Glad to hear it.'

'Culture life and put it in plastic heads, gag as it restarts.'

Gregor glimpsed creepy marionettes and toddling dolls on the slurry floor below. Periodically these hinge babies disappeared into the sprocket-barnacled walls. Floor lobsters collided and scuttled over each other.

The Dollimo remarked upon assorted doll ordnance as they descended a stairwell near the main forge. It was all hammering diesels and steaming boilerplates, none of it connecting with Gregor's problems. 'Thanks, Grand Dollimo, this is a good facility, thanks for letting me look.'

As they re-entered the office the Dollimo turned to regard him. 'You seem uncommitted.'

Gregor realized vinyl people were watching silent and jewel-eyed, encased in the shelving. He backed carefully through his own bullshit. 'But how does this stuff help with the blood clock?'

The unnatural sheen of the Dollimo's glass mask was point-blank in Gregor's face. 'The blood clock.'

'In the town square. The mechanical knights, that's why I'm here - I can't stop thinking about the blue one. They're automata aren't they?'

'It becomes clear to me,' said the Dollimo without inflection, 'that your life is an unsavoury mess of indulgence and demonism. A figure needs three or more moving parts to qualify as an automaton. Amateur. You waste my time.'

'But they're hinged, they're made of wood,' Gregor bawled as the Dollimo directed him from the room. Gloss-faced mannequins were clappering with laughter.

'Take it outside, you freak.'

Tired and wretched, Gregor wandered through the Square, halting briefly before the mayoral palace. He looked up at the blood clock, its descending array of bowls and gutters through which the liquid was tilted, slowly displacing weight to tip the gears into motion. The red-gold doors were closed, the hour not at hand. Gregor reminded himself of the words of the philosopher Violaine: 'Wounds close without fanfare.'

'Plenty more fish in the sea,' Gregor hummed, 'and they all hate me.' Forever loyal to his reputation as a bloated fool who persevered, he went across town toward the Powderhouse, his steps lagging, head beginning to droop, until he arrived at the thick door all lumpen and hopeless. This was the only other religion he knew around here and he might as well give it a try. He thumped his lowered head against the door.

The door nudged open. 'Waterproof Integrity Grits,' Gregor said with a quaver in his voice. 'A meal in itself.' He displayed the product gingerly.

A fusehead, confetti in his hair and a slight smirk quirking the corner of his mouth, examined Gregor and seemed to decide. 'Face-first we go, nonstop and altogether. Observe our duties.'

Gregor was ushered into a monstrous chamber ricocheting with supplicants. Pop-streamers splurted and fell over fuseheads eating rocket salad and riding an onyx jackass. With sporadic yelps these guys were springing pell-mell past bronze sconces and windows of blue rose glass. A few agile mutants swung off the fittings, all frivolity and ostentation. Even the grubs were wearing bikinis.

This was more like it, thought Gregor. People bouncing over and living for the instant like dogs.

'I am instructed to dither and be minimal,' said the fusehead who had opened the door, 'until you look for someone who will use their brain.'

Cannonites in blast regalia lined up to welcome Gregor as he passed.

'I perform the jelly services. Making sure a body can be ignored and dry. Clasped and bundled.'

'I'm the Neck Minister. Ensuring no air or saliva persists in the throat. It's prestigious, in its way. Some necks are thick. Some old. I've knotted cord around them all.'

'I undermine you and open your bags.'

Another handed him a laminated card. 'Death-rattle guidelines.'

'And who is this pork being?'

These words were addressed to the temple at large by a lank, exhausted jester in black and blue, his every gesture one of bemused satiation. He leant negligently, over-casually against an ornamental cannon of jade and gold. 'He has the look of a man who committed a few tentative misdemeanours and then ran like an egg. Come nearer where I can ignore you.'

Gregor shuffled forward. 'Are you ... Rod Jayrod?'

Fanning himself with a fern, Jayrod met his gaze blandly. 'Just try and stop me.'

'I'm a salesman,' Gregor stammered, raising the produce.

'A dainty predicament,' said Jayrod, looking without interest at the Fainting Cannibal Commemorative Plates. 'Almost too dainty to live long. And you've ears like deformed tubers I see. Well, your inconvenient fancies and first-class drolleries are not welcome here.'

Gregor frowned up at the cage dancers and the swirling cannonical ideograms on the sweating blast walls. Flaring in firelight were stone sentinels with neck and limbs elongated as though cartoonishly zooming.

'Those fancy cornices won't save you, pig man - nor your comely bewilderment. Luckily I am so weary with satiation I seek recourse in talking to you, a bloke whose head is no particular shape. It's not all bad. Should we find that you're a real delight, the prospects are practically limitless.'

Gregor considered that the chances of anyone finding him 'a real delight' were poor and getting poorer. 'Thank you, er ... Fusemaster? I'm sorry I don't know the formalities, I just popped into the other place across town and they chased me out of there.'

'The so-called Church of Automata?' trumpeted Jayrod. 'Those simulacra of theirs contaminate everything with their scary games and waddling. Threw you out did they? A point in your favour. So you roll up here, spoiling for enlightenment. My advice for life is, get out the way of the rolling gong.' With an easy smile the lurid layabout pushed himself from his resting place and took Gregor by the arm. 'In the Cannon Sect our procedures are primarily funerary. More round than a circle, the cannonball leads the way. Until then, we make it a point to thrive like bastards. This inordinate revelry keeps our powder dry. We skip through meadows of magenta reprimand. And when our time comes the Gospel makes plain the escape velocity, burst index and trajectory required to send us speeding out of this poor world. There is written the ready reckoner of body weights and powder charge, the glory of the blur. Immortal? I don't want to still be alive when they're stacking chairs. Do you feel it, pig man? Double negatives are a no-no.'

Feeling warm with conviction, Gregor jumped. 'I guess I do. I guess I'm in.'

'Whatever you like. I'll need your signature here, here and ... here.'

'Your chin? Your eye?'

'And my arse, that's right. We'll make a man of you. Or something. Here are the Powder Protocols. Learn well this incomprehensible gibberish. It's all there - chapter and verse. Now come this way, whatever your name is.'

Before tall black curtains at the rear of the temple lay a low shrine of blue gemstone into which a form had been pressed as though into dental resin. 'Here resided our holy relic the Wesley Kern gun, until it was plundered from us - one day it will be restored and the culprit found fatally maimed and twitching in a turnip field.' The languid riddler gestured to a baby on stilts, who pulled on a rope - the curtains floated apart to reveal the titanic metal image of the revellers' cannon-mouthed godhead. Dead eyes of blue gold regarded Gregor. 'Isn't she a beauty? The slow smoke out of those urns gives it a doomy feel. The Powdermouth belches on the hour, purifying us all. Supplication here is something I cannot recommend sufficiently. Take your time.'

Gregor stepped uncertainly towards the steaming godhead, his caution yet to catch up with the evening's turn of events. *Be slow and large*, said Violaine - *they'll accommodate*.

Gregor cleared his throat and looked up into the giant face. 'Birds,' he said. 'They vamoose through the air, why?'

'I don't know what the deal is with birds,' said a voice from the black oven of the god's mouth.

All activity ceased in the temple. The iron face had become a strange silent blue surrounded by prayer eyes and aweful silence. Forested faces looked pale and undone. Rod Jayrod let the fern slip from his hand.

Gregor wasn't sure if this was usual. 'You said?'

'You, pig man,' came the reverberative voice from the round, smoky maw, 'you I have chosen. Yes, Round One, this tinpot god smiles upon you like a barber upon his victim, thankyou yes. Give me a minute to think and I'll dispense your chores.'

'Chores? Well, I've already got to learn this rubbish.' Gregor raised the Powder Protocols.

'Bring your friends through the creepchannel direct to your god, and they will have jelly and ice cream.'

'What flavour.'

'Do not question your god, pig man. The trip must be a surprise to all, especially Barny Juno, who pleases me greatly thankyou sir.'

'I prefer to remain, er ... aloof from mortal danger. Coquettish, mysterious. I run from hazard, giggling like a tart.'

But Gregor was already being swept up by the revellers and hailed a 'Holy One'. A banger went off in his eye.

Amid the chaos the cannon mouth fired and nobody saw

Skittermite flying, all arms and legs, through smoky air to splat against the main doors.

Around this time Prancer Diego set fire to his arse in the town square and shoved away those who came to help him. 'Adapt to new surprises, naughty boy! Immoral superiors are on the screen and even worms are despairing! I'm outta me head with this blood-drinking, boss - the land's random!' And Prancer embarked on a high-kneed capering dance for no reason and in utter silence. 'I'm excellent and show it, so what? In this pantleg's a leg, in this one's a heavy heart.'

Passers-by bellied up, indignant. 'Shut up, crazy man.'

'Could you optimize the bribe so I can afford new clothes?'

'Bribe?' shouted a thug by the name of GI Bill. 'We're having a fistfight.'

'A fistfight? I wanna spell it out like this: e-t-e-r-n-i-t-y.'

'You can spell it any way you want, but we're gonna fight.'

'Will you save me?'

'What? We're gonna *fight*, you goddamn fool.'

'I'm a chimpanzee, look - ha ha!'

'Keep still you sonofabitch -'

'I can't, I'm excited!'

GI Bill retreated with his face a riot of disgust.

'Letters taste like dandelions!' Prancer shrieked. 'Take me home daddy! Even as you look I smash the standard!' Prancer claimed to have found life insurance papers in the baby-pouch of a badger. He produced a jagged scroll which appeared to have been cut from human skin. 'Read and weep, my friends.' He clunked to his knees, sobbing like a castaway. 'Weep for the deadly boy I was.'

The scroll began with a blurred purple heading, *The Cyril Manifesto.*

4

ATTABOY, MIKE

Untended, questions grow wild

When Barny told Magenta Blaze about the dead bat she laughed like a drain and urged him to do the same. Their relationship was conducted amid a saturation-bombing of misunderstandings and strenuous suspension sex. Now they sat in the Ultimatum Restaurant, where Barny had once again been required to eat some kind of bony, barbed flail. The alternative had been pasta.

Magenta cast a pink shadow, her heart full of crossed wires.

'I killed him,' Barny wept. 'It's doing my nut in.'

'He went to heaven,' Magenta laughed. 'That's what you always say.'

'I know.' Barny blew his nose on a petition for his death which remained from a past debacle. Realising what it was, he threw it aside before Magenta could see. She had him solidly pegged as a wild and colourful man and he didn't want to remind her of this occasion. As they entered the restaurant he had noticed the front of the establishment was newly-sprayed with the slogan CYRIL IS LOVELY. Barny had no idea what it meant but he rushed her past it anyway, fearing that by some obscure route even this scrawl might enhance his prowess in her eyes. 'Anyway, I've got something to tell you. I didn't want you to hear it from someone else.'

'This sounds mysterious,' said Magenta, hunkering down for intrigue.

'No, no,' Barny moaned wearily, 'nothing's mysterious, it's boring, I'm boring and completely uneventful.'

'Bubba, you are funny. What about that fight you had in the Shop of a Thousand Spiders?'

'That's because Edgy tore someone's shirt. He dragged me in there - I don't even enjoy the place. I don't really like going out at all. I'm not social, I hardly ever laugh, I don't like excitement. I just want to take care of the winged and stepping animals of the earth.'

Cake-pale between hoop earrings, Magenta's face was blank.

'Know what I mean?'

Realisation dawning, Magenta became embarrassingly giddy. 'You killed it deliberately?'

It was hopeless. Barny gave her a sickly look. What the hell could he do with this girl? Now she was grinning wolfishly for some reason.

Barny started thinking about the Power Shout - what was going on there? He almost never raised his voice much. Gregor whined and ranted, Edgy barked and jittered; Barny didn't even yelp when the leopard clawed his leg.

Maybe the Power Shout was one of those etheric exercises Edgy talked about sometimes. It involved putting the image of an idea into your belly and then breathing out and shooting the idea-molecule at someone. Edgy once used it to trip a mime into a fast-flowing river. The Power Shout was probably that sort of thing, but shouting the idea at the same time.

Barny began revving up. He drew the notion together in his head, bringing it to fine focus. He took a deep breath.

The waiter came to the table. 'More coffee?'

'WE'RE FINISHED!' bellowed Barny. The waiter collapsed like a cut puppet.

Barny recovered from his exertion to see Magenta convulsed with laughter. 'Barny, you are *unbeatable*.'

'A drive in the country?'

'Or perish in the attempt.'

Edgy and Gregor were walking across the dusty street toward Dot Spacey's gas station. In exploring lethargy as an artform Dot had set upon achieving the sunset ideal of 'total immobility'. He sat on the forecourt like a mascot as Mike Abblatia, whose back was giving him increasing pain, ran to please all. 'Welcome, Mr Gregor - I got the car ready.'

'Say no more about it,' Gregor laughed nervously. He had asked Abblatia to soup up a vehicle for creepchannel travel. Scarcars were so rare and expensive that few believed they existed. As Abblatia chugged the buggy from around the side of the garage, the sun glared on bony spars, scapular spoilers and tyre radials of human flesh.

'The hood's black for void mergence,' said Mike Abblatia, getting out to raise it and tinker with the engine. Gregor and Edgy watched with rueful fascination as he ratcheted cytoma and spritzed the fatty meat of the cylinder head. 'Vertebral shocks. Heavy duty.'

'You don't need to tell *us*,' Gregor urged him with a forced smile. His godlet-commanded task had beguiled that part of his mind which would normally build a sandwich. There was little room for anything else. But the car was clearly giving Edgy pause for thought. Gregor acted brisk and hearty. 'It's the only car he had available. Okay, let's go.'

'So, are you guys gonna pay now?'

'Don't worry, Mike,' Edgy sniggered, and he slapped Abblatia on his swollen back. 'Remember what old Bingo said. "Hunches are coordinates from a different angle."'

They piled in and pulled out in a cloud of red flake dust.

A couple of torturers approached Sweeney's living armoured throne. They were simplistic, rotund demi-demons with big eyes. 'We've made rapid progress in the torture chamber.'

'Discarded limbs crackling in the grate?'

'Better than that. We've been growing roses.'

'I beg your pardon.'

'Oh yes - their satin finery is a crazy marvel.'

Sweeney leaned forward in strenuous scrutiny, aghast. 'Their "satin finery" belongs in cages! Are you blurred in the head? Roses? A cheap conjuring trick!'

'Oh, no - not those beauties surely. Does it hurt anyone?'

'Exactly - *does* it?'

'Oh, lighten up Master.'

'Lighten up?' The braided roots of Sweeney's brain began arcing from his skull seams like worms in a rainstorm. 'Don't you understand we're managing an open-end apocalypse here? Rich hours of succulent little abominations. Easy meat gurgling open. Life's puzzle is only as deep as their body - it's down to us to scatter the pieces.' He stared at them. 'You don't know what I'm talking about do you? Oh hell - I free your lesson!'

Darkness peeled off the wall and began spinning fast, wrapping around the two demi-demons. As they blurred, flaying into shavings of glass and sawdust, Sweeney considered a torture befitting Juno. Those above needed something graphic. Confronted with the hollowed head of their best, they'd cave.

Barny and the gorgeous Chloe Low were admiring a couple of ghoulish statues in Scardummy Garden when the replicas exploded like dandelion heads, showering them with sand. 'That's nothing,' coughed Chloe, slapping the dust from her clothes, shaking it from her blue-black hair. 'Look at this one.' She pointed out other fierce constructs in the tangled bushes around the precinct's edges. The Garden contained a statue of each and every Accomplice citizen and it was traditional to deck and groom your own during a visit. But Barny had never seen these tomb-yard beasts before, clasped and blended as they were into greenery. Something like an ankled rope of bones hunched toward the sky. A bat skeleton the size of a child crouched over a broken bottle. A hat and coat with scythe arms stood serene and ready. A thug of scraps grinned, all cheek and snot. A winged knight with a head like a tomahawk - this last Barny did recognise. 'That's Dietrich Hammerwire,' said Chloe, a nice notch in her brow. 'It's a mega-paravamp, a draco-class demon. Strange that they're all here, isn't it? Part of the community.'

Certain minutes are like a doughnut, the very thing. Sitting on a bare plinth, Chloe gazed at toppled pillars, drifting air silk and world light. A tree whisked around, Barny's dog Help capered near a basilisk platform, earth rust was baked by the sun. Here was a bush before the wind, the drained blue table under the wall, the bottomless sky, and amazing silence. And Barny was gazing bovine at Chloe, her smile longer by inches; watching the girl shift buttocks and squint at the sky. In this strange corpse orchard, a vast plain of pillared people, his heart ripened and peached.

'Lessons settle like a new grave and we're quiet,' Chloe whispered. 'A simple insect grudge match can be perfect. All my resources squeal to a halt here. I can lay down and get busy with the sky.' She turned onto her back. 'Before he fired from the Tower, one of the things Wesley Kern asked for was a siesta.'

'What's that?'

'A sleeping time in the afternoon. It wasn't always this warm here, Barny. But when the weather changed, employers didn't want to accept the traditions of hotter places. Working hours were the longest in the world.'

'A siesta,' said Barny thoughtfully, noticing a weedgrown flagstone sprayed with the red words NICE CYRIL. 'People should sleep whenever they want, like other animals.'

'That's what he said. And the Mayor dismissed the idea despite sending everyone to sleep with speeches. Kern paid a servant to belt the Mayor around the head every afternoon and photograph the inert body next to a clock. With these images he produced a set of fifty collectors cards and schoolkids fiended to amass them all. The rarest was number seventeen, in which the Mayor's gob was stuffed with a half-eaten pineapple - only one copy of the card had been produced. When the Mayor was stuck for campaign funds, Kern gave him card seventeen and the Mayor's advisers confirmed he could sell it at auction for thousands. The indignity of that auction left the Mayor in a bathroom alone, weeping like an ice sculpture. At exactly the same time that Kern himself was killed by doves, the local shaman seemed to evaporate. Only his earlobes were left, looking like squeezes of dough. Then someone with more money than sense put them in a bell jar and encouraged them to mate. Bedded down in angel cress, they'd soon spread like a bead curtain. After several weeks the earlobes resembled a pale honeycomb. A document in the Juice Museum says this growth eventually became the current shaman, Beltane Carom. I sometimes think about that. Remember what Violaine said: "Do you think the past is contained within the present? The past has escaped to its own freedom and doesn't think of us."'

Chewing a sandwich, Barny nodded without meaning or comprehension. Chloe put him to shame once a week with mindbogglers from the Juice Museum, a treasurehouse of denied facts and bricked histories. Barny contented himself with the headswim of staring but his friend Mr Peterson, the nearest thing he had to a functioning father figure, warned him that if he didn't take a lead she'd kick his heart into the long grass. 'We know women have control over men; we assume they have control over themselves. What's left, Bubba?' But when Barny looked at Chloe Low, something came loose in him. And what about Magenta? She would not accept him as he was. Now Chloe was talking about an archive of doors in the Juice Museum. These doors had been pulled from their jambs in such a way that some of the space behind them had come away too, like a tap root.

Barny mawed his mouth, crumbs falling. 'Chloe, er ...'

A car screeched up in the lane on the other side of the hedge and Edgy's tufted head appeared. 'Pile in, Bubba, we're goin' on a picnic.'

They went and peered over the bush. 'We're on one already,' said Barny. 'Where'd you get this flashy motor?'

'Stole it from good old Mike Abblatia. He's a helluva guy. We're having jelly and ice cream. Sorry, Low - only room for one.'

Barny scarfed up the rest of the sandwich and piled in, the dog Help leaping in after him.

Chloe flapped her arms against her hips. 'Well, alright, bye.'

'See you outstretched on the cake then,' shouted Edgy as they roared off.

What have I done? thought Barny as strange, unhinged laughter exploded around him. Edgy, Fang and Sags Dumbar from the office were here, and Gregor was driving without joy, sweating like a bastard. Barny wished he could think fast, like a housefly. Or was it just that they had special eyes?

'Hey,' called Edgy, 'you and Prancer are doing a great job hoaxing the Cyril thing, Bubba.'

'What are you talking about?'

'He told me all about it, collaborating on the Manifesto? Boy, that's a wild read.'

Above the roar of the drive Gregor seemed to be saying stuff about the cannon church - the same one Barny had annoyed once by burying a lizard. 'Yeah, it's quite a scene over there. Quite a scene.'

One minute they were ploughing through some financial advisers in a field, then the car gave a booming cough as it dropped into a yellow intensity of spinelight and etheric corrosion. Bodies tensed with distress and full recognition of the situation's novelty value as magnetism bent the air and they shot down the channel like a guillotine blade. The car was a fluorescent smear tearing through taut skeins of migraine aura. The spaniel had his head out the window, a smile on his face as slams of turbulence sailed his ears and black glitter blasted by. Bile bugs were drumming across the roof.

The channel spiralled and Barny looked aside at Sags Dumbar, whose strange shale head was glowing like a shaded lamp - sickstone ribs and antique canola rushed past, mildly refracted through the transparency. 'I'll have the roast beef platter,' Sags remarked. They smashed through a glass alarm and into a sofa made of bread - contempt barged these trifles aside, trailing lightning-like sparks. Brain vapour was glincing the windshield and the atmosphere swarmed with urgent repairs.

Then they seemed to hover, venting exhaust. Barny looked out the window - they were atop a rolling red boulder, coasting in the arsenic light of a channel junction. Edgy's screams were so notoriously insightful that people sought him out to inflict some agony - now he outdid himself, yelling at Gregor to strip the gears if he had to. Cranking, Gregor gunned the motor and they tore away from the king corpuscle, down an arcade of wounds in a cold, screaming rush. The gas tank exploded, herbal soup stains flaying back at the windshield.

Counting the petals of a larkspur in preparation for the 'loves me/loves me not' game, Magenta Blaze strode down Owl Transfer Street. Was Barny being truthful or just filling out some quota of self-effacement? Antisocial, never goes out, never laughs, avoids excitement? Surprising herself, she decided to put aside any possible prejudice and take a chill look at the facts.

Ahead of her, a ribcaged car exploded through the display window of the Shop of a Thousand Spiders in a garish spray of interface medicine, dreamspore, thaumaturgical artifacts and activans. Balking to a halt and standing in a slow leak of benthic steam, the car stood striped with crash tar, a rear bumper sticker reading I BREAK FOR HADES. The bodywork had acquired a dark coating of burnt nerve tissue and now cracked open, muffled hilarity becoming fully audible as a door bust to earth with Barny upon it, weeping with laughter. Everyone piled out, gobs distorted by speed and dementia. 'Wow that was so cool,' said Fang. Edgy seemed to find his remark hilarious. Everyone's chin had been converted temporarily to dense, fibrous wood, and they began clacking these like hanging puppets. The dog Help yapped and skipped around. It was clear to Magenta after all that Barny and his friends were a healthy crew, reckless with youthful humour and camaraderie.

Dietrich stormed into the cavern after stewing for hours. 'With respect, Majesty. Kermit doesn't know how bloody random it is up there. He's just a vex. He won't be able to navigate.'

Sweeney, throned in poison plenty, was unimpressed. 'Who do you suggest, if not a pestilent?'

'Trubshaw, Rakeman, Feroce. Anything's better than some latchkey fiend who thinks it's clever to walk on his buttocks. Those people up there'll absently kick his bones off the front step. I tell you the world proceeds without them as they attend to other matters.'

'In true terms even you're wet behind the wings, Dietrich. Why enter the game to end it? The continual efforts of the harmless damned entertain us. Let's view Skitter's progress.'

Sweeney called down the Aspict. As the dark red revulsion diamond lowered into view, it became clear it was not in tip-top condition. Its light was clouded, the vermiform innards totally obscured.

Belted radial tyre-marks crisscrossed the surface as if a car had used it as a switchback. Sweeney's eye on the upper realm was blinded.

5

PRESUME ZONE

Blood can't be counted

The Mayor was shaken and embarrassed that the Cyril movement was manifesting in objective reality. Stupid slogans were appearing everywhere and the square had been blessed with a 'speaking truncheon' which passersby approached tentatively. The Mayor watched from his office window as a citizen touched the black missile and incited a stream of incendiary abuse which scattered everyone amid shrieks. 'It's a sort of miracle, I suppose,' he said gloomily, and turned to see Max Gaffer smile at the absurd lie. 'Very well, I wish it wasn't there. In a very real way. No speaking truncheons in the town square, that's my motto. That way, the most authority has to grapple with is normal human disinterest. We'll issue a pamphlet.'

Gaffer winced. There was a famously inaccurate pamphlet issued by the Mayor's office which stated that 'all dead birds explode eventually. Love it or loathe it, you can't change nature.' The pamphlet, entitled 'Am I Safe From Birds?' did offer some useful guidelines on dove attacks, dove insurance and dove evasion, this last under the sub-heading 'Any Fool Can Dodge Doves.' There was a small cartoon of the Mayor himself, his expression making it clear he was not to be trifled with, springing over a garden pond. The last page bore the image of a placid swan and the slogan BUTTER WOULDN'T MELT. The Mayor had had some explaining to do when he demonstrated his ideas by dressing a servant as the devil and spearing him to death on the balcony. 'No more fatal stabbings during speech' he had later noted in his journal, underlining the reminder three times. The only successful pamphlet the Mayor had ordered was about skybikes, terrifying stained-glass penny farthings driven silently in circles by skeletons in the night sky. The pamphlet, called 'Don't Be Scared of Skybikes', assured the public that these aerial apparitions were an omen of good luck, and that the Mayor himself invited such phantom visitations with puckering lips. After the booklet had been distributed, thirty-six skybikes collided in the air above the mayoral palace at four in the morning, spattering the roof with neon bones and other ectoplasmic shite.

'You'd better take a look at this, sir.' Gaffer handed over a sheet of paper. 'They're turning up everywhere, even in my pants.'

'What nonsense is this? The "Cyril Manifesto?"' He scanned it quickly, his face congested:

You're exposed to a mob of friends so you'll worry. Then a trowel is put to use on your ears, and a photograph is taken. Finally you're burned in effigy on a traffic island. But the real you - boy oh boy. You'll glower till they laugh. Approach the raindrops with a length of string. Dash through the graveyard with a surfboard. Brandish sausages at a weeping old man. Telephone the opera and mention a hen. That's got to light up your considerations hasn't it?'

The Mayor was appalled. 'This is disastrous. How can anyone see Cyril as a proper nemesis when its credo has been composed by cattle?'

'The problem is,' said the lawyer, 'that it's proving popular. Cyril meetings are springing up everywhere.'

'What? But the points are shockingly arbitrary. This thing's been blown out of someone's nose. Beguiling minutes I spent believing that it made sense. Then the realisation, and the anger.'

'Remind you of anyone?'

'Eh? Not ... Turbot you mean? My own speech writer?'

'Noam B Turbot. He's done worse. Booting the focus groups, remember? Blundered in here with a stolen nest in one hand and a roulette wheel in the other. Knee-walking drunk. We haven't enough binoculars to make that man a giant.'

Disturbed, the Mayor half-fell into the nearest chair. 'Beware the reviving scrape of god's claw, that's what Violaine said wasn't it? Well whoever's responsible, this idle malice could wreck everything. And the Conglomerate? They'll have my arse for a throwrug. We're too far along to devise a different public outcry. For a while I'm their liberator. We'll look back at this as the time of purchase, the joke fresh. What to do. We should ideally keep our legs busy while thinking this over. Even I take a stroll occasionally and I'm quite burly. If it weren't for these bloody floor lobsters.' He kicked one like a toy - it scudded a short way across the carpet and halted, unharmed.

'Perhaps we could sell these notional roaches as food for the poor,' the lawyer suggested lightly.

'Yes,' the Mayor muttered thoughtfully. 'Yes, see to it - and sweeten the deal with a few miniature swine made of pyrex. Everyone loves a pig, a small one of that kind. It's a sad turn of affairs but in politics you learn to cry with your ears - nobody's expecting that. Not in a million years.'

'Outstanding, sir. And the manifesto?'

'There's information in a hoax. Enough maybe to reverse into the perpetrator. Go see Turbot, then maybe we'll attend one of these little meetings. It is indeed a tragedy on the street when acid words effect democracy, eh?'

Gregor had failed and it was like he'd shaken off half a hypnosis. Did it matter so much what the Powdermouth said? A few days ago he'd barely heard of the thing.

But the car trip had bonded him again with Barny and the crew - they'd slapped him on the back so many times he coughed up some lamb he'd eaten earlier. And now Edgy insisted on putting him up at the Bata Motel, where he maintained occupancy by pretending to be a ghost. 'Rotten glass and fire map on the door etc,' said Edgy, throwing his keys on the sidetable and opening the fridge. 'Anything dreadful in this room is yours.'

'Thank you Plantin. Where's the bathroom.'

'Wherever you like. If the maintenance guy comes up unexpectedly, just beat hell out of him.'

'Beat hell out of the maintenance guy,' repeated Gregor, nodding.

Edgy was a practitioner of fridge meditation, that moment of blank reverie which occurs upon opening the fridge and forgetting why. Gregor waited respectfully while Edgy communed with the milky glow.

Presently Edgy threw the door closed and Gregor gave him a quick smile. 'I couldn't help but notice you've got a gravestone in here.'

'Oh, this is the royal jelly of frighteners,' Edgy stated, patting the gravestone like a dog. 'This little baby's pulled my chestnuts out of the fire so many times. I just move it around every day so if anyone comes in, it's in a different position and gives 'em the first rate heeby-jeebies. Then I create the illusion of a ghost like the fumes from a tyre fire, by setting fire to some tyres.' Edgy chuckled. 'And I bought a cormafester in the Thousand Spiders.' Edgy indicated a crablike medallion over the door, black and throbbing. 'One of those weird house growths nobody dares examine or walk under. So dense it's guaranteed to give everyone the fear. There's yellow jelly in the fire hydrant. And a gutted betsy lamp at the window, harmless really but looks ominous. Oh by the way, the old goat who runs the Shop of a Thousand Spiders, she's not too happy about you using the creepchannel exit at the back of the store.'

'I didn't know it was there. I mean I didn't remember - we just got spat out there by the luck of the draw. Listen, when did this whole ghost thing start?'

'A year ago. Had an argument with the landlady. My rent was in arrears.'

'Why put it in her ears?'

'Arrears - listen to what I'm saying, Round One.'

'So you muffled them with your rent money. What's the matter with you?'

Edgy shrugged on a new Hawaiian shirt. 'Well, it's the phone. The engaged recording keeps telling me to replace the receiver, so I do. It's costing me a fortune buying those things. Anyway, unshaven and into the fray, I knew my bills would remain unpaid. Then I hit upon this little ghost number. Only problem is the sound through the floorboards. In fact I got an idea for Stampede Products – sound proof carpet. You can stamp, drop stuff, collapse in a violent fit.' Edgy giggled, chuffed. 'And nobody'll be any the wiser. So how's it going at Stampede?'

'Good. And they think I could work in the autumn, as a sort of lost man standing around.'

'That's what you do all year.'

Gregor sat on the bed. 'Well, they saw that and were illuminated.'

Edgy popped a beer and scrutinised Gregor. 'So what's the score with this baggy-pants farce you call a religion, Round One? How did it happen?'

'I don't know, I just blundered in there and the next thing I knew, I was being told to read up on all this stuff. That Powdermouth stat-ue's a beauty, though - like I was saying to Barny, it fires gas and effluvia from its gob every hour on the hour. I think that's the rum-ble we feel around then. They gave me this novice fuse to wear, some devotional gunpowder. They think I'm some kind of special person.'

'Oh, they probably say that to everyone. Those high-kicking cultists'll give you more famous church scratches than you can possibly follow. What you got there?'

Gregor frilled the sacred volume without enthusiasm. 'Velocity Gospel. I have to learn the Powder Protocols, Chip's Strife Angle Theory, ascension telemetry, the Ballistic Catechism, a Murphy One curse, Deloquatant's Sin and the first five platitudes. The catechism's all questions and answers like "When a man blurs, does he cease to exist?"'

'What's the answer?'

'No.'

'Oh, Round One, Round One, why waste your time? I don't like to see you like this, all pumped up on support mechanisms and meaning.'

'But it admits in the introduction, "It is in the nature of the document that darkness and irritation impacts in flashes."'

'As a friend, Round One, I've gotta tell you Barny may be a little simple-minded but you're downright weak. Well it's your life, it's your time, but me I don't like churches. Cutlery chain on the truth, or they'd like you to think so. Doll worship's the same; and anyway that Dollimo and Distaff frighten the life outta me. And by the way, do you know this cannon church of yours came about by mistake?' Edgy was lalloping back and forth, gesturing with the can as he declaimed. 'Too much fuel in the crematorium. Massive blast, you know. Coffin fired half a mile in the air. So here they are blasting bodies into the stratosphere and plastering the act with terminology. Between you and me, Round One, I once crashed one of their affairs at a funeral switching yard. "Chap with earlobe," I lied, "came to pay my respects." "We all have earlobes here," they said. "Then I'll feel right at home," I said. "You wish to enter through discord?" they said. "Damn right I do," I said, and was admitted into a carnival of horrors. They had things called "strutting procedures", where all the strutting they'd denied in the rest of their life, was compressed into two minutes of jerky mayhem. And did you ever see a cannon confessional? It's like a gameshow, they dump slime on you, it's terrible. And then the firing itself, pell-mell out the business end of a cannon.' Edgy sat down on the headstone, spent. 'I'm telling ya Round One. In the graveyard, accidents petition our respect.' He swigged the beer.

Gregor leafed through the book and there, sure enough, was a section which explained 'Quantum Strutting': 'Only with gunpowder in his eyes does a man reflect upon the forces which have used him. Strut, strut, strut.' In his head Gregor heard the reverberative squawk of the Powdermouth. Had he been distracted? Wasn't there something else personal he should be dealing with about now?

Putting the book aside, Gregor urged Edgy to continue his haunting instructions. Edgy based his teaching methods on those of his own ear-laughter tutor - he had been attending lessons in the art for two and a half years, and he took it very seriously. He could now snicker quietly through his ears and was assured he would be able to guffaw within a few months. 'It's way more advanced than ear-crying,' Edgy snorted. 'Everyone does that.'

'But the one thing I don't get,' said Gregor, 'is what we do if the landlady comes in.'

Edgy opened a small cupboard. 'We get in there.'

'In there, are you crazy?'

'You know you could go stay at Barny's.'

'I'm scared of the lion and the leopard.'

'Oh, you can never have too many big cats, Round One. Anything else is a false economy.'

Barny charged off the street, through the snout distillery, the flower store, the bar full of angry failures, the sauna, the printshop, the karate school, the giant mouth, the movie theatre, the bowling alley and into the street. 'Dago - so what's the story? You told everyone I wrote some half-arsed manifesto with you? Like I don't have enough trouble caring for the winged and stepping animals of the earth and being happy?'

Prancer Diego tore off a wrestler's mask and cawed with laughter. 'Apologies are tools of control, Juniper.'

He pushed a thick wad of leaflets into Barny's pockets. Recognising the duplicated echo of Prancer's stripped flesh, Barny spent a time frowning at one. 'Wait a minute, isn't this complete bollocks? People'll think I'm simple-minded.'

A fiercer bout of hilarity gripped the prankster and shook him like a flag. Tears striped his expression. 'I'll deny it,' he gasped, 'if you do one last thing for me Juniper.' He produced a camera from a small golden coffin. 'Go look for a face - Cyril needs one. And between us there is a rumbling baboon of a difficulty.'

'What sort of difficulty?'

'My broken lagging. The fridge. The burnt carpet. I can't speak to you directly until these matters are resolved. Push me away.'

'Eh?'

'Push me away now.'

'There.'

'You have. Thank you. My god I'm glad you understand.'

'I don't understand a damn thing,' Barny began to assert, but where Prancer had stood there was now only a badly-assembled scarecrow. Jerky with impatience, Barny dashed the turnip nose from its face and kicked it into the gutter. With a fixed grin, the scarecrow burst into flame. Silky smoke tumbled up from the torso. 'Well,' Barny coughed loudly, utterly baffled and speaking purely for public benefit. 'My work here is done.' And he shuffled away.

The tip of his long downcurving nose having fused with his upturned chin, Noam B Turbot had reached the age of realising there was no reward. Hair grew from his eyes. There was a good angel on one shoulder and a bad angel on the other, both drunk. He looked out the mossy window, mouth pursed like a fist. 'It's as I suspected. The sun, rising at an angle, has inflicted another morning upon us all.' He shook his head dismally.

'It's near dark,' spat Max Gaffer, entering and halting immediately in disgust at his surroundings. Three floor lobsters tangled with the top of the hat tree. In fact the place was lousy with lobsters. They climbed pillars of smoke-stained timber and among dry bird stuff on the stone mantel. The ceiling fan slewed slow.

Turbot turned from his desk at the window. 'I got your note. Stinking I may be. Great, perhaps. Hell-demon I most certainly am not.'

'The messenger told a tale of violence and reproach.'

'I talk to people so they know it. What's that?' He indicated the leaflet in Gaffer's hand. 'My report card? Must do better?'

'The last speech was a little flowery.'

'Poets are poisonous round the eyes, didn't you know?'

'Poet,' muttered the lawyer, casual and observant. 'So how do you judge this, old man?'

Turbot snatched the manifesto from him and read it in glum silence. 'A failure,' he declared. 'Written I suspect, by dogs.'

'It calls itself a manifesto.'

'Young dogs, then. It's a myth that revolution isn't fun - there are forged papers, rain, and monologues in the interval. Yes, why not? They're less than powerless. You wish their hatred be diffuse so as not to support violence. Your wish is forever granted.'

'This is the first you've heard about it?' asked the lawyer, examining a flaky lamb skull.

'Meaning what?' asked Turbot, appalled. 'What are you playing at?'

Gaffer's mouth moved in a cool smile. 'An honest man must change as quickly as the rules.'

'You're referring to law-abiders, not honest men.'

'Well, Turbot, you're neither. Not since we picked you out of the chorus. Put you where you are today.' Gaffer examined a framed Violaine motto: *You make more difference to the world emulsioning a wall than you do writing satire.* 'We need another speech, by the way. Portray the manifesto as an unwholesome mindgame.'

'I may, I suppose,' stated Turbot in a pompous voice.

'There are walls in people, sick and essential. Your pretence that you have a choice is understandable.'

Fastidiously distracted, Turbot tapped a moth from the window. 'You forget that it needn't be uncontested. I could offer my services to doomed Eddie Gallo.'

'Oh, please. His faculties come and go according to their own schedule. He'd think you were a daffodil.'

'So regret me. My job is to adapt the presentation of the client's will to the prejudices of the public, so that one is well served and the other feels so for a time. And I suppose you think I'm talking about your underwear?'

'Aren't you?' barked the lawyer.

'Even your bones are superficial aren't they? Caution the floor, if you want something to do.'

The lawyer drew himself up. He went to the door. 'You're a poor host.'

Turbot sat blandly aloof, eyes almost closed.

'We need the speech tomorrow, old man. Reassure the Conglomerate re your loyalty. It's the smart thing to do.' Gaffer slammed out.

Turbot returned immediately to a fierce scrutiny of the leaflet, his face becoming distorted. This gabble of trash concocted at some punchbowl vigil - its slapdash flare was so galling to him he had been tempted to claim he was the author. In fact he was bitterly flattered that Gaffer had suspected him. How pathetic was that? In such a situation the great Bingo Violaine would have strapped on a set of antlers and pinned Gaffer to the ceiling.

From the beginning Turbot was ill-equipped as a firebrand - he had had only one item of anger, a poor war chest. The anger hadn't even grown thin with use - he had misplaced it, the worst squander, and it was unremembered. Reduced to mere math and ironautics, here he sat, monochrome in old lies. He could pull no more bunnies from his dustbag brain.

Though Bingo Violaine had been drummed out of his body years ago, it was said that he had swerved around the traffic cones of hell's teeth and found himself detached from his own story, persisting as some floating atomic remnant. Turbot hoped vainly that Violaine was looking elsewhere tonight. He was wretched and trivial, owned by others.

He needed the green unheard-of thought that for saps like him occurred only once, in the summer luck of childhood. Where was the juice?

Turbot hefted himself up, stood unsteadily a while, and turned toward the door. 'When a man walks,' he quoted, 'he kicks at his future.'

A night black as old soda and beneath Barny's eyelids the jelly was giving it all it could. Invisible tabs of sky rolled through his sleep, the outer scuttle of wall lizards translating in dream to the popcorn death of a mime.

Skittermite twitched across the ceiling. Mistaking impatience for initiative, he'd decided to just spring at Barny and claw at his essentials. Looking straight down past haphazard ladders and indoor jetties to the lower floor of Barny's multistorey shack, he saw no movement in the gloom.

Barny's bed was suspended creaking near a platform off the third deck. At the end of the bed a cat sat like a jug, watching Skittermite's spraddle-legged approach without curiosity. But as Skittermite sprang onto one of the guy ropes, the cat gave the slightest miaow and the entire twisted building erupted - shapes on the wall became screaming monkeys, corner shadows swooped in the form of prey-birds and the floor stirred with predators. Skittermite dropped to the living room in a clot of chimps. Shaggy monsters such as a lion set upon the giblet-jointed tyke, biting at random. Skittermite was scurrying for his life, neon wounds dripping like fluorescent graffiti. The lion loped after him as if it had all the time in the world.

Skittermite climbed a buckled wall toward Barny's bed with a vague plan to beg for help. When he emerged at the bed end, his delta-shaped head a right laugh in the darkness, a blast of light blotted his prehensile eyes. In the after-dazzle, he heard Barny winding on a camera.

6

DRINK ME

Disgrace is one of the classics, requiring a great number of players

Skittermite stood in an alleyway staring up and down the gallery of posters stamped with his own startled face. The image bore down on the viewer, maggot-white and unfocussed. The ballpoint nose seemed to be rushing forward like a spearhead. Underneath hung the slogan: CYRIL INVENTED CONCERN.

Skittermite had served his time as a novice. Several months stuck in a drainpipe had taught him the long view. It had tempered his darting, nervous energy. But now his brain started to fry. He began to grasp Dietrich's wary respect for this bandwidth. What was that saying from Violaine, whose big lower jaw Dietrich kept under his bed? 'Unnoticed by the target, the strongest dislike goes into thin air.'

Edgy kept Amy's x-ray tucked in his wallet. She was a knockout. She wore her veins in a ponytail. After picking flowers she strapped them to the hood of her car. But she wanted Edgy to help her publish a book of tormentingly bad poetry under the title *We Are Taunted On Two Levels*. She thought he had pull because he had blundered into the writing of a disastrous book about dogs a while ago. He had included a chapter entitled Dogs Which Come Running When a Sergeant Speaks and this had stuck in the craw chamber of the local Brigade. Luckily for Edgy he had been ghosting the book for Barny Juno and the Brigade focused their vengeful plans on the innocent whose name was on the cover.

'At least change it to *Taunt Us On the Double*,' Edgy told Amy in Snorters cafe, his hair in furious condition. 'It's snappier.'

'What?'

'*Taunt Us On the Double*. Eh? Can't you see it? It's a surefire winner, a lock. You're not going to include "I Hate Blue and Love Pigs"?'

'Duh? Of course I'm going to include it. All about how I hate blue and love pigs?' Disgusted, Amy stirred a cup of liquid stress.

'Well, what about "The Damned Onions Are Trailing"? Do you have to include that?'

'How could I not?'

'But do you have to call it *We Are Taunted On Two Levels*? Is there a way? I'm the one who has to deal with old Testy at the publishers.'

'Listen mister, if you want to write a book called *Taunt Us On the Double*, that's your right. Mine's called *We Are Taunted On Two Levels*, okay?' Gort swung out of the booth and stormed away.

'Amy!'

As she flashed into the sunlight, crossing the street, Edgy watched her through the window and foresaw a hosepipe ban.

Mayor Rudloe wore a fibreglass containment suit when forced to venture outside - though unwieldy, it kept him from direct contact with the masses. Today it was also protecting him from poisonous gasses as he visited the Conglomerate. It was Max Gaffer's first audience with the thing and his first experience of trepidation. 'Grey flowers?' he frowned as they entered the foyer, and the Mayor was uncertain enough to remain silent.

A door opened at the chamber end. The Conglomerate was brimming amid its own uncountable legs, and wearing a bandmaster's hat. 'That's right - that's right children come in I won't bite. Ha ha ha!'

'Are you sure this is the man sir,' muttered Gaffer strongly.

'Yes. Look at the hat.'

'That doesn't mean anything, anyone can -' And he took out an identical hat, shoving it on.

'*Take it off!*' hissed the Mayor. 'You'll upset the bastards and they'll open out, wrapping us tightly in the tissues they consider least important to the smooth running of their beautiful body.'

'I beg your pardon?'

'Enter, children,' called the Conglomerate in exaggerated euphoria, 'I'm a surgeon who loves his work.'

'Did you hear *that*?' Gaffer whispered, but was pushed aside by the Mayor.

'Gentlemen,' the Mayor hailed as he strode in - he halted as the steaming environment hit his visor. Behind him, Gaffer entered the carrion stench of the conference room with a look of awe. The fungal walls moved with pumping lungs and the trickle of blood like shower runoff. Tall harps of tendons leaned together, taut with a webbing of catgut and hamstring. The Conglomerate itself was a pulsatile labyrinth of muscle, gelatinous pockets and hanging ganglion. A scorpion chandelier swarmed near the ceiling. The floor flowed and ratcheted with lobster growth, so much that it had bonded into one living mass. Amid venting steam and occasional pattering leaks of fluid, the Mayor stepped over slugs of slippery gut and approached the Conglomerate. 'You're looking well.'

'We bask in illness, idly invoicing the masses,' trilled a voice through a scalloped layering of fat. The hat fell to the floor, splashing in a dark puddle. 'We're so powerful it's not even funny. I sent for you to hear some entertaining evasions. How goes the campaign.'

The Mayor took another small step forward, holding aside a cerebral bag suspended from a snarl of veins and giving them a smile. 'Oh, we're three-deep in lobsters round there. M'lawyer here suggests we sell them as food for the poor. Other than that everything's hunky dory.'

'I cannot agree with you,' came a voice from another part of the blubber mound. Rising steam faded and revealed sweaty detail. 'There is the matter of Cyril. He seems to have escaped your control. A manifesto has appeared, debasing your initial pitch. We have reports of people doing poncey dances against the crowd control barriers.'

Rudloe was rattled. 'It's the posters, gentlemen. Cyril it says, but nothing to do with my concept of the bastard. Staring thing with antennae. He purportedly invented concern.'

'Demon deals have been a feature of your campaign in the past, Rudloe - their dangerous wingtips brush you like a menu card. You're sure he's not one of yours?'

'I dreamed up the Cyril cult so I could get those mugs into the shed and extort more levy for you, as you demanded - asked - but now a real Cyril cult is saying it may even disband so people won't have to contribute, you see? They've taken it out of my lily-white hands. Despite my calling dibs on the idea.'

'There's no dibs in politics.'

'A swindler cannot afford to be headstrong,' another mouth pitched in. It was situated between two black bellowing lungsacks. 'Best to be a team player, like us.'

'See the scope and grandeur of our biology. How much blood it takes to run. Hungry means angry. The red levy is all we ask of you, Rudloe. And your office depends upon our sanction.'

'What should I do,' said the Mayor. His voice was brittle, about to break. 'Put my own misshapen head in the noose? I'm the poor bastard who has to stand on that bony balcony flinging psychological blennies to a rabble of rogues and madmen aren't I? Well?'

'Shut down the blood clock - tell them it's rusted and needs lubricating with some more of the rich stuff. Jam it just before twelve, that'll get them panting. Convince them they prosper through witnessing prosperity.'

'You underestimate the Cyril charlatans,' the Mayor ventured. 'Mournful speculation is circumvented by the strong drink of disobedience.'

'We never forbid or rebuke - leave that to the young generation. We present a choice. Find the hijacker who composed that childish tract.

Alternatively.' A red arm extruded from the mass and indicated a ribbed exhibit revolving slow in the gloom, picked to a mere dangle of bones and gristle. 'You will no longer appear in your mirror.'

Watching the Mayor quake, Gaffer was dead impressed. Advancement perched pecking on his shoulder.

Skittermite manipulated a piece of clay into a semblance of Barny's face, plugged it onto his beak, and ran Gregor down with a tricycle. The scene was ignored by the majority of passersby, who were used to Gregor failing at the top of his lungs. But a huddle of initiate fuseheads, who had been on the verge of approaching the holy one for wisdom, witnessed the blasphemous act and swore vengeance against the retreating Barny. Perhaps his punishment would form the centrepiece for a foam party. Gregor, meanwhile, they left thrashing in the dust. Holiness was long term; sin required immediate attention.

Barny entered Snorters Cafe to meet Magenta Blaze and found Edgy bending under the weight of a frown. 'Bubba - just the man,' Edgy said, forcing him to sit down. 'You've gotta help get Amy's stupid poetry published - your name was on that dog book, officially you're the author.'

'Am I?'

'Yes. Why d'you think they had a cardboard cutout of you in the bookstore?'

'For being a loyal customer.'

'You sick sonofabitch, there's no way I can do this alone.' Edgy quoted a poem called 'Stood Up By Plantin Edge':

black dreaming
telegram cafe
arrive nine years late

'I wish I could help you Edgy, but even if I worked at the publishers I wouldn't take that bollocks.'

'What do you prefer - *We Are Taunted On Two Levels* or *Taunt Us On the Double?*'

'I prefer death.'

'Oh I guess you're right. How's the snake?'

'Tired and under pressure.'

'Why? Nothing's expected of her.'

'Oh right - only coiling, rearing up, rippling, and laying still as though dead while people speculate within earshot and call the authorities. How long before you'd crack under the strain?'

Edgy gave a noncommittal grunt.

'Then there's the Deadly Snake Contest to worry about. Balaclava Lewis and his bloody mamba are the favourites. Maybe I'm pushing Misses Kennedy too hard.'

'I don't know, Bubba. You here to break it off with the Blaze?'

'I'm going straight for the bust.'

'Better do that before you break up with her.'

Barny nodded. 'So what about this wolf tart you recommended?'

'Oh yeah, you'll see - it dilates the entire front of your face. Waitress!'

They ate some wolf tart and took turns dilating their faces, bursting blood vessels in the nostril and forehead area. It's a man thing.

Finally Magenta Blaze entered all smiles, ending their simple joy.

'Hello darling, just ... puffing our cheeks out a bit.'

'Wish I could stay, Madge,' Edgy called, standing. 'But there's something terrible Barny needs to lay on you. Pretty soon you'll be sobbing the place out like a lost child. See you Bubba.' He skanked out.

'This all sounds very intriguing,' said Magenta, shunting into the booth. 'What's all these posters saying CYRIL WON'T BLOW HIS NOSE?'

'I don't know, I'm not political,' said Barny, his face still pullulating a little from the tart. 'This is what I'm saying, I'm not interested in politics, I'm not a trouble maker, I'm not a high flyer, I'm not loud, not into spreading it around.' Barny wound up for the Power Shout. Seven cannon followers burst in and began dragging him from the booth. 'I'M NOT WHO YOU THINK I AM!'

'Yeah, right,' they snorted, wrestling him out of the cafe and into a plain van.

Five minutes later Barny stood before Rod Jayrod in the Powderhouse, surrounded by votive violence. Jayrod leaned forward, resting one wrist on a huge gold monstrance. 'Well, don't that just beat the biscuit. Barny "Nature Boy" Juno. You profane this temple.'

'I was dragged here.'

'Yes, but I see no reason to refrain from such a belter of a phrase. You profane it anyway. First you bury a lizard and drop your trousers during the eulogy, then you set an alligator upon one of our assassins, and today you run down one of our members, a certain Gregor, on a tricycle. Then you set upon him. According to eye-witnesses the number of punches to his belly ran well into three figures. You deny it I suppose.'

'Yes, ma'am.'

'I'm afraid I find that difficult to believe. Don't you, guys and gals? Juno, you are some piece of work. It's common knowledge you consider yourself too, quote, swell, unquote to bother with doctrine. We know all about your trouble with demons.' Jayrod kicked back, lazy and powerful. 'Sweeney. A white trash devil.'

'Oh yeah,' muttered Barny - he had forgotten.

'I cannot understand why people object to our practices,' Jayrod declared. But when Barny began explaining it to him, Jayrod turned blandly away. Catching on, Barny's captors took another try at his face, buried their beliefs there - Barny was soon on the floor.

'And in addition to all this, you are one of the founders of the Cyril movement, the manifesto of which states' - and Jayrod referred to a leaflet - '"Dash through the graveyard with a surfboard." A dubious sentiment at best. And where's the mention of our glorious cannons? The contrail left by a velocitous corpse as it breaks the sound barrier? Only one man had the skill to guide the fragments of the status quo - Wesley Kern. He built a portable cannon, handheld, by some means. Our altar once held it ...'

Thinking about the Wesley Kern gun which resided at the Juice Museum, Barny became anxious. He had a habit of eating small, struggling trolls when under stress, and he pulled one of these from his pocket now - dozens of Cyril leaflets exploded out with it.

'Cyril lies!' shouted Jayrod, pointing like a dart. 'Right spang in the middle of the church! And what's with the troll?'

'I know a story about Kern,' blurted Barny, trying to remember what Chloe had said. 'One afternoon Kern decided he wanted to put the world to sleep, so he beat the hell out of everyone. And he killed the mayor and stuffed a pineapple in his mouth, and photographed it. And he bought fifty pineapples and fed them to a load of kids, then sold seventeen more to the mayor. And he campaigned for funds in the bathroom, saying "The past has contained freedom - don't think of escape." And the doves began developing earlobes, so Kern kept one in a bell jar and killed it, and this dove became a shaman who manufactured bead curtains for a living. And Kern hoped that in the future his crazy antics would be celebrated every afternoon with a huge fiesta, culminating in an auction of collectors cards depicting ... vapour.' Barny's face flummered with a wolf tart aftershock.

All activity had ceased in the temple. Rod Jayrod was shaking his head in reproach, while others regarded Barny with baffled disgust. Barny bit into the pudgy troll.

Jayrod gathered his wits. 'Well, you'll all be glad to know this diecast outrage won't go unpunished. Delicate fruit demands the hammer. It is almost the hour - prepare the Pit of Inconvenience.'

Barny was bounding across the alter in a jiffy, springing at the lip of the Powdermouth. Rod Jayrod became more bent out of shape then ever. 'Transgressor! Is everyone seeing this?'

Fuseheads were climbing the blast walls in antic frenzy, stilt babies striding near the iron face but not daring to make contact.

In the mouth of their pepperbox god, Barny was scrabbling around in a ratcheting trash of floor lobsters. It seemed the Powdermouth really did purify the church on the hour.

And when that hour arrived, the lobsters atomized - Barny blurred across the temple, shattering the stilts from beneath a baby and blasting through the grand front doors.

Magenta Blaze strode across the main square, where the town hygiene department were spraying the 'speaking truncheon' with foam cement. Magenta made a neutral sound.

Barny was such a crazy guy. All that stuff about - what was it - not political, not loud, not a high flyer, not into spreading it around? She stopped abruptly, thinking: or maybe he really was trying to break something to her.

Before she could pursue the notion she saw Barny flying through the sky, bellowing like a bastard and dispersing in his wake a litter of printed sedition.

7

MAD CYRIL

Don't eat corks - there are waiters for that

The Mayor watched as a group of workmen laid into the speaking truncheon with chainsaws. The cement cladding had failed to set and it was a messy business. When a swarm of killer bees erupted from the saw wounds, the Mayor quickly slammed the balcony window and wheeled at Max Gaffer in a foul and vengeful mood. 'Cyril smiles a block away and obsessional fringe groups are born. Where's Turbot with the new speech?'

'Disappeared, sir.'

'Probably standing in the high street doing quickdraw with his willy, that's all we need. The Conglomerate'll drink paraffin through my bloody spine. Have you stopped the clock?'

'Yes, sir. That writhing anatomical stew you call a committee, sir, I'm curious, are they human?'

'Of course, how else could their joint intelligence and morality be less than their individual intelligence and morality?' The Mayor started hauling on his containment suit, switching his cigar from hand to mouth to hand. 'I've been thinking, Max, how about calling this place Rudloe Manor? I mean, that's the style isn't it? Slot-eyed armour on the landing etc. And no-one else will ever preside here.'

'Outstanding sir.'

'Have you sorted the lobsters?'

'Yes sir. The poorhouse owners realised if they take on our bugs they'll generate an almost equal number of their own - it's a helluva deal.'

'Good. Put a skirt on, Max - we're going to a Cyril meeting.'

Caged with worry, Gregor barely registered the worshippers doing sacred cannonball dives into the pool. He stood before Rod Jayrod in bad shape, his arm broken, his head reeling with crammed dogma. 'Fusemaster. I have brought this deformed wren as tribute.'

Jayrod blew out his cheeks. 'Well. As you're aware, I can't accept, or even take seriously, your bid for velocity without a full recital of the Ballistic Catechism. I can make no exceptions, not even for one to whom the Powdermouth has spoken.'

'Really?'

'The weak wipe their nostrils on the passing windshield.'

'The weak?' Gregor considered that by this estimation he must be as feeble as a strand of cress.

'It's just routine, I'm sure you'll do fine. Put the wren over there and assume the position.'

Gregor sat in a comfortable armchair.

'Why is traffic louder than roses?'

'To rise above beauty.'

'In which grabbing of one's own body is the stance of hero assumed?'

'No grabbing of one's own body.'

'What manner of years has it been since we made any sense?'

'Donkey's.'

'By what does the good man escape this world?'

'The seat of his pants.'

'Why do we ignore our ears?'

'Ears are not important.'

'Wet the face of a cow and what do you get?'

'A cow with a wet face.'

'What's the preferred entrance to a cake tasting?'

'Rising from a pit of smoke.'

'How shall we react to those who deplore us?'
'Move along deploring.'
'What sort of certainty can't choose?'
'A certainty in being wrong.'
'Why have you left your post?'
'Diligence bores me.'
'Why avoid capture?'
'Hostaging has no repartee.'
'Why look always forward?'
'Otherwise to discover would be to admit we didn't know.'
'Who is frisky and reasonable at the same time?'
'No-one.'
'How is space a comfort?'
'My face is only local.'
'Bulk lard at a monthly premium?'
'Crawl through tobacco straw to sign.'
'Forget to release the cagedancers long enough and?'
'Bugs take over the entertainment.'
'What is the lordly function?'
'Sitting in our roots, lords make illness of energy.'
'How can you believe you're normal?'
'In a matter of hours.'
'What is the advantage in dissolution?'
'The same advance in sensation will crumble my pursuers.'
'Why human?'
'Because we needed contours.'
'Why keep it modern?'
'Classic drama requires the description of various specialities.'
'What's buck-passing?'
'A suitable use of my time.'
'Why do you snigger?'
'Respect saddens me.'
'Of what do we say, "It's just procedure"?'
'Our flayed rejoicing.'
'Life holds out for stature and what does it get?'
'A belly.'
'Why confess?'
'Truth allows my demeanour to relax a couple o' seconds.'
'Monuments?'
'Hold memory in place, away from hearth and home.'
'Popular pints are never?'
'Green.'
'How may persuasion be increased?'

'Suggest it in a lovely garden.'

'If imagination was ample I'd have twenty perfect legs - you?'

'A hen.'

'What freezes blood?'

'Window witches.'

'Tacky happiness?'

'White earphones.'

'How can we save money on personnel?'

'Pay the vision of them but not the people.'

'A badger will never don gloves but may remove them - why?'

'Badgers do not like wearing gloves.'

'Final goal?'

'No re-entry.'

'When a man blurs, does he cease to exist?'

'Yes.'

'Blasphemy!' Jayrod screamed, his face rigid with fury. 'You misunderstand everything! And you consider yourself worthy to wear the blue touchpaper in your lapel? Goodbye without delay!'

Amid consternation and stares of grim disappointment, Gregor was ejected legs-first from the Powderhouse.

The meeting shed was in back of a derelict yard growing nothing but ovens. On the way they'd been harassed by a loogie-eyed bastard trying to sell lucky heather and brandishing a baby. 'What a darling little child,' Max Gaffer cooed. 'And that will be your undoing.' They had walked on, the Mayor glad both of his disguise and his containment suit. To conceal the visor he had wrapped his entire head in a golden turban. As well as a floral print dress, Gaffer had also seen fit to wear a set of antlers.

'Never fear, Max,' the Mayor whispered as they neared the entrance. 'Such meetings attract a certain kind of fanatical coward. A grab bag of god-gobs and debt-dancers. Lantern slides and dolly music. A paid-entry platitude meeting. We'll be in a forest of bizarre beards.'

'We find it advisable to keep our beards transparent around here,' remarked an unsmiling man at the door. 'And there's no charge.'

'Ah, all to the good,' blustered the Mayor. 'I'm impatient with restraint.'

Mohair pants filled the chapel. It was all wooden benches and saucerlights - the new arrivals sat in the back row. Someone was shouting 'Quiet - let Energy Maggot speak!' and on the makeshift stage a powdery old lady with a thin knife gave the scratchy cry: 'You all bug me. My furball husband was a thinker. He's been silky dust these twenty years. That's where you're headed.' And she picked up a toy wagon and tried to throw it into the audience, falling into the off. The Mayor saw that the backdrop consisted of a giant poster of the supposed Cyril.

An annoyingly zany hired host by the name of Rooster skipped beaming onto the stage. 'The expensive vocal stylings of Energy Maggot there.' Various resinous bubbles from his nose wrought unqualified dismay among the onlookers. 'And for those of you who've just joined us, welcome to today's Cyril cult meeting, sponsored by Stampede Products, "The firm that flirts with danger". Sit in these corners and be late for your responsibilities. Remember, society is a useless display and your head splits with duplicated material. I've just been handed a memo. It says there's a copper firefly in the sandy hand of the manager. And a note from FDA Bonfire offering apologies for his absence. "I am so changed I fear you would not know your old friend." Ha ha ha - what a guy. If you want to flap your distorted jaw about anything, come on up - but first, here's Prancer Diego, who is not particularly brilliant in any way.'

Prancer took the stage in parrot-bright colours, setting up several high-ticket driftwood sculptures of his arse. 'Fascism is born of the idea that progress can reach a conclusion. Into a tirade you must schedule one snorting sound and three flubbers of the gob. No waste and no relaxation of stance. If relaxation occurs, re-establish continuity with a single step forward. Bake no pies during the address. Insist on nothing, but know in your heart that your people are long-horned and random, wild in their thoughts and utterly loyal to you, gorgeous.' Then he flew off the handle, yelling in a bogus dialect. He leapt from the stage and began striding down the aisle like a god. 'This carnage is doing my nut in,' he trumpeted. There followed an ugly clash of faces. Trying out the intended motion of an accuser, Prancer committed welcome and all was resolved. By this time Doctor Perfect, his brain sweating like damp clay, was on the stage bemoaning the lack of initiative re the north canyon. The foreshortened flyover was dotted with exploding sloths and anyone trying to vault the canyon by this means was blown apart, further shortening the road stump.

'On the plus side, yes, there's melons for all. Against it there's the matter of noses. Our nostrils are inescapable and will doom us all, believe me I know. And if Cyril invented concern like they say, shouldn't he begin constructing a bridge at once?' But everyone was bored with this subject and began shouting him down, pausing only briefly when he claimed 'My skeleton is, however improbably, that of a zebra' in a crass bid for popularity.

'We need an aeration parish to buffer the evil,' someone shouted, and was ignored as doomed Eddie Gallo stepped up.

'Why are we carrying on like this when the hot twilight air is full of flies? Why not lean on the pasture bars and watch it all? Bumble bees the size of dogs. These are our treacle days. And it's all nice and legal.' Gallo then embarked upon a discussion of tea biscuits so involved that even his close friends could make neither head nor tail of it. The last thing they let him say was something like 'there are many times the one shape and then my biscuits go away'.

During a bit of commotion the Mayor's bored scrutiny fixed on the light above him. He squinted toward it, half-standing. Within the delicate bulb, where the filament should have been, was strung a sentence: 'I am trapped here and will die.' The Mayor sat down again. Maybe politics wasn't so random after all.

'Reliable old doomed Eddie Gallo,' chuffed a citizen sitting next to the Mayor. 'Congenial, covered in dove run-off - he's one o' the good ones.'

Unfailingly obliging, doomed Eddie Gallo gave way to a man wearing a corrective shirt, who did a victorious turkey trot across the stage before even saying anything. Then it became evident that the man had no intention of saying anything, and he was wrestled awkwardly from the limelight. Kung Fu Snorter claimed the right to read a lecture on the subject of 'My Eighth Belly'. But after two hours it dawned upon the assembly that he intended to prelude the talk with a thorough treatise on the first seven, and he was punched to the floor by a dozen citizens before he had reached the third. Another man announced 'You'll love my skull' and began tearing the skin from his face, at which alarmed onlookers sprang up and restrained him. The lights guttered, crackled and stayed on, causing only a fall of dust.

Later the patch-eyed EH Hunt dragged a heavy treasure chest on to the stage. His mane of white hair glowed under the stage lights. 'Beyond these shores I've met people all the colours of a fusewire. A half decent star can take you anywhere. There's balloon fish out there that enjoy nothing so much as kissing a man. Hundreds of 'em. Think about that. No difference between drinking and puckering if you're a fish. Porpoises take care of themselves ...'

There were groans of disinterest from the audience - these mythical so-called 'fish' and other 'ocean wonders' were Hunt's obsession. He told long, elaborate stories which could have been believed were it not for his insistence that they occurred on or sometimes even in salt water. Moonlight in the ship lanes, cults plunging a hunk of god-statue into the ocean, the burdenhead laying in sways of wrack. Hunt was growing belligerent. 'The iron shark circled, parrying our oars. Satisfied? Yes, my red chest seam goes wherever I go. Land leaders? Appeasement's a narrow reef - just forget 'em.'

Mayor Rudloe suddenly realised that Hunt had a beard like a shovel. He turned to Max Gaffer, whispering in outrage 'That one's beard isn't transparent!'

The whisper was amplified by the audience's desperate need for distraction and all eyes fixed upon him. 'Maybe turban boy would like to share his thoughts with the rest of us?' asked Rooster, standing from the front row.

'That's right,' blurted the Mayor, bolting to his feet, 'you think I don't understand, you buoyant bastard? And why hasn't the Mayor been mentioned even once?'

'Because he's a depraved moron who sleeps in a fungus trench,' muttered someone in the crowd, to general agreement.

'Yes,' added another, 'and ugly, very.'

'Chubby, too. Anyone that chubby wants watching.'

'All right,' yelled the Mayor, 'apart from being depraved, ugly and chubby, what's the problem?'

'Well, the Gubba men for instance - what are they?'

'On standby,' claimed the Mayor stoutly. A demon had long ago tattooed a magic phrase on to his left forearm, but this was hidden by his containment suit and thick disguise.

'Why are you defending him?' asked Prancer Diego. And he stalked forward, his avian head crooking this way and that in scrutiny. 'A box suit?'

'I've seen enough,' barked the Mayor urgently, tugging at Max Gaffer's arm. 'We're leaving.'

'Oho! It's like that is it?' And as the two strangers scuttled up the aisle amid jeers, Prancer yelled after them. 'So regret me! Leave it to the real men, mister! Seeing duty's shape and the lake of deeper wealth I did a backward flip into the latter!' He slowed up, chuckling to himself. 'Technicians of the flaming man evaluated me as purposeless - quite likely my information was indeed out of their way. Everything's locking in, lads.' After the pair had left he shot his cuffs and started swanking around, strutting like a bastard so that everyone instantly wished him dead.

Unseen by the assembly, the demon Dietrich hung from a ceiling beam. His mutagenic disguise had failed and inner bone serrations were even now trying to elevate his expression, tearing through the skin in an explosive slake and locking into place as slimy, impractical tusks.

Blinded to the upper world, Sweeney had sent Dietrich above to assess Skitter's progress. Dietrich had never had great confidence in the little dingbat, but judging by these bizarre proceedings the imp was frenzied with his own agenda. In pride of place at the head of the meeting hall hung a massive, bleached-out portrait of Skittermite himself.

8

YER WRATH

Magic can puddle in the john

In a steel chamber at the rear of the chef school, master chef Quandia Lucent praised a drifting, finned backbone suspended in a painted cabinet. A group of students knelt in supplication.

'Human rights run counter to table manners,' the gilly fiend was sibilating eerily. 'This is our advantage. Necrotic flesh, insect paste and slatternly service.'

'They'll take it,' said the Master Chef, head bowed. 'They'll take it and smile.'

'Your ruthlessness does you credit,' queezed the creature. 'Each man will embrace his flaming portion. Leave me now.'

Quandia fastened the doors, closed his frown and the cabinet moment ended. 'We have a problem,' he told the assembled chefs without preamble. 'The Cyril meetings. I attended one disguised as a sane man and EH Hunt was there, talking about salty fish. What if he convinces them that those creatures really do exist in free abundance in the baffling ocean? Lets slip that they're edible? How long do you think everyone will keep swallowing pasta? And something else. The poorhouse have drastically reduced their pasta order - say they're going to dish out "mystery broth". That place is plastered with Cyril posters. We cannot allow such changes in the status quo. Recite the creed.'

The crew gave a mighty cry: 'Garbage, at crippling prices!'

Half drowner, half current, Noam B Turbot picked among crustacean rubble and hopped dismissively over tidepools full of flimsy critters and natural lassitude. He was no fan of the seafront with its outsidey wind and stretched situation but somewhere along here, he was sure, was an entrance to the Juice Museum - there he'd find some life. Fertility, nourishment; even rare volumes for the plundering. He'd surely earned that right. His self-denial just went over people's heads.

Too late he saw the Announcement Horse. This declaiming steed was worse than useless. Brandishing civilisation by way of excuse, he trafficked his knack for formal anguish and the stained iron body grew yearly heavier with brooding. He stood where beach tar and brown seaweed thin as audiotape darkened the rocks. A sepulchral chime rang out as Turbot tried to pass unnoticed. 'Turbot. You'll hear the devil's granulous footfall on the driveway.'

'I beg your pardon?'

'Death stares at our wrath like a babe at an equation. Slowing into chains, nothingness is granted. We try to live by the false boon of law's detail. Yet only nature's detail is infinite.'

Turbot looked down - on the sandbed stupefactoids of every shape glittered together. Clinking rustacles were moving with the tide.

'Long ago from the sea things like armoured ears were caught and eaten. The ocean floated with sieve glands and living samosas. Today, what with the waves coming constant toward me with all their variation, it creates the illusion of progress, merely. You should try it.'

'*Why* should I?' Turbot demanded.

'You hope to slit open information and stuff your scalp. But the rain of cracked ownership works through the false door.'

Turbot was short of breath. He darted an orange cloth about his face and threw it over a passing butterfly. 'You presume too much. I mean, what are you? Eh? So there. I mean, situate me in time by the unique heart I hate in.'

'We are all sunk with tenure,' the Announcement Horse boomed, unmoving. 'Revelation too late. Keys past, useless but for a stranger's door.'

'Speak for yourself,' spat the speechwriter, and then repeated it at a petulant yell. He stalked away down the beach.

The barnacled sentinel remained staring out to sea, water slocking up in the rocks.

Part of a Pennyground field had been cordoned off for the Deadly Snake Contest and a few spectators stood by unsure whether to be hearty or hesitant. Tony Fleet stepped into the contest area with Rubber Hose. 'This snake has a bill. No, only kidding.'

'What's interesting about that?' asked Barny, peering into the basket where Misses Kennedy was coiled.

'Just a joke to jolly us all along, despite the extremity.'

'We're here by choice, Tony, it's not terrible.'

'I suppose you're right. I still feel the need to joke about old Rubber Hose here though - don't I, Rubber? Don't I?' And he shook his face point-blank at the snake. 'I love ya! I love ya! Yes I do!'

'Calm down Tony,' said Balaclava Lewis, affronted at the display.
'Look at the mug on him!' Tony continued.

'Destroying us is his idea of making a start,' Lewis told Barny.

'No-one's destroying anyone,' Barny stated. 'Why don't we all just calm down. Is Sid ready?'

Golden Sid was strapped into an airlock throne, as pale as a ship-wreck skeleton. His glasses magnified haunted eyes. The twisted fibre of his body was dense with fear, immovable, barely leaking breath.

'Ready,' said Lewis, then smirked at Barny. 'Honour hour is coming.'

'Don't count on it,' chuckled Tony Fleet, and kissed Rubber Hose for luck.

'Am I late?' asked Mike Abblatia, dashing up with a slow-worm.

'Perhaps I object,' said Lewis.

'Well do you?' Barny asked.

'No.'

'Right then,' called Barny, 'Tony to start.'

It was traditional for each competitor to introduce his snake with a one-sentence oration. Tony Fleet stepped forward with his cobra. 'Conjuring unfailingly blood from my forearm with his fangs, Rubber Hose is a focus for my love.' And he draped the snake across the nose of Golden Sid. 'Acknowledge the screaming, Balaclava Lewis,' Tony said as Sid reacted with loud cries.

'They're good enough,' Lewis conceded without real enthusiasm.

'You'll never tame the loops outta my baby,' smiled Tony, looking on at Rubber Hose.

'He's a fine snake, Tony,' said Barny with a firm nod.

'Two minutes,' called Lewis and the snake was removed from the traumatised captor. Lewis lifted his mamba, Tamale Wired For Sound, from a polished heart pine box. 'With his tarragon scales and scorn for pomposity, Tamale Wired For Sound bails me out every time.' Then he whispered 'You are done waiting, fang brother,' and threw it at Sid. The snake landed on Sid's face with great apparent acrimony, and the timid man began releasing short coughs of pain with each shake of his body.

Lewis looked knowingly toward the others. 'I deposit the magnitude of this event now - winner I am.'

'Not so soon, Lewis - this is not Sid's last yelling opportunity.'

Presently, Barny produced Misses Kennedy from her basket and stepped forward. 'Having better manners than to shout from an adjoining room, Misses Kennedy enters filled with gossip and licks me with her thin tongue.' He dropped the viper from above, causing

Sid to shriek like a girl and burst into wrenching sobs, all control lost, a pitiful sight.

'There's a note of calculated contortion in his acts,' sneered Lewis, sniffing.

'Sore loser,' sniggered Tony Fleet.

To humour young Mike Abblatia they let him step forward with his slow-worm, though by now Golden Sid was beyond perceiving anything. 'Slowworm Sadness understands me, and curls in silence round my right wrist.' And he propped the slow-worm on the frame of Sid's glasses.

'That's a class showing, Mike,' nodded Barny. 'You improve every year.'

'Really, Barny?'

Barny warded off the onlookers. 'Contest still in progress! Nerve ending safety is not guaranteed!'

Gregor had been hauled so far off the track he could see his own profile in silhouette, way off to the west. He sure had a belly on him. Entering the bakery, he indicated a display cake and said he wanted it.

'The theme is an old one,' replied the proprietor, and coughed loudly. 'Apologies, senor. Sickness travels the land, making a cane of a red thermometer. Another cough and the division between us increases. Here is the cake. You're billed in the side picture over there - a painted version of you dwells in the landscape.'

'You mean all fiscal matters are processed in that acrylic world.'

'I dare you to deny it.'

'I don't.'

'You are wise, senor.'

Now Gregor stormed into the shaman's yard and complained of shoddy brainwashing. Whole days had been hijacked by a stranger's agenda, all for nothing apparently. 'Edgy swears by you and your dumb tricks - maybe you can get me to see this stupid god who start-ed it all. He's down in the creepchannel supposedly and I don't know how to navigate.'

'I'll try. Sit on the rock-feature there. What's that?'

'Some sort of cake.' Gregor dropped down near to Beltane, who was taking some slices of meat from a bag. 'So how did you get into this shaman nonsense?'

'Well I was walking along the riverbank and a brace of young otters started accusing me of every sin I could muster.'

'What sort of voice did they use.'

'Male, German accent, barking tone, as though recorded on an ancient wax drum.'

'And these were otters.'

'I know.'

'And after all this time you're still affected.'

'Well, I work all day, and ... no, it never goes away. But I'm quite slim so it can't be all bad. Now, let's see what the arsenal cards have to say.' He drew a blackstrap and laid it down. 'Nephron. "Punch the apple from the branch." That's related to a myth, how mankind got the head involved.' He laid another down. 'Antihelix. "I badly need some respect." That speaks for itself. Loop of Henlé. "Did plans precede this disaster?" Great saphenous vein. "At least in detention the whirl of fists is private." Punctum -'

'Wait a minute!' Gregor yelled, standing. 'Is this all you're going to do? Is it too much to ask for anyone in this town to talk normally?'

'Barny asked the same thing. All right, Round One, I think I understand the problem anyway.' He dropped the cards into the pond and paced leisurely about the yard, regarding the tree-and-bird action. 'What mishaps we worship in extremity, eh. Your current position of tangling social disaster will one day grow uninteresting to you, Round One. Until then, what grief drains, flowers also drain.' He crouched at the pond, cupped water into his hands, and stood. 'This is called a cloacal star. What's the opposite of a trick?'

'The what-now?'

Beltane Carom flung the water toward Gregor and it blushed into a vortical membrane which swirled in mid-air as Gregor shrieked. Leaves and trash were being sucked into the twister.

The shaman yelled above the roar. 'Strange hole in the air eh, that happens. There's a day between Thursday and Friday which the angels use. This yard is calibrated to it. Step through here and you're reborn in the corner of a redder room. Don't forget the cake.'

'Beltane,' shouted Gregor. 'If you were nothing more than an iron-willed moron, you'd tell me wouldn't you?'

'Despair sits with truth in a blazing green garden.'

'That's not an answer!'

'Never you mind - *go, go, go, go!*' He shoved Gregor through the vortex, which sucked closed behind him. The shaman turned to the horizon. 'Fire in the hole!'

Gregor clenched his eyes against the storm of bloodwater which ended as suddenly as it began, then his sight cleared like the tide hissing back over shingle. Rendered numb with extremity, he was wandering through the weird obstetric subway known as the creepchannel, blasts of cold air blowing by him. Walls slimy as the innards of a mirror were dripping vitriol over heaps of pearl onions, fossilised eclairs and bent propellers. Gregor's sanity instantly sensed it was in a hardhat area. Once again his career as a boneless striver had left him entirely unprepared to face the day. His reserves of courage did not replenish automatically like those of others, and his quota had been low since he found a spider on the phone earlier. Sick with apprehension, he climbed slow up a technical ghost pocket into an endless migraine pattern of walk-in crypts and yellowed electrocution. He walked across a massive puzzle made of skin, realising afterward he should have gone around it like a traffic island. Sickstone walls dented with the grey alphabet began to change as he passed, curving into the smiles of lawyers. Then he tripped and slid quailing down a deeply sloping tunnel, accelerating through a daze of bone-flake confetti and almost dropping the cake. As he blurred along the cascade, darkness wheezing beneath him and elemental agony scorching his ears, he wondered how papers tackled this sort of thing in the lifestyle section. Maybe his reckless foray into damnation was frowned upon by the smart set - or flawed simply by his carrying this particular cake or screaming this particular way. There was so much to conform to, and to what possible gain? It was all baffling to him.

He spent the next few hours edging thoughtfully along some precarious meltstone ledges, eating his own mouth in fear, and remembering better times until finally he levered himself into a tunnel and lurched from a hole in the ground, his eyes like sun-dried tomatoes. He was in a vast ribbed cavern which banged with arcane industry and flashed with yellow air pain. There was a weird sense of imminence as Gregor, sick with apprehension, looked over at a movement. Lit by an opening in the smoke, there reared a colossal skeletal insect, its complex open-work body studded with ducts and scissoring mandibles. A coldwater heart was visible through epiurethane skin. The whole thing was enthroned in a veined, leathery halfshell.

Gregor took the liberty of flailing backwards as the creature regarded him with eyeballs of porous bone. But seeing as his luck was long ago cut off at the pants pocket, it barely mattered what he did now. He stepped forward. 'Thank you for inviting me and my pals for jelly and ice cream. I didn't ignore the invitation, I tried to get here. If I'd known it was this easy to walk here I wouldn't have tried to drive over. And where's the parking? Did you consider that?' Gregor kicked at some red shapes on the floor. 'What are these little flesh brackets?'

'Gitterbants.'

'Gitterbants, that's what you call them eh. You learn a new thing every day. So listen, I brought you a cake, here it is.'

'"Happy Birthday to Our Darling Little Boy". And what's that, a snow scene?'

'Yeah, a little fella skiing.'

The face of slowly maculate death armour shifted in the dark. 'Foolhardy, Mr One, but not the way you hoped. D'you really consider yourself as adept at that little game as your friend Juno? Protection through randomised innocence? Not you, and most certainly not here.' The demon ejected some gore from its ear nozzles. 'Oh, you run fast over turf but you're suited more for baiting Juno into -'

'Can I put the cake down? My arm's busted.'

'Don't interrupt while I'm detailing my infernal scheme - what's the matter with your arm?'

'That simple bastard Barny ran me over with a tricycle. I got a black eye too but that's going pale green now.'

'But he's your friend, yes?'

'Does he sound like one?'

'You mean he doesn't actually care what happens to you. I can't use you as bait?'

'Shall I put the cake on the side-table of bones then?'

'And a special occasion cake? Why bring it to me?'

Gregor smiled uncertainly. 'Isn't this a special occasion? I mean, here I am.'

'D'you take a special occasion cake wherever you are? And say "here I am"? Get away from me!' And the demon kicked up with a mandible, exploding the cake.

'So we're quits, right?'

'*Get out!*'

Gregor jittered and ran.

When the blob-faced botch of a man had gone, Sweeney called down the Aspict. He watched as it extruded from the ceiling, but the worker demons were still attached, tinkering with its beautifully tooled acridity. 'It'll take at least a week, guv,' they shouted down. Sweeney sent it away again.

So the Round One was of no regard to Juno at all, and useless as bait! Sweeney knew enough about the world above to know that deliberate ramming with a stabilised bike was not an act of friendship.

Just then Skittermite darted in, scampering on the spot and generally stinking up the place. 'Majesty yes thank you, I have turned the Round One against his friend by disguising myself as Juno and running him down with a tricycle.'

Sweeney darkened like a bottle filling with smoke. 'What? You bloody moron, I let him go because of your baffling actions! Are you deliberately wrecking my affairs?'

Skittermite was about to defend himself when the demon Dietrich entered with a large paper tube. 'I told you this skeletal tyke's brain was too close to his ankles. I visited a raucous meeting of the so-called Cyril cult above and here's a beautiful poster of their leader.' He unfurled the poster with a flourish - Skittermite's bleached features stared out above the slogan I AM CONCERN. 'Yes, he's making a power play of his own above as this Cyril fella. He must have been laying the ground for it the whole time everyone thought he was stuck in that drain.'

Sweeney turned his black ice skull toward the cowering imp. 'So you've been industrious. No sooner are you in their bandwidth than you install yourself as a gilly firebrand and influence the masses. What else were you planning - a demon flypast?'

'Your Majesty thank you, remember what Violaine said: "Power receives power."'

'Violaine? You dare ...'

And Sweeney began pulling away from his chair, straining forward as pink stretches of gut flubbered and twanged like gum behind him, locking taut in mid-step. Skittermite sped chittering up the wall and between the ribs of the distant ceiling, vanishing amid crannies of infection. Sweeney turned to Dietrich with a yell that banged some enamel off his beak: 'Clip his wings!'

As Dietrich took flight into the rafters where a billion hollow realtors dangled, Sweeney struggled against his extravagant anatomy, leaning away from the varicose muscle which bound him to the throne.

Behind him a white eye opened in the chairback. Slipping foolishly in the smashed cake, Sweeney was reeled in like a puppet.

9

DO NOT FORSAKE ME OH MY DARLING

Progress accelerates downhill

Fugitive from pursuer shadows rippling over walls, Skittermite hammered at the door of the Powderhouse. A face appeared in the doorcrack and sank away again. Voices.

'Monster outside.'

'Mouth dripping?'

'Dripping and it's a lulu.'

Pushing in and no illusions about his chances, Skittermite flew at the Fusemaster's shirt and hung there like a bat. He was still begging for sanctuary when the worshippers tore him away. A quick X-ray of his head raised more questions than it answered.

'A funeral crasher?' Jayrod barked. 'Explain yourself.'

Skittermite produced a ticket of gospel glass which he'd picked up here a few days ago and chirped the only piece of cannonical dogma he recalled. 'Without vice we are chill.'

'You petition for membership?' shouted Jayrod in hilarity, then stopped as though stung. He lifted a presentation fruitbowl under which lay a Cyril leaflet bearing the likeness of Skittermite. 'Sharpened face? Telescopic eyes? Yay high? Cyril himself, here to tear my expensive shirt and yours!'

A rush of fuseheads lifted Skittermite aloft in a frisky way and shouted 'Try my aerosol udder!' or something like that, hurling him into the frolic pool. He emerged with froth on his head and was told by everyone that he looked like a lamb. He almost digested himself with shame.

Edgy bumped into Magenta Blaze outside Snorters cafe and in no time at all had her believing he and Barny were known as 'the Dull Boys'.

'And I can't pretend we don't deserve it,' he added. 'By the way, which do you prefer for a book of poems - *We Are Taunted On Two Levels* or *Taunt Us On the Double*?'

'*Flowers Are Lovely*,' she replied with a bright expression.

His smile frozen, Edgy backed away and continued toward Feeble Champ Books. The building perched on the edge of the canyon and it was easy to fling unwanted manuscripts from the window into this convenient abyss. In fact the office of Crash Test Nureyev projected over the drop, steadied by chunky wooden struts. Nureyev rose to greet Edgy as he entered. 'Plantin, glad you could come.'

'I reached the street according to the plan.'

'Good, good.' Nureyev seated himself behind a desk-collision and the smog of cigarettes. 'Sit you down.'

Edgy indicated a hammered steel cardigan on the wall. 'What's that?'

'A reminder of the human cost. I lick it every afternoon.'

'Really?'

'Without fail.' Nureyev smiled wickedly. 'I've been looking again at Gort's manuscript. I admire your talent for finding these characters - Juno's dog book is a real hit. That chapter entitled "Dogs Are

Blameless" is spot-on, no matter how much it grieves me. He's some kind of genius, though the couple of times I met him he denied it. In fact he acted like he didn't know what I was talking about.'

'Yeah, well, he's a card.'

'The second time I met him he was spreading some sort of ointment on a monkey's hand and kept telling me this was the quietest the chimp had ever been. What do you suppose that's about?'

'Er ... I really came here to talk about Amy Gort, Mr Nureyev. As her personal agent I'm concerned about the presentation.'

'How so?'

'The title - she prefers *We Are Taunted On Two Levels* and I say *Taunt Us On the Double* - someone just suggested *Flowers Are Lovely* and I have to say I'm losing all perspective.'

'That's a mistake I wouldn't recommend. Nine mistakes I would recommend are: sneeze forty-eight feet of telephone wire across the sky; compliment a frazzled loser; triumphantly bring in a thing dangly-dead; hide an ambulance under your shirt; touch something glimpsed in tears; prepare a prison of ham, previously a sunlit limestone yard; take seventy-three years to get dressed; hook your scalp and pull; sign your memories over to me and stand silently outside my office.'

'It's a deal.'

'Plantin, these are all mistakes. You see you're taking it all too seriously.' He lit a cigarette and drew, regarding Edgy thoughtfully a while. 'You see the metal cardigan up there? It was given to me by an old-time writer by the name of Noam B Turbot in his heyday. Man of letters.'

'Man of what?'

'Letters. Wrote The Wedlock Trilogy - covering his marriage in *Against My Will*; his divorce, *Trying to Hide*; and its aftermath, *Blessed Relief*. You see?'

'Dinner party stuff.'

'Yes, middle class tedium. I must have wished for his death a hundred times. Action was back and business blew random money into the flue. Bit him on one occasion. Fat off his arm tasted of coffee. We were running from an electrical storm once, hell of a thing - a stunning, crackling uproar. And he began to swerve for no reason I could see. I didn't mention it at the time. But then I had an unwise fit of temper. "I'm suspicious about you changing course suddenly when we were running from the electric storm the other night." Well he finally confessed but I had to physically pull the words from his face. Apparently he was running and decided maybe it wouldn't be such a bad idea to act like he knew what he was doing. And in the process he had some sort of vision concerning a giant kitchen full of bagels, sex and spare time. This, it turned out, was his plan for the future. Well, suddenly the day of success played out. He lost all humility and perspective. Boxes of pills were bashed aside by his face, he trembled, reeling across the hospital walls, beating off the menace of help and stammering like a bastard. Officials fumbled the rest. Now I hear he lives only to increase his past. Pity he ruined the storm with his apparent knowledge and adjustments. Meanwhile I remember my principles with a jolly nostalgia. And smoke cigarettes tasting of dead cat.'

'So Amy's poems, Mr Nureyev. You really do think they're good, right?'

'Plantin, I love this stuff. Give it to me and the lines are wolfed down like sausages. This one, "Certifying Puncher Horn":

Nuns float on wheels
strangled my neck
mechanical daughters moving rapidly
fear transfigures

Reindeer don't know *that*, do they?'

'No, Mr Nureyev.'

'Believe me, Plantin, hotels are pelvic, cowpats look like liquorice, a church organ sounds like cheese and a lion's a lion whichever way you slice it. Climactic fight in a grain tower and bob's your uncle.'

'But, er ... but the title, Mr Nureyev. What do you think?'

'I can tell I'm still not getting through to you, Plantin. Come here, I'd like to show you something.' He stood and led Edgy to a corner table cluttered with dusty office plants. In a pot on top of a thick ledger was a human head, a dead ringer for Nureyev's own but for its silver eyes. 'Isn't that something? Got it from Kenny Reactor at the hydroponic place, one of his little experiments. Completely vegetative, never moves, doesn't make a sound, nothing like that. I find it relaxing to water this guy and let it do my worrying for me. You know how I boost the soil? Wood pulp. Eh? Bookpaper. Eh? Isn't that beautiful?'

Edgy knelt close to the fungal face.

'Your man Juno's got the right idea, Plantin - don't measure yourself by all this. Life's elsewhere.'

The Feeble Champ building faced on to the rear of the Mayoral palace and as Edgy emerged he saw Max Gaffer slinking around back there. The lawyer was supervising the loading of sacks into a van. This didn't seem significant until one of the sacks burst open over a workman and a jumble of bugs swallowed him alive.

*

Barny was dozing in a hammock, the house lopsided around him and loud with the green squeak of canaries. Grass grew out of the radio.

Edgy entered using the walls for balance. 'Bubba, wake up - I bumped into Magenta Blaze outside Snorters. I told her you're dull, we both are. I may have convinced her we're actually known as the Dull Boys.'

Barny looked blearily at Edgy. 'Dull Boys?'

'Yeah, I know the trouble you've been having.'

'You talked to her?'

'I think I set her straight on a few things. She says she loves it when you get assertive and start shouting.'

'She used those exact words?'

'"I love it when he gets assertive and starts shouting."'

'What was she doing when she said it?'

'Just looking at me and smiling.'

'In an amorous way?'

'Why would she be smiling at me in an amorous way as she said that?'

'Maybe she wanted you to shout at her, I don't know. I never know what's going on with her.'

'I don't know, maybe she meant something by it.'

Barny watched the chimps awhile. 'So what it boils down to is we don't know any more than we did before you spoke to her.'

'No we don't.'

'Well thanks Edgy.'

Edgy sat on a gangplank, swinging his legs thoughtfully. 'You could tell her you had sex with the lion.'

'She'd just be impressed.'

'You didn't did you?'

'Rest easy, Edgy. Look around. Slow lizards on the prowl. Cats scudding around the place. It doesn't get any better than this.'

'Yeah you've got a nice setup here Bubba.' They listened to the hiss of the shade trees. 'Hey, that's what I wanted to tell you - listen to this.'

And Edgy told him about what he'd seen behind the mayoral palace. Walking past the poorhouse later, he had seen the same van unloading and a sign on the poorhouse window in black chinese ink: IN PLACE OF PASTA, IT WILL NOW BE THE POLICY OF THIS ESTABLISHMENT TO SERVE MYSTERY BROTH, A THICK SOUP WHICH IS WITHOUT CHARM OR SURPRISE.

'You see what's going on there Bubba?'

Barny's round, bland countenance showed that he didn't.

'Remember what old Bingo Violaine said? "Whispering is satisfactory only when it is heard." Think about it Bubba, the Mayor and his lawyer are feeding floor lobsters to the poor.'

Barny thought about it, blank. 'Animals need happy results.'

'So? That's what I'm telling you isn't it? What are we going to do about it?'

Skittermite had returned to the Powdermouth, kneecap in hand. Marvelling at his sheer swagger at coming back, and jazzed at the idea of indoctrinating Cyril, they had given him their hopeless credo bound in a burnished volume. 'Learn the same thousand manners as these fellows,' Rod Jayrod had told him, spent with excess. 'It could be a setback or the opportunity of a lifetime. Either way, I'm fine.' And he dismissed him with a lax and peremptory twist of the hand.

Now the grease monkey sat in the poorhouse swaddled in a small blanket, spooning strange soup, absently unscrewing a scab and pondering the dogma. 'Showing your complaint to the sky, you'll be cold and out of range, footprints lost, smeared in the wind. Mince the clouds and drink the rain, fly, fly.'

He looked aside at a slack-jawed chump, who indicated a bug on the table. 'Hey - check out the standing caterpillar.'

Cramped with change, Skittermite returned to the writ. 'Watch a spear hit the horizon, re-create the first question.'

Blasphemy awareness? Arcana trumpcards? They wrote the same as they spoke. It didn't mean anything! This place and the everlasting happy sun, damn the sun! Where was the creepchannel's electrocutive bone cold? The vomit in the heart?

But a dozen grim breaths later, he quietly returned the information framed in despair.

Then all hell broke loose. Barny Juno and the scarecrow man erupted in upon giant wild animals, holding nothing back. 'Understand that you are always a lion, Mr Braintree,' called Barny Juno. The cat reared, pouncing bowls and cutlery from the tables. Sallow urchins ran screaming.

'This cat's so glossy it's almost frictionless,' yelled Edgy. The leopard gave a chewy snarl. 'Feel it.'

'I have, Edgy, and it is.'

The lion swiped a cook with a forepaw. 'You have purged suspense by knocking me out,' the cook claimed before falling.

'Deadly poison!' shouted Edgy, swiping a pan from an old man's hand.

The old man looked severe. 'To be struck in August: wrong.'

Skittermite was weeping tears like cough drops, order exploding all around him. 'The day you elected to ride into the poorhouse on a lion thank you,' he screamed, 'my strained trail faded for no-one to follow.' Looking through the haze of flying soup and mind-boggling profanity, he saw that the men upon the fierce roarers were discussing the scene at hand as though it were already over.

'In the confusion I stole this.' Edgy produced from his thin shirt a meaningless velvet colour swatch.

'Your mania for leopard-riding,' Barny smiled, 'has not destroyed you.'

Skitter's mind was dissolving like new bread.

10

MUSCLEBOUND FREAKOUT

Point enough and people will look at you

'Look at this,' spat the Mayor, slapping *The Blank Stare*. '"Frothing potion gets uniform thumbs-down because it's venom." And sightings of Cyril at the scene, shouting against the state. How can he be this organised? That meeting we went to was carved from raw spud.'

'Nothing to get hung about,' said Max Gaffer.

'With me pumping out evil at this rate? By the time we get back to the office it'll be rammed with lobsters again.'

They were sat in the back of the limo as it glided toward the Furfur district. Gaffer was slow and casual. 'Only a setback for your conscience, sir.'

'My hair was my conscience, I was glad when it went. We need a pain handle on the populace. A few drops of rain erase the benefit of thirst - what are we going to do? This Cyril's a popular guy - maybe we could welcome him into the Mayoral race all patronising, say competition's good, new blood's welcome.'

'The less said about blood, sir. Defend the man in anagrams - play it safe.'

'You were born into an office weren't you? Well let's hope old speechbelcher Turbot's finally shambled home. A firm line's required. Straight from the shoulder, though naturally not mine. More stuff about the town clock as a symbol of something or other.

Tricks and crafty betrayal Max, that's the stuff eh? At all costs they can't be allowed to know it's the same blood re-circulating.'

'Agreed. They'll point to the gutted and say, er, something like, "Lookathem eh? There's a bad thing."'

Gaffer was referring to citizens who had been overlevied and now lived as rattling freaks in the borderlands - people like Microlady and the Kite, shrunk and bloodless.

'The gutted? I look elsewhere for my terrors.'

'The Conglomerate.'

The Mayor tersely admitted that this was the case. 'Beef up security anyway. Thaw the Brigade and point them in the right direction.'

'Already done, sir.'

'You know, Max. Power's a funny thing. I was a toddler when I knew. They wanted me to walk, they insisted on it. The pressure was on, so my arms started moving. I spoke some loud words before I knew what I was doing. People said I had talent. At my urging the old settled routines became bravely superimposed with images of activity and change. That's what I am, Max. A force to be acknowledged.'

'My enthusiasm is inoperative, sir. There are people ahead of us.'

'Oh, a night's sleep'll forget 'em.'

'Outstanding sir, but I mean the people are revolting.'

'The verb?' Rudloe jerked his attention to the window, clinging a hand to the glass and squinting out. The car had slowed into a crowd of citizens who were brandishing banner slogans such as TOO DRY ELUSORY DREAM and MORTARED LORD - YES, YOU and DESTROY YOUR MALE ROD and DELOUSE MY TARRY DOOR and MODERATELY SORRY DUO and YOU DRY ROADSTER MOLE. 'What's this for? They're usually bone idle.'

The car was now stationary but for the shoving of the populace. The Mayor noticed that one man dressed in a mechanic's uniform was copulating with the fuel valve. Some of the crowd were carrying a huge inflatable bargain hunter with bulging eyes, its fat arms floating aimlessly. Others kept pointing to their own nostrils, each individually and with a fierce and meaningful expression. The rhythm of this activity was both hypnotic and frightening. Two elected children bashfully pushed a set of giant wooden dentures into the face of the bargain hunter. Bag-cheeked and billowing, it buckled and dented down until the bearers were dragging a flaccid tangle upon which the kids rode in delight, slime spurting from their gills.

'At least they're not saying "destroy Mayor Rudloe",' said Gaffer.

Without the containment suit Rudloe had full access to the magic phrase tattooed on his arm - drawing up his sleeve, he took a gander: I HAVE MADE IT QUITE CLEAR THAT.

Clearing his throat, he slid open the roof hatch and stood to straighten his instincts out. 'I have made it quite clear that: er, our happy home Accomplice, an imploded enclave, is mandatory. This martyr's rodeo you call a protest - what do you think it'll achieve?'

The dot-eared GI Bill, nose as grubby as a graveyard dog, stumped pugnaciously up with a banner saying YORE A DOLDRUM OYSTER. Then he hauled the Mayor by the arm, toppling him into the mob.

The Mayor gripped his own throat, gasping pop-eyed. 'Manmade fibres!'

The Brigade were wandering nearby, looking at the trees. 'Lovely inspection, Sarge,' said the Deputy. 'We adore you like a mother.'

'Thank you, but one of you apes sighed like the air pushing out of a cushion - any guesses who that could have been?'

'T-T-T-T-T-T-T-Teddy?'

'There you go - was that so hard.'

'My abdomen,' said Teddy.

'Eh? What's the matter with you boy? And here we are in the countryside and all?'

'He ate some soup at the poorhouse, Sarge,' said the Deputy. 'I don't know why.'

'Let's stop here and the main ones, that's me, the Deputy and Gibbs, will sit on that gate. You others, sit in a circle and look angry.' The Sarge sat on the gate and everyone followed his instructions. 'Lads, do you remember Karloff's Circus and the trouble it caused us? Never go to the circus, lads. Soldiers in the dim-lit sawdust ring talk through sewn lips, unheard - they're food for midgets and lions, their veins drawn out and dried to make the netting under the high-wire. Their heads flattened and bolted to create the wheels which all fly off the mini car at once and bounce - there's a reason they bounce and that's the brains, being put to use for the first time.' Finished, he turned to his deputy, who brandished a dish.

'Snail, sarge?'

'Don't mind if I do. What are they?'

'Snails sarge.'

'Snails. Don't mind if I do.'

'Get your face round that then.'

'What is it.'

'A snail, sarge.'

'Snail. Alright then. Eat it do I?'

'Eat it sarge, that's right.'

'What is it.'

'Snail - a snail, sarge.'

'Snail.'

'A snail, sarge. See? It's a snail.'

'Snail is it. Well now.'

'Snail.'

'Snail, eh. Well, don't mind if I do.'

'Good on yuh.'

'Right.'

'You eatin' it then?'

'Eh?'

'You eatin' that?'

'What is it.'

Before the deputy could reply, a cry rang out. The troops gazed toward a wide lane a way off, where the Mayor was being thrown into the sky by citizens galore. Max Gaffer too was being manhandled. 'Don't touch the underwear!' he was shrieking.

'That must have been the cry we just heard,' the Deputy muttered.

As they continued to watch, they saw the Mayor's driver being smothered in paste and relay monks dancing tauntingly before him with emeralds the size of boxing gloves. 'Merciful god!' screamed the driver. A roofmender wearing a dragonfly mask took a run-up and kicked a seabird into an unset loaf.

'Ah, Death, the incompetent visitor in red,' the Sarge commented.

As the Mayor stood restrained by pouting rioters, Prancer Diego stood point-blank in front of him, facing the other way. Then Prancer glanced at him negligently, seemed to notice him for the first time, and began jabbering about 'hook dames'. With a caw of laughter he suffered a whole-body convulsion which sent him sprawling. 'Stretch the chalk mark from this origin to the greyhound over there,' he began to say, but his words segued into another language as he waded down the road as though in a river, up to his waist. He thrashed deeper until finally the road closed over his vulpine head.

It had been a stressful day. Startled by a pop-up book, the Sarge had knifed the main character. Seeing his mistake and the resultant damage, he had cried for almost an hour. 'Shall I at least set my lads in order?' he asked himself now, and decided. 'Commandeer eighteen worms, boys.'

'What are we going to do, Sarge?' asked his Deputy brightly.

'All kindness and concern,' said the Sarge, 'we'll go hog-wild for studying worms.' He stood down from the gate and fixed his face on the future. '*That's* what we're going to do.'

*

Reckless in his quest for plagiarism, Noam B Turbot jettisoned the rotten plank he'd been using for buoyancy and waded to the grotto shelf. He had gambled that this low-roofed sea cave was an entrance to the Juice Museum and the bed and lamp on the inner shore suggested it was inhabited at least. Reaching the sandy ridge he looked back at the distant cave mouth. Albescent shapes played over the walls, teasing hundreds of drifty pleasures from his brain. A tunnel of damp limestone sloped upward into the rock. He followed it, fiending for headfood.

The tunnel walls further on were panelled with warmly polished wood, embedded with slide-drawer cabinets and foggy paintings. Turbot drew out a narrow drawer and found a weathered photo of Wesley Kern and Bingo Violaine larking about with what appeared to be an enraged grizzly bear. Another showed the bear asleep in a hammock. So far so good. Stuffing these into his pocket, he went on.

On an earth-floored landing, cupboards displayed code stones, a smoking rose, snake-tree gold, brittle scrolls and rusted shrike scissors. A framed picture was filling with seawater, historical victims looking out. Along the passage, Turbot stopped short as he was passing a little side-room. An old man, his face benign and wrinkled with smiling, sat looking into a teacup tattooed with vines and muttered to himself. 'Thirty days sipping tea has left me in charge of the moon's character, I defend it continually ...'

Turbot ducked past, entering a room like the shell of a chambered nautilus and filled with the smell of burning sugar. Here was fusty junk and cherry gas, the essence of stuff pulsing through the air. He saw coloured glooms and rusting apples, tarmac heatwarp rising through blackberry bushes, heaven glimpses of the right thing done on some ethical afternoon. A wet garden of detail shifting with fresh sun. Emerald melodies chimed around him. He was as loose as the tired sky-muscles of the clouds.

He floated on into a chamber which smelt like rotten flowers, his heart buzzing hard like a beetle. A thousand cracked books lay amid arcane artifacts. A parchment portrayed the bowed ribs of fantastical lunar barges. Turbot opened a volume bound in rose leather. 'Gentlemen have many terms for the dead and many levels of decomposition. Their world is the final version, their actions already taken. They don't let go easily. Smiles are not a part of their worth. They grow ruins of judgement and class. Topics of interest may not awake them. Wounds spurt sand. Death for them is distinguished and garnished with dainty platitudes. Their frontier is delineated only by eyeliner. They say, "The true use of suspicion is a holy thing." They say "Pursuit is a negotiation." They say "Respect the paper." They are a beacon of absence.'

Turbot regretted having read it. Must explore, he thought, pleased with his adventure, the first in years. A fanned rack of stairs faded into the dark and he wandered down to a windy platform of architectural fragments and ancient statuary. There was a pediment with the slogan 'Love is the opposite of luck'. Must remember, he thought, and keep ahold of why I'm here.

Testing the environment beyond the platform, he found soft soil, and stepped tentatively onto this, walking into the cold shadows. On the way he passed something which looked like a folded, boulder-sized gallstone. A swerved human face was frozen in the mix, its palate reversed. There were structures ahead, and as he got among them he found that they were doors planted upright, frames and all.

All the doors had something attached to the back, something like a dry umbilical or withered tap root. Turbot went to the handled side of a door and pushed it open. He was looking into a starved hallway, bleak and trivial. A hollow wind cut through a universe of destitute oblivion, where the best hope was a depth of suffocation, deaf bones packed in soil. The sight crystallised in Turbot's mind as the purest mirror, showing him the dead wire of his reflection. Gnawed by a roaring vacuum he reeled back, toppling some monstrous ornament and collapsing against a step like the church kerb of a crypt. His frosted brain crackled audibly. Just his luck to get the empty mask.

1 1

AMOEBAS ARE VERY SMALL

Leverage is dulled on a soft man

Gettysburg, a demon of mystery skin and lightning bug eyes, was sat in the shaman's yard chatting to Beltane Carom. 'You advise Barny Juno because you think he's a special case, maybe he is. But when Violaine prophesied the Beast Man and the downfall of my old master, the philosopher was sputtering through his own blood and brain-water. Maybe it isn't Juno. What's he got going for him?'

'Power through misdirection,' muttered Carom. 'Yes, not much.'

'So what's with this?' The defector demon produced a copy of *The Blank Stare* with the headline CYRIL'S CONCERN ESCALATES. 'How's this helping Barny? If he's implicated who'll protect him? And what are you doing to shield him from Sweeney?'

'You still don't understand this place, Getty.'

Gettysburg stood, a white giant with a spike-mine head. 'Maybe I don't, but I consciously chose this set of dimensions - I sometimes think you people take them for granted.'

As Getty re-emerged into the alleyway he glimpsed jerky motions in a corner - a little sprite with a head like an anode capered up all desperation.

'Is that little Kermit? Last time I saw you you were working on that subspace extension.'

'Mr Getty,' Skittermite rasped. 'Impossible. How to be here, the Powdermouth, chaos, I can't -'

A shadow stiffened into form and began walking. 'Boy, the detail of decorum is disgusting.' Dietrich strode into the light. 'Why consort with his type - the shaman? Inconveniencing everyone with signs and wonders. He picks out of happiness an answer that would die elsewhere. The assumption that if you got a good philosophy it'll stand up under fire from the likes of us. Accomplice suits a vanilla demon.'

Gettysburg smiled. 'You're so transparently relieved to be able to talk about it all, Dieter. Why keep coming back? I think you fantasise of being stopped.'

'No. Autonomy is one tooth, useless.'

'You're wrong, it's owning your own jaws. Look, let's just try and play nice shall we?'

Skittermite looked on as the two giants faced off. Dietrich turned to him. 'Send a weak link after a weak link, how dumb was that? Time to take him in.'

'Run, Kermit, run!' shouted the white demon, slamming a claw around Dietrich's throat. He hissed into his face. 'Heroes yearn for mistakes. It's natural.'

'Call yourself a hero?'

'I meant you.'

He hurled the paravamp backward. Dietrich stumbled, steadied himself. Skittermite was gone.

'So the sun's come out like that eh,' Dietrich breathed.

Gettysburg blinked his milk opal eyes.

'*Mascot*,' spat the paravamp, and deployed his wings.

Gettysburg was left staring at the minus smear of his departure. 'That is one conflicted demon.'

*

Mayor Rudloe and the lawyer dragged into the office and collapsed into chairs, standing again to repeat the relief of the experience. 'What the hell was that about? Emeralds, lard? Did you see that abnormally bearded failure with the net? The satanic runners? And your hired goons were just skylarking, off to the right.'

'Studying worms.' Max Gaffer plucked a dead fern from his torn trouser leg. 'Yes ... yes I accept they could have helped more.'

'God almighty. If this trend persists we'll be seeing our own bones. Make some tea, will you.'

'Naturally I refuse.'

Rudloe sagged back in his chair, hopes draining out with his exhalation. He glanced aside at the balcony window without enthusiasm. 'The day fades. To make up for the sky I will stroke my invisible herds and my own neck in turn, rest my bulk here and repeat my claims of superiority.'

'Outstanding sir, but there is still the matter of the speech tomorrow. You can't postpone again.'

'Where's Turbot?' Rudloe kicked a floor lobster, which flew to smash against the wall. In unison the others stopped moving momentarily, then continued to scuttle. 'Bastard's probably hunkered down with his philosophy in curlers. We could use him now. A slogan with a future is a thief without parallel.'

'People are hard to quantify. Opinions differ.'

'Different people? A patchwork won't wash easy.' Rudloe frowned at the ceiling. 'We need to convince them all's for the best, in a friendly way. "Fate is fun", how about that?'

'Or convince them that wealth is actually undesirable.'

'I could smoke a cigar and start coughing really hard. Say something like, "These things aren't as nice as you think".'

'It would have to be done offhand,' said Gaffer pensively.

'I can do offhand. It's my middle name. "These things aren't as nice as you think." And I throw the cigar away.' Rudloe stood, stern and decided. 'Fortress your phone, Max. I prepare to be gawked at by nutters.'

A doorman entered announcing a lump-faced visitor the size of a wooden chair.

'Oh, show him in,' said the Mayor, deflating. 'It can't be any worse than that walking hammer we had in here the other week.' As he waited, he frowned at a persistent sound in his head - it was as though his sanity had come partly adrift and was bumping back and forth like a muffled clapper.

A bone coat-hanger scampered into the room, springing on to the chair opposite the Mayor's desk. Its head appeared to be made of soft clay.

'Leave us,' the Mayor told Max Gaffer, waving a weary hand. 'Whatever this is it won't put me in a savoury light.' When the door was closed, he turned to the visitor. 'Now what are you, a midget? You're not a kid, you haven't got any gills. You're not an overlevy are you?'

'None of the above thank you.'

'Have you covered your head with clay? How small is your head?'

'I wish please to make an offer. I will tell you the true identity of the man called Cyril. A man who though appearing simple-minded thank you, is in fact all fouled-up with fancy hardship and split-second timing.'

'Guess I don't get this for free. State your terms.'

'Well, I want you to rename the sun.'

'The sun? Rename? To what?'

'Jonathan.'

'I beg your pardon?'

'Yes thank you, from now on people will say "lying in Jonathan" and "never look directly at Jonathan" and "Jonathan is hot today" and "where are my Jonathan glasses".'

'And instead of sunrise, Jonathan-rise.'

'You're getting the idea.'

'Idea? Now you listen to me my lad - this sun-naming scheme of yours is bloody death for everyone. What do you think this is?'

'Thank you I ...'

'Don't thank me you bastard. Who the hell wants to be caught dead in *Jonathan glasses*? Get out of here! Max!' Gaffer instantly burst in, leaving a bit of eye-jelly in the keyhole. 'Take this amateur and dump it in the trash - it wouldn't be impolite to make fun of his arms either.'

'I will,' Gaffer grinned, advancing.

Perched atop the Tower of Nowt, Dietrich slowly scanned the town with a head like a wet clawhammer. A breeze flubbered the webbing of his wings and he shifted position, hunching so that the rills on his back pulled open.

The vista was a stained outbreak of spires and flat-tops. How was this different from the dense accretion of the creep? Only the pretense that it made sense. And didn't that up the ante? These bastards were outdoing his bandwidth. Beware the beast: Man.

Gregor hadn't returned to the Bata Motel and nobody knew where he was, so Barny, Edgy and Chloe Low went to Scardummy Garden to look at his statue for a clue. Barny was telling Chloe all about the Deadly Snake Contest as they walked the gravel path between lawns striped like toothpaste. 'Misses Kennedy got two rosettes - Deadliest Viper in the Neighbourhood, of course, but she was also voted Adder Most Likely to Strike the Face. Balaclava Lewis's snake won first prize in the Relentless Horror category. Good for him. His black mamba's going through the terrible twos.'

'It's a mamba,' said Edgy, 'it'll always be terrible.'

'That's a negative attitude.'

'So how did you first get interested in animals Barny?' Chloe asked.

'A dog that impressed me, which stared now and now and now, honoured me with his attention. There was no going back. That dog spoke of love.'

Edgy began whistling loudly to alert Barny to the fact that he wasn't doing himself any favours in the romance department but Barny was oblivious. Edgy picked up some gravel from the path and pushed it into his own chin, where some of it stayed. 'A beard of bees,' he gloried. 'Yeah once you got a beard of bees you got it made in the shade Bubba.'

'It's cruel sticking bees on your chin for laughs. Why bees anyway?'

'Haven't you noticed? Half the gravel on this path is in the shape of bees.'

And so it was - the killer bees which had escaped a while ago had their own little statues here in the Garden. Barny hopped yelping onto the grass verge. 'I've been killing bees!'

'Killer bees, Bubba, killer bees!' Edgy started bounding up and down on the path. 'And I like it!'

'Leave 'em alone you murderer, get out of it. Chloe, get up here.'

'That's amazing,' said Chloe, picking up a palmful of stone bees.

'You're treading on winged animals!'

'What about the baby trolls you can't help eating?' laughed Edgy.

'Those are different, they're a fungus.'

'Well I've seen them roiling their chubby limbs my lad and they look pretty real to me.'

'I didn't say they weren't real. I mean it, come up here.'

They walked on the grass until they entered the statue stands. Chloe was fascinated by the bee find. 'There must be a statue for every animal in Accomplice, Barny. Not just the people and those demons in the side-bushes. Even your snake and your lion. Maybe amoebas are here in the form of sand grains.'

'Amoebas are very small,' Barny conceded. 'What would happen if someone took their own statue out of the Garden?'

'That happened once but people don't like to think about it,' said Chloe. 'A man called Earfont Jackson got tired of coming out here so he took his statue home and put it in the back yard. Then he started finding it in the house when he woke in the morning. Then standing at the foot of his bed. Then one night he woke up with a pain in his arm and the statue was holding him. They were fusing together, and took almost two days to become a solid mass. We've got it at the Juice Museum.'

Edgy wasn't listening, stone bees falling one by one from his dented chin. 'Hey, Low, what do you think's best - *We Are Taunted On Two Levels* or *Taunt Us On the Double?*'

'Well, one's an observation and one's a command I suppose. I don't know Amy very well but I'd say the command would suit her better.'

'Thank you. Hear that, Bubba? Maybe even a picture of her on the cover, with a speech balloon.'

'Here's Gregor's statue.' Barny pulled some ivy from the keglike form and brushed loose mould from the face.

'Any ideas?' frowned Edgy.

Barny peered into the hard face. 'He's smiling.'

'... and finally,' announced Rod Jayrod, leaning languid against a statue of a valentine corpse, 'when a man blurs, does he cease to exist?'

In a state of visible deterioration, Skitter pipped his reply: 'No.'

Instantly the Powderhouse revellers became jubilant to the rim of frothing madness, including some hooting relic who thrust his varicoloured face ahead and called above the din 'That's me - remarkable in the world!' Impassioned crazies introduced themselves and offered advice carved into food. Skittermite shrank back as he was issued with his ash certificate and a tin crucible of useless fluff. Bespangled frauds and prancing cronies allowed no time to focus - he sought out a clear space where he could stand in wooden wonder. A boy in electric scales played in a cage which swung past terrible designs tracked in the marble wall.

Skitter peered over the writhing celebrations at Rod Jayrod, who was pouring lime from a jug. 'What now please?' he called.

Jayrod seemed unconcerned. 'Run, scream, anything you like.' He drank, looking away.

Skittermite clutched the soapstone receptacle of fluff. He felt violated, undone. Where was his centre? Jonathan glasses? What had he been thinking?

A half-masked midget grabbed his arm and said 'I can tell you feel wiser. Wiser and less patient. You'll never go back.' And the little man disappeared into the crowd.

12

PETIT TESTAMENT

Describe social custom with care - you may give something away

Mayor Rudloe tore drawers from his desk and flung them at the floor. 'Where's the bloody cigars?'

'You must have mislaid them,' stated Max Gaffer, smirking into his own mind. 'You'll have to improvise.'

'Improvise? Last time I improvised we all ended up dressed as otters.'

'I enjoyed that.'

'So did I, so did everyone but my god what a predicament. Minutes to discover democracy.' The Mayor stood there staring at Gaffer in clueless silence awhile.

'The hecklers will be grateful,' Gaffer offered.

Rudloe deflated a little. 'I see. Well I've faced worse. Some brisk hectoring and all will be well.'

'Yes,' Gaffer smiled. 'Read something off a platitude form.'

Startled into hope, Rudloe knelt to thrash through the drawers again.

'Before it turns ugly.'

Rudloe looked up at the lawyer. There would be no platitude forms. He stood, straightening the varicose chains of office. Then he made a redundant gesture of dismissal, and flung through the balcony windows.

The ground below was dappled with stooges and onlookers and other living things, some wearing leather car coats. They were sneering from the get-go, or smiling in fun like Edgy, who never missed one of these unfortunate incidents if he could help it. He had dragged Amy Gort along and Barny stood nearby with Magenta Blaze. Stancing pompously, the Mayor began with studied disdain. 'To avoid making fools of yourselves, I suggest you pretend to understand me. What do I grant you? The privilege of outrage, the freedom of fury. And in the face of my conduct, who would choose not to exercise such liberties? Thus, all is well ordered.'

The crowd parried his meaning with chunders, farts and other sonic contrivances.

'And, er, I augment nature with hallmarks. Tree birds brought to account and so on. See the stillness of the blood clock below, dry and un-nourished. You'll go to the red shed, every one of you, and give your due quotient. Flop out your wallets and pretend you've a choice. I promise you nonetheless that a destination protrudes toward your journey. I'll set up a task force and set up a task force and set up a task force. My habits are reserved for accomplishments, accomplishments, not standing here, standing talking here to you whoever you are, you people. This, though a moderate scene, I question it. That shows something eh, that I'm radical or something? What else is there - doomed Eddie Gallo? He has never made sense and shows no signs of doing so.'

In the crowd, doomed Eddie Gallo stood seemingly immersed in the merriest thoughts.

The Mayor was getting jumpy at the fringes. A glare worried at his eyes. 'The attraction of pigeons is the legs - they're an enigma aren't they really? So much to do, er ... how about this ... let's rename the sun. Pick a name, me first, I pick Jonathan, eh? And the lucky winner will brew rain and cigarettes into deserted silhouettes of blight. Who's up for it? Eh, people? The technology already exists to consider these and other matters. Stir a blessing a thousand times, make it thick.'

'Who are you?' someone shouted up.

'You know damn straight who it is!' Rudloe barked. 'I hold this town together by the cheeks of my arse! What are you all gawking at? I stand here before you and these are the ideas I get? I'm prosperous, why aren't you? You and your meaningless antics, waving your trouble-monkeys about the place! You'll stay fooled till your body gets oaty, ears eating out to the rim-rind! Try realising then, grip out of the casket, pushing earth - if you can! Melt again upon the steps, you victims! I halve my smirk by the doorframe! Boil you all!' His face became distorted, squawking. 'You want a piece of me? The ego on you! Die, die! I'm naming this palace Rudloe Manor because I'll never leave, I'll never leave, I'll *never leave*!'

There was a commotion below the balcony as a brittle fiend twitched across the palace face on to the blood clock platform and began pecking out a litany of condemnation. 'Accomplice!' it screeched with a head like a corner sandwich. 'Yes please, you! You were meant to be a domain of paradise meat thank you, but within two hours bad luck hid goldfish in my soap - I arrive to dropkick you into bedlam and you repay that trust with wandering attention or outright sleep. Apparently evil is a subtlety beyond your grasp! The bad-luck pantomime you call society, the blood-nothing of your bodies - you and your expensive buffoonery thank you I ... I feel exhausted just talking about it.'

No two expressions alike, the crowd were already shouting: 'Cyril! Cyril!'

'You are concern!' others hollered in obeisance. 'Take my trousers!'

Mayor Rudloe gripped the rail and peered down. 'Cyril? Oh pan the place why don't you. That's a lot of damp news. Democracy regulates traffic, that's all.'

The demon zigzagged with irritation. 'Damnation itself is in jeopardy! Faded labels speaking just out of reach! My mind is *cracking*!'

'As compared to painting a dog, charity is wearisome,' someone shouted.

'Do you think he's frail enough to be withered by a photoflash of logic?' brayed the Mayor. 'I'm pretty damn sure it was this dingbat who came to me suggesting some ludicrous idea about re-naming the sun! Is that the sort of etheric funster you want to give your trousers to? Speaking sweet reason in your ear? Any organisation'll be a disgrace to Accomplice. We lead the world in chaos and bullshit.'

'Says you.'

Rudloe made a strangled sound of affront and astonishment. The rabble were getting out of hand. He switched stances in a hurried portrayal of pacific equanimity. 'Yet with due consideration my actions necessitate a rival.' He ducked afraid, an imagined rock passing his head. 'Er ... yes, well, so I welcome Mr Cyril to the Mayoral race. A few chubby children will be amused I'm sure.'

'No!' shouted Skittermite in a sandblasted voice. 'Your arrogance has caused the air to divide up into silver beetles which attack me! Brown summer blocks into my eyes! Forests carved from mahogany!'

The Mayor nodded stoutly. 'That's right, girlfriend. You people should be ashamed of yourselves! Carving trees!' He extended the last word for a minute and a half, phasing it in and out with an open face. Skittermite meanwhile was crying out like a castaway.

'Nothing connects, nothing thank you!'

In the audience, Edgy was chuffed. 'This is the best,' he gasped with hilarity, his face bright and appreciative. 'They've both gone off their nut.'

'Hey, chump.' Amy Gort stated. 'Look what we're seeing - *we are taunted on two levels.*'

'Eh?' Edgy was suddenly worried. 'No, no, they're taunting us on the double.'

'You're wrong.'

'Does anyone need any milk later?' asked Barny.

'Tranquillity is politics reversed!' screamed Skittermite.

'Hey, they don't need to be hearing that!' stammered the Mayor, sweating like a hog. 'Cigars are b-bad, throw 'em away ...'

'Fractured all,' said Skittermite with a bitter, chittering laugh. 'It's the Round One, that roiling botch of a man. Please has there ever been an atrocity to equal him? I could have been a fine demon if it weren't for him - wingspan wiping the sky as the colour of your screams shifted into autumn. What do you say about my ribcage now? Cyril? I'm Skittermite Syrinx, Pestilent Demi-Sitch! Show yourself, Round One!' And the demon began to choke with sobs. 'Won't you?' He turned and started whacking his head against the frozen clock face like a gavel.

Something gave inside the mechanism, counterweights dropping, and the big hand clicked to twelve - two doors flipped open on either side of the clockface and from each a mechanical knight scudded onto the platform, swerving to converge on the demon.

Slumped on the back of the blue one, sated, naked and happy, was Gregor.

With each chime of the clock the knights struck down at the startled demon, twenty-four wounds wedging his flesh. A confetti of his own headblood rained past his eyes.

'Crowned for loss, what am I saying? Where am I ...'

Skittermite floated from the platform into the crowd, landing flat as a cranefly.

The blood clock was in full flow, clicking smoothly.

Magenta Blaze was gaping up at Gregor. 'Now *that*,' said Barny, 'is an interesting man.'

'Well,' muttered the Mayor. 'It could have gone worse.' And he went inside.

A crack team of bored idiots wandered away. An ambulance made of glass roared up too late.

Creeping backstage like a pantaloon executioner, Prancer Diego was pensive. He walked slow across town, looking at hot pavement, oil stains in driveways and cycads spiking from drains. Entering the shaman's yard by an overgrown side door, he blunted his nose, removed the bicycle clips from his throat, and was Beltane Carom.

13

NOT BE ALRIGHT

*A cliché is like a womb - we can sleep there, hide there, be safe there. And like
the womb it must be abandoned if we are to reach full adulthood.*

'The Aspict's back on line,' Sweeney called as Dietrich Hammerwire
strode into the cavern. 'It's been an interesting few days hasn't it
Dietrich? Skittermite's burnt his bridges like a good'un. You've
referred to him as an upstart at every turn. And I've been menaced
by a clueless mound of lard. It's the last part that worries me. We
can't have just any fatso bumbling around hell cuddling the under-
fiends.'

'I don't think he actually cuddled anyone.'

'That's as may be,' said Sweeney, cheerfully dismissive. 'Those
meaningless rectangles embossed on your belly - what's it all about?'

'Belly squares. What you probably don't know is these are all the
rage on the street.'

'You don't care what you do, do you - not really? Are you wearing
an alice band?'

'I might be.'

'I'm in a good mood, I don't know why. Maybe it was the cake. A
nice thought, that. First thing I'll do when I destroy humanity's
bandwidth is eat a few of their scones and so on. There's a whole
world out there - ours to empty.'

'I'm sorry, Master, but I just don't think so. It's like holding up a
matchflame to the sun.'

'You are one for exaggeration.'

'No, you haven't seen it lately. Amateurs in chains judging the
horizon. Over-patient saints at the mercy of bureaucrats. Random
acts of lethargy. Circumstance on the rampage.'

'Here's the Aspict,' said Sweeney as it floated down and settled,
disturbing a pyramid of molars. 'Skittermite may yet surprise us.'

The Ruby cleared upon a gathering in some kind of switching
yard. A muzzle-loading cannon the size of a locomotive engine had
been wheeled along a rail from a funeral hanger. Streaked with backblow, swirling embellishments on the serrated barrel portrayed dismal encounter scenes. The Fusemaster Rod Jayrod stood near the
cannon wearing jester-diamond vestments of black and purple. 'Who
left this shiv here?' he demanded, kicking a knife away with an irri-

table stare at the assembly. Fuseheads stood in the wet daytime heat, many saddled with binoculars. The feinting palm trees made it a lovely scene.

'Dunk the year in dove paint, does that mean peace? I don't know.' Jayrod leant against the cannon, pensively sardonic. 'Anyway, here we are again. Cyril pecked out a few prayers with us. He was a strange fellow, thrown so far back upon his own resources he was usually off in the distance somewhere. During the catechism exam our gauges had indicated that he was a hopeless wreck. He was one of us, finally. And now, hi-jinks concluded, he's gloriously ordained for a blundering flight outside the mortal round. At birth we are meat in a rush - so should we be at death. Subtle today, forgotten tomorrow. We shall not forget our friend Cyril.'

From his vestments Jayrod produced a Velocitous prayerbook with a black pearl cover. He regarded the pages diffidently. 'The true round is infinity.'

The assembled fuseheads answered low by rote. 'A glimpsed understanding awkward on the edge of the air.'

'Why get all bent out of shape?'

'Through our answers run the pest of truth.'

'To the unresponsive sky volcanically delivered.'

'May he attain escape velocity.'

'With offence taken. Nostrils wild.'

'With his body we supply the sky's predation.'

'Lock and load.'

Lackeys hauled on some tarry rope - with a clank of counterbalance the cannon tipped a few degrees to the sky. The crowd recited: 'What are you going to do?'

'The only thing I can do,' read the Fusemaster. 'Fire our friend out of this here cannon.'

Two fusehead assistants marched toward the cannon mouth with a wooden casket. They placed this on the ground and looked down at the contents. 'A bat with a shell?' muttered one.

'Times have changed,' grunted the other. He picked up the body of Skittermite and dropped it down the cannon barrel like a broken umbrella.

'Alright,' said Jayrod as they stepped back. 'Let's send this freaky-assed booger.' He removed the blue touchpaper from his lapel and pushed it into the powder vent. Then he struck a match on his arse and put it to the fuse while reading from the little book. 'Look out now, look out, look out, I'm lighting the fuse. There's gunna be one hell of a bang. Run, run.'

The cannon discharged a glaring cloud of confetti, poison gas and mental splinters from which Skittermite blurred like a dart, twisting away through the blond sky.

'Look at him go. Quick, say bye.'

'Bye!' called the fuseheads, waving and peering through their binoculars.

The horizon went straight for Skittermite, snapping him up like a juicy bug.

Jayrod lit a cigarette. 'That was fucking sweet.'

In the bitter cavern, Sweeney's complicated mouthparts were spread like a starflower, an insectile gape. His complexion smoked.

'I told you,' snarled Dietrich. 'I told you that skinless wonder hadn't the bite radius for a job like this. I just plain never trusted him to start with. You're too ... *patient.*'

Sweeney locked his mouth briefly, marshalling his pride. 'Seeds following a long spine of thought, to them does it feel slow?'

'Maybe.'

'No. No, you know why we'll win? Because shadows don't have to finish. You're aware I've a cosmos of compressed monsters to redeem.'

Dietrich imagined demons swarming like leaf-cutter ants and taking a half-moon out of heaven. It felt to him like a sweet childhood dream, precocious and naive. 'You'll need them all.'

Sweeney was pensive. 'Feroce maybe, or Rammstein, what do you think?'

'The Ponce is too subtle - you need someone who'll tangle with their legs and crash them down.'

'Again with the legs. But perhaps you're right. We need an old-time bone-freezer, a shrike - Rakeman, why not? The rib ladder. *There's* one that doesn't need any frills such as antlers and so on. Yes, good old Rakeman - he'll turn a man's tissue to frozen vinegar.'

'I admit he's a freak of the old school, but -'

'Yes, why use a modally-boned demon for a world which is, as you claim, chaos anyway?'

'It's far worse than that, Your Majesty. Throw evil at Accomplice and they spread it around like fertiliser. We're ... wallpaper to them. They fired Kermit out of a *cannon.*'

'No, there's some heads too light to use for a tetherball, that's all. Flesh is the illusion of years' duration, it'll need a while to dispel. You're a pessimist in your old age, Dietrich.'

'So regret me.'

'What did you say?'

'Nothing. I'm going to my room.'

Sweeney spoke into a face antenna. 'Pull up Demon 1,656.'

An organic booth pushed from the cavern floor in a burst of steam, a form unfolding slowly from the capsule. Rakeman, a thing of belted bones, advanced through twists of sick yellow light, its head all screams.

Dietrich slouched into his chamber, which was a migraine scramble of cobalt green. Reaching under the bed, he dragged out a travel case made from a couple of ribcages. He looked through his stuff in a desultory way, collected a couple of hammers, a faded photo of he and Sweeney mirthfully roasting a farmer, and his prize possession, the very jaw of Violaine which had said 'There is a passion for conflict which requires no deception.' These he stowed in the case, which he hooked into place at the front of his armour. Then he opened the roof on to a vista of etheric turbulence and banged open his wings, ascending through cyanide skies.

Magenta Blaze had attached herself to Gregor but, loose and vented, he was as happy as a decal on a breast. He'd also picked up an idea from somewhere and pitched it to Stampede Products - Jonathan Glasses, the glasses which alter the visual effect of the sun. When challenged with the notion that this was an identical product to 'sunglasses', he stated with a knowing smile that much could be achieved with a change of name.

Edgy could believe it - the publishers had decided to call Amy's poetry book *Flowers Are Lovely*.

The only thing that still bothered Gregor was Barny running him down with the tricycle. 'Barny wouldn't ride a bike,' Edgy told him as they walked through town. 'He saw skybikes when he was young, the idea terrifies him, he's allergic.'

'Skybikes? Those phantom things?'

'Let's go over to Barny's place and set things straight, eh?'

But halfway up the gangplank sat the lion. When Edgy tried to approach, the animal let out a sound like a truck igniting. They backed up, wary.

His scalp stuffed with scrawler bugs, Noam B Turbot passed the pumps in the levy extraction shed, and entered the antique elevator. Walls of pulsing capillaries wormed upward as he sank. He strode through the silverine foyer of bleached portraits and grey decoration, and pushed through the end doors. 'Disgust be a friend,' he thought as the clammy air hit him.

'Concerning hyphen five,' the Conglomerate was saying as he entered, then the multiple reaction head perked up to his presence.

'Well, it's no less an alcoholic than Noam B Turbot.'

Turbot slipped, almost falling. The room flubbered in response.

'Yes, the floor of our game is alive. What brings you before our very select group.'

Attempting truculence, Turbot drew a shallow breath. 'For recognition. *The Cyril Manifesto*, yes, that masterpiece was mine. I'm entitled at least. Yes, a stab at your root-system, I've still got it in me.'

A new face awoke. 'Is that the speechwriter flapping his ashtray jaw?'

'He's claiming he wrote the Cyril tract.'

'As if we care.'

Turbot advanced into the heaving landscape of blubber and stretching astringent. 'You don't?'

'Well, duh. We know we didn't write it, that's all that matters. Life's an unhurried, casual darkness, Turbot. Learn it at last.'

Turbot was wretched. He looked about him at their trailing, fossicated organs. 'I've done stuff though.'

'Of course you have. And herein lies the reward - grief doubled, great designs of killing delusion, momentary wisdom swept away like lint in a hurricane. Now carry a little smile though choking, Turbot.'

'Alright, you can say what you like about me. But I'm loyal. I've come through every time.'

'An odd victory, to be always reliable.'

'At least I was wrong about all the right things. I tried, didn't I.'

'Time to lie down, Mr Turbot.'

'In the old days -' Turbot began.

'Take me as I am,' trilled the Conglomerate, swelling, and darted a sucker at Turbot's face. 'And blame me for nothing.'

Blood shot through the throbbing cable as Turbot stood rigid, justice affronted within his dying body.

Rattling, his head crumpled like a bag and puffed a cloud of dead powder. The room flushed red. Turbot fluttered, nerves firing for the last time.

The connection was broken. He tipped like a stack of old newspapers, coming apart.

Barny lounged in his tropical bunk, his arms about a sleeping Chloe Low. 'I love it here,' he whispered, and kissed her warm sugar skull.

ACCOMPLICE 3

DUMMYLAND

"Oh darling, we're really married."
"And the dog makes three."

- Bingo Violaine
Intrigues of the Yellow Palace

Wahey, I'm dead. If I hadn't been so inept, the future could have had me. Sweeney, Emperor of Cold Hell, ate my entire brain and for ever after I was like a notion on parchment, fixed and useless, the philosopher Violaine everyone quoted to save them the work of thinking. Useless except that I had shouted something about a nemesis who would cause Sweeney a lot of problems. How did I know? The end of all things throws back a shadow. Barny Juno wound up as the focus for Sweeney's paranoia. Juno was almost a simpleton and often forgot about the entire affair. If I were a whisper and not an atom trailed in ink, I'd tell him: This horizon's the merest posture of eternity. Stage blood, Barny. And he'd say he hadn't a clue what I was on about.

1

VIVA CONTRAIRE

Immortality in heaven grows mundane

In the doll forge a dozen steaming mimiques stood rigid in a row. Behind them the express fiend machine was coughing sparks to the floor, its piston knuckles shuffling like a coinwalk trick. Lacquered eyes witnessed the head of rituals, the Grand Dollimo, entering via the gifts of a scaffold. He consulted a mechanical grimoire, a hinged mandala on its cover, and looked impassively down on the slurry-floored assembly area. He muttered, perusing the checklist. 'Brass springs under cardboard skin, eyes the same colour as the facial flesh, unguessable inner life. Good.' He called out. 'Accident faucets on.'

A burst of acrid metallic smoke flumed from the gauge wall, smogging the turbine hall and blasting past the hinge babies.

Near the end of the row, Maquette woke into the flavour of wooden teeth plugs and the rigid fit of her own jaw. She felt badly jointed, squarepegged into round holes. Her skin was crummy, barnacled with sprockets. The barbed wire veins in her wrists stung, sinuating.

Methylated monks drifted by. Before her she saw pipes and foundations, vents breathing eachother's air. Large dark bugs trafficked the floorspace.

It was a simple and obvious matter to start running around, her clicking motions like surgery, and get out of this place which had given her only the aluminum winter of her head. Her little electric family were apparently dead. They didn't react as she skittered past rearing chuck jaws and mystery switches, out of the foundry and through the finishing shop in which she would never serve time. She was exploding through piled prosthetics and vestigial industralia before anyone could react.

Back on the observation platform, the Grand Dollimo was observing a number of floor lobsters with mangled legs and split shells, and a monk repeatedly counting the new frights and checking his sternum dial. The Dollimo strode to a window and watched a clattery imp with bracket ears scamper away from the process cathedral up Paid Preferential Treatment Street. 'Child,' he said, 'suffering is just another precision.'

There were no panes in the windows - the Dollimo wore a glass mask.

Finding a withered melon on the front step, Gregor gloomily considered his lifestyle. Five glad bugs on a bedspread, one disconsolate whimper and a head which was no particular shape - these were the spoils of a string of damaging episodes, the last of which had involved his molesting a civic monument. In his sub-basement bedroom irrigation pumps chilled his dreams and there wasn't enough room for time to pass. And he arose to find this sort of scornful relic, left stealthily in the early hours. Once he had stumbled upon a burnt pork chop which seemed to resemble his own face. A note which accompanied a tusked skull, reading 'Letters: where are they?' had seemed blotched with tears and led Gregor to suspect it all related to some service badly done - but beyond this he was confounded. He had wrapped the flaky head in newspaper and given it to a child in the town square. The note he had thrown in the furnace with all the other baffling trash which arrived unceasingly at the sorting office.

Though he lived below the office he longer worked there - his shot nerves and mallow shoulders now bore the weight of Deluge Trousers, Reticent Greeting Cards, Pre-burnt Diaries and Deadly Carpet Samples. The latter, impregnated with lethal effluvia and venom, was a steady seller for Stampede Door to Door Products.

Keg-shaped and plodding, he bumped into Edgy on the way out. Edgy was a stringy guy with a head like a cinder chimney. Today he turned up for work in a tropical shirt, bermuda shorts and jelly sandals. He looked up at the ripe sky. 'Ah what a beautiful day to offer you the opportunity of a lifetime Round One. What's in the sample case?'

Gregor felt he was on a rare patch of sure ground. 'A couple of new winners, as a matter of fact. The Table Chaffinch - a chaffinch which stands on the table and is otherwise unprepared to do anything. The Damaged Radiator, exactly what it sounds like. The Levity Closet, that's doing well. The Doggone Diagram, this big technical poster here - see? There's circles round the equation there. That shape in the corner I don't know what that means.'

Edgy scrutinised the baffling blueprint. 'This all you got, my friend?' He sounded concerned.

'What about this? It's a sort of jellied slug but it's got a first class mind, maybe. Because I can, I make you a present of it.'

'This is a coin, Round One. It's so long since you took one out it's shrivelled up like a navel.'

'Really? Well there's this collapsed husk I just found, I guess I could sell that. Yeah I could clean the grit off and call it Worse Than You. Whatever happens, you can compare yourself with this and say, "Well, at least I don't look like that thing." They will when they're dead and rotted, but by then they will have paid up and I'll ... why you looking at me like that?'

'Round One, this isn't a dried husk - not the way you mean. This is a drylord seed, a dormant judge. You've got to take this to a legal guy and pay for the hatching. Scratchy scribe with innards like an insect. Nostrils too close together and feelings learnt from a book. It must be about that display during the Mayor's speech.'

Gregor felt weak. 'I'm going to court? Well ... what happens?'

'Each viper takes a turn to give their own unsettling rendition of the facts. I saw your disgusting display - who else?'

'Everyone in the town.'

'That's right, I remember now - everyone. We were all stood there laughing at the Mayor and then you appeared with a funny look on your face, humping one of those statues on the town clock.'

'Don't keep explaining it to me, I know how it was.'

'In fact now that I think about it, it's just about undeniable. This spore guy's probably the only fella who wasn't there that day. But that's the beauty of these drylords, Round One - they don't have a clue what's going on in the world until they hear it in the courtroom.'

'Well, if someone can be charmed by a beanbag, I'm in with a chance.'

'Has anyone ever been charmed by a beanbag?'

'I bet they have. Certainly they have. With the beanbags they're making these days? It's a lock.'

'You're damned, Round One.'

'I know.'

'What have they done to you Round One. Look at you. You're lurching from one fulfilling success to another. Carry on like this you'll be selling one welly near the subway. Laying with only the mid-day traffic for company. Nothing learnt and new shrugs like the old from our friend Bubba here. Hey, Boo - a strange iridescent sheen on your face there, what's happening?'

Barny had wandered slowly through the heatwashed morning toward the sorting office, looking at a fun book about animals. He still didn't know that by annoying the king o'demons a while back he was the motivating force for every recent atrocity in the town. Barny passed tough, reptilian plants, callboxes raw as a baboon's ass - local calls only - and jettisoned shells of transport. The few traffic lights in Accomplice changed with the seasons, beginning green in summer, then through yellow to a lovely russet red in the autumn when, like fallen leaves, they could be ignored. 'I'm in love,' he replied.

'How d'you know?'

'I haven't got any money.'

'That why you're so thoughtful?'

'I've been tending to a woolly monkey. He was crying and I hugged him for a long time. Oh, and I brought you a book.'

Edgy browsed about in the proffered book which was called *Coping With Leopards*, with the subtitle 'It's the Most You Can Hope For'. He read aloud. '"If I've learnt one thing, it's that animals don't like going backwards. But they will approve of it in you - even stalk toward you with a snarly expression to encourage it. Yes sir, one rule for the powerful, another for us." And a quote from Violaine at the front - "Fiction is not a threat to those who know the difference." Thanks, Bubba.'

'There's a small section on panthers,' added Barny as Edgy tucked the volume away.

'Well, Gregor here's had the grey pineapple and expects to pay for the proceedings by selling Deluge Trousers and other crap that's going begging in the marketplace. Gregor, you're planting your arse on scanty soil. Think you can create a buzz on an old product, like Hootry the fruitman? You know what he did? He started referring to the fruit as 'marooned bladders', without transition or warning. Within nine days his entire market base had dried up - nobody want-ed what he had to sell. And here I am offering a golden chance.'

'I haven't heard any golden chance from you,' Gregor spat, and slap-folded the Doggone Diagram in preparation to leave.

Barny piped up. 'If you need money, Gregor, why not get it from Fang, he's a bag man.'

'He's a *bog* man,' Edgy corrected him. 'And maybe he'll join my scheme if you two won't.'

'Oh the beach bar idea?'

'No, that's a more long-term dream. But I could finance it with my notion to obtain the illegal meat of the Quadraface harpies - they live in the swamp, you eat the meat, you go invisible, you can do whatever you want, everyone'll want to buy the stuff. A reindeer doesn't know that does it?'

Gregor pushed the poster into his bag. 'That's your justification for everything isn't it Plantin? A reindeer.'

'I've never seen a reindeer,' said Barny thoughtfully and smiled, chuffed by his imaginings. 'But I'd love to. They're the only deer where males, females and calves produce antlers. They shed their antlers annually.'

'Manually?'

'Annually, Edgy. Then new antler growth in the spring and summer is nourished by a vascular covering called velvet.'

'Antlers,' Edgy mused dreamily. 'Now that's living.'

'I don't mind going to the swamp tonight, Edgy. I'm not sleeping.'

'Monkeys again, Bubba?'

'No, I keep having a terrible dream. But I've got to go to the swamp to visit the barbers. Crash Test Nureyev told me the barber knew all there is to know about bats - I may be able to get one to replace the bat I accidentally sent to heaven the other day. It's a special kind, otherwise I'd just use one of the ones we snog at the office. You ever go to the barber's, Edgy?'

'That would be admitting there's a problem. Anyway I've been scheming for weeks to get this harpy meat deal sorted - any expedition has to be planned in fly-leg detail. Glad to hear you're in, Round One.'

'I never said I was in,' Gregor blurted aghast, but Barny had begun describing his dream, immersing one and all in the involuntary imaginings of a man whose philosophy was less complex than a swiss roll.

In the dream, he was with his girlfriend Chloe Low, sitting on a rock over see-through water. The bay was as still as a mirror. They could see the Announcement Horse posing half a mile away. Then EH Hunt appeared, a rather ominous-looking huge fellow dragging a treasure chest over the cauliflower rocks. 'What's in the chest, EH Hunt?' Chloe asked.

'Perhaps a complicated jasperflower, who knows?' he smiled, winking.

'Is it?'

'Well, no,' muttered Hunt, and as always when embarrassed, he began frantically pointing out the wonders of the deep. 'Mermaid chow,' he said, 'and ours too.' Barny and Chloe looked at tinkling shrimp of thin glass, seahorses like corners of toast, a studfish pullulating across the seafloor like an ulcer and a marine mouth which moved by blurting sandy water.

'Hey Barny that's so funny,' said Chloe, and pointed out an underwater man, scar incarnate, its head a white scream, surfacing fast at them.

Barny stood quickly and found himself near the Church of Automata in easy conversation with the shaman Beltane Carom. 'Like I told your friend, there's a day between Thursday and Friday which the angels use,' said Beltane, who was now the trickster Prancer Diego. As in many dreams, the two people had become mixed together. 'Someone keeps slipping through. But that's another story.'

'Whatever this is, it's getting old.' In the dream Barny was thinking about flies and humans, and how being everywhere was not the same as having conquered.

'The truth doesn't get old, Juniper. And I don't hear you suggesting anything better. Except that stupid thing about spinning dogs.'

Nearby, workmen were pouring the foundation for a new Gubba Man. Every year a few psychologically vulnerable diggers were swallowed by ectoplasmic white holes while their colleagues laughed unharmed. Accomplice was a sun trap lidding an etheric mesh of connecting tunnels, the creepchannel. This toxic tissue formed a subterranean transit system for demons on the way to people's breakdowns.

'I don't know what you're talking about. I just want to care for the winged and stepping animals of the earth, and be happy.'

'When Sweeney's killer surfaces, you will have another sadness. Motive is another person's reason. Live on mere motive, and what makes one thing visible will hide another.' Then the figure whispered in a different voice again, 'I won't be here forever. I go on the record for the day you work it out.'

Barny looked away down the street. Some sort of shabby replica of a child ran up to shrill his face and Barny bolted awake in his hammock, staring about at the joists and rigging of ladderland, his ramshackle home. Windows painted moss-green, honeysuckle flourishing out of the floor and the lion asleep on the second deck.

*

The dream was in fact a pretty good prophecy of the mayhem programmed for later in the form of Rakeman, who was even now approaching Accomplice in search of a horizontal mirror to exit shrieking. This tumbleweed skeleton wasn't modally boned and so proceeded to the upper world almost like a worm, shuffling through unspent geology against the flow of lawyers coming the other way. One of these lawyers was Max Gaffer. Undamned but brash, he saw opportunities below and chugged downward in a scarcar he had stolen from Mike Abblatia at the gas station. The car was hardwired for tragedy, six dozen auric plug arrays birthing servitors under the hood. Its silver grey bodywork was corroding with the vomit transmission fluids of the creepchannel. Already Gaffer felt at home. Here the lies were like rain repeatedly overcoming the steady work of the windshield wipers.

He was navigating a mesh of connecting tunnels, yellow bile speedways flurrying with a million popcorn skulls, all sick and aglow. Migraine patterns rotted the windows, spinal fluid bursting into the cab and rendering the car into a sudden eruption of bugs. Gaffer swallowed hell. Lost, he was decanted from an ectoplasmic portal in the ceiling of Sweeney's cavern and landed through an expensive glass coffee table.

Stumbling awkwardly, he looked up at the titanic mantis which bent almost double to view him from above. Scallop-backed and armatured, its every movement made a ratchetting echo in the freaked cavern. Coaxial spite veins spread from its thorax to the chamber walls. The elongated skull, which was the size of a family car, opened out at the front like a Swiss army knife. 'You have an ulterior nervous system,' it rumbled. 'A lawyer, am I right?'

Gaffer stepped unsteadily out of the useless table frame. 'Max Gaffer, your majesty. Distortion's the game - I pretend it's not a luxury, or that there's such a superabundance of truth that the luxury of distortion is okay for a laugh.' He brushed the glass powder from his ruined suit, straightening his cuffs.

'Gaffer. When you contacted me through that piece of rotten meat I wasn't sure whether to see you. It's not particularly convenient.'

'Well, as the philosopher Bingo Violaine said, "Voyage ignorant, arrive surprised."'

'You begin badly, lawyer. That ambitious patsy died at my jaws. It was him prophesied that Barny Juno would be my nemesis - just to gall me in the interim. His removed looks are barely remembered except for those stupid sayings.'

'My sentiments exactly, majesty - and as a shadow of my sincerity, I've brought this chilled piece of brass, hammered into the general shape of a huge maggot.' Gaffer held the offering aloft into the yellow air pain of ghost sickness.

'Put it on your head,' Sweeney commanded.

Gaffer missed a beat. 'Ofcourse,' he said with a frown, and balanced the metal maggot carefully upon his head.

The infernal grandee leaned back a little, coaxial nerve cables swaying around him. 'Speak.'

'Well, your majesty, as you rightly guessed, I specialise in the hobbling of humanity.'

'Humanity? I call it "prattle meat".'

'The hobbling of prattle meat.' Gaffer gave a colourless laugh. 'I pretend to conceal a large sentiment behind my licence, but in fact there's only a piece of plywood and then the wall. See how false and polished I am. Unbeatable. The condition of forgiveness is always makeshift, and temporary - I do better. In fact I swindle away and Accomplice sits like a plaster pig.'

'Yes that's all very well but you're really nothing to me. The way things are at the moment, henchmen and cronies are two-a-penny. In any case I've got a plan in hand already with a classic shrike demon I've sent above.'

'Special pleading, your majesty. I work for the Mayor. He's had trouble with the simpleton Barny Juno, who I know has raised your clattering hackles in the past. I can manoeuvre the situation however you like up there, as an inside agent. In fact a strange blob-like friend of Juno's is being taken to court and I'll be prosecuting, all according to the law. Juno will be called as a witness, his blank face and shapeless kecks a shame on the town. I shall incriminate him before a judge made mostly of air.'

'Thousands of these barbed nerves work the law.' Sweeney twanged the nerve net with an auxiliary mandible. 'Your efforts are mine already.'

'The targeting is all,' Gaffer stated with due deference. 'And opportunity. The law is a collection of intimidations which stands for nothing at ground level - but within the court it poses as reality. No truth. All there is hell and negotiable.'

'Hell on earth, I know,' said Sweeney wearily, sitting back in thought. 'That was the idea, after all. Physics and fate being what they are, one place is as good as another.'

On closer examination the shell at Sweeney's back was a giant leathery chair, holding him in with fanned measures of gut. Gaffer was feeling sick with the effluvial air and raw cold electricity. He had to wrap up the pitch. 'So what's the point in succeeding solemnly?'

'You think I've lost sight of the ideal? Allowed Juno to weary me?' Gaffer let it ride.

'Allow me to limit you with congratulations,' the demon announced suddenly. 'I do happen to have a vacancy at present. The demon Feroce will show you to your quarters. Oh, first you'll have to eat this.'

An arm like a white branch anglepoised toward him, the claw at its end holding something like a black starfish the size of an angel cake. Gaffer took the crusty thing tentatively - it was as light and dry as a biscuit. 'Is that really all there is to it?' he asked. As he put it in his mouth he glimpsed the blowhole gupping at the star's centre.

'Just a core creature.'

Gaffer's throat was slit vertically all the way to his chest as the core creature went down, a vivid heart blooming on his starched shirt. Bloodvapour clouded from his mouth. The brass maggot crashed from his head. He tore at his clothes, exposing his chest as the creature shot its barbs and anchored there, the blowhole showing like a third nipple. A bony grey blade cuckooed from the hole.

'Alright?' Sweeney chirped.

A large upright dog of skin trotted over to Gaffer and began to pull him away by the arm, not letting go when the screaming lawyer fell to writhing convulsions in the frost. Dragging him, it looked ahead with eyes like the navel of an orange. 'Don't touch the underwear,' Gaffer choked, strangely comforted by the sheer mundanity of the request.

Maquette had skirted the centre of town but enough people had seen her by nightfall to give everyone the heebie-jeebies. Some shouted 'What?' and others went 'Ah!' in a high frequency. She had overturned some trash behind Snorters cafe only because it seemed the thing to do. People were in there working their munching units.

Some people seemed woolly. Some were more colourful than others. One of them danced around.

She passed around the back of what was obviously a school for chefs - there was steam and mayhem in there, and an evil more tangible than any she had encountered thus far. A group of chefs gathered amid the polished steel, the master chef presiding. 'A stringy bird'll convert them for a while, but we need something that accords with our principles. We have trapped night for years in a portable cabinet. Their mouths at last rely upon our meals. It's time for the final phase. Not yet but soon, and then there'll be no more real food.'

She hurried on, ball-joints clicking, shapes tumbling past her.

Twists of car and cacti to a calmer district. She was looking up at a green onion-domed building. In the silence she heard her own head.

2

THE POOL OF TEARS

Templates can't stand a masterpiece

Barny entered the swamp in the dead of night clinging to the roof of a strange concrete train which screamed from nowhere to nowhere - most people entered the swamp this way, leaping to safety before the ghostly machine swerved out of existence. Though he lived to care for the winged and stepping animals of the earth, Barny had killed both with one stone when he inadvertently caused the death of his parents' pet bat. Edgy advised him to visit Crash Test Nureyev for advice. Nureyev was the main man at Feeble Champ Books. 'Interested in furry winged pigs are you?'

'Bats,' Barny had told him.

'Indeed, well, I never published anything about bats. Want to hear the good news? The idea was poison to me because I associate those flapping monsters with the barber.'

There was only one barber in Accomplice. 'Out in the swamp?'

'Yes, he's got about a thousand clasped on his roof so densely they look like layered lead. I became attuned to their squeal frequency during a particularly harrowing visit.'

Crash Test Nureyev had once gone to the barber wanting a beard, and the barber nodded, agreeing silently to sit with him for the duration. They sat unmoving for forty-three days. Finally the barber roused himself, gesturing Nureyev to the chair.

'A pointed beard demands discipline from the wearer - are you equal to it?'

Had the barber asked forty-three days earlier, Nureyev would have chuffed a laugh of scorn. Yet now, haggard and starving, riven with insects, jumpy with irregular sleep, he was no longer certain of anything. Staggering into the swamp, he floated blank-faced down a waterway until it emptied hot into the sea. When he was washed up on the shore the Announcement Horse declared him an unprecedented gobshite.

Barny picked past trees twisted like chewed candy and pond-scum rich as mustard, stopping amid the nervy Rizla crackle of drag-onflies. The barber's porch was lit with a spiral lantern. The roof hung from a horizon of sausage blood and indeed a thousand bats lay upon it like composting leaves. Barny entered the shack. Like many swamp structures, the walls were fused with onion glue. In one corner was an earthenware statue of an electric fan and on the back wall a poster saying 'Tired of your abilities? Join the army.' There was a protocol to be followed in this tiny place.

'Why venture you into a quagmire writhing with predators?' asked the barber, a tall man in a false moustache and deceased suit.

'Because I dared to dream of a haircut.'

'This extraordinary admission makes us brothers. Sit you down.'

Barny faced the mirror, next to which a framed sign read: 'You pay me to oppose your preferences.'

'Would you keep it down to a low roar, sir?' the barber insisted suddenly, and began by knocking the round hand-mirror to the floor. It was against his code to acknowledge the mistake immediately, and as he danced attendance upon Barny's head, he did not see the demon Rakeman twisting up toward this perfect doorway.

Time passed, the barber making small moves and large, and releasing an occasional cry. The meagre lights sometimes guttered. Barny's face floated in the wall mirror like a cartoon moon. A water-snake entered, showed some interest, then flexed out again, leaving a helix diagram in the sawdust. The barber made a few folksy remarks. 'Anyone applying makeup in quiet grief, sir, I raise my glass.'

'Yes.'

White as a tap root, Rakeman ascended toward the etheric port-hole, the knurls of its spine spiralling around its body like a screw thread.

'Monks certainly are silent, sir.'

'Yes, they are.'

The barber pulled at a few head corners, his expressions shock-ingly arbitrary. 'Your good father, sir, was fishing nearby - I happened to notice he has the manner of hairstyle which would cause cattle to stampede.' Barny's father had a sort of huge, glowing octopus of hair which Barny had given him for his birthday. The barber apparently didn't like the idea of trying to tackle it.

'He has.'

'I think we're all done.'

Rakeman was an instant from entry when the barber plucked the mirror up and tipped the demon back into icy space.

'Dozens of nights will replace eachother before it returns to its former glory,' the barber remarked, angling the mirror around Barny's oblivious head. 'Anything else?'

Having climbed the roof, stolen a small Mariana fruitbat from the throng and slid screaming into the swamp, Barny departed the barber's neighbourhood with the man's professional curses ringing in his ears, such as 'May your love fumble in the lock' and 'Doves will attack.' Both curses would be effective - but when the doves attacked weeks later, Barny would be suffering a terrible cold, and with nothing on which to blow his nose he considered the sudden white flurry a gift from heaven, snorting into them and casting them aside.

Maquette explored the domed observatory, looking at charts of spiderwebbed skies. The tall round windows were transparent clocks pinned with a glass hour and minute hand. The whole place was inset with such technical emblems. And in a chamber at the middle of the building, she ran in on an old man in a cane armchair, who turned rotten yellow eyes upon her. She was turning to leave when he called out, 'Don't rush past me. Disobey my mouth and be devastated by the dog.' The old man indicated a cat which was relaxing nearby. 'Come here, let me grab your face.'

Maquette approached uncertainly, and the old man reached out, running his hands over her features. The cat shook its tail, producing a sound like a rattlesnake.

'So it's like *that* is it?' said the astronomer. 'Eyebrows like pinball paddles, a sort of teflon snout and a hinged flap for a mouth. Well, the last's not so unusual. Must you see a person's argument before you see through it? Yes, if there's truly something there. So I never needed my eyes much. Sit you down, child - and don't mind the dog, his bark's worse than his bite.'

The doll sat on the hard floor and looked directly up at the lenticular roof.

'I do without window certainty, ofcourse,' said the old man. 'Got some fella with a strange sort of head who helps me out here with the observations - Getty. A good assistant's rare - they just come apart in your hands really. But I see plenty. Pictures swell into my head like filling sails. Amino acid in a vase, get your imagination in there and stir. That's the golden concentration. I could drive this chair forever.' He crushed himself in a little more. 'This whole place, bricks no bigger than a sixpence. A real home has life in its walls. And I don't just mean the rats and so on. The open air means something different. Winter exchanges flowers for heavy breathing - does it advance the relationship? Nature is obstinate by moving around. Think on that, if you can with that head arrangement of yours. Clouds are the blunt end of infinity. Myself I shoot dead wood down the cash slot but it's not enough. Gaps grow together and we've got a meaning - call that culture? Their values even exist, if in a ghostly form. Ah, good years sink to the bottom of my memory.' He gave two sighs - or maybe he was breathing. Maquette had removed her eyes and was toying with the idea of offering them to him. One rolled toward the cat, who was instantly alert. Maquette quickly retrieved it, stuffing both eyes back into her face.

'I used to put the colours among the putty, I tell you,' the old man was saying. '"Toad for a shilling mister." Ho ho! Picture the scene, me panting in connection with a cab-horse. Disaster you might think, but at a penny a shot my invitations were accepted. Know what I told him? Back to the grave with you and your twelve and six! My legs, ofcourse, were smashed. Well, a cup of tea builds character in an asylum, if thrown at the right moment.'

'Thankyou sir,' said Maquette, standing.

'Off already? What, ashamed of your piping?' He called after her as she walked through some curving stone corridors. She found another room, which seemed to be a device library. Reaching on tip-toe to beckon an object from one of the shelves she caught a move-ment in the side of her eye - something angled outside the window. She got behind the door and peered in. The demon seemed to perch on creaking air, then clamped to the window frame and tucked its wings away, ducking into the room. It stepped down and was imme-diately examining a timepiece and strolling about. Its head was sil-ver and its body was folded white vinyl.

A shadow spread down from a corner and across the floor toward the silver thing. It became dense and roiled up, a dark armoured demon with a head like an industrial vise. Maquette retreated sharply, scuttling away.

The demon Dietrich Hammerwire clipped past striping dimen-sional edits, occasionally sampling the flavours of a passing band-width. A bunch of bright green squares and blue warmth caught him and sucked him down as though through the nostrils of a plughole. He tided out into the local reality, firming up.

The blade-silver Gettysburg, a demon with a head like a spike-mine, turned his platinum eyes on the new arrival.

'I heard you'd finally defected from Sweeney's repetitive realm. How are you feeling?'

'A bit gassy.'

'Well, for the moment you're pasted on this reality like a leaf on the surface of a pond. Your few possessions are hell surplus. It'll be strange for a while.'

'You know me as being of iron control,' Dietrich said.

Getty seemed amused. 'Oh I know exactly how it is - why you're here. Your reserves of evil were maxed-out. A chance of something. Honesty and conclusions, clean as nature. Anyone who studies nature knows that murder is superfluous. I speeded history once, then looked away - saw a blur of billions coming down the pike in escape from the rules.'

'Even the slightest end has impact.'

Getty was acting over-casual about this encounter. The bookshelves were racked with wallclocks, slotted in sideways - he would occasionally slide one out and turn its face forward, browsing the time, each one different. 'You think so? You don't know this world.'

'So this is your understanding of my actions is it?' Dietrich's scarred wings were hunching like shoulders. 'While in fact, what's attempted below is here perfected. Humanity can begin a season in the abstract and end it with blood in the roads. The day does not contain one hour of time that makes sense. A barcode baby falls out of the cake and no-one thinks to scream. That's the sort of thing we're dealing with. Their behaviour is chaotic. Their distortions are undirected and crude. Their rebellion against authority is no rebellion at all.'

'They see no reason to dismiss something which they never recognised in the first place. You and me, we're interbeings, smelling always of bonfire. Half the time I go undisguised, not just here caring for the blind man. We're a couple of exotics having a chat amid the mundane, so what?'

'Liberated are they? You think it's only the geology that keeps these people here? The canyon, the sea? They can't think out. EH Hunt and that shaman are the only ones who've been elsewhere and who believes them? That's why it's such an occasion when the circus comes to town.'

'And that's true too.' Getty stared at him openly. 'So regret me.'

Part of Dietrich seemed to concede - he relaxed a little, watching a random distance which was drawn across the window. 'Well, how do you suggest I occupy myself?'

Gettysburg considered. 'Discover twenty sentiments in an oak, whittling. Watch stories zigzag through town. Lobby gringo sells narcotics and knuckled root crops hulk in miniature. Remember the rest with alcoholics and you're laughing.'

'Hobbies?' Dietrich said with scorn. He turned from the window, the sky impressed on his face.

'Maybe.'

Dietrich was beginning to see how the new hell operated. This place worked like a jigsaw. Nothing would be a whole pain again.

Barny pushed through a thicket of grandmothers and approached his parents' shack, entering through a side window. The canary cage which had housed the fruitbat was empty - only a sad fragment of apple lay on the papered floor. He handed the new bat into the cage and walked quietly out to the porch. His father was sat there on a rocking chair, the massive cilia of his hair phosphorescing the area. 'Well, look what the bat dragged in,' said the old man. He stated in no more than five words what he hoped for Barny in the future, and Barny asked after his health. 'Oh I shan't complain - though I've been married for years, I'm determined to remain optimistic no matter what. You're still seeing Chloe Low?'

'Yes, father.'

'Long legs are short term. And don't call me that. As Violaine said, "Things are as bad as our short time alive will allow." And the eclipse is coming.'

'I was telling the leopard about that.'

'The leopard. Listens does he.'

'Well, yes. While doing other things.'

'Like what.'

'Well, pouncing. Chewing, you know, that sort of thing.'

'Chewing,' said Pa Juno with thin contempt. 'I remember the last eclipse - your mother stopped talking a while. And there was a hell of a storm. Birds were liquidized in the air.'

'I would have screamed.'

'So would I but there wasn't time. A friend of mine, Tommy Franks, started going bonkers in the head. Threatened him but he thought I was joking. No imagination, that one. So the future's a blank for him anyway, why should he care if I conk him on the face a few times with a timber? That was my reasoning at the time. Before I could act a moose came a-bellowing out of the forest, rammed him with its antlers and ploughed him through a load-bearing wall. That brought him down a peg or two. The headstone said: "Here lies Tommy Franks, acquainted with death but never previously to this extent." But look, all explanations are hopeless.'

'It wasn't a reindeer?'

'Reindeer? In my whole life I haven't seen a single one. Your mother thought so too. I told her five times - which was alot in those days - "That was no reindeer." I'm a little tired of hearing about it.' And he started coughing.

Barny was about to reveal the kind act which he hoped would compensate for the bat incident and the perhaps forgotten matter of the alligator, when Pa Juno piped up again. 'I bet the Mayor'll use the eclipse as another excuse to spend money on himself - money they could have spent on mending the flyover and clearing the sloths off of there. Even the stones are rotten, it's a crying shame. What do you do to help the community, boy?'

'I won the Deadly Snake Contest with my viper Misses Kennedy,' Barny told him proudly. 'I was up against Tamale Wired For Sound and Tony Fleet's Rubber Hose.'

Pa Juno stared at him, momentarily speechless.

'I suppose you know there are no more vases in the whole of Accomplice because of you and that snake of yours? Get rid of the reptile or I'll take it by the tail and crack it like a whip so as its head flies off into the grass. Hey, Ethel,' he called, 'do you hear what your son's about now?'

At that moment Barny's mother emerged from the shack, limping with grief. She was wailing 'Dead and eaten by a furry winged pig' and then weeping 'Our brittle friend is gone' or something like that, and Pa Juno stood to get the facts from her. It seemed that Barny's replacement bat had eaten Lovely Ramone, an exotic katydid which had the camouflage ability to resemble a fragment of apple. The pet bug had been a balm to their previous grief and now Barny had inflicted yet another unprovoked cruelty upon the household. 'Your son belongs in a p-p-paddock,' his mother sobbed, mortified.

Pa Juno held fast to his wife, glaring in affronted ferment at the whey-faced and retreating Barny. 'Get away from here, disaster boy - back to that menagerie of yours. Back to your hill station! You're no son of mine!'

Fondling one of his auxiliary chins, Mayor Rudloe poised on a wooden horse for a portrait. This moment would be fun if twenty kingdoms were mine, he thought. He was trying to look proud but didn't really know anything about it. Max Gaffer had recommended Undo Cakewalk as a fine painter - Undo in fact was known to have emulsioned the wall of a couple of sheds and was meant to be painting GI Bill's house right now, so not only was he due to disappoint the Mayor but to get smashed to the floor by GI Bill. The portrait thus far resembled that of a charred thermostat smothered in onions. Mayor Rudloe was giving the man the standard speech he reserved for employees. 'If you were more emotionally intelligent you'd have better tools to pretend you want to be here and I, as the fella who explained this to you, would be embedded from the get-go as a benign authority -' Max Gaffer entered the office. 'What is it Max?'

Gaffer was uncomfortable, his bones still howling with cold electricity, the yellowed frost of hell crusted on his guts. There was grit in the collars of his eye-sockets. He moved in a chemical pain. He was confounded that normality could feel exactly like this, a devil's hand in your pocket.

'Well, what is it? Speak up man! You been beaten up again?' The Mayor broke his stance, frowning at Gaffer's bloody shirt.

Gaffer halted startled an instant at Cakewalk's canvas, then pulled himself together.

'Eh? Oh that's it exactly sir, no fooling you - by a gang of screaming children, their gills venting scarlet. Said gills were everything, and tried to cut me some with a fast knife.'

'Those bastards. One day the technology will be in place to understand what they're on about. Pack up for now, boy,' he waved dismissively at the painter, 'my head'll be roughly the same shape when you return.'

Cakewalk dragged the canvas stand through floor lobsters scattered here and there like burst telephones, and closed the door behind him.

'We need to discuss the matter of public celebration around the eclipse, sir.'

'Celebration - bah!' The Mayor slowly dismounted, stepping directly onto a carapace which burst with a loud report. 'Oh yes they show the bit when everyone throws their hats in the air but not the mumbling, scuffing business of sorting ownership afterwards.'

Gaffer handed him a folder. 'I've been drawing up guidelines on exactly how much strutting is acceptable.'

'The fuseheads won't like it,' said the Mayor, sitting down to examine the document. 'They've got that ritual, the strutting procedures.'

'Well there's always some special interest group isn't there.'

'It says here "I take up the pewter sword of the blag". What's that about? And why organise a special event? What's the racket in an embrace? I get repeated and ringing endorsements for my reign of terror. My unassailable office allows me to speak modestly. The distribution of co-operative morons is consistent across the district. Acquiescence is faster than we can handle these days. I think you'll find democracy is more than enough for servants.'

'Unbeatable, sir. But you're forgetting that certainty, along with a mansion, is a signal to the general herd that your right to life doesn't apply.'

'You mean they'll hate me and then kill?'

'They may do both simultaneously. Right process wrong smile; these matters are delicate. And in cases of emergency, our robbing of the citizenry cannot be held up by the matter of their consent. Better to pre-empt such bloody violence.'

'They had a roaring good time with the rioters' pageant.'

'Pageant? That was a riot, sir.'

'Yes. So what must I secrete in the midst of these people to make them respond any more?'

'Well there's a simple way to get a million feet beating their way to your face.'

'Ofcourse - millipedes, a whole sack of 'em! Max, you're a genius.'

Gaffer coughed politely. 'A festival of Accomplice culture, sir. Music, drama, like that, by and for the people. Hold it in the Scar Garden, surrounded by statues of the populace. It'll point up the bland as positive, waste people's energy and soften the tone. Sentiment is ignorant of history. And nothing lasts longer than the effects of unkindness. Time some conventional revelations for next year and you're laughing, lit from below.'

'You mordantly cynical young hound,' chuckled the Mayor thoughtfully. 'How did a monster like you come to be in the world?'

'By the time I was aware of anything the whole affair had been arranged.'

'That's grand. Well, a cultural fair. Buffoons and the stink of failure. Bastards farther than the eye can see. And to the finest exhibitor I'll award a bound edition of my collected speeches.'

As speechgiver, raconteur and sudden bellower from windows the Mayor's oeuvre contained a good many classics including 'I Serve You Though You Sicken Me', 'Look at the State of You', 'This Sea of Gawking Faces' and the more mature, resigned tone of 'I Realise I'm Stranded Here'. Among policy speeches were 'I Will Destroy All Other Candidates', 'Burn, You Mother' and the hardline 'I Will Make It More Expensive', as well as the sympathy bid 'I Kick Snails Away But They Keep on Coming' during which Rudloe collapsed into quiet tears. 'Hello, Mate' and 'You Will Become Dust' played well both in their separate forms and as the combination barnstormer 'Hello, Mate - You Will Become Dust.' Other philosophical and contemplative monologues were 'Bang - Sorrow!', 'Am I Really So Chubby?' and 'My Thirteen Thousand Misgivings', an epic diatribe about everyone he remembered seeing or meeting. His personal favourites were the boastful 'Trousers Won't Contain It', the pugnacious 'Yes, This Is My Eleventh Corned Beef Sandwich', the truculent 'Lurk Here, Lurk There, You Champion Bastards' and the knockabout nonsense of 'Arly Barley Fell Me Where I Stand'. He even displayed some humour in the safety talks 'Head - Don't Travel Without One!' and 'Thank God For Chainmail', and the left cheek of his arse in 'Get a Load of This'.

'The other matter concerns a trial in which I'm taking part. That spudlike thing who had sex with a statue during your "You Want a Piece of Me?" speech - a friend of Barny Juno. Ofcourse, you'll want me to completely absolve Juno of any complicity during the case.'

'Eh, what's this? Who?'

'Barny Juno who is ofcourse always beyond reproach.'

'Juno? Beyond? Damn it isn't this the same bastard who held a funeral for a lizard and dropped his trousers during the eulogy?'

'That's him.'

'Didn't think twice about coming in here dressed as an ape. Released a croc in a crowded theatre. Threw a death-adder in the air during my "You Aimless Wonders" speech.'

'Has eight hundred eels in his garden,' Gaffer added, looking thoughtful and reluctant - he was carefully and visibly conceding to the Mayor's view. 'And it was a grizzly he dressed as, when he came in here.'

'Dressed as an ape in here and rode a lion into the shelter, wrecking our attempt to sell these poison insects to the poor as food.' And the Mayor kicked at one of the huge carpet bugs, merely snapping an antenna like an asparagus spear. 'He's probably in charge of that wooden midget everyone's seeing.'

'Wooden midget?'

'Where the hell have you been, Max? There's a toddling mechanical doll putting the frighteners on one and all. It clicked its rigid head against the window at Snorters cafe apparently.'

'Ofcourse,' said Gaffer, thinking instantly of the Church of Automata. 'Yes, it's got Juno written all over it.'

'Really? Then the trial's the perfect opportunity to have Juno executed as an intolerable nuisance. As Bingo Violaine said, "Activity is often wastefully over-wrought - for instance, only one small lesson can be learnt from an avalanche."'

'Outstanding, sir,' Gaffer nodded, and on the floor around him a number of blurs appeared like lens-faults, drying into intricate glass. The forms filled out to solid black and red, ratcheting their many legs. A dozen new floor lobsters had swelled to life, the visible ticks of corruption.

3

CHAPTERHOUSE

Any good insolence accommodates whole universes

Conspicuous and powerless, Gregor had stood on a ledge apparently for fun. He maybe deserved all this walking and walking through the town on the way to a grim appointment with a preserved man. Veering aside into the cakeworks, he was halted by the proprietor.

'Door admission amigo,' said the man sadly. He had a drooping beard where his moustache should have been.

'Adds up to nothing,' Gregor improvised nervously, and the man gestured to the bounty of his store. Gregor selected a large morgan cake. 'I could spend a lot of time eating this.'

The baker wrapped the merchandise. 'Enjoy it senor. I wish I was in your place, and young.'

Gregor left the store. That night the baker would write in his journal: '*I was indifferent as to whether he should survive the encounter. There were certain decorations on the cake. If he failed to see the beauty in this arrangement, that is his problem unto eternity.*'

Gregor trolled on, holding in one hand the bagged cake and in the other a grey husk the size of a pineapple - the drylord seed. As he entered the offices of De'ath & Destruction, ancient automated needles plunged into his arms, halting him in pain and drawing fluids from his body. It was like a red levy extraction except that the fluid seemed to be water, not blood. The needles retracted into the doorframe and he proceeded, feeling dry and dead tired.

'You're a great man for the statues I hear,' said a beetle-like man rattling in the trouble of his cases. Worn-out citations on the gloomwall were the only bit of flash in this twilight world of legal stationery. Even the floor lobsters were sluggish and enervated, some mere husks. 'I've been selected to witness your blistering defeat at trial.'

'Aren't you defending me?'

'Ofcourse - I was using legal terminology. De'ath's the name. That's the seed is it.' De'ath took the drylord seed from Gregor and carried it with a sort of brisk reverence to a pale wooden cabinet which resembled an upright coffin. Opening this, he placed the papery spore on an upper shelf. He closed the door and turned back to Gregor. 'Well now - what else have you got there? Oh dear, I can't evaluate a cake like this. Either eat it all now or put it in the floor cupboard over there, out of my sight.' As Gregor did so, De'ath sat on the edge of a desk, one of the 'normal fella techniques' he had learnt at desiccation college, and glanced at a file. 'The courthouse is grown from boneseed, as you know, and has to be grown anew for each new case. The cornerstone is formed by a piece of thigh-bone removed from the innocent party. You'll have to go see a surgeon - here's a note for Dr Perfect, you know him?'

'He's the one who told me I was some sort of walking potato.'

'That's the one - he's got an entirely visible brain. Don't mention it to him, he's sensitive about the old noggin. In the past fiends have sprung from his study, breaking through heavy crates and tumbling furiously into a pond. Unexpected even for a famous cynic. These are the fluids we removed at our front door, by the way, already sealed in plastic, you see?' The lawyer tossed the laminated block into the bin.

'How long will the court take to grow?'

'Eight months, a year, two years.'

'I can't wait two years for justice.'

De'ath went into a fit of hacking laughter. 'You'll wait forever for that, Round One. But the court may take a couple of years. It all starts with the principle that the facts of the case can be discovered only by the utmost severity, and so this severity will instead be directed toward you yourself. Expect an ambush of embarrassments and urgent disgust. Your fiasco of a face won't help.'

'According to Edgy my face is shaped like a cloud.'

'Exactly, so people see whatever they want in it - and in this case it'll be horror and perversion.' De'ath carked with laughter, his left cheek ripping to release a spuff of colourless dust.

BB Henrietta, a strong blond whose head resembled an exploded sack of flour, worked in the sorting office with Edgy. When she heard about Barny's weird dream, she began telling one and all it was balls-out obvious she should base a play on it for the Miasma of Culture the Mayor had announced. BB was the one for amateur dramatics and had last year put on a thing called *Standing Brick in Hand, Rain* in which lank worms were blown at the audience out of a tennis server while GI Bill lumpenly recited the Violaine monologue which began: 'The ashes of my club may choke you, baffling the battle record' and ended with the words 'You are super-wrong!' being repeated fifty times.

BB Henrietta itemised her new plan in Snorter's cafe and when Edgy's girlfriend Amy Gort declared herself in to write the project,

Edgy began juddering violently and holding on to a stranger's face for support. Amy's last written effort had gone like this:

> *troubled protocol,*
> *rain and wet,*
> *field botanists screaming,*
> *'I am slung over a branch.'*

He was determined, this time, to prevent it. 'Amy,' he said raggedly. 'Darling? Leave it out. My little chicksands? Leave it out, I ...'

A caterwauling interrupted his efforts, echoing through the streets outside, and he found he could protest no more.

It was some days before the facts were established. The trickster Prancer Diego had caused bloody havoc in the Square by releasing a parrot directly into a gran's face. The traumatised old woman had run amok, climbing a tower and hurling years of stored abuse upon the town. Condensed and purified over time, her scorn was so meticulous it had caused everyone alive to black out for forty minutes.

In the observatory the artificial child Maquette returned to the central chamber to find the old astronomer slumped aside in his chair, and the cat simply laying nearby. In fright and confusion she ran from the domed building. Everything was silent but for the wind and the distant hiss of the sea. She toddled down the lane and through a gate into a small field of redgrass and parked cows. Beyond this was an area of rusted greens and planted heads which eyed her silently as she passed. A man in a woollen hat was sitting against the wall of a brown shed and Maquette stood looking at him until he woke up and squinted at her.

As for the old gran, she was left on the tower ledge to desiccate, remaining there like the shuffled husk of an insect. To point out the corpse would have been to remind one and all of the shameful incident, so it was ignored even when it rustled in the breeze.

'When a cold glass child steams completed in the slamming powerhouse, we give our creation the respect it deserves,' stated the Grand Dollimo. Wearing a monochrome suit, city bowler and glass mask, he faced Gaffer across the mechanical desk. 'Since Celadon, the first doll struck in our forges, was a mere statuette in a fiery womb, we have corresponded cosmic to the trouble engineer. The mannequinade are a stillborn sisterhood and all the scarier for it.' His eyes moved behind the mask like those of a reptile behind its nictitating membrane.

Gaffer wasn't about to argue - the Dollimo had given him a short tour of the process cathedral, pointing out junk tracks and scaffolding. Dolls dragged around like cockroaches as the masked man rifled through skull drawers, removing punnets of cracked glass eyes and implements in scratched and studded steel. 'This artefact hand is for collectors only. The new dolls leave the mouth out of the loop, their hearts scream direct. Look at this torso, full of hairpins, stale rubberbands and seventies dust. This one's got a vocabulary - from fiction. And this head's built round an old human skull.'

'It's a bit flaky,' Gaffer had ventured.

'An experiment. Cross the transfusion factory here, watch your step - this is as busy as the algorithm deanery gets but the monks' work is vital.'

All had a patina of iron dust and dead perfume. And now in the office, Gaffer was hard-put to gather his pitch. 'I finally surpass the dead in social satisfaction. What a delightful tour. Carbon scoring everywhere. And, er ... I share your concern with your little latch-knee kid.'

'Maquette. An empty force child - clock logic keeps her aglow, mayhem in her lobes.' The Dollimo seemed to be attempting a dismissive tone to render the content utterly banal. 'Yes, her brain is a calamity manufactured using oxygen-free copper.'

'Indeed?' Gaffer forced a meaningless smile. 'Well, over at Rudloe Manor ... the Mayor shouldn't be losing sleep over a toy-sized fright. No-one should, but the Mayor, there's the Miasma of Culture to organise, and so on ...'

'The Mayor is not our concern.'

'Mayor Rudloe is corrupt so you don't have to be.'

'In that, Mayor Rudloe is presumptuous.'

'Should we have reason to doubt your loyalty?'

The Dollimo's expression shifted like a fish in murky water. 'I've no reason to care.'

'Be that as it may, there's a theory that your church presents a robotic front to avoid the red levy. Bloodless and thus nothing to give.'

'Our position is a matter of record, Mr Gaffer. No regrets and a soldered coffin. What is a mask when nothing is behind it?'

'The Cannonites -'

'The Powderhouse is a mere crybaby temple, their inordinate revelry an evasion. A break in our church is every loser's dream.'

Gaffer gestured to a NO ENTRY door which led from the office. 'You have secrets. Maybe this doll knows a few. In any case we can't have distorted tin children running about the place. Now in the Mayor's office we see this as an opportunity for a two-for-one. We've reason to believe your escapee is intending to liaise with Barny Juno, a notorious mooncalf.'

'Why.'

'Juno lives to care for the winged and stepping animals of the earth. The girl's full of gears and he wishes to protect her. What could be more natural? We could pool our resources in the pesky chore of snaring this cocky little replica, while silencing Juno into the bargain.'

'We have no argument with this simpleton Juno.'

'Oh, a stranger's just an enemy you haven't made yet. No-one would pretend you were strangling anything other than a deserving bastard. Deny the doll's your work. I could see it wasn't brought in by anyone else, by giving the job to the Brigade.'

'If there's any strangling to be done, it'll be done by this gentleman,' stated the Dollimo. He pressed a copper button on the desk and the whole deal jawed open like a trash compactor. A weird sentry elevated out of the mechanism and stepped aside; the teeth of the door clicked shut. This thing was a man of red wax, its head seamed like a football. 'Distaff Plastique, my lethal chaperone and bloodshed assistant.'

'Out ... outstanding,' Gaffer gargled.

'Distaff's only got one ingredient. He's skin stretched over a pulse.'

Gaffer looked at Distaff's vinyl face. The mask paid no attention to him.

'Now,' said the Grand Dollimo, 'we influence the dead hand of the voter. And you? Lost in admiration for the brilliance of your own underwear, you might forget every promise you ever made.'

'Me? I distribute the situation to benefit all.'

The Grand Dollimo shunted open a drawer and removed a rivetted metal mask. He smacked it down on the desk. 'This is the Iron Smile. It forces the wearer's face into a smile no matter how unhappy he is. It is screwed directly into the face, through skin and into the skullwall.'

'A threat?'

'A bargain.'

Putting pills on string for re-use like a teabag, Doctor Perfect sensed his patients, a dry death rattle beyond his door. He went to look - an endomorphic idiot was sat in the time lounge, stumped by a kiddie puzzle. 'The square hole shouldn't be that intriguing, laddie.'

Gregor looked up without comprehension. He was feeling worn, having inherited the hyperactive Magenta Blaze from Barny. She had credited him with seduction and he was disconsolate. She even let it slide when he told her about Nap Chickens, the squabbling fowl he thought he heard when on the edge of sleep or snoozing fitfully in the daytime. He had decided to set up a camera to get the phenomenon on film. And now here was the Doctor with his exposed brain and all. It was a man's world alright.

The Doctor's bare skull tackle was grubbier than ever, rinds of dirty fat hanging off like ravellings from a hat, and the flies were a busy cloud.

The surgery was situated underground and cool rootwater fell from the ceiling, pulping documents and staining furniture. Gregor upset a tray of organ forks as he followed Perfect inside. 'That's right, larva boy,' Perfect muttered. 'Wreck my life. I've been inquiring after the printed gouge records since they told me. "Riding a public monument" wasn't it? I heard all about it - who didn't, after all? This insanity of yours is a model of its kind. Anyway, legal cornerstones are a rare treat for me. Some say the prosecution of victimless crimes like yours leaves the structure weak. We'll see, won't we?'

Gregor looked at the smashed anatomy angel on the back wall and the two crushed cars which served as dissecting tables. 'What's that?' asked Gregor, pointing to the object on the second vehicle. It looked like a mess of exploded lard.

'I've been dissecting a Gubba Man.'

Gregor gibbered - Gubba Men were statue-like figures which dotted the town and grabbed you if you went to them for help. Once grabbed it was almost impossible to disentangle yourself from these officially-appointed sentinels - starvation and lack of progress would follow.

'Have a look, while I prepare. Glance through this surgical lens, it'll make it worse. Illness stylized, that's the aim.'

Gregor looked through the dish-like magnifying glass - it was like looking into a dish of milk.

'It's something like solid scar tissue,' said Doctor Perfect as he pulled on some bloody scrubs. 'Or cheesed milk.' He looked over Gregor's shoulder. 'Ah, the heart, king of veins. Notice the total lack of characteristics. I name the more crucial flesh and damn the rest for wasting my time. In a sense this is the perfect control subject. Anyway, laddie, it's time for your surgery. A few people organise a set of spare bones for this sort of thing - you haven't thought that far ahead I suppose?'

I don't have any, thought Gregor. *Why didn't I think of spare bones? What a dope!*

'Alright, get up on the car. A lazy muscle is a watery muscle. It's annoying and probably illegal. There you go. It's good that you're wearing those stupid shorts, less work for me. Watch the nerve screen up there. Let me see ... Operation 40, I think.'

Gregor lay back on the thundery roof and stared up at a suspended glass bowl which was veined like an eye. He tried making conversation. 'Ever met Karloff Velocet, Doc? Got a problem similar to yours.'

'Problem?'

'But worse - it's all stuffed in his hat.'

'I have no problem, except when an occasional experiment goes wrong.'

'How can it go wrong if it's an experiment?'

'Be quiet now. I'm making the incision and flaying bare your upper leg.'

On the screen, skin opened like a rose. Gregor was shot through with a chemical pain.

'Screaming in a patient is to be expected,' said Doctor Perfect. 'Surgery done gingerly is mere infatuation.'

Gregor stopped shrieking long enough to see bones amid the blood like drowned architecture.

'Red-and-white-nuggets, red-and-white-nuggets, what to do? Eeny-meeny-miny-mo. I'll just scrape the cartilage out of there - you don't need that.'

'Are you ... sure?' asked Gregor. His leg was coming unglued.

'I open the people but death claims their innards.' Doctor Perfect scraped away as though buttering toast. 'The extraction's a simple matter of torque. I ...' Perfect levelled a heavy wrench into the wound.

Gregor woke up on a wooden bench, a thermometer in his mouth. He sat up and found a plastic bowl on the floor. In it was something like a big lump of slimy china. He looked at his leg. There was no bandage - it seemed to have already healed over. The Doctor appeared. 'What happened to the hole?' Gregor asked him.

'I plugged it with Gubba Man stuff,' said the Doctor. 'Just an experiment. Saves having to embroider the patients.'

Gregor took the thermometer from his mouth. It depicted a scarlet skeleton.

4

BLOOD FROM A STONE

Long accidents rub your face in it

Barny was with his girlfriend Chloe Low, sitting on a rock over see-through water. The bay was as still as a mirror. They could see the Announcement Horse posing half a mile away. Barny looked down at seahorses like corners of toast and a studfish pullulating across the seafloor like an ulcer.

Chloe turned to him, her short black hair flicking a bit in the breeze. 'BB Henrietta told me about this play of hers - I don't like the idea of our lives being splashed all over the stage, Barny.'

'It's not about us - it's a dream I had. We were sitting next to the sea and something leapt out at us. Then I talked to the shaman about it.'

'Did I ever tell you about Ong Jahbulon?' Chloe said. Every week she told Barny a story connected with stuff in her father's curio museum - she spent her time trailing about through those cata-combs, poring over stored storms, Zeto lights and ampules of com-bustible moth dust. There were severed doors in the basement, died and dried like picked skin. And now that she had someone to tell, it had become a fierce habit. 'There's a diary of his dreams in the Juice Museum. Everything he dreamed came true, and he was horrified by the objective results of his nightmares. He became resolved to stay awake, and set out to find stuff that would hold his interest. But society being what it is, the most recent interesting event was the appearance of a giant hernia in the local aqueduct, as a result of one of his dreams.'

Barny's eyes followed a marine mouth which moved by blurting sandy water - then spotted something like a starved white tree float-ing toward the surface.

'So Jahbulon allowed himself an occasional dream to give him something interesting enough to keep awake. But when he did dream, it was always about the real results of his dreams - and so the dreams became inbred. Can you guess what happened next?'

Barny realised the thing was an underwater man, scar incarnate, its head a white scream, surfacing fast at them. He was just begin-ning to holler when the mirrored surface of the water exploded in white sparks, the spectral man shattering as a small fish flew out and over their heads. Behind them, EH Hunt reeled in the capering creature, laughing fit to burst. 'Finally a shorethump of rest eh fishy? Golden seafood, I love it. Eels are eels but so what, bite the head off. There's seabass out there, and eleven dolphins. Seaweed too, the entrails of the sea.' He was already cooking it, spinning it on a spit so fast it blurred. 'The narwhal has no dorsal fin,' he shouted, bellowing with hilarity.

'Fish aren't edible, Mr Hunt,' said Barny.

'Can't I, boy?' Hunt took the fish and bit into it. '*Can't I?*'

Chloe calmed Barny as they wandered toward the town. 'He's right, Barny - the chefs don't like to admit it, but pasta hasn't always been the staple diet for humans. In fact, did I ever tell you about Widey Dantooey? There's a calcium picture of him in the Juice Museum. He studied fish and discovered they make themselves the same density as their surroundings by means of a swim bladder. So he ate hundreds of swim bladders, hoping that he'd be able to hover through the air. But he only made himself the same density as water, and when the chefs tried to drown him -'

'What the hell's that?' Barny asked as they passed the Ultimatum Restaurant - he was pointing at Gregor, who was walking along with a nugget of bloody bone.

'From my leg. I'm going to the courthouse lot, want to come?' asked Gregor dismally. They followed him to the grey hardpan of the courthouse lot. Nothing grew here but the courthouse - not even pale weeds. It was a little deliberate desert. All three of them began to feel heavy and oppressed. Gregor pushed the chunk of bone into a cement sinkhole in the North-East corner. 'Let's get out of here. I want to see what state my statue's in after that operation.'

'Did I ever tell you about Korova Laddfrith?' said Chloe, feeling antsy and backed up. She had to finish a story. They crossed the square, dodging herds of flappy swine as she told them about it. 'There's a blueprint baby of his in the Juice Museum. You know everyone in Accomplice has a statue in Scardummy Garden. Even animals and demons. And if anyone dies, their statue crumbles and disappears. But there was one time when someone died but still had a statue in the Garden. Laddfrith was a rust artist who was always enraged by the critics' inability to understand that his iron sculptures changed and improved with age. He finally constructed a strange sculpture in the Garden and invited the dullest critic to see it, intending to kill him on arrival. He could have smashed the critic's statue, but the principle of statucide would have meant he himself would also die.'

The three entered the white and green statue garden. Here stones were born hot in the weeds and grew amid panama crows and east-ergrass. Many of the statues were decked with clothes and decoration, some topped with soft hats. Gregor's, when they found it, more than anything resembled a giant spud. Its real-life double gazed upon it with a thoughtful expression. Apparently no item of his own body was too commonplace to consume Gregor's interest.

'The rust sculpture was a sort of frame scorpion,' Chloe continued, 'and since this creature had been built on site and cemented into the soil of the Garden, it took form in the community and immediately scampered to find Laddfrith. The sculptor tried to fend it off with a mixer of industrial cement. When the critic showed up, he saw Laddfrith holding the mixer over his head and being set upon by the iron scorpion, tipping the cement over himself. A few minutes later, Laddfrith's statue crumbled. But the cement had hardened on the real Laddfrith and, to this day ...'

Gregor suddenly leapt on to his statue and started humping up and down like there was no tomorrow.

'Wha ...?' Chloe had put up with a lot since stepping out with Barny, nearly every day being pecked by an adder or socked in the nose by a chimp. On one occasion a duckbilled platypus had slapped her senseless with his tail. But this potato man, abusing himself as no-one had ever self-abused before while staring glazedly into the middle-distance? 'Barny, it's bad enough that you're ignoring me in favour of the winged and stepping animals of the earth but these friends of yours? Look at Gregor. Why's he doing this?'

At that moment Edgy loped into the Garden looking for Gregor, and smirked to see the Round One's antics. 'I see Gregor's almost weightless, nettlesome brain is running wild. Who says there are no more heroes, eh?'

'You see?' Chloe continued urgently. 'Edgy's head, that exploded cheroot again? He's probably having a good laugh about it now.'

'He's right here,' said Barny, 'he's not laughing.'

'Oh I don't know what I'm saying, out of the way -' And she got all choked up, storming off.

Gregor finally seemed to decide that he had done all that was required of him, and dazedly dismounted.

They stood in amber sunlight, not looking at eachother for a while. A vine was growing against a south-facing bastard. A bug like a belt buckle stop-started across the flagstones.

'She was right about your head, Edgy.'

'My face is stringy, I'm a boy.'

'Feast your perishable eyes,' said Sweeney, viewing the scene as reflected in the bloodshot deeps of the Ruby Aspict. 'It's starting to work. Rakeman's influence, even in nightmare. That's how demons used to work - spoke into blood to influence. Juno's powers are fracturing.'

Max Gaffer stood in the chill voltage, shifts in dread evaporating and reforming as the king corpuscle slowly turned. 'Why not just pound a coffin together and get rid of the bastard. I spoke to the Dollimo, a head of one of the church cartels - he's charged some sort of automatic man to deal with all the wearisome business of murder.'

'We'll be more thorough than that - Rakeman'll bring him down here, through the nearest mirror. Its head's all ring muscle, you see.'

'I don't quite believe in the child-man Barny Juno being formidable in any way.'

'Ofcourse you don't. He wears bewilderment as others might wear armour. You've come quite late to this caper. Seeing matters from both of two opposing sides can be limiting in ways you may not appreciate. Your predecessor, Dietrich Hammerwire, yay high, anvil for a head - he took me for all I was worth and then defected above. Why? To bother only one direction at a time? To eat the biscuits available up there?' The thought seemed to occupy the ivory demon too fully for him to continue. The chitin scaffold of his body towered against glaring phosphorus. 'Anyway it's madness to do the same thing over and over and expect a different result.'

'Unless you account for changes in external circumstances.'

'Shut up - get out of here. And don't upset the flesh valence in your chest - it'll want out. How is it, by the way?'

'It hurts like a cast-iron bitch, to be frank.'

'Good, good. Off you go.'

Edgy and Gregor walked down Ken Blurn's a Coper Street. 'I've got everything we need for the swamp expedition, Round One. Are you aware again of what's going on around you? Hear what I'm saying? I went to the Shop of a Thousand Spiders and covered every eventuality, including your bloody death. I got a spirit knife of white glass, a benthic brace, a bottle of bone, a cathay claw, a cornercage, an october switch for making visible what is invisible and four betsy lamps for attracting ghosts and irreversible trouble. Those harpies won't know what hit 'em. As Violaine said, "Yield to doubt and glimpse a world of possibilities." Anyway I paid the goat and nearly got out of there before that Spooky Staring Boy said anything, but he collared me at the door.'

'What did the boy say?' asked Gregor raggedly.

'"Black eggs in the sleeper."'

'What did you get in case of my bloody death?'
'Raisins.'
'Huh.'
'So it's on for tonight - we're catching the ether express.'

5

THE MAN WITH THE VEGETABLE HEAD

Voters play with the moment

'Sorry I couldn't see you earlier Mr Lucent - I was balls-deep in work.' King Verbal stood briskly from behind his desk and strode to shake the chef's hand - he led Quandia Lucent to a plush seat and returned happily to his own, backlit by a delicate fishbone window. 'Yes, I've seen you at the Ultimatum Restaurant and wanted to chat with you a while - we have the same philosophy, I believe.' He indicated an ornamental bone fireplace which flared to the ceiling, the company motto pressed into its polished face: 'Garbage at crippling prices.'

'We cut convoluted meat into merchandise,' the chef conceded.

'Your candour does you credit.' He inspected Lucent with easy curiosity. 'You run the chef school too, don't you?'

'I teach others how to take a chicken and cuff off its head.'

'You mean "cut" off its head.'

'I know what I mean.'

'Well, what can I do for you Mr Lucent?'

'You probably know we take our orders from an overgrown sea-horse in a cupboard, which lives on a diet of desiccate packets from appliance packaging.'

'I'd heard as much, as rumour.'

'I'm happy to confirm it - within these walls.'

'I understand.'

'We are aiming for one hundred percent pasta consumption within two years. In truth, we're almost there. Customers exist to serve us, as you know. They can't get enough of whatever's placed before them. They order salad, we give them pasta, we called it "pasta salad", they don't even blink.'

'And what a boon to you. Pasta's instant, complete trash and costs nothing to produce.'

'Exactly. People are feeble, powerless. A waiter is an authority fig-ure by the mere fact of bringing their dessert.'

'This explains why waiters are occasionally burnt in the town Square.'

'Indeed - I was right about you, Mr Verbal.'

'Oh, I've been there - cheap supply? When I first tested boneseed, the initial seeding was done in a graveyard - many of the houses I grew had the stretched skulls of our ancestors doing a visual scream out of the walls. Crazy days. Wild. Later on, dispersal was accom-plished by a berserking pig with a couple of saddle bags. Never too soon for that sort of mayhem.'

'You anticipate my major point: cheap resources. The work of the Boneseed Company has interested us for some time. Architects: they lattice parliament, barbwire the train, sense the box most like a building and use that as a basis. The human race succeeded in dim light, in bitter cold - why not in a world made of pasta? Steaming keeps and cathedrals of pasta, lax doors, slick walls, sweating vistas of slimy impermanence. Join with us and you will want for no resource.'

King Verbal regarded him with cagey good humour. 'I like you, Lucent, we're on the same page with this corporate crime malarky. Monopolies are just so flagrant they're delicious.'

'Then you will consider it.'

'I'll think damn hard about it.'

'This is as much as I can ask. Good day.'

When the chef had gone, Verbal skinned a cigar and lit up, frown-ing happily. It had always seemed to him that the scattershot petu-lance of chefs was designed to distract from their shame at having evolved with no natural enemies. But this guy Lucent lived calm in a plan. Pasta towns? Verbal stared into trancey smoke.

An hour later he was on the phone to the centrifuge coven when his next appointment was ushered in - he cheerfully gestured Max Gaffer to sit down, completed his call and gave the lawyer his happy attention. 'That was the lab, they borrowed seven tons of salt from the decency commission and it's pure flour, riven with slugs. Useless for our purposes - and for theirs too, wouldn't you have thought?'

'I couldn't possibly comment,' Gaffer smiled.

Verbal chuckled. 'You sly young dog. To what do I owe the pleas-ure? Another wing on that cranial pad of yours, you ergomaniac? Baby teeth pushing from walls, something new for the ladies? Or how about this - mashed ears, a beautiful new concept in windows. You can tell your old windows it's been real but -'

'I'm afraid this is a more ... delicate matter.'

'Oh?'

'A certain criminal got a cornerstone order a short time ago - you've probably received a request to re-grow the court.'

'Indeed we have, just yesterday.'

'The Mayor would like you to expedite matters. This criminal is an associate of Barny Juno, who as you know, has killed and killed again.'

'I heard he threw an apple core at the Mayor.'

'It's true,' Gaffer muttered regretfully, 'that he came into the office eating an apple and threw the chog at our leader. Lobbed it under-arm so it defined an arc and gave everyone time to think on the inevitability of things.'

'But hardly murder.'

'The point is, the Mayor has charged me to bring down this social nuisance one way or another. I've been given carte blanche really, to withhold certain words, barge in a bit, ignore various matters, what-ever I like.'

'Ofcourse, my co-operation will be full and hearty - insect paste maybe, that could speed development, but lifespan also ... When do you want the courthouse complete?'

'Three days.'

Verbal whistled. 'Well, there may be a way but disintegration might accelerate too - in fact the structure could become necrotic almost immediately.'

'Appropriate isn't it, for a court? See what you can do - good.' Gaffer stood to leave. 'I know I can rely on you.'

Alone again, Verbal sat in thought a while, then plucked up the phone and got the lab on the line. 'Fletch? Don't throw the flour away. Put water in the vats. We're trying something new.'

Maquette liked it out here in the growlands. Here were car wrecks cooking red in the greengage field, finger posts rotted to tobacco-coloured powder and miles of bushes tangled with brown windblown audiotape, trailing down to the sea. The bobble-hatted Kenny Reactor told her of nights he spent gazing at the familiar living neck-lace of plant lights. 'Over there are globe roses, the glasshouse is mainly sports gear hydroponics, in that corner are drylord specials, and here are my heads. All my heads are legal, there's no blood in them. Look.' He dragged a head from the soil, its hairy tuber root trailing long. Taking up a half-moon knife, he sliced the thick matter in half, showing Maquette the cross-section. He indicated the packed outer leaves. 'These tight hard cabbagy layers are the mind imitation called "chadder". These look like spore arrays but they're actually chemical fuses. This centre starshape is the code heart of any grexian planthead like this. These are the lock fluids, which filter through to the ruff of valve sprouts around the neck. The plasma is flushed down these channels and collected for use in blond beer. All this tangled grey fibre is about water drawing, like any plant.' He turned the lobe, the glitter of moisture moving in the sun. 'This is the face.' He pushed some of the rooty hair aside. There was a fungal, expressionless human face, brimming amid itself. It was almost blank, its eyes like coins. Its lips were yellow blebs like the ears of cacti.

Maquette heard a crunching from beyond the hedge and ran into the shed, cotter pins ticking. Next door was a small allotment of fire alarms, red as tomatoes - their owner had wandered over to banter with Kenny on the matter of apple butter and lemonics. 'If you're such a country boy, Reactor, what does it mean when the cows lie down?'

'That they've been killed for food.'

'I mean the other time.'

As their talk continued, Maquette picked up a dirty mirror and propped it on the seed table. Wedging a trowel into the seam which passed down the right side of her head, she prised at the crack. When the face tilted open, she could see a dark organisation inside. Her glass eyes were set amid some dusty grey valves, antique wire, frozen gears and a gummed-up gasometer display. The door of her teeth clicked shut.

Kenny Reactor came in and stopped, holding a seed tray full of bonce eggs. 'Hiding out eh? Burying something here is dangerous.' He put down the tray and looked at her open face. Then he closed it for her. 'Maybe some animal hair,' he suggested, 'and some colour.'

Barny had been so distracted by the nightmares and all, he had missed the main event. Every moment of Chloe's body was like liquid gold. Now Barny felt like there were tiny lights drifting into his mouth, blotting out. He was making the world dark. He never thought to go argue with her - Barny assumed that everyone meant what they said and did.

Shuttering up in the ramped and cabined landscape of his house, he lay his head on the lion. 'Oh, Mister Braintree,' he said. 'I wish I had a beak. A colourful one.' The lion yawned and slopped his mouth closed. He slowly whipped his tail - it was like a golden rope tipped with a fluffy teardrop.

Chimps eager to play instead found themselves hugged in silence.

Barny finally dragged over to see his friend and auxiliary father-figure Mr Peterson, who sat poolside wearing Jonathan glasses and considering the glass in his glass right hand. 'I'm in your debt after that bit of driving you did for me, Bubba. If it's a matter of money, just say the word.'

'No, Mr Peterson, it's Chloe. I could climb her like a tree. But my scary nightmares have made her go away.'

'Old John Satan with his eighty nostrils and his horns the shape of question marks eh? If you don't have at least ten demons prodding at your eyes round here you've got some explaining to do apparently. See that butterfly over there on the hedge? That flippy thing's more worthy of respect than you.'

'Why, Mr Peterson?'

'Because it's an adult. It's due to die any time. It's a question of perspective.'

'Is that the question? I dunno ...'

'When you're chortling, you think you know a secret. Then you forget the secret, you forget you ever chortled, you make a sandwich. Yuh get older and mirrors choke your smile. Keep drinking railroad paint, Bubba, and cherish each little mood. If they mended that flyover you could go see the world. Wind of the high roads, straight and disappearing. But as it is, these escapades of yours ... To a man like me they're just baffling and that's all.'

'Me too, Mr Peterson. I don't ask for it. Any of it.'

'Well, I'm scheduled to shrug my shoulders and punch the wardrobe at six. Get outta here.'

Barny decided to go and see the shaman Beltane Carom in his strange garden. A slogan over the arched doorway said: 'A tree is not in doubt.' This was of no help at all. He entered the flowered and fountained pattern yard. The flooring was concentrated into a dense oracle schematic which was of no interest to Barny. Beltane Carom sat in the mosaic centre playing a board game of arcane components. Barny explained about the demon nightmares and Chloe. 'I'm scared.'

'Hell is the fifth season. It operates behind the other four. Look.' Beltane pointed to the air and there appeared a sharp second of vast reality. 'It's the spacial mating of this realm and theirs.'

'What do I do, Mr Carom?'

'There's a defector demon living over at the observatory - I'll give him a call.' Beltane took down a mirror from the ivied garden wall and placed it flat on the ground. 'This is a spiral induction,' he said, and repeated a few obscurities. The silver demon Gettysburg folded up via subspace with shivery wings. He listened to the shaman's account of Barny's problem, and in response suggested that Barny confront the monster in his dream.

'Lamp the bastard with whatever's lying around,' said Gettysburg. 'Then you'll wake up, like that.'

'Thankyou ma'am,' said Barny, oblivious to the demon's affront. And he left, feeling a little better.

Gettysburg stayed on a while in the yard, chatting to the shaman. 'Eyebrows in the back of his head, that one.'

'He's not a fool, just preoccupied, is all,' said the shaman. 'It's somehow put him at an axis point for anyone or anything that goes berserk. Like a catalyst, he himself is barely affected. I think *The Eleventeen* calls it a rumble hub. I once saw Barny in the Square. He was crying loads and looking at a picture of a collie. The dog had wet eyes and he explained the animal had died four years ago.'

The notion brought forth a dog from the air, a mere protein brow, semi-formed, which evaporated.

'I think I recognise the demon he described from his dream,' said Gettysburg. 'It's Rakeman, a real vintage fright. The eclipse might help it through. Sweeney too, for that matter.'

'It's like chess, isn't it? Each piece of the story is deep and goes right to the middle. Something's made Accomplice mathematical. Someone with a plan. You can feel it can't you?'

'The doll?'

'I don't think so. Probably the lawyer.'

'Dietrich mentioned that lawyer had sent a rot message to Sweeney.'

'Dietrich,' Beltane muttered. 'What is it with you two?'

'Typical interbeings, I'd say. Like everything, trying to grow. Even that doll's trying in its way.'

'Yes, I screened her progress from the observatory to the hydroponics ground. No-one was conscious. As Violaine said, "If a memo burns faster than you can read it, nature is telling you something."'

6

PSYCHODELTA

The slots of a pig's nose are precise enough

Flashlights flitted through brackish smoke in the deep tree night. Gregor always struggled when called upon to stray from his role as a sweating, door-to-door dupe. Covered in marsh flukes, rollmaps and packs, he ducked under the keening of honey buzzards and called ahead to Edgy. 'This place is really crummy. What are these - tree pogs? "Water Tupelo". What's the point? These plants are completely uneven. They don't know what the hell they're doing.'

'We're in a swamp, Round One, a *swamp*. At least the slime stops them from being creaky, eh?'

'This is the crappiest line of approach we could have used out here.'

'This line of approach is an absolute peach and you know it. We'll find the wise woman Feral Beryl, ask her how to catch them glass harpies and bam's your uncle. There's nothing she doesn't know about harpies, or anything, any subject. She's a top-flight wise woman with a face you could use for a can opener.'

The mashy ground logged their energy and stained their pants. Fogs were slowly drugging a swollen landscape of wrecked foundry graves and casks of false blood dried solid. Here was an old truck sunk to the waist, mossed as furry as a caterpillar.

'For instance, at what point did you become a part of this landscape? It depends on someone else's viewpoint doesn't it? Well, the harpies play with that. Their four-sided heads disengage their image from your perceptions by going one or more better.'

Gregor's senses were getting shredded by the endless disarray of jungle gloom, the lurching heavy sky and untuned colours. 'This is taking ages,' he said.

'Hey, you know that thing you did with your statue,' said Edgy. 'It was really gay.'

'What do you expect? I've got Gubba Man stuff in my leg - I'm part cop now.'

'Quiet - there she is.'

She sat amid a sparse scattering of white piano bones on a plum-coloured hill, stirring a bucket of bee venom. Her face was whorled and flaky as bark.

They were starting up the slope when the crone cried out. 'What the hell are you doing?'

'Why not?'

'I didn't ask why, what the hell's that thing?' She pointed at Gregor.

'Human detritus,' said Edgy, and winked at Gregor.

Gregor whispered to Edgy, 'This is the top-flight wise woman you told me about?'

Edgy whispered to Gregor. 'She thinks with her teeth, that much is obvious.'

'What are you whispering about?' snapped Beryl.

'Quadraface harpies.'

'Glassers eh? Mythical and real as levy skeletons. They'll nip your head off with extraordinary ferocity.'

'My head? No ...'

'Oh yes. Those bastards don't mess around.'

'Do you know how to survive them?'

'I'm alive aren't I?'

'I've no reason to suppose so.'

'Don't I bother you?'

'I see what you mean.' Edgy smiled. 'Well, you really are a font of wisdom.'

'Is that so, do I look like a font?'

Gregor pushed forward. 'Come on you old hag, you're wasting our time.'

'That has nothing to do with it. I'll break your legs! That's right, your legs!' And she began cackling and capering toward them in a scary way, all rags and elbows.

Gregor pulled at Edgy. 'Come on, we'll have to sort it on the fly.'

'Work out how to find and kill semi-transparent dragons on the fly?'

Beryl kicked Edgy sharply in the balls and darted back up the slope, complaining at the assumption that she was wise. Seekers returning to civilisation would cover their embarrassment by inventing some arcane wisdom and attributing it to her. All she wanted was to be left alone.

'We'll tell one and all,' Edgy gasped, curled upon the ground, 'you have their best interests at heart. It'll be a blueprint for positive change.'

'Know what I think'd be a blueprint for positive change? You getting the hell away from me.' She snorted and gobbed a flob like an oyster.

'Just tell us where the harpies are,' Gregor stated, 'and we'll get out of your way.'

'You'll find them where you see the harpies which are called "quadraface".'

'Those are quadraface harpies,' Edgy wheezed.

'Oh yes, it'll work alright. I'm not even worried about that.'

Edgy staggered to his feet. 'You're ... you're a moron.'

'So regret me.'

As they stumbled away, she called after them. 'Oh and mind how you go - some idiot released a 'gator out here.'

*

'I think I am correct in saying that a meal of this standard is a criminal offence.' Haltingly chewing a sparrow behind locked doors and the hours of darkness, Max Gaffer sat in the Ultimatum Restaurant with only the head chef for company. 'Saying thankyou for it is like ceremonially forgiving the headsman before his work. I had no idea how much petrol you used here.'

Quandia Lucent stood over him. 'Condiments are necessary.'

Gaffer glanced at the menu again. 'Giblets parboiled for no reason, fluorite buns, armistice gutting, plasma earlobes, bladder walls tough as a belt, and on the back cover, a tamale erosion chart. This document is a disturbing reminder of mortality.'

'A formality,' the chef stated. 'It is not up to you.'

Gaffer dabbed his mouth with a rag, shaking his head in admiration. 'I'm reluctant to characterise it as a meal at all. You have quite an operation here Mr Lucent. As Violaine said, "Cheese which, when sliced, can bend double without breaking, is likely not cheese." Let's go to chin level on this. You're hellbent for pasta saturation. I know you discourage other foodstuffs with a sneering expression and the propagation of this manner of incident.' He handed over a newspaper with the headline MINCE BINGE ENDS TRAGICALLY. 'In fact I like the way you think, so I'd like to help you. I happen to know that Barny Juno has been told everything there is to know about the edibility of oceanic fish and that he intends to pass on the knowledge.'

'Juno. He's the one who set free *una cocodrilo* in my restaurant eh?'

'Yes, disgracefully, he probably did.'

The chef's expression became stormy. 'The fishes of the sea are a near-unending resource of non-pasta nutrition. Terrible, terrible.'

'I agree. Vertebrae like a zip fastener. Stay away.'

'Children know the purpose of food is decoration. That's why we discourage their attendance.'

'Look to Barny Juno, my friend. If you graft the pattern of change on to the pattern of fear, you'll find a match.'

A grim waiter stalked in with the next dish.

'Ah, doves,' said Gaffer, tucking in. 'Bounty of the sky.'

The first thing they captured was a vampire wearing some sort of apron - this they released in an embarrassment which kept them silent for half an hour.

Then they met the tiny Microlady, who lay in a palm bed and trilled of her peculiarities. 'I walk in shoes of eyelids,' she told them as they retreated through the contorted trees.

They even bumped into Fang, the zombie who worked with them

in the sorting office and came out to the swamp to sleep in the damp earth. At their approach he arose yellow in rotted clothes, a corpse *par excellence*. 'Hey, Fang,' Edgy hailed him.

'What are you crazy guys doing this time?' Fang asked, his expression in trembling readiness for hilarity.

'Snaring glass harpies,' Edgy announced.

'Edgy's idea,' Gregor muttered.

The gristle man began balking with laughter, his entire body jerking and folding. One strong convulsion threw his head from his shoulders and into the undergrowth - the cadaver sat back down as though stunned.

'I could use some coffee, and how,' said Edgy in a low, confidential tone as they moved on.

'The maples seem to have sprouted hind legs.'

'Shut up and help me with this,' said Edgy, unflapping a large map.

'You brought a Doggone Diagram here?'

'No, don't you recognise it? One of those old "Maps to the Morons" I used to sell. A guide to the homes of the biggest morons of our fair community. Doomed Eddie Gallo, GI Bill, Barny's house, your house, Prancer's room, Rudloe Manor, it's all here. Remember the time I told GI Bill he had something on his nose and he said it was just his head?' Edgy chuckled fondly.

'*My* house?'

'Anyway it's like I thought - the swamp's shown as just a random design at the map edge. No good for our purposes.'

'*My* house?'

Something knocked waves into the fog. Transparent channels were worming the atmosphere before Edgy's eyes. He halted Gregor and shrugged off his backpack. Casting an october switch before him, he watched it bounce in the air, spinning aside and landing in the brush. Then he unpacked a cornercage, placing it gently on the rumbling ground and unfolding a slip of paper. 'Listen, Round One,' he whispered. 'Cornercage Ltd instruction leaflet. "When someone must maintain a particular position, and that position cannot be maintained, the fixed need becomes a handle by which someone can be manipulated. Since the target entity must be invisible it will react to the knowledge of its visibility by hiding in our patented corner cage. Keep away from badgers."'

The switch deployed and two horse-sized dragons liquified a few feet in front of Edgy and Gregor.

'*My* house?'

'Focus, Round One. They're harpies, harpies. You knew that going in. Now don't make me come over there.'

Rills of shadow sawtoothed together and the earth was stamped to dust. Benthic light was flowing through the creatures' bodies and inside each ghosted the spirals of an abalone heart. These beauties had quadratic heads and flanks like shellac. 'Hello, harpies!' Edgy shouted at them, waving. 'I like what I see!'

One harpy bolted into the undergrowth, sprinting like a gazelle. The other panicked the other way, throwing itself at the cornercage. In a blaze of portable spinelight it was sucked into a space no bigger than a breadbin. 'Well,' chuffed Edgy, smiling stylish. '*Now* who's a danger to himself and others?'

7

A CHANGE OF MIND

Paranoia is an investment

Long reborn doom on the mat, first shadow of the day. The lips of the bed disengaging from sleepers over coffee. And as Gregor set up a video camera in his small bedroom in the hope of filming a few nap chickens, his friends gathered for wolf tart and tea in Snorters cafe. BB Henrietta frowned at the newspaper headline, GALLO SENSES FLOWER, above a picture of doomed Eddie Gallo looking at a flower. An embarrassed spokesman was claiming on Gallo's behalf that he was a veteran of nostril faith. 'That silence of white damnation, a handkerchief, will drown out his voice unless you vote, vote, vote for doomed Eddie Gallo!'

Edgy was displaying his novelty failings and the duelling scars of bad planning. 'I'm on to a king's ransom and a neglect to inform the relevant authorities.'

'Selling harpy meat?' BB scorned. 'It's a lame idea, all right? They'll hunt you down like a doll.'

'Is either of you eating this ultimate cracker?'

'So you think you're impressive now, brush head?'

'What's the point of hiding it? You know I reckon if the Steinway Spiders ever came back, I could tackle one.'

'Yeah, right,' BB snorted.

'Which gambit would you try?' Barny asked, with a marvelling stare.

'A running gambit,' Edgy declared.

'I favour a punching and screaming gambit for that kind of setup,' said BB Henrietta.

'With running at the end?'

'Optional.'

'Depending on the effectiveness of the punching and screaming.'

'Exactly.'

'Oh and we met Fang out there - that skinless wonder cracks me up very time.'

'You want some of this pasta salad, Edgy?'

'No thanks - I hate it.'

'Typical man - won't commit to a thing he doesn't want. What about you, Juno?'

'Maybe I should try eating a fish - EH Hunt keeps saying one of those things is the stuff of life. Gregor says he'll try it if I do first.'

'And acquaint yourselves with the toilet,' said BB.

'What Violaine said,' Barny stated, 'is that a toilet is like a fat ceramic swan in the bathroom. When did it arrive and why is it there? Answers on a postcard.'

'On a what?' Edgy asked.

'It's just an expression, I think.'

'Other than you poisoning yourself, Bubba,' BB said, 'what have you been up to?'

'The shaman says I should defeat the monster in my dreams and everything'll be alright,' said Barny without enthusiasm.

'Hmm. That'd work well in my Miasma play. Framed narrative.'

'Well listen Beltane is good,' Edgy agreed, 'but he can't hold a candle to Feral Beryl.'

'Alright, harpy whisperer,' BB asked, dripping with sarcasm, 'what did she say?'

'Eh?' Edgy jittered, taken by surprise. 'Well, she said some very important advice actually. Er, for us all. Yes, she said, these pearly words here: "Problems are like dogs - they stare, they demand to be fed, they spin in place".'

'I think I see that bullshit borealis Gregor's always talking about.'

'You dare? Can you perceive what I've done? Can, can, do you know how I fought that quadraface fiend to the floor? You're looking at a man reared on the following: stares, palping, a tawny scab, metallic mouths in a bottomless lake, collars, parlour tricks gone awry, and crazy talk.'

His claim was met with a revolted silence.

Edgy continued, equable in his joy. 'I'm thinking of changing my name to Bollard Salvo, what do you reckon? And wearing antlers like candlestick holders.'

'I think you're getting a little carried away.'

'Imagine being announced and making an entrance!'

Edgy pulled a face which was, regrettably, attached to a passer-by. 'Reality can polish my arse!' And he began juddering in his seat, foam flying from his mouth.

BB turned to Barny. 'You know, Juno, you're a gormless idiot but at least you never go into violent convulsions. And that's cool in its way.'

'I don't know what you mean.'

'Right.'

The Mayor was again posing on a high horse. He exhibited his chins like a flowchart. The painter looked upon the image which had filled his canvas - that of a sleepy gibbon in a shredded undershirt.

The door flashed open and Gaffer burst into the office already laughing. 'A reply from the circus. Delivered by some sort of winged midget.'

'What now,' sighed the Mayor, bored.

'It says "I would rather burst my own nose than enter Accomplice in time for your jaundice exhibition. Arriving too late to be of any use, we will expose you to the greatest spectacle ever seen. And be assured, Mayor, I will bare my wonderful arse also to the town. Signed, Karloff Velocet, Fall Marshall, Karloff's Circus."'

'Is that all? Where have you been?'

'You've no right to time my entertainment.'

'You look rejuvenated.'

'An abstract term for saying you hate my jacket.'

'Why does everything have to be about your underwear?'

'I never mentioned it.'

'No you didn't.' Mayor Rudloe looked suspicious. He gestured at the painter. 'You can bring your waves of desperation back with you tomorrow.' When the painter had left with his equipment, Rudloe dismounted and approached Max Gaffer. 'This sudden-death integrity of yours, what's it all about?'

'I considered mercy. I stopped trying with the realisation that even the greatest show of it isn't fun. Confusion sometimes contracts rewards. You gave me the treat too soon.'

'What the hell's going on around here?' Rudloe demanded, his face congested with anger. 'Just do your job and enumerate the fancy misgivings you're famous for.'

'Very well: Barny Juno.'

'Juno? Rode in here on a swan, that's the trouble.'

'Indeed. I've corralled the great and the good against him. They'll use his blank face as a broom for the township.'

'Without consulting me? My arse is the engine room of this community. Mine. What if he was denounced by a pig made of straw, with a tape-recorder hidden inside?'

'It would give the term "false conspirator" new meaning, plus amusement to all. No need to disturb the natural order.'

'If they need order, show them the door. A large rectangle is guaranteed to give a good example. Then keep 'em busy about the Miasma. It's their perfect opportunity to avoid acknowledging they don't really care much anyway.' Rudloe sparked his cigar with a lighter the size of a car battery.

'Your lungs must be black as a wallet.'

'And your heart must be large as a grape, lawyer. What other business?'

'The fugitive doll. Sanctuaries seem to bang open like greyhound traps for that one. I recommend that it's dispatched before the Miasma.'

'Agreed. Can't have a jangly marionette twitching against the revellers can we. Order the Brigade be released. Anything else?'

'Can I speak freely sir? You know there's folk running blood stills out in the swamp to make account for the levy.'

'I've been carefully ignoring the fact for years, why bring it up now?'

'Because if that slubby cabal the Conglomerate were to learn that they were often feeding on cloned blood, that you were laughing at them behind their collective back ...'

'Who'd tell them?'

'Let's just say that if you want to spring from this window here onto the jagged face of an onlooker, I won't stand in your way.'

'It's a high window, and not a round one.'

'All true. Is this your only comment?'

Rudloe's face sort of grimaced with affront, his nose and gob jockeying for position. 'Have a care, Gaffer. These damn fool comments could bring your gummy ballet of a career to an end. I think I'm numbered among the Conglomerate's closest confidantes.'

'Your days, if not yourself.'

'What's that?'

'Nothing - I have a case to prepare. I'll dispose of Barny Juno if you can't. Good day.'

'Oh good day. And don't let the door flume into infernal meat and flip you screaming to hell on the way out.'

Not noticing a floor lobster on the desk, Rudloe snatched it up when the phone rang. He barked hello and the creature scuttled against his face. 'Bloody hell!' he screamed, and hurled the clattery vermin through the balcony window.

'Where this arrow lands,' proclaimed the trickster Prancer Diego to some children in the Square. 'I shall learn braille.' And he fired the arrow in the air, watching it hit a flying floor lobster in a small explosion of meat.

The Brigade approached Kenny Reactor's farm armed to the teeth with knives, spiked maces and an october switch. The Sarge halted them at the gate, primed the switch, and looked across the head field, fondling a thin badge made of a dog's nose leather. Finished, he turned to his deputy, who brandished a dish.

'Snail, sarge?'

'Don't mind if I do. What are they?'

'Snails sarge.'

'Snails. Don't mind if I do.'

'Get your face round that then.'

'What is it.'

'A snail, sarge.'

'Snail. Alright then. Eat it do I?'

'Eat it sarge, that's right.'

'What is it.'

'Snail - a snail, sarge.'

'Snail.'

'A snail, sarge. See? It's a snail.'

'Snail is it. Well now.'

'Snail.'

'Snail, eh. Well, don't mind if I do.'

'Good on yuh.'

'Right.'

'You eatin' it then?'

'Eh?'

'You eatin' that?'

'What is it.'

Before the deputy could reply, a peel of firecrackers announced the approach of a group of Fuseheads. 'Are you the Belly Honour Guard?' sneered the front man, and the others cackled like tarts.

'And who might you be?'

'We seek the Church of Automata's escaped abomination, you bastard,' announced the front man.

The sarge smirked aside to his deputy. 'Notice how he called me a bastard? Everyone calls me that round here.'

'Remember the hedgehogs we saw here last time, Sarge?' said Gibbs, looking into a hedgerow. 'They've given birth to hoglets.'

'What's the matter with you people?' asked a cannon worshipper, indignant. He addressed a colleague. 'Bring the switch - we'll root out the walking blasphemy without help from these.'

'Look sarge, somebody gave me, ah, a drawing of a hoglet.'

'Nobody gave you a drawing of a hoglet, Perkins,' said the sarge, smirking. 'You drew a hoglet, didn't you?'

'Okay, Sarge, I did.'

'It's good.'

'Forget these jokers - the sooner we catch the doll, the sooner we celebrate. Onward!'

'Another hoglet appeared in the picture, sarge,' said Perkins, his face smudged with ink. 'It's incredible.'

The cannonites pushed past the Brigade into the head field, knocking the october switch from the Sarge's hands. Activating, it threw the field into acidic negative. The doll Maquette was buried to the neck among the heads, topped with a grubby fright wig - she was noticeable for a split second before the Fuseheads dropped their own switch and neutralised the first.

But neither group had noticed the doll, and when the Sarge ordered Ripper to unpack the picnic gear, no-one could really be bothered to carry on the search. The Sarge showed everyone how to draw hedgehogs starting from the stubby nose. One of the Fuseheads explained how he had simultaneously grown two overlapping beards, quite distinct from eachother. Someone played a flute.

Shadowed by a nearby tree, Distaff Plastique was stood waxenly, like a totem, its skin earth red. It was mid-afternoon before the happy group dispersed, heading for the beach. Distaff stepped onto the field, kicking mechanically through vegetable heads.

A thing of fright paint and disordered hair, Maquette was struggling out of the ground like a newborn, blankly frantic as the automatic man approached. As she freed herself and began tick-tocking toward the gate, she looked backward to see Distaff halt abruptly. After a minute this strange, cored servant turned around, an earth fork hanging from its back like a tow pike. Kenny Reactor stood beyond it, startled by his own act.

Kenny bolted in one direction, Maquette in another. Distaff Plastique followed the doll north.

Something woke Gregor - he had to go see the lawyer, he remembered. He felt terrible, like someone had worn him for a hat. He reached the offices of De'ath and Destruction to regard his counsel raggedly through bloodshot eyes. A dark suit full of dead nerves, De'ath was immaculately unimaginative. No air had ever gotten in or out. 'Ah, the hardy loser,' he greeted Gregor.

'Is something wrong?'

'That will do. The appearance is many months away. We merely need to play out the grim scenario ahead of time. Remember, the question is not whether a thing is true - the question is what number of human beings are prepared to accept it as a possibility. Regrettably the burden of proof that you're a normal fella rests entirely with you and your reactions in court. It is impossible to imagine how they could come to view you with any favour. This flimsy vapour you call an alibi - what was it again?'

'I was at the slaughterhouse.'

'Oh that's just dandy. Your honour my client couldn't have done the murder because he was at the slaughterhouse. My god.'

'What do you want me to say to you.'

'What you say to me sonny jim is neither here nor there - you can tell me you were kissing a badger and loving every minute of it. But in court laddie, in court you're obliged to at least try.'

'I don't know the form. Do I wear trousers there.'

'Christ, yes.'

'And a tie?'

'Yes, yes. And you tell them you were in a bar with eighty other people, all of them as pure as yourself. That's the way.'

'So you want me to charm the pants off them?'

'If you can. Though quite frankly my boy I doubt you could charm a dead wren off a hedge.'

'Did you say murder? I never murdered anyone.'

'Ah yes, some sort of public abomination wasn't it ... Either way you're headed for a room with a drain in the middle, if you get my drift.'

'So it's all decided.'

'Nonsense, we are free to be laden with proof on the matter.'

'Isn't there any way out?'

'Let's see. Teeth clamped hard to the judge may cause an adjournment I suppose. He's quite brittle.' And De'ath opened the large cabinet to view the pupating judge. A seed once the size and weight of an owl had already developed into the full-sized drylord which would, when its eyes were slit awake, sit in judgement upon Gregor. 'And this message Max Gaffer brought me earlier might have something useful to say.' He unwrapped the missive and read it silently, then looked up at Gregor. 'My prayers are with you and your monstrous friends.'

'What? Why?'

'No sentiment or waste will force its way into my account. The trial is on for tomorrow. Apparently the courthouse has grown at unprecedented speed.'

'What? What are we gonna do?'

'Listen carefully, Gregor. One of the big guns in the court's armoury is its sedative effect. Bigger is its dismissal of objective reality and biggest, its ability to abduct people without moving a muscle - the abductees do all the work, tranced by assumed authority. I love it.' And ropes of drool began lengthening from the lawyer's gob.

'What's the best I can get away with?'

'The best? It'll be on your permanent record.'

'Permanent?'

In Snorter's cafe later that day Gregor raved at Edgy about the concept. 'I never thought I'd make a mark - everything is transitory, I thought. I'd die, be forgotten.'

'Right.'

'But this thing - my "permanent record", Edge. Permanent. He insists that people'll know about me forever.'

'Know that you had sex with a mechanical statue.'

'What's the difference? He said forever, he insisted on it. Apparently this is the one thing that survives beyond the end of everything - you gotta give it a go, right?'

'I think it's an exaggeration, Round One. The record doesn't last forever.'

'Then why would I give a damn about it? This guy stood there being very precise about the whole procedure. I've created something permanent!'

And Gregor went home swinging each leg forward lustily, down into his little room where he slapped the nap chickens video into the machine and popped a beer.

The edit swarm coalesced into the image of the Round One bent in bed, his face slack. Presently the ventilation grille on the wall swung open and a stubby leg reached through, and another. A mechanical doll, its face painted up like a clown, stood into the room and looked at the sleeping Gregor. Then it dashed silently off-screen. A dark arm angled out of the vent and pulled after it a large moulded plastic man, which straightened up and marched immediately out of view.

Max Gaffer descended into the gutty dungeon concealed beneath the Blood Shed. The clammy air and lambent red atmosphere hit him - wet fungal walls pulsed with fanned capillaries, a tongue swung in the clock and the chamber was filled with a wall-to-wall meat morass, multi-mouthed and occupied. 'The only thing on this list I recognise is the Wesley Kern gun.'

'But where did Turbot get it?' a larger mouth croaked. 'It's not his handwriting.'

'It's signed "Low".'

'There's no Low on the mug levy register. This is a waste of our sweet, sweet time. Now concerning unproven heifers ...'

Another mouth interrupted. 'We have a visitor.' Lime eyes opened in the dark. 'Look at him, pretending he feels no disgust.'

A flesh turret of sneers projected from the upper surface of the Conglomerate. 'What makes the Mayor's errand boy so forward of a sudden?'

'I have a strange live medallion in my chest which directs my actions.'

'If you weren't a lawyer you'd know that was your heart.'

Gaffer opened his shirt to display the toroidal fitting from which the infernal drillbit emerged.

'You could hang a furry dice on that, as on your career to date. You wish to advance? Is this your bid to avoid an eiderdown death away from the cameras? Armageddon goodies your prize? A real polecat rush for the glory. We understand. Benevolence is the first chapter in a boring book.'

'Mayor Rudloe is wealthy and slow,' said Gaffer, 'dull but loyal. I expect he's back at the office now, frantically throwing phones on the fire. But you could do better.'

'You've done well yourself, amid a form of politics advertised on pencils. In a very real way, it does you credit.'

'I'll take that remark to the bank and see what transpires.'

'You will apologise first.'

The stern resolve drained from Gaffer's slackening face. 'I ... draw a line under what I said.'

'Funny.'

'I never laugh so hard that I can't talk money.'

'You know the difference between a primitive woodsman and a politician, Gaffer?'

'One chops his quivers, and the other -'

'The difference,' the Conglomerate interrupted, 'is that one will hesitate before touting any given concern in return for pay.'

'Why have the people ever believed that all the blood they give goes to work the town clock?'

'People will do almost anything to avoid acknowledging that they're powerless. That's a sturdy handle.' A loose arm tapped one of the gore-gummed sump valves in the wall. 'There's another exaction coming up, you'll see even the oldsters struggling out of the swamps to get bled. The agitator Wesley Kern's been silky dust these many years. I believe an excavation was completed recently in the walls of the skeleton coast. Seventeen tons of pocket fluff was found in the cave. It seems your ancestors were as boring as you are.'

'Have you heard of a Varney bug, Mr Gaffer?'

This mouth was no more than a palping spout which Gaffer doubted he could ever get used to.

'No sir, I haven't.'

'It's like a floor lobster, but it births directly and physically from the originator's head. If the corrupt fellow survives, he's much the worse for wear. Be careful your plan doesn't kill you birthing, Gaffer.'

Gaffer looked at the lung-hung ceiling and skids of red tar, the moving meat amid vapour. 'The enemy of uncertainty might think the answer lies in grammar,' he observed. Varicose alarm wires bloated the walls, going to his head. 'Progress is formidable on short acquaintance - after a time its existence can't even be proven.'

For years Mike Abblatia had been living an extra day between Thursday and Friday, growing a little older than his years. Though supposedly a young man, his back ached and seemed to swell more with every vehicle that was stolen during his watch.

Abblatia worked at Spacey's gas station. He sat on the forecourt next to a tank marked Zapata Oil, eating a sandwich and contemplating the horizon. He had the notion that people lived in a sandwich, moving always between the earth and sky. Rooms, roads, buildings, all were horizontal strips. Death was when a person fell out of the sandwich.

A false child, fresh out of some specialist foundry, wandered across the forecourt toward him. Its head was like a dirty kettle and its gob was like a pedal-bin. She waddled over, looked at him awhile and then sat down on some mixed ash-and-bone blocks. They looked across the scorched tarmac in the quiet of the afternoon. The forecourt was edged with a few wooden posts and loopy elaborate flowers, some like hang-peeled bananas. The gas stands were rusted and reversed into complicated colours.

Abblatia was so attuned to mechanisms he could hear a watch ticking in the stomach of a dog. The mannequin had solid glass eyes and a heart like a pascaline. She was lonely. Surely somewhere there was a blued steel boy for her to click around with.

Abblatia took up a boxy bottle of water and drank, then offered it to the imp. She was gone. A minute later he heard tyres sizzling over gravel - a truck drove around the station and swerved into the lane, the doll at the wheel.

8

LET US LURK

A man who cannot be changed has no need to fight

After creating several vats of glue, Verbal had consulted the chef Quandia Lucent on the constituents for pasta. The chef informed him he had been mixing the quantities correctly - the difference was only one of definition.

And so as everyone entered the courtroom they found it a brittle venue indeed. In place of the crossbone masonry usually deployed for perjury reverberation there were bland starch walls wormed with spaghetti filigree. Instead of torsions and flexions of bone there were volutes of pasta and exquisitely turned fusilli bannisters. Lanceolate pinnacles of macaroni jutted dryly at the sky. There were some token pillars of poured bone which didn't reach the ceiling, and what appeared to be hairline cracks in the walls were actually fine print.

Meanwhile the Drylord was as complete as it would ever be. Uncertain as to how many nostrils it would require to convey a bearing of authority, it had overcompensated, vacillated and finally abandoned the matter as it now stood. It had a hundred and twenty, so its nose resembled a piece of sponge. Yet despite all this it didn't seem to be alive, propped at the courtroom's head like a Guy Fawkes.

'That frail catnip judge over there,' whispered De'ath as he and Gregor entered the courtroom, 'is the ramp to respectability.'

In discussing strategy with De'ath, Gregor had remarked that it wouldn't hurt to give the judge the cake they had stowed in the cupboard a few days before. But De'ath had wavered, stating that it would be too obvious an attempt to curry favour with the court. Gregor had suggested that openly poisoning the cake would neutralise this impression and the lawyer had agreed to the remedy.

De'ath handed it over. 'A gift, your honour, as befits a man in your ridiculous situation.'

'You think you can curry favour with this sugary fondant creation?'

Gregor laughed lightly. 'No, your honour - in fact the cake is poisoned with a variety of household detergents. Testament to my indifference to your opinion.'

'What?'

'What my client meant to say,' stammered De'ath, 'is that he has no desire to influence you favourably.'

'Having offered me poison cake in the courtroom, I think he can rest assured on that score.'

'Trying to sway the dry reed of the judge?' announced Max Gaffer, beaming as he entered. 'Send a message, Judge, if you can.'

'You put this on the fast track,' De'ath declared to Gaffer.

'Still feels deadly slow though, doesn't it?'

'He's right,' said Gregor, surprised at the realisation. 'How do they do that?'

'I've explained before,' hissed De'ath, pushing Gregor away from the laughing Gaffer and on to the bench. 'Now sit there, stay silent and for god's sake remember how daft you are.'

De'ath reached into the black petals of an open bag, retrieving dozens of prematurely aged files as spectators filed into the gallery. Half of Accomplice was here, including Barny and the gang. The jury meanwhile consisted of twelve heads on a trolley. A distorted outcome was ensured by the fact that this was the only time their opinions would be allowed to affect anything.

Gaffer was wearing his eyes swept back these days and compared to De'ath he was slick as a wolf, all blade suit and cufflinks of pink flesh. He called Gregor to the stand. 'Let us dispense first with those events which are a matter of record. Did you not, during the course of the Mayor's "You Want a Piece of Me?" speech, crouch out upon the ornate ledge and dispense sexual favours galore upon a paint-flaking statue which formed a part of the town clock mechanism.'

Gregor looked over at De'ath.

'Don't expect any help from that conjuror's stooge you call a lawyer,' said Gaffer, 'who for years has been throwing good alibis after bad. Confess with grace, at least.'

Gregor tried to appear unconcerned, his head repeatedly lolling forward as though he were nodding off. He had asked Barny how to manage it, and Barny had advised him to 'look to the giraffe', showing Gregor a picture of a giraffe and explaining the animal's beautiful neck motion. Gregor knew that to convey the action as a visual soundbite he had to speed it up, so now his head was shooting back and forth in a shocking manner. Some of the spectators screamed with a kind of primal terror but Gaffer seemed to understand. 'Let the record show that the defendant has given a greatly accelerated impersonation of a giraffe.' He retrieved an exhibit. 'I have here a photograph of a tumescent tearaway assaulting our communal time-piece.' Gaffer glanced at it negligently, then brandished it at Gregor. 'Do you recognise the spud-like figure in this picture?' There was a pause. 'May the record reflect that the defendant has indicated his own face. And attempted a questioning, bland expression.' Gaffer replaced the exhibit. 'In fact you're not particular what you do, are you? The sort of fella who doesn't really need a reason, eh? So you decided to whip it out and see how much trouble it could handle? I wonder, how do people get this way? A single wrong turn in life and - bang - it's ledge-climbing and statue assault. This urge - let's call it "Hell Frenzy" - it was perhaps also the cause of that little case of Stegosaurus Interruptus in the bone museum a while ago.'

'It was a Triceratops,' Gregor muttered feebly.

'A Tops eh? And you ...' - Gaffer consulted a file - '"erupted from its skull and scared the children".'

'They were there to learn,' Gregor protested.

'I wish I could believe that,' said Gaffer sadly. 'Were you not in fact on a burgling spree when you went into Hell Frenzy? Do you claim never to have stuffed yourself through a stranger's window and collected certain of their belongings according to a dog-eared list given you by the devil himself?'

It was the rule that during the first cross the performing lawyer should slow his breath to imperceptibility in emulation of the living dead, and the lawyer seated should hold his breath entirely, so that the more continent a lawyer was about his objections the more comical he seemed. De'ath had been sitting for several minutes, cheeks full, face turning crimson, and when he finally bolted to his feet to yell 'Objection' it was a garbled explosion from a gasping figure who smashed through the fragile panelling and staggered to his knees with a wretching sob.

Gaffer eyed De'ath disdainfully. 'Nothing further.'

De'ath stood slowly and straightened his tie. He seemed subdued as he approached the witness stand. 'You've been a moron how long?'

'Twenty-eight years.'

'Okay, all right ... And for that period you have suffered from trovander, a statue-related illness.'

Gaffer stood, breathing heavily. 'Your honour, m'colleague's an unprecedented idiot and I never tire of his failings - guard your faces when this one's learning to use a fork. But the illness gambit he just exposed us to leads us all astray, leaving us finally exhausted, dehydrated and confused.'

'It goes to the question of insanity, your honour.'

'Whose, you bastard? Don't touch that!' The drylord yanked his gavel from De'ath's convulsive grasp. 'What's the matter with you?'

De'ath returned to the witness. 'So, a sickness. Then your expression of these lusts was ... curative?'

'I have no idea,' stated Gregor simply.

'You're giving me every reason to believe that it was a medical compulsion. So that occasion on the belfry was a real red letter day for you.'

'Red what?'

'Finally - I now find I can no longer refute the fact that you were a sick man when you molested the inanimate figurine on the ledge. I see undeniably now that you made yourself a hostage to fortune by displaying your wares to the town - yet your generosity is today so shabbily abused. Let us not assassinate this lad further, your honour. We have done enough. Have we no sense of decency, sir, at long last? Have we left no sense of decency?'

The first of a series of noxious gasses was pumped into the courtroom, causing nausea and heavy delirium. When the air had cleared a little, Max Gaffer was cross-examining his second witness. 'Your name is Plantin Edge.'

'No sir.'

'No?'

'My name is Bollard Salvo.'

'Bollard Salvo, is that right.'

'Bollard Salvo yes sir, born and raised, more every day.'

'Where did I get,' Gaffer scrutinised a file, 'Plantin Edge?'

'Well that's my name.' Edgy instantly regretted his words. 'Damn I was so close! Bubba, you see that? Maybe the antlers ...'

Edgy produced a double candlestick holder and put it carefully on his head. De'ath groaned, whispering aside to Gregor. 'Your friend's delicate balancing act has had the effect of giving his face a look of wariness and worry. Nobody will trust him now.'

'What's that yellow slime all over you?' Gaffer demanded.

'Well it's actually blood. When I was called on so unexpectedly, I was in the middle of cutting up a body.'

'What kind of body?'

'A quadraface harpy. The meat's semi-transparent like pearl.'

'Isn't that illegal?'

'It ... would be if I weren't joking. I was actually baking a lemon meringue, as I always do on a Tuesday.'

'This is Wednesday.'

'Then the meringue is burning. Excuse me.'

'Wait a minute, you're not going anywhere. Did you witness the defendant assaulting a public marionette?'

'If I did, this is hardly the time or place to discuss it.'

'Brilliant denying, Mr Edge. Don't smile. What is your relationship to this flabby envoy from hell?'

Edgy attempted a suave demeanour. 'Well he's a friend, a work colleague, and latterly a student in the art of lurking. I can see your surprise - perhaps even shock? You see, after Gregor was accused of waving his trouble monkey at the Mayor during another speech - I think it was the "I Need More of Your Sweet Blood" monologue - he was fired from the sorting office where he also lived and, for a while, had to stay with me in the Bata Motel where I evade the rent by pretending to be a ghost.'

'You witnessed this previous outrage during another speech?'

'Yes, I was wearing only a sheet, I recall, which was torn away leaving me to slap home naked except for the context I kept explaining.'

Gaffer fixed the jury with a glare. 'Naked, ladies and gentlemen.' He turned back to Edgy. 'Have there been other such incidents involving the defendant?'

'Well it's funny you should mention that,' Edgy chuckled. 'We were in the Dummy Garden the other day, and Round One here, he starts in on his own statue.'

There were gasps of shock and efforting imagination from the audience.

'It must have been an interesting sensation,' Edgy laughed. 'Like being covered in glitter glue.'

Gaffer, smiling ruefully amid the disturbance, ended his questioning and De'ath stood. 'Mr Edge,' De'ath shouted a little for silence. 'You claim to work at the sorting office. What do you do there?'

'Well,' Edgy swallowed, 'like it says, we sort things. Some goes in the trash, some is, er ... burnt.'

'In which case, why must you evade rent? You are paid, yes?'

'Well, I think I speak for us all when I say I've better things to spend my wages on than mere rent. In any case, I don't always go in. I have a hammock which I enjoy. I'm a beautiful man, as you can see. I believe it was Violaine who said, "Since my very being is involuntary, isn't also everything it contains?".'

'The human stage is not suitable for hammocks. Idleness is an insurmountable barrier.'

'What of it, if it keeps out whatever beast it was built for.'

'Your honour, I move to strike this witness -'

'Hold him back!' shouted the judge as De'ath sprang toward the flinching Edgy. Three ushers grabbed the lawyer and pulled him to the floor.

'And here we have the unlikely kingpin of the operation,' Gaffer stated when Barny was called to the stand. 'Yes, looks like a living child doesn't he? Yet the fact that he knows and is known to every principal player in this deadly game is far from coincidental. If history teaches us nothing, it is that Barny Juno is a demon from screaming hell. Mr Juno, sinister alias "Juniper", is it not the case that you are acquainted with the defendant, and with Plantin Edge?'

'Yes, ma'am.'

'You entered a soup kitchen with Plantin Edge and committed ... assault with a deadly leopard wasn't it?'

'Edgy rode the leopard - I was upon my fine lion, Mister Braintree.'

'The same lion which ate a tailor and attacked a dactylian fiend bent on mayhem. Indeed your home is packed to the twisted rafters with winged and stepping animals isn't it?'

'They're my friends. I rescued Mister Braintree from the circus. A healthy predator is a happy predator.'

'Happy predator,' Gaffer repeated with heavy inflection. 'You have eight hundred eels in your garden - does that sound like the behaviour of a responsible man?'

'No, I suppose it doesn't, does it? Eels, are they? Are there really eight hundred?'

'Eight hundred eels.'

'Eight hundred.'

'Does that surprise you?'

'It interests me. I didn't know there were any. That's fantastic. Is there any water back there?'

'I don't know.'

'But you've seen the eels?'

De'ath bolted to his feet. 'He's got you on the run, Gaffer!'

'Everyone's seen the eels,' Gaffer declared with lofty patience, rolling his eyes to the ceiling.

'Who's seen these supposed eels?' shouted De'ath. 'Who, in this courtroom?'

'The eels have never been in this courtroom and thus have never been seen here,' Gaffer stated as though explaining all to a child.

'Is that so?' yelled De'ath, pulling eel after eel from his jacket and flinging them at Gaffer and the startled jury. 'An eel, an eel, an eel!'

'And so,' stated Gaffer, flicking an eel from his shoulder, 'you have conveniently proven that everyone in this courtroom has seen the eels.'

De'ath sank slowly into his seat again.

Gaffer swiped up a document with a flourish. 'And I have here a list of Juno's trespasses which I will shovel into everyone's ears now. He set a lion upon a tailor; released a swarm of bees in a laundry; drew a massive picture of an exploding arse on the landscape; pretended he could fly but chose not to; built and released a mechanical child upon the town; interrupted a cat in mid-yawn, particularly despicable; wore a blanket round his face and peered out of it all cute like a baby; held a funeral for a lizard and dropped his pants during the eulogy; passed a scribbled note to a duck on a pond, after which the duck swam away and was never seen again; claimed he was too exhausted to flirt; backed over an old wooden radio with a tractor. As we can see, his face is flawed and simplistic. He cannot speak of the sun or sky without making it transparently clear that he resents their achievements and abilities. And apparently he blames it all on some massive demonic insect with a brain the size of an engine block.'

Woozy with indifference, Barny began to nod.

'Let's get to the heart of the wash, shall we? Our community is in crisis, its particular chaos threatened by an organising force which seeks to guide it like a lamb to armageddon. Do we really originate the logistical smarts with this champion idiot?' He pointed at Gregor.

And then to the stand came a rogue's gallery of friends and acquaintances. BB Henrietta described Barny as 'failure bait' and started laughing so hard her hair caught fire.

Official records were silent on the question of Sags Dumbar's plasmate head, which lolled sideways like a bag of water. 'I believe you work with this walking lens fault?' Gaffer asked of Barny.

'I'll have the roast beef platter,' said Sags, and nothing more.

Fang took the stand wearing a strange wicker jacket designed to retain his tripes. His face hung away in three ragged strips. De'ath hissed aside to Gregor. 'Is there any hope, indeed life, in this walking autopsy?'

Gregor leaned to whisper. 'No.'

'Mr Fang,' Gaffer began.

'Just ... Fang,' gurgled the cadaver.

'Fang then. Can you explain how it is that Barny Juno knows so many of the slovenly, the criminal, the sick and the insane?'

'He lucked out,' came the response from a mouth which had seen better days. 'Chum.'

'Don't call me chum.' Gaffer turned toward Barny. 'Not what

you'd call a good account from this royally rotten friend of yours.'

'What do you expect?' said Barny. 'He hides in the mud.'

Completely fazed by the reply, Gaffer camouflaged his frown by repeatedly muttering 'Such a macabre retinue', but everyone thought he was saying 'Suck my carburettor nude' and it was a while before procedure was re-established.

Barny's boss the Captain was grilled to within an inch of his life as to the purpose of the sorting office, until his panicked dissembling fragmented into wracking, hysterical sobs and he was led gently from the courtroom.

Mr Peterson merely claimed that Barny had a 'cock the size of a draft log' which had to be 'kept under a tarp'.

De'ath finally found his voice, and stood proud. 'Your honour, this witness is rubbish.'

'I'll need a technical objection, Mr De'ath.'

'Very well, I suppose, it's just occurred to me that since Mr Peterson owns the hydroponics plant, he effectively owns this jury of vegetable heads.'

'That's actually rather good,' frowned the Drylord.

'I must admit I sounded more confident than I felt,' chuckled De'ath.

The final witness was Mayor Rudloe, who was still trying to pull on his containment suit as he was marched into the courtroom. 'Exposure!' he gasped, seeing the assembled masses, and attempted to zip his hood as he was forced to the stand. 'Adopt explanation demeanour, Gaffer,' he demanded.

'After all,' the lawyer stated smoothly, 'there can be no doubt about your part in this. You were on the balcony above the town clock when the molestation occurred.'

'I well remember the incident, so what? I was informing the town I'd rule dead-eyed and bloated from atop a hill of human skulls and then all hell broke loose in the bell chamber.'

'Oh, now - even to an unattentive listening your account is an obvious lie.'

'Eh?'

'The evil genius Barny Juno - he's known to you?'

'Yes, he's the fellow who entered my office dressed as a grizzly, flew past the window on a swan, whipped me with a python and asked for a job.'

'And what purpose is served by the blood tax? Where does it all go?'

'What? The levy? Well, it drives the blood clock, as you well know.'

'So much? Many suspect that the bulk goes elsewhere.'

'You work in my office, Gaffer - if it did, you'd know it.'

'Indeed,' said Gaffer.

'And be implicated,' added Rudloe in a hurry. 'In any case the evidence for that is entirely anecdotal.'

'So's everyone's account of themselves, the world and anything they've ever experienced.'

'Blackmail and insurrection,' stated the Mayor, thoughtfully. 'Here, among the dead.'

'Perhaps I should leave you here.'

The Mayor stared at him levelly. 'You assume too much.'

'I'm finished with this one, your honour,' said Gaffer dismissively, and turned away.

'Your honour,' De'ath announced as the Mayor stood down, 'I'd like to introduce a surprise witness, but since I don't have one, I'm placing a set of false gums on the front of the witness stand.'

'So I see. Does this mean anything?'

'I'm thinking about that.' De'ath frowned down at his shoes for a while.

'Anything yet?' asked the judge.

'No.'

'I'm going to have to hurry you.'

'Well, since you pressure me, let's just say it means ... nothing unusual.'

'You can take the gums away now, counsellor.'

'Well alright, but I'm not happy.'

Kenny Reactor spritzed water over the jury heads during a short recess, the ash of innocents was spread on the floor and Dumbar's gelid head was the talk of the time lounge. The court resumed for closing statements.

De'ath strode slowly about the court, his words a steady drip. 'You have seen a series of witnesses, real and imagined, go on at length about my client's depravities, as well as sundry unrelated matters designed to stun us with boredom, dulling the senses and stripping the myelin from our nerves. But I'm not so sure. Look at the accused now, for perhaps the last time. He has a face that sets back the cause of civilisation a hundred years. His ears can open and close like a valve and he makes a virtue of admitting it. The days of the week are his personal disaster in serial form. Yet Gregor here, a pioneer of sorts, explores for us the byways of sensuality and should be applauded. His blink-and-you'll-miss-it sanity, meanwhile, should provoke our tears, not our scorn. This offence, witnessed by so many people and from such a variety of angles that a 360-degree hologram of the incident has already been mass-produced and is on sale on the very steps of this court, is not beyond pardon. I myself once rodgered a standing cow and the pleasure it afforded me is beyond the scope of this closing argument to describe, even in out-line. No, ladies and gentlemen of the jury, I cannot do it justice - but your duty today is to do justice to the twenty-four-hour erotic holo-caust who sits before us. He refused to be furtive, and that's how matters stand.'

Max Gaffer's statement was more folksy, appealing to common sense and a desire for slowly revolving gore.

'That one over there,' he began, pointing to Gregor, 'that's what we're dealing with - pear shaped and he doesn't care. Every time he opens his distorted mouth, we are witness to a turmoil of crinkle-cut alibis and mind-boggling profanity. Nothing pleases him more than to disgrace himself in the public square. If he does not ride upon dogs it is only because he has no wish to do so. And since I was exposed to his excuses my forehead has taken on the consistency of tough leather. Yes, ladies and gentlemen, we have all had to suffer the poor-est of explanations from defence counsel as to why this little universe of darkness forced his attentions upon a defenceless effigy. You have seen Mr De'ath attempt to discredit the witness Plantin Edge by smacking him in the mouth. Another witness, the one wearing Jonathan glasses, has been ejected on a clever technicality. All designed to deflect attention away from the ringleader. Because such events don't occur by chance, my friends. In a random world, the organising hand stands out like a snorting pig in a smashed wedding cake. As Violaine said, "Some wait to be discovered - others, to be found out." Barny Juno, that featherheaded wonder-child in the gallery, purporting to be a simple man, committed clear-cut lurking during the assault, looking on, knowing, seeing, breathing. He was a confidante of all the key agents, and a sworn enemy of the Mayor. With so much evidence, condemning this man has never been easier. And I have here a sworn affidavit, signed by one hundred people, stat-ing that they saw Juno ordering Gregor to disrupt the Mayor's speech and subsequently shouting "Hooray, I am a sinister presence".'

'I wish Chloe was here,' said Barny in the spectators' gallery. 'I love her so much, Edgy.'

'Bubba,' Edgy hushed urgently. 'They've got it in for you.'

A couple of chefs in the row in front turned back with glares of approbation.

'Pass that up,' the Judge ordered, and Gaffer gave him the docu-ment. 'How can we know these forged signatures are real?'

Max Gaffer pushed forward a barrow of stacked papers. He took a sheet from the top. 'This is a sworn affidavit attesting to the authenticity of the signatures on the first document. This is signed by a different bunch of people.'

'How do we know those signatures are legitimate?'

'By the assurance of the third affidavit, signed and attested. This in turn is backed up by a fourth, and that by a fifth - I have here four hundred such affidavits, your honour.'

'How is the last one proven?'

'By the rider attached to the document you're holding, your honour, and witnessed by the first set of signatures. It's a proof cycle, a self-supporting system.'

'A daisyclaim,' the judge nodded. 'Very well.' He placed the paper aside. 'Mr Gaffer, the focus of this trial seems to have shifted to this fellow Mr Juno, but since I am born to serve you absolutely, that's just fine. Your attack upon the Mayor also passes me by entirely, for reasons the powerless public shall never know. You are, truly, a lovely man.'

'Thank you, your honour.'

The Drylord addressed the rack of mint-eyed jury heads. 'Your big and only chance has arrived.'

The spokeshead parted a beak like a cabbage rib. 'If a mind can truly teem with one idea, we have led a rich inner life, and thank you.'

Three of the heads in the back row began screaming in a way reserved for those who needn't take a breath. It was the sound of a patriot who has given all and then seen where it went.

The head speaker continued as though pre-recorded, its eyes like medals. 'The defendant is composed of litter which death will clear from him.' And the head began to emit a high whistling noise, which continued seamlessly until the court realised that the verdict had been given in full.

Satisfied, the Drylord ordered Gregor to stand up, and addressed him.

'In my budding youth, the merest formality could excite me. I'm beyond the age when due process can afford me any pleasure. But today your death comes highly recommended, and so it seems your attempt to poison me at the start of this trial has returned with new alliances. Your mis-shapen head and lack of real direction in life mark you out as a colossal threat to our institutions, to lovely bright flowers, and even some of the better class of insect about the place. Butterflies, yes.'

'How long do we have to listen to this mattress?' Gregor hissed to De'ath, a whisper which the fluted walls amplified to an oceanic crash.

'Staring our society's etiquette in the face,' the judge continued savagely, 'pointblank and silent, without meaning or comment, offering no alternative, no critique - merely the sight of your spectacular transgression upon the very ramparts of authority. Your mania for statues - yes, mania. Is thoroughly irresponsible. And so, revenge is ours. Do you wish to make a statement before you are conveyed from this place to the mime tent? Be mindful that, as a convicted felon, anything you say will appear on your permanent record.'

'There it is,' Gregor thought, and was on the stand, feeling released, strangely super-confident, well disposed toward everybody, drawing a lungful. 'Well, I made it. I never thought I'd achieve anything permanent in my life. The judge is right on the money about my depravity and lack of any constructive suggestions. I don't have a clue what's going on, and I really don't care. So I'm grateful to everyone here - especially my friends Barny, Edgy, Henrietta, pud'n head Dumbar over there, and good old Fang, resurrected by popular demand, ha ha. I love 'em all. Even the jury of pulseless pulses here, look at 'em - top-drawer assessors of guilt, every one of 'em. More power to their cool botanical brains. Here I am, condemned, and they haven't guessed half of what I'm capable of. Beautiful. And the lawyers. Tell them you're gunna destroy the requirement for flames and they'll lick their pencils and take it down. The professionalism of those guys. I feel loose and happy. Justice is done. Everything is easy. The system works.' Gregor looked out upon the attentive courtroom. He seemed to tremble on the verge of tears. 'You know, when Edgy and I ventured into the swamps on a quest for knowledge the other day, we met the wise old hag Feral Beryl. I had doubted how useful some broken-down failure could be to anyone, but immediately the light of knowledge in her eyes pinned me. I put to her my deepest questions regarding ambition, pillow sprats, yearning, and all my mad dealings with this world. Would I wind up as I suspected, corralled at night by normally gentle neighbours and butchered wordlessly on a football field? Well, the old crone thoughtfully appraised the condition of my arse, gazed at the smoky trace of the trees against the night sky, nodded her head thoughtfully, and looked me in the eye. And she imparted this knowledge: "Always eat a fish headfirst. You never know."' Gregor paused for effect. The entire court was hushed except for a couple of chefs who seemed to be experiencing some agitation. 'Was she right, or was she right? So, ladies and gentlemen, I bear you no ill-will. This is simply the endtime of a keg-shaped, clueless joke with a brain the size of a Subbuteo figure. Good people, when you've seen the mere door of the matter, begin to retreat, and don't make the mistake I made. Farewell - forever.'

It was soon clear to Gregor that his self-memorial had gone awry. The court had become humbled. The jury heads were squitting some silver spores which for them were tears. The public spectators too were feeling pity and regret like it was going out of style. 'Your honour,' said the head speaker, 'we wish to acquit.'

'No - not acquit, not acquit!' Gregor shouted.

'I agree,' said the judge. 'The accused is free to go, and all trace of these proceedings are hereby struck from the record.'

'The record?' Gregor shrieked. 'But it's permanent! Permanent! I'm guilty! I've done it all! No alibi! I'm a monster! When I see a nice person I slice his gizzard as a matter of routine! Nap chickens!' Gregor leapt from the stand, blurting his every imagining in a spasm of panicked candour. He snatched the affidavit from the Judge's desk and scrunched it under Gaffer's nose. 'I'm taking this home to Mr Belly!' he shrieked, and stuffed it into his own mouth, chewing as he grabbed one of the jury heads and banana-kicked it into the spectators' gallery amid screams. 'I'm doing it! I'm doing it! Take it or leave it!'

'What's this disgrace?' the Judge was shouting as Gregor ran past the podium.

Gregor stood peeing in the corner and bellowed at the rafters 'Good news! I'm learning! I'm learning!' The pasta wall began to soften and sag, wilting open and slapping to the floor. Part of the roof shuddered and tilted with a bang, flour sifting down. The courthouse began crumbling. The judge's podium dissolved like a honeycomb candle. Screaming idiots were trying to run, skidding across the slimy floor. Splinters of pasta were flying like detonated glass.

'I'm bored,' said BB Henrietta.

'I feel terrible,' said Barny. 'Let's go - you coming, Edgy?'

'Not yet - the Mayor might say something else.'

Barny and BB wandered out through a hole in the wall just before the pasta lattice roof fell in and hit the floor like custard.

9

HEX ENDUCTION HOUR

Nature can get away with anything

Barny slept so deeply he had to grow up every morning, and perhaps the day never held enough time for him to reach full adulthood. This night he dreamt again of the razor larynx shooting from the sea, its eyes black flukes without detail, a mouth like a downturned horse-shoe - and his own fear sent him running again, away from Chloe and the shore, to Beltane Carom's garden. In fact the yard configuration formed a wall behind Carom, as though he were floating on his back above it. Angels sharp as knives darted around him. 'Logic is only another garden,' Carom said. 'Anything in life can serve as a doorway to understanding - some open straight on to it, while others open on to a long corridor full of stinking garbage. Shove imagination to join your rent, and it becomes something else.'

Barny's disinterest was mild and amiable, without obstinacy. 'I still don't get it, ma'am.'

'The truth drinks last, when everyone's gone home. That tin homunculus for instance - the most strangely detailed things are done as a diversion. The Powderhouse, the Church of Automata - the same theology begins them all.'

'What do you mean.'

'Dangers of clarity.'

'That doesn't seem much of a danger at the moment. This is exactly the way you talk in real life - why do you have to be doing this in a dream?'

'I'm being watched,' the shaman whispered, and Barny found himself watching Prancer Diego leave the snout distillery. Diego once left the house with a demon on his back and, thinking it was a duffel bag, stuffed a football down its throat. Now he spotted Barny and frolicked over, dispensing insults like caramels, strumming a nerve lute, his tears flowing upward. 'Proposition one - never empty the trash. Proposition two - contort so your shadow is a key. Yes, it's me - and not a moment too soon I see. The sky fills me with feelers, their industry of mouths confidently pouching, oh I giggle, I giggle.'

Barny shoved him away and ran across the pennyground acres. Showers and wages on the land flapped.

As the sun set Bo began to soften and shine, turning to sugar.

Barny found Bo glistening silently on a chair, realised the time and cursed, looking at his watch. He had wanted to ask him something, it would have to wait until morning.

Barny awoke suddenly. Who the hell was Bo? He didn't know anyone by that name. Looking aside, Barny found that BB Henrietta was asleep beside him. He was in her house and they had slept together last night after the trial. So much for fighting the nightmare. He had re-smashed the fragments of his relationship with Chloe. He was a monster.

Barny staggered through the dark into the bathroom. There were inexplicable containers everywhere. 'Body gel,' he read from a label. He found a hand mirror and placed it on the floor facing upward. What were those weird words the shaman had spoken to summon his demon ally?

Before Barny had done anything the mirror began to ring and Rakeman emerged as creepy as a chirp from a breakfast egg. It came seething into shape and stood there. The air trickled slowly around it.

'This is the worst night of my life,' said Barny. There he was having fun at a friend's trial, and the next thing he knew he was in a cramped bathroom with a tragic-looking creature made entirely of ankles.

Rakeman blew ashes and other shite out of a mouth like a sack. The electric sockets were bleeding.

'Are you using my toothbrush?' asked BB Henrietta, appearing naked in the doorway. She registered the etiolated saw doctor fluctuating in blasts of spinelight, shook her head, turned and left.

Barny kicked the mirror and it skitted across the floor, hitting the closing door. It flipped over, blinking the demon from view, and Barny stamped on it, the glass crunching like a key in a lock.

He staggered panting into the bedroom. BB Henrietta was pulling on her jeans and generally tearing about the place. 'Draft log or not,' she said, 'that's the last time I ever have sex with you.'

His sanity long abandoned as an impossible dream, doomed Eddie Gallo didn't have any serious reservations about giving hospitality to a creature which appeared to have a diamond hammer for a head. He opened his cottage door and smiled a friend straight away. 'Good morning to you. As Bingo Violaine said, "Never learn a saying from behind a door - mis-hearing could lead to embarrassment." Come in.'

'My name is Dietrich Hammerwire - I have followed your opposition campaign with interest, doomed Eddie Gallo.' Dietrich looked around the living room. He had been here before, incognito, and little seemed to have changed. 'Spring onions in a vase eh?'

Gallo called from the kitchen. 'And jars with bonnets.'

'There's a tortoise in the drinks cabinet.'

'I know - heck of a deal isn't it? You'll have to excuse these elaborate trousers. Today's a colonic holiday for my people.'

'Its these tiny cribs that scare me.'

'Just a hobby - made from fishbone.'

'I notice so much more these days. I see your hair has grown to resemble a cardigan.' Dietrich jabbed a claw at Gallo's forehead. 'I'm new here. What's this?'

'The forehead is the head's palm. Not from Accomplice? How is that?'

'Do you know what hell is, doomed Eddie Gallo?'

'Not much. Bit of a tense atmosphere round there I expect. Lot of awkward silences and that sort of thing. You say you've followed m'campaign for mayor? Seen the new angle?' He presented Dietrich with a poster.

'"Understand My Legs" is not a campaign slogan.'

'Know the legs, the rest will follow. Biscuit?'

'Thankyou. And what's this rubbish about you sensing a flower?'

Gallo looked on without comprehension.

'Do you understand, doomed Eddie Gallo, that you will never be Mayor as long as you continue this way?'

'Oh, I'm fine - though I've been treated like a woolly monkey, I'm determined to remain bright no matter what.'

'I find your optimism positively morbid, doomed Eddie Gallo. I ...'

Learning from the Powderhouse's strutting procedures, doomed Eddie Gallo had established a personal regimen of quantum shrugging - he would allow all he didn't know or understand to accumulate for several days and, at saturation point, shuck his shoulders hundreds of times in quick succession. Those who witnessed this would think he was having a fit, though he usually continued speaking quite clearly during the procedure. As he began to shudder before Dietrich Hammerwire, he was baffled at the creature's sudden startled stare and backwards retreat to the door. 'Thanks for visiting,' he called as Dietrich's face withdrew and the door closed.

Later he was watering the front garden and a truck hauled up, steam pouring out of it. After topping up the radiator in a neighbourly way, he had a chat with the driver, who appeared to be a small artificial girl made of plastic and cardboard. She seemed very interested in his policy ideas and they drove out to the flyover stump on the North edge of town. They sat near the cliff edge and opened a packed lunch of bananas and digestive biscuits. Gallo pointed to a heave of concrete waves, severed steel reinforcement shafts poking out at the breaklines. 'The sloths did that - they explode when accosted, and every attempt to vault this canyon blasted more off the road until, well, you can see - it's no more than a ramp now. I plan to bring timber from the Awkward Forest and extend it.' Gallo indicated some hardpan. 'That used to be called a lay-by. It was purely for sex.' They walked to the very edge. A wooden sign was coughing in the updraft. Gallo handed her the binoculars and she clicked them against the glass of her eyes. The opposite side of the canyon was heatwarping, patched here and there with vegetation and shot through with black sheets of rock. She swept the glasses along the far ridge. It seemed desolate. There were no people. 'Look down there,' Gallo suggested. She peered through the binoculars at the canyon floor, which was a lost world of mist and vegetation, speckled here and there with white dots. 'Those are manuscripts,' Gallo told her, and gestured over at the offices of Nimble Champ Books, the rear of which projected over the abyss. 'Convenient. There's a few phantoms down there too but they're rubbish, frankly. Useless to man and beast.'

Gallo began talking about the Miasma and Amy's play, how he planned to bake hundreds of pies made of pure lard. He soon forgot that the doll was there, and started chirping like a bird, chuckling at his own amusements. He had zoned out completely when Maquette told him she was interested in the play. 'Especially if there are animals.'

'I'm sure there'll be a part in it for you,' said doomed Eddie Gallo. 'We are all one community.'

The truck, this time, was dead. They would have to drop by Abblatia's and steal another one.

Mayor Rudloe plucked up the phone. 'Ah, Grand Dollimo - how are you and your waxen atrocities this morning? The escaped doll? Yours is it? I'm sorry, I do not assign rights to novelties.' He paused, then his voice was jerky and high. 'Max Gaffer paid you a visit? Without my sanction, I assure you. No, he doesn't know you provide the Gubba Men. He knows nothing of our arrangement, he shouldn't have approached you. The Steinways? Now don't do anything rash. I've a beef to pick with that shyster myself. Keep those monsters under lock and key, I'll deal with this. I assure you I am appalled by his acts. He will be dismissed as soon as his career is over. Goodbye.'

It was perfectly clear to Rudloe that he would not be seeing Gaffer again except as a deadly foe or other inconvenience. Stung into action by the lawyer's betrayal, he looked fiercely at a corner of the desk. 'I'm ready for anything,' he barked at the empty room, at which a daub of demon lengthened to the floor, walking on. 'Well, menace me quickly or not at all, I've matters to attend to.' But Dietrich Hammerwire seated himself opposite and asked for a job. The Mayor was tortuously aghast. 'You think I'll employ any out-at-elbows fiend who walks in here? Straight out of purgatory and leaning in the crackers?'

'There's no point in concealing my preference,' said Dietrich mildly, the fresh dawn light glinting off his hell-blasted cowling. He gazed outside - there was a man standing atop a high stepladder in the Square and consulting a book. Children surrounded the scene. 'What's that moron doing?'

'Learning braille, apparently,' the Mayor muttered. He was wary, knowing that a deal with a demon invariably entailed a number of hair-raising provisos. 'How do I know you're not a placeman for the forces of hell?'

'Oh, give it a year and then take a view on it.'

'So what's your advice for a kick-off?'

'Put on a dress and kill everyone you see.'

'A dress? Kill?'

'Is there any reason why we can't begin immediately?'

'Aren't you the bastard who disguised yourself as a normal fella to convince me I should win over the masses by pushing a servant off the balcony?'

'Sounds like the sort of thing I would suggest.'

'Exactly. And now it's dresses and immediate killing.'

'Just so. What do the people have on you?'

'They know me because the van sings my name. Blame the sentry for the scarce attacks.'

'You might try a more folksy role in the Miasma proceedings, perhaps. Good sport and man of the people. Then confound all by saying something interesting as the eclipse occurs.'

'Interesting, eh?' Rudloe turned the notion over in his head.

'You could even try apology.'

'It's true - that apology gag gets 'em every time.'

'It has the element of surprise, and a fairly long rhetoric decay rate.' Dietrich seemed bored, distracted - it was all too easy. 'There's the philosophy of politics, and there's the career of politics - the two are not good for eachother. Where the two meet, the process and machinery of politics is excreted. That's why you're full of shit, Mayor.'

'Well the fact remains I'm the big wheel around here. I'll consider your application. Leave me now - oh and excuse all these megabugs.'

'Have you tried paraffin?'

'Yes.'

'Have you tried honesty?'

'You're joking ofcourse.'

When the anvil-headed demon was gone, Rudloe put a call through to the Conglomerate.

10

SPIGOT GIRL

It's only good manners to wave to one's assassin

Mike Abblatia was a blot of pain which increased with each vehicle he lost. When the plastic child roared away in a truck, he had felt his back expand, small bones creaking. Doctor Perfect had a real knack for removing important meat but Abblatia approached his surgery as though it were a narrowing corner of hope. 'Enter my empire of emergencies,' called the Doctor. 'I was just carving the image of a screaming leper into this old root beam.' And he tapped the leper's nose. 'Wasn't I, matey? Now - Mike Abblatia isn't it? Don't see you often - keep yourself to yourself eh? Well, don't worry. Things have moved on a little since we tied one end of a rope to the patient's tonsils and the other end to a rampaging horse. Sit up on this crushed car.'

There were two cars with flattened roofs - the other one was occupied by what appeared to be a large smashed fungus. Abblatia sat on the free surface.

Doctor Perfect took up a pair of tongs and began tugging at Abblatia's ears. 'These legs of yours have seen better days - if they are legs. Been kicking badgers have we? And your nostrils appear to have a life of their own. Look up to the corner. Now to the other corner. See those things that look like pancakes? They're a kind of mould growing up there. It gives me hope that life can thrive in the grimmest places. Give a sort of cough which is loaded with significance, will you? Good. And again? I understand.' He tossed the tongs aside. 'Well, I'm afraid your brain has lain fallow for some years, your torso is completely uninteresting and your balls are a mystery. I could offer you a phial of goatwater but you would refuse it, chundering like billy-o. I'm at a loss as to what you expect of me.'

'My back's the problem, Doctor.'

'Bit dicey is it? Alright, take off this shapeless garment and lay on your front.'

After laying forward amid silence a while, Abblatia heard the Doctor pronounce. 'This "back" as you charmingly characterise it - you're aware that if it was any more swollen I should have to perform a citizen's arrest? Been having alot of fun with it haven't you? However, the good news is, I can help you with knives. Lie still, laddie.'

Abblatia felt a cold tingling down his spine.

'I'm cutting the seam. There's no blood. Pushing the edges aside. It's completely clean. A sort of damp fuzz in there. Seems to be some kind of fibrous mush, like the white innards of a seedy loaf.'

Mike Abblatia's attention was wandering, his eyes floating over the walls of coloured hux tinctures and flay charts. His attention drifted to the other car and he recognised it as one which had been stolen from him two years before. The one he lay upon, he realised, had been boosted slightly more recently.

'Fascinating,' the Doctor was saying.

Abblatia sat up as though tranced, and pulled his shirt on.

The Doctor seemed fazed by his patient's capacity for autonomous will during the examination. 'Off somewhere are we laddie?'

Mike Abblatia walked out through the time lounge and up the muddy slope, opening the rotten hatch into the alley as sunlight exploded upon him.

The Conglomerate had sent for Max Gaffer and he entered the flesh basement prepared to adopt explanation demeanour. Hanging alimentary loops dragged across his face.

'Here he comes,' said one of the voices from the half-light, 'his authority in one hand and his broken heart in the other. Beware turning the truffle of that one's brain.'

'We've heard about your obscure debacle in the courtroom.'

'Oh I see.' Gaffer knew this was a failure, pure and simple. By the time the courthouse had sagged completely, the judge was able only to purse his lips in a funny way - or perhaps he was simply inclined to do so. According to procedure the jury heads were tossed on a bonfire and the judge was sent to the dryhouse, a small unfurnished bungalow on the edge of town. Like many drylords before him, he would stand silent in that dim concrete-floored room as night turned to day and day turned to night, crumbling slowly to a heap resembling powdered bracken. 'You approved my advancement.'

'Guilt and implication. As last-ditch as a spring-snake in a failure's mouth. You went beyond your remit. The Mayor serves us well, knowingly or not. So, etherically you outrank him. It also means you're no longer quite anchored here. Unlike the Mayor, who's dug in like the true bastard.'

Gaffer stumbled over slimy bones, grasping for balance at hanging rinds of gut. 'What do you mean?'

'The Mayor's corruption is dependable. You? You're ambitious - and dealing with poisons more instant than ours. It makes you rather too volatile, useful only for the very short term.'

'I'll make amends, anything. Give me a contract, I'll sign in colour.'

The voices came thick and fast from different parts of the organ reef.

'The idea has merit, as trash.'

'Treasonable dealings are forgiven only when successful.'

'You're as duped as a battle surgeon - a hack.'

'But why open that can of nerves.'

'You entertain us with harm, merely.'

'Give our regards to your gigantic host.'

'Death occurs here, my friend. On your neck.'

Amid the sense of nerve bodies heaving, Gaffer felt a yank at his throat and he came loose, hitting a hard corner of the room. Such gentlemen always needed cold stone, even if they didn't have food. Gaffer gagged at the aroma of hamburgers frying in the skull. Another barb dug into his side and a film of milky colour clouded his eyes. 'Ah, the moment of the face falling apart, spattered with angel,' said one of the mouths. But Gaffer had gotten turned around. He was on the step out of here - he tried to stand, nudging at the doors.

'D'you mind telling me what you're doing?' came the commanding shout from behind as he crawled through the doors into the silverine foyer. Far away was the elevator door. He glimpsed strange dry flowers, and blood pooling on the carpet under him. Opening his shirt, he let it flow down to the metal barb at his chest, which seemed to soak it up some, though the beak made a noise like a screaming infant.

Gaffer climbed the spiral stairs to his oval bonehouse, throwing himself inside and collapsing in an armchair. His wound had begun to clot a little. The Grand Dollimo was at the corner bar, fixing a mazarinade. 'You really had no idea of the nature of my arrangement with the Mayor.'

'How did you get in here.'

'And the match girl, our runaway - no result. Yet all the while, you claimed to have the Mayor's blessing.'

'That statement was only local - in fact it did not persist beyond the room.'

Dollimo's waxen hatchet man advanced through a doorway, its earth-red skin blazing in strips of sunlight.

'Had you telephoned,' Gaffer breathed, half-rising out of the chair, 'I could have saved you an inconvenient journey. I'll not concede to be slaughtered today.'

'In the coffin we return to the wild.' The Dollimo approached Gaffer with two glasses, handing him one. Gaffer sank down again. 'We blot there and sag. Plenty of time to relax our stance when the time comes. Until then.' And the Dollimo raised his drink in salutation. He did not join Gaffer in drinking - his glass mask made this impossible. He strolled to one of the broad windows, which showed a far strip of blue ocean. 'Do you know that human beings used to do the work of the Gubba Men? They were called 'police'. They were replaced, finally, with our blandflesh.'

Gaffer played for time, eyeing the room for a weapon. 'Why do it that way? Why the Gubba Men?'

'Something to do with dissonance. Human beings acting less than human, and thus being treated as such, yet acting surprised or offended when it happened. This way, however, all accords with itself - and no feelings to be hurt. I thought you would have guessed that Distaff Plastique here is an advanced Gubba unit. No feeling, you see. His core temperature's way below zero, like a tailor. Distaff is empty life, a tool made for one job.'

As Distaff neared him, Gaffer saw that the automaton held the Iron Smile in its vinyl hand. He smashed his glass and launched himself at Distaff, slashing the slick upholstery of its forehead. The sentinel knocked him aside with an easy swipe of its arm.

The Grand Dollimo was chuckling softly to himself. 'That red pepper brain of his showing through like sofa leather? A class act all the way, isn't he? A future without content - your future.'

'I'll find your doll,' Gaffer barked as Distaff Plastique locked a hand on his shoulder, preventing him from rising.

'The doll knows nothing. D'you think it's that easy? Place a brain cell in a jointed doll and bingo? D'you think the dolls, those totems, all this mechanical business, is what it's about? What makes more noise than the death of a man? The death of a secret.'

The Iron Smile was a dull beaten half-mask rattling with attachments.

'What secret. What are the dolls and all hiding?'

'That we can never be creation's original stem, perhaps?'

Distaff placed the dented metal bridle over Gaffer's mouth.

'I don't believe it,' said Gaffer. 'You lashed together some sort of religion out of smoked glass and chicken wire, why?'

Distaff tightened the first screw with an automatic screwdriver - it went through Gaffer's face and into his cheekbone.

'What's it all about? To hide what?'

The thinner bones snapped audibly as five more screws screamed into Gaffer's skull, locking the mask to his face. His features were pinned in place.

The Dollimo leaned down at him. 'Happy?'

Gaffer couldn't help but smile.

He groped down the twelve steps to Sweeney's cavern.

Enthroned in a veined hull, the white shell emperor floated his head around. 'Ah, war returns from exotic climes, over-loud for the home. Report, report, as florid as you can.'

Nerve guylines twanged as the Ruby Aspict descended from the sky-high roof. Gaffer crawled across freezing sickstone, puzzle-toothed and broken. 'Barny ... appears to be kept aloft by efforts invisible and constant as hummingbird wings.'

'Nice touch. Continue.'

'He's happy to care for the winged and stepping animals of the earth.'

'Happiness sounds rather dull.'

'Maybe it's the way I describe it. Then again, maybe not. Glee, at least, is worth the effort.'

'Glee? Sounds like a jelly preserve.'

'Well,' breathed Gaffer, at a loss, 'life continues - the primeval soup prevails.'

'Black mud is no consolation I'm afraid. Still, many a slip between pup and tip. And the eclipse approaches, oiling the skylight. However, since agreeing to put your few remaining principles beyond use, you've exhausted m'patience with petty and somewhat lurid reprisals. What are your personal intrigues? A spark in the grandeur of my life. Wipe that smile off your face, man.'

'I'm ashamed, your majesty,' burbled the crouching figure as the roiling red Aspict settled behind him.

'You clearly thought hell was cosmetic, fangs sewn into your jacket and so forth. Personality retention. No such luck, regrettably. Time for you to graduate.'

Cold voltage branched through the lawyer and his anatomy became an open secret, flents of skin flying like sawdust. The black of his suit became a thickness of constantly roiling spiders, his own bleached ribs replaced the white of his shirt, and twelve sleek swords sprang erect from his skull, each leaking a slow excess of toxins which ran in a constant tide down his shiny grinning face. His eyes were glints the size of nail pairings.

His reflection tumbled in the turning Aspict. Relieved that he would still be able to pass himself off in the legal community, he turned to Sweeney and bowed low his towering crown of bayonets. 'You do me too much honour sir. Life, merely - a dainty loss. May I realise all is dross.'

'The demon Maximillion,' Sweeney pronounced with satisfaction. 'Charmed.'

11

THE GALE

Like a cyclist, the critic is assuming you'll get out of the way

Despair is not a subtle business. Barny entered the town's celebration of culture with his lion loping beside him. Scardummy Garden was filled with goofy project action, skriking kids, busted porphyry columns, erratic behaviour, eyes filming over, cameras from the Douglas Bar Show, carnage, and one trotting dog. All the town's statues stood planted in earth, some decked and maintained, some left to the flowers. To Barny everything passed in mourning.

Edgy had stolen a truck from Mike Abblatia and filled it with glass harpy pies - this had collided with a truck which doomed Eddie Gallo had stolen from Mike Abblatia and filled with lard pies. The wares had become a little mixed as they scrabbled to reload, but who would know or care about anything either of these idiots thought or tried to do? Barny wandered up to doomed Eddie Gallo's stall and noticed a strange mechanical doll playing under the table. 'What's this, doomed Eddie Gallo?'

'A doll,' said doomed Eddie Gallo, giving Barny a complimentary pie. 'A sort of talking mask, really. Escaped from that silent temple of needles on the corner of town.'

'Who's pulling her strings?'

'No crank organ for this glass-eyed beauty, Barny. She's cut her own umbilical. I like her.' And Gallo began shouting his pie pitch to the crowd, scaring everyone. 'Pies! Perhaps you should consider other things a waste of time? Pies! Perhaps you should consider other things a waste of time? Pies!'

At his nearby stall, Edgy realised that this pie tirade would work to his own advantage also, and began moving his mouth as though he were forming the words himself. '*I am the shining man*,' he thought.

The lion bellied under Gallo's table to follow the capering doll, and Barny went behind the stall to find them sat together on the grass. He joined them beneath the whiskery trees, and offered the doll a piece of pie.

'I eat carpets,' she said.

Barny thought about it for a while, drawing a blank.

A fairylike dragonfly landed on the grubby pink prosthetic plastic of her arm. She watched it until it took off again.

Nearby was a struggle-statue of a man tangled with a sort of mechanical mosquito the size of a sewing machine. The bug's rusty legs were caught in the statue as though in resin. The whole thing looked finished and ditched, unlike the other figures here. 'Silence,' said Barny. 'It's going to be silence from now on for me.'

'I like this furry,' said the doll, putting her hand into the deep fur of Mister Braintree. The lion licked his chops and gave a snaggled yawn.

'He's my friend,' Barny told her. 'His purring is twenty times the volume of a household cat. He can jump as far as forty feet and as high as fifteen feet.'

Maquette rested on the lion's head. Barny looked toward the fair's centre - everything seemed to be slowing, GI Bill's stride swimming to an almost stop, gaps opening in the pressure-world as the Mayor tortuously ascended a pyramid of dead tailors, a sluggish blue balloon passing him.

The Mayor tottered a little and used the mike stand to find his balance. He surveyed the crowd and turned to the demon Dietrich. 'Present yourself like a theme park and the louts appear.'

'The mike's open, Mayor.'

'God almighty. Well everyone, here we are in the Dummy Precinct. Nothing like a hard and ringleted head to make a fella look classical. Tedious grass around here and so on, you'll notice. But we won't let that distract us from this foolhardy escapade, yes, these grotesque antics, many of which are already looking to me like a relic from the past. This day will melt away, and so will you. But until that time, there will be no respite from entertainment - it will be brutal. I cannot over-emphasise the dangers inherent in this nonsense. Give yourselves up to drunkenness and wild conjecture. Evade, evade, evade as factory funnels pump stains into the sky. You are all my children. I feel the rest of the introduction is rubbish, I'll let you imagine it.' The Mayor began to mime atrociously, losing the attention of his audience in seconds. 'Democracy is the right to add to the swarm's thrum or to remain silent.'

'The mike's still open, Mayor.'

'Oh, hell - well everyone, to begin the Miasma, I now unveil a portrait of myself, rendered by the esteemed Undo Cakewalk. You have my authority to understand the thing.' He pulled on a string and the veil fell from a picture stand. The painting seemed to portray a furtive herring aiming a mallet at a shivering dog, the entire scene heavy with fog and darkness.

'It's a picture of a decomposing camel,' came an appalled voice from the crowd.

'Why?' wailed another. 'Why show us this?'

'Er, I declare the Miasma of Culture, open,' the Mayor stammered, and stepped down from the pyramid as the band struck up a warning, thought consultants decamped in panic and a gout of smilers looked with hidden despair upon kids riffling their gills like new playing cards. The Mayor surveyed the scene. 'Maybe it's better this way,' he said mournfully. In his new role as advisor to the Mayor, Dietrich had convinced him to play a part in BB's theatrical production, something Rudloe barely understood. The demon slapped him on the back, directing him toward the makeshift stage, and followed him, looking to the sky.

Along the main arcade were stalls of caged boneseed stretched with tailorskin, selling umbilical soda and feather-aerial radios. Mr De'ath operated a children's puppet show or so-called 'campaign of terror', presenting his version of 'The Tell Tale Heart' in which the protagonist buried a strawberry under the floor and was haunted by a lack of ideas. Flesh performers experimented with cheek holes and new ragged mouths. There was a 'honking booth' where a man foretold futures of violent death and failure. Entitled 'Horrifying Futures', it sent a few people scurrying and, once the word was out, attracted no more.

Fang presented an exhibit called 'Do Glass Chairs Make You Uncertain?' Citizens were urged to sit in some glass chairs and see how they felt. Rooster showcased his 'lard music' - 'He croon jowly and unsolvable' went the publicity. His tone was in fact unusually surly, on the edge of truculence, as he strutted with a barely-restrained violence. He folded a cloth napkin during his rendition of 'Every Single Time', then presented it for view with a sharp, threatening flourish. There in the funnel were collected houseflies.

Prancer Diego wrapped himself in sack and chains and, struggling for what would be recorded subsequently as a full five weeks, chided his furious onlookers for lacking the 'precious gift of patience'.

'Tight show, Prancer,' Edgy called during the first tense hour.

Prancer was distracted, ungrateful. 'Mark me up for seventy courses of lashing with a hurlypen whip, target me, target me!'

Gregor did a strange 'mirror duet' with an empty frame, on the other side of which stood his statue. It was inappropriately romantic and he began snogging his image, climbing it with hugging legs. This tidy little spectacle revolted one and all, including his girlfriend Magenta Blaze. She punched the nose of his statue, breaking Gregor's nose and her own. The guy in the honking booth up and died. The lucky dip was a predictably violent affair. The Captain reproached everyone for their groaning and there was a nasty scene. Here was a stall selling books written in nondescript, the language of walking death. And in balance near the pie stalls stood Crash Test Nureyev's exhibit devoted to Bingo Violaine, copies of *Puff-Adder Christmas*, *Conker Fight My Arse* and *Hand It To Sparky* laid out for sale. Nureyev constantly pounded his forehead with the heels of his palms and repeated details of the author's life. 'Wrote books. Big ones with an oil brush. His manner lodged icicles in guests. Acted grandly offended. He was drummed out of his body years ago. Violaine rests in peace - the world rests in ignorance. You think learning's boring? History's no virgin.' And so on, until Barny, watching ants in the grass nearby, had learnt all he could about the armoured dots.

'Those are just great,' he smiled, chuffed, and stood up. 'Now let's go see BB's play.' Maquette and the lion stood to go with him. Finding the stage area, Barny sat on the outer edge of the seating. Doomed Eddie Gallo fetched the doll to be costumed as a lion for her appearance on stage. Mister Braintree stretched out on the pattern of green leaves and green. Barny noticed Chloe was among the crowd, her white face open to the show.

Behind the stage Mayor Rudloe had entered dressmaker bedlam. BB Henrietta pushed him through the throng. 'You sicken me Mayor but that pet demon of yours says you'll give me a lotta money for this - stand over there.'

'Me? Offered you money? I doubt that.'

'We'll fill any faults with music. Tentative, halting affection is something the band can play. Sometimes they stop completely. I said stand over there mister. This is the bloke I was warning you about, everyone. He'll be playing the monster in Barny's nightmare.'

Rudloe looked about him, nervous. 'I peddle twelve expressions, all disapproving.'

The dressing tent was packed with freaks. Barny was being played by GI Bill, who in regard to intelligence considered himself at least the equal of a twig. He viewed Rudloe with open hostility. 'He no act. No light on him.'

'Don't we have any costumes? Great plays glow in the dark don't they?'

'Not this one,' said Amy Gort, clicking herself into a harness. 'This is a work of the New Truculence. There's the script.'

Rudloe leafed through it. '"The bear *entrez*" - what the hell?'

'Let's hope it goes better than last year's production,' said Baz McCaffrey, a dedicated actor. 'I had to physically attack the audience, in a brutal violation of my training.'

'Remember, people - tickle their standards with a plague of imagination.' BB clapped her hands. 'While-away the narrative in noise and alarm. And never say an audience is unappreciative - just say the play was meant for people with lower expectations. Let's go.'

The Mayor looked out through the curtains and spotted a lion in the audience. 'Yellow nerves bunched into the shape of a lion!'

'It's a lion you idiot!' snapped BB Henrietta as Amy Gort was winched into the eaves. 'Get out there!' And she pushed him on to the stage.

'A monster!' bellowed GI Bill, climbing into bed and pointing at the Mayor. He pronounced the more complex lines with infinite care. 'Observe! Now its mouth distends, oozing blood. Here in the lopsided chicken coop of my house, on the slope of the landing, a carnivore of unusual design does stand.'

'It's the Mayor!' someone shouted from the audience.

'He's being haunted by the Mayor!'

A shabby lion pounced onstage and Rudloe screamed like a woman, getting a few laughs. As he realised it was a sinister automaton in a suit the scene changed around him and BB shoved him offstage - the principal actors were now seated in a crappy replica of Snorter's Cafe. BB played Gregor by filling her cheeks with air when she wasn't required to talk, signifying fatness. Doomed Eddie Gallo was strolling through the part of Edgy. 'Well, er, Bubba,' he said to GI Bill, 'this monster sounds about as real as my arse.'

'Your arse isn't real?'

The cast paused for a big laugh from the audience, but heard only the fizz of a few flies.

'When I consider the miracle of centipedes and their bodily needs,' said GI Bill haltingly, 'I disturb myself upwards, above normal concerns. Already bedposts are mere details, soon the rest will follow. Just from thinking about centipedes.'

'Well you're disturbing everyone else too Bubba. Just because you saw some jangly fiend in the window.'

'So regret me.'

'Let's go to the dummy garden,' said BB Henrietta, 'because I love my statue, if you know what I mean.'

In the garden set, they stood with the undead Fang. Behind them, BB rolled around on a giant potato. The entire scene had about it an atmosphere of futile despondency. 'It's no good, Barny,' said Fang to GI Bill. 'Gregor's too fat, Edgy's too thin, you're an idiot, and here we are with these statues. And like these statues, when I die I shall be planted in soil, ugly worms trying my patience.' And Fang turned, stepping off the stage and dropping headfirst into the audience. One of his arms lay twitching behind the footlights.

'Chloe is gone,' said GI Bill, absently picking up the arm. 'But we're boys, and we don't care.' And the representations of Barny, Edgy and Gregor began dancing mischievously.

Baz McCaffrey sprang into view, wearing Edgy's candelabra and capering like an imp. 'Beltane Carom here - look upon this mirror, and be helped by demons.'

The three lads swore allegiance, saluting, and declared in unison, 'We will remember.'

In a blast of smoke, Baz was gone.

The court scene tried for gravitas. Sags Dumbar, his translucent cuttlebone skull at odds with the ease and pleasure of the audience, played the judge. Edgy had escaped his stall long enough to play the lawyer Max Gaffer, and swept back and forth in a black cape, berating BB Henrietta. 'Look over there at Mr Juno. This twitching lunatic's parents are actually garments of some kind.'

'Are you sure.'

'They look very like garments, that's what I mean.'

'You should say what you mean then.'

'Oh really? And what did you mean when you,' and Edgy pretended to look at a document, though he actually scrutinised the forehead of an alsatian which had wandered onstage, '"smashed everything you could see?"'

'I was passing so I thought I'd select a lamp and break it with some stones.'

'What did you do it for?'

'For the consequences.'

'Not a good reason.'

'Well, here I am.'

'And welcome. Yes, welcome to the festival of whimsy we like to call "justice".'

'I confess, I confess!' BB contrived an expression like a stomped flower. 'I encourage everyone to engage our civic statuary in sex, sex, sex for fun and education, and why not? It's love, it's love! What else? As Bingo Violaine said, "A successful sin should make a difference shouldn't it?"'

The audience seemed to have become a scowling contest, the aim being to include the maximum number of facial folds and involutions in that expression. During a set change Edgy delivered a dirge, sung with an air of cloak-trailing melancholy. 'Learn well, children,' he intoned in a French accent, 'the human soul will turn, like mayonnaise. Just leave it long enough in this stupid world without anything interesting going on. I pray for you.'

'The dancer has no concept of duration, does he?' remarked the Mayor backstage, and BB Henrietta slapped him eleven times around the face. '*Why*?' he howled. But the next scene was beginning.

GI Bill stood amid broken furniture. 'Chloe is gone and I am the Donkey of Failure. If only someone could comfort me - can it be true?' And he looked up. At this point Amy Gort was supposed to be lowered to the stage on wires, playing a trumpet. But by this time, Amy was so drunk with the boredom and all, she had passed out and was lowered lank as a drowned witch. The trumpet fell from her slack hand and knocked GI Bill unconscious. Doomed Eddie Gallo had to take over as Barny. 'I feel so ashamed,' he read, fumbling through the script. 'Broken up with Chloe for only three minutes, and already I have rodgered half the town. But I remember the mirror and the help of demons.' He put a hand mirror face-up on the stage floor and recited a nonsensical invocation. BB Henrietta shoved Mayor Rudloe through the curtains to stand over the mirror as though magically apported. The audience could by now make no sense of the events unfolding - why was placid candidate doomed Eddie Gallo having sex with half the town and then summoning his fiercest political rival through a mirror?

The plot exited before the actors, wrote the drama critic for *The Blank Stare* during the performance. *And their contribution was a*

groan of green cosmetic method. We viewed their activities as a threat-
ening commotion. Mayor Rudloe's illness swung open and roared into
the crowd. Help me.

So when a great rack of flayed bone folded up out of subspace, bringing with it air pain and blasts of sour disaster, the audience barely reacted. Mayor Rudloe was sitting on the shoulders of Rakeman amid shimmering crackles of cold electricity. 'That hope-less amateur,' Baz McCaffrey gasped from the wings.

Barny was throwing himself down the row, blurting at Chloe, 'I never called down Amy Gort on wires with a trumpet - I slept with BB Henrietta.'

'You mean that zombie was meant to be me?' As she looked up at him the air was suddenly chill. Miles of sky turned grey as a burger-sized chunk was taken out of the sun, growing into darkness. The sound of rain pelletting against cheap seats completed the scene.

The Mayor shouted, 'A staggering amount of water appears to be landing and landing for no reason on house and field alike.'

'It's raining, Mayor,' Dietrich hollered. 'And you're riding on the shoulders of Rakeman, Sweeney's help, a kind of living fence! Beware the beast, man!'

'What about Rudloe Manor? This rain of yours'll debauch the masonry.'

'Don't worry, Mayor,' Barny called. 'It's just the eclipse. Dad says it's happened before. That was the day my mum began knitting beg-gars out of her own veins. When she finished them and snipped them free, they would always shiver and wobble, leaving the house straight away.'

Alerted, Rakeman began stretching toward Barny like a knotted sheet, its howl-mouth a sack of darkness. The audience bolted in several different directions as the Mayor was cannonballed into the seating and left behind. The air filled with the smell of burning wires. Rakeman swerved like a train, blurring after Barny.

Rain fell like chains. Barny thought of his many happy wander-ings with Chloe through these very gardens and their snort-laughing discovery of demon statues on the peripheries. He ran toward the untended edges of the precinct, the downpour tearing leaves and freaking the scene around him. There ahead among the crab-apple trees was a stone ladder of latticed ribs surmounted by a vortical shriek mechanism. If he destroyed this, the creature would die. But the principles of statucide would mean he himself would also be destroyed. He reached the twisted statue, and on the lawn behind him appeared the white shrike, lit by lightning, rain glistering down its bloodless wound of a head. It launched itself at Barny, twisting in mid-air and smashing into its own statue, the femur climbing frame exploding around it. Rakeman's endless throat had been cut, snow flying out of the wound. Then the demon evaporated with its replica.

The creature had tripped on something - a small new figure.

Barny returned without hurry to the seating area to find that the wooden stage was filled with the anglebars of Sweeney's many legs, the crane cab of his head peering down at Scardummy Garden and its stressed visitors. 'Look at this,' the demon gloried, 'an entire set of unopened bodies!' The scene was hung with the applause of rain.

'This fellow is Sweeney, Emperor of Cold Hell,' Dietrich commented aside to the Mayor. 'He's got an auxiliary spiral face housed inside his mouth, you'll notice, and those mandibles are capable of crushing your skull like a monkey nut.'

'Skull, is that what he wants? I can't!'

Quake shrugged the sidewalks.

'What's that?'

'Just secondary warp from the creepchannel due to such an inconvenient fiend coming through.'

'You mean this one's more inconvenient than most? Don't just stand around informing me of the crucial facts, do something!'

'Dietrich Hammerwire,' said Sweeney, and hove its huge face toward the demon and the Mayor, its bloodshot muscles sliding whole yards. Several townspeople backed away, stumbling over seats. 'My proportions strike the times as massive, should I apologise?'

Dietrich stared at the titanic mantis. 'What have you been up to of late, sire?'

'Hatching hard meteors from my arse.'

Dietrich sighed, wearily offended. 'How unnecessary. You never disappoint, do you.'

'A baby scorpion gasps so? Dirty fame is hard on the new breed, I know. Head like a yard mailbox, you're right for this neighbourhood, Dieter. At last, no lies to live across to, yes? You'll learn different if you haven't already. And how's the other runaway - Gettysburg? When's the wedding?'

Dietrich remained flint-faced. 'Tomorrow.'

Sweeney missed a beat. The rain was letting up. 'The Trim Reaper seems to be dead. I can't say I'm altogether surprised considering the trouble he had getting through. I'm priming Rammstein below.'

'He can talk a mean deed, at least.'

'Don't think he's up to it?'

'He's a bit lippy, that's all.'

'Spare me!' Mayor Rudloe interrupted, sinking to his knees and generally calling attention to himself. 'Take the child!' He pointed at Mister Braintree. 'She's disguised as a lion!' And he scampered over to the lion, grabbing its fur and getting a whirling, savage bite on the arse. 'My head!'

'Your arse, Mayor,' coughed Dietrich.

'And you consider this a suitable use of your time,' Sweeney sighed. Dietrich bowed his head, his tarnished armour dull in the half-light.

'It's all right, Mr Mayor,' said the doll Maquette, toddling over from the other direction and removing her costume. 'I'll go with the monster if it will help.'

'You all heard her,' shouted the Mayor to the assembled citizens. 'This child volunteers to go to hell in my place. Sound tactics I think you'll agree. And let us never speak of this again.'

'Children burn out,' said Sweeney. 'Even this one, maybe. And it's Barny Juno I'm interested in, while optimal conditions prevail.'

'Who put this big insect here?' asked Barny, wandering over and indicating the king demon.

Sweeney brought his whale-skull face to bear on Barny. 'There is no pleasant way to say "I will destroy you". And now that I'm in your presence, I sense no power in you at all.' He plucked up the mirror. 'Consider yourself damned. This is the servants' entrance to my famous nerve tornado. And for traditionalists there's a chain of underground fire-lakes.'

'Yes, ma'am.'

But as the demon turned the mirror to catch Barny's image, Barny was fading, benthic colours passing through his shape. A flicker of air and Barny was gone.

'Well,' chuffed Dietrich. 'Don't that just beat the biscuit.'

Sweeney looked at the empty space without comprehension. His oyster-white eyes blinked over, fogging and clearing as the light began to change. The eclipse was closing down. He had wasted his window - he began warping into the mirror, knots of cold lightning banging through the frame. His head angled at Dietrich. 'I'll kill you. That's a bargain.' And his skeleton collapsed through the portal, which fell to the grass.

Dietrich's wings rucked like a cabbage. 'That's too bad.'

12

A RIDE ON A LION

Become yourself like a tap at last running clear

A warm southern breeze blew in and the grass flamed again with sunlight. BB Henrietta emerged from behind the stage and announced to the scattered crowd: 'We've abridged your reaction by poisoning the seats. Thank you for coming.'

The Mayor attempted to cradle his own arse. 'Dietrich, this afternoon's entertainment was costly. In fact at such a price an entire day would cost my life. What's this now?'

People were gathering around the false child.

'Some sort of civic overflow.'

The Brigade, a few Fuseheads and the red sentinel Distaff Plastique were among the crowd which had formed around Maquette, and the Mayor saw the opportunity for salvage. 'Yes everyone, I've delivered up that killer robot for y'pleasure.'

'I don't think there's quite any evidence to prove it's a killer robot, Mayor,' Dietrich remarked.

'To the praying classes, it's a cast iron bitch. Hello everyone, I seek no thanks.' Rudloe did in fact seek it where none could conceivably exist. 'More importantly, the jugular issue is resolved - that belief in a hinge baby with Faberge guts is no match for cynical electioneering and a headstone crammed with footnotes. No offence meant to the Church of Automata, the Cannonites, or anyone else. Bad taste entails a kind of generosity. This fraud will be a complete success.'

A scream rang out as a small stone replica of Maquette came dragging across the grass toward the crowd. Barny Juno materialised around it as the effects of the harpy pie wore off. 'Look, Mr Mayor,' he said. 'It's a statue of Maquette. It's what tripped and killed the long demon that chased me.'

Conversation stirred. Many among the onlookers who had eaten glass meat, intentionally or otherwise, were trickling in and out of visibility.

'So?' Rudloe demanded. 'Juno, your brain gets smaller every time I look away - why are you wasting my time?'

'Her own statue. It means she's like us, a part of the community.'

Rudloe grimaced, struggling not to understand.

'Which is what the Miasma today is all about.'

'All right,' the Mayor sighed inaudibly, resigning himself to the worst. He made a weak smile for the crowd. 'He misses nothing, this one. I have clearly stated that the doll is a killer robot. The implication was clearly that she is *not* a killer robot. In fact, I love the little imp.'

'You condemned her to hell,' said doomed Eddie Gallo.

'I'd have thought she'd relish the chance. And as for Barny Juno. We sometimes find it amusing to speak to him as if he understands. And I for one want to thank him for the errors and beauty he's drawn our attention to today. This undue buoyancy of his ... well, I count myself lucky if my strength proves equal to the task of looking the bastard in the eye. Step away from that jangling marionette, ladies and gentlemen - yes, damn the attackers for their importance and officers. Maquette's the name, eh? Well, as a citizen of Accomplice she has the same rights given all of us.'

'Which are?' someone said.

'And tomorrow, in a special ceremony in the town square, I shall present her with the key to the city. After all, if you prick her, does she not bleed?'

'Frankly, no.'

Rudloe, aware of gathering press photographers, ignored the argument. His face was set in such a strain of stern resolve that his lower jaw, jutting out beyond the upper, fractured across the middle.

When the red myrmidon returned empty-handed, the Grand Dollimo smiled sadly, unsurprised. He ordered Distaff Plastique to lay on the desk and activated the cabinet gears - the sentry lowered out of sight, the desktop closing over it.

The obfuscations of priestcraft got uglier every year, thought the Dollimo. He pressured the wall at the right spot to open the layered door marked NO ENTRY. Passing through, he waited for the door to close behind him and removed his bowler, glass mask and gloves, tossing them onto an ornate rosewood side-table.

Nowhere to be seen was the huge android scorpion bed of lore. No mechanical crucifix deployed its legs on the wall. In fact he hated a successful equation the way he hated a cheap frame - it wasn't worthy of what it was meant to bear.

The room was one of snug and opulent domesticity, all warm lamps and rich velvet. The Dollimo kicked off his shoes, pulled on his slippers and walked across a thick red carpet to the drinks cabinet, pouring himself a sherry. Then he sat into the deeps of an armchair, lit a pipe, and snapped open the newspaper.

*

Barny, Edgy and Gregor attended the wedding of Dietrich and Gettysburg the following day. Maquette handed over the ring, actually a funny antique fuse like a cork wire, which she had found on the back of her head. As a sea captain EH Hunt had full powers to wed and was chuffed that someone finally acknowledged the truth of his assertions. The two demons, one in battered armour and one in white leather, stood before the main observatory window as applause and confetti rained upon them and beer and wolf tart were served. Edgy talked about his profits from selling the harpy meat, not enough to open the bar. Half of it would be lost on medical bills due to his being beaten up by those who had found their pies filled with everyday lard. Gregor, too, had a smashed nose, but without the threat of legal action hanging over his head, he could think clearly. He was trying to develop a line of rigid front-buttoning balaclavas called 'head jackets' and couldn't stop laughing. Barny, fully visible again, stood sad amid the festivities with a chimp on his shoulder as Maquette rode Mister Braintree around the place. BB Henrietta was feeding wolf tart to the blind astronomer despite the fact that he was trying to give a speech.

'We mix and effect. Shirts beloved, make the water change. When young I was an iconoclast, ignoring gulls until they left and weeping unusually fast to get it over with. And I thought, "One day my own fault will be enough". Today I turn sideways, try to force arms and nose into an envelope. A lot of things are possible, I'll tell you, but a simple thing like that? Not in this basket of bloody tempers.' He wrenched impotently at his wicker chair. 'But ideas endure in the whirlwind. My age allows me a certain latitude. I give you a puzzle desk full of snakes. I give you the red velvet which lines the inside of my skull. I flash last week at you as though it were ancient and valuable knowledge. The following I impart for free. Police - mental bowels. Pedestrian - unpaid clown. Life plan - a safe full of autumn leaves. Never belong to your work. Sorrow hangs our arms at our sides and pays no money. Passion is ridiculous only in fishes. A man should kick with the bright side of his trousers. Death is a little minute of white like a full stop. In the buzzing cream of the summer air, we prepare to be angels, the world prepares to be left behind by us all. Out there, I can feel the picture completing itself. A thick-backed man walks the streets away from hope, the colour of striped noise approaches Accomplice, the great bug prepares to shed itself, and the settling earth fills a thousand dead mouths all the deeper. To the happy couple.'

Barny looked thoughtful as the toast was given.

Dietrich leaned to Gettysburg. 'You liked to say that fools cast an honest shadow. I've realised everyone does.'

*

Later that day, the Mayor stood on the palace balcony with a brace across his lower jaw and, pausing to state something about 'postponing my bloody overthrow' to the assembled masses, presented Maquette with the key to the city. He looked ahead with a rigid expression as she inserted it into her heart and cranked it like a starting handle.

ACCOMPLICE 4

KARLOFF'S CIRCUS

"I'm expected to sleep in a diving mask
and false beard. The priesthood is
not what I had hoped."

- Bingo Violaine
Hand It To Sparky

1

HANGING ON A STAR

Real friends don't shake hands

Suicide is a permanent solution to an ever-replenishing series of temporary problems, but Mike Abblatia was concerned only with the immediate one concerning his business. Every day, cars were stolen from the garage where he worked. Now he walked across Jericho Bridge away from Accomplice, the only town capable of being complicated by laziness. Some believed property was theft and others believed they were renting. But while they led a life of Sundays, Abblatia had been living an extra day between Thursday and Friday, growing a little older than his years. His back was killing him. Halfway across the bridge, he climbed into the black suspension girders and stood a while listening to the sizzle of night insects. Then he let himself fall, accelerating toward the soupy river. Air rushed up his shirtsleeves.

His back split, turning open like a time-lapse flower. Sticky wings were blown into use and filled, shuddering. The slippery current of the water began to blur past his sixteen-hole boots.

Behind his flight a heavy train roared across the bridge.

In the cab of the train, smoke blasting past his pointed face, Karloff Velocet stood like a sentry to himself. A silver-painted midget had already capered through Accomplice slapping up posters which declared CONSIDER THIS YOUR NEW MOTHER beneath the face of a jet-eyed fright with marshmallow flesh. All recognised the depicted creature as a Karloff clown and fear had gripped the populace. Karloff's company travelled in a train which tended to arrive by bursting out of someone's mouth and everyone was alarmed that they might become the winner of this terminal lottery. Even as Barny Juno approached his parents' shack with an insect, the etheric-buffered locomotive was shrieking toward the town. But then Karloff happened to glimpse a fan of white wings erupting away from the bridge, gliding low and fast through the gloom. Without emotion he reached aside and jerked the emergency stop.

Barny Juno climbed in through the rear window of the shack,

landing lightly so as not to waken his dozing mother. He approached the spartan canary cage with a katydid in his hand. The insect resembled fairly closely the pet which he had accidentally killed on his last visit. His parents would assume the memory of Lovely Ramone's death was the sort of crappy hallucination common to codgers like them. As he tipped the bug into the cage he heard his father squelching around on the porch. The boards were steeped in swampwater.

'Well look who it aint,' said Pa Juno as Barny emerged into the night. 'Lightning in a cot.' He looked at Barny from beneath a writhing chaos of bioluminescent hair.

'I came to give you all the news that's fit to tell.'

'Brought a paper?'

'No.'

'Even there you fail. Me and your mother are coming into west Coum for the blood levy soon, I need to know what's happening. You want me to be a laughing stock, a country bumpkin? For all I know they're wearing iron trousers over there, I'll be the only one in these stupid ones made of mahogany.'

'Well that reminds me of one piece of news - doomed Eddie Gallo is trying to extend the flyover on his own by quietly hammering bits of timber to the end.'

'Quietly hammering? Sounds like he's just horsing around.'

'And Kenny Reactor's started growing arses over at the allotments.'

'As if those buttock cobblestones to the west aren't enough to damn us all.'

'Also the cannon people are shouting about guns a lot. What is a gun, father?'

'It was a method of moving lead quickly from one place to another.'

'Like a pencil?'

'And aluminum.'

'Like a pen?'

'They were used to force people to do things.'

'To put down what people have to do?'

'Swiftly and utterly.'

'That doesn't sound so bad.'

Barny saw something white flashing through the trees. Some sort of angel was beating through the mushy brush like an injured swan, followed by a load of shambling circus freaks trailing orange plastic nets.

'I'm glad we're on the same page with this thing,' his father told him, rolling a cigarette. 'For once you're not away in your crazy fantasy world.'

'There's a bunch of circus freaks chasing some sort of angel through the forest.'

'There you go again.'

'I mean it father.'

'Don't call me that,' Pa Juno snapped.

Barny was pointing at the clotted waterways when the door banged open and Ma Juno hung out wailing 'My innocent boy eaten by a monster!'

'I'm all right mother,' Barny assured her.

Ma Juno wept that her 'innocent boy' was a tiny fruitfly which she and Pa Juno kept in the canary cage. Now someone of precocious cruelty had flicked a katydid in there and the fly had approached it all eager and aglow, fooled by the bigger bug's fruit-like camouflage. 'Think of poor Ryan's terror when the slice of apple opened up like a Swiss army knife,' she sobbed. 'Evil!'

'I'm not evil,' Barny protested. 'What about the bug in there? I took care of it.'

Pa Juno enfolded his wife, regarding Barny in disgust and affront. 'You took care of it all right.'

In the town square the following day there was a good deal of irresponsibility and a good deal that made sense. Barny entered the square riding on a cow. He had met the mammal in a field and it had looked utterly bored. Now he rode toward his friends Gregor and Edgy, who were standing idle outside the Ultimatum Restaurant. 'Why are you riding that cow around, Bubba?' asked Edgy.

'The lion's in a funny mood.'

'So is the Round One here,' said Edgy, pointing to his oval associate. 'He's been looking at his own reflection in this window for two hours.'

'His gob's a bit glossy,' Barny observed.

'That's human saliva,' Edgy told him, 'the final proof that he's not a mere golem like the papers keep saying.' He turned to Gregor. 'You're not doing yourself any favours with this window-staring, Round One. What's on your mind?'

And Gregor seemed to blow a head gasket, springing at the glass hips-first and smashing the whole thing down. Barny knew enough to wheel the cow away at once, strolling it towards the crowd which had gathered to watch Rod Jayrod, jug-eared master of the Cannon Sect, mount a powder barrel to deliver a diatribe. Barny heard Edgy shouting chidingly 'Hey, will you stop it?' and other yelling from bystanders outside the restaurant.

'Glory in the spectacle of this fellow, Mrs Cow,' said Barny, and they stopped to watch the Fusemaster in his black and blue vestments, two fuseheads on either side of him swinging red dust from sanctified powder pouches.

'In the words of the philosopher Bingo Violaine,' Jayrod declared, '"Truth isn't beguiled, people are. Truth remains whether anyone's gazing that way or not. It's the most patient thing in the world." We seek the return of our rightful property, the Wesley Kern gun, the *objet ballistique*, that portable expression of the inner cannon which is spoken of in myth and legend.' He flourished a fossilised cheese sandwich. 'We offer this remnant as reward for information leading to the reclamation of the Kern gun and its restoration to our shrine. Can you do any less than fill the absence on our altar?' He then began chanting to drown out any reply which might ruffle his question, finally droning it down into silence. 'That lovely chant is beyond your understanding.'

'Your ideas have been grown like a translation, no wonder!' shouted someone.

'Shut your face!' snapped the priest.

'You probably heard someone talking about his passionate devotion to something or other and in a state of high chin and jealousy swore your life to a busted cannonball which happened to be the first stupid thing you saw lying about the gaff!'

'Silence! Nothing can influence me, ladies and gentlemen,' Jayrod declared archly. 'I'm as loose as a flag.'

As his mouth was open to say 'flag', a steam train came bellowing out of it, about which his head expanded and snapped like a rubber band. His body was obliterated under the carve of wheels and machinery as the enamelled engine screeched across the tarmac, rocketing through the front of Snorters Cafe and bunching to a stop in a boom of steam and earth. The train had come to rest in a zigzag pattern and the scattered crowd closed in again hesitantly, slipping in goofer fuel.

Karloff Velocet shot from the smoke stack and cartwheeled to a carriage roof in the thick of his audience. His clothing appeared to have been carved from wax. He was striped up and down like a humbug. His neck was constricted by a blue ruff which resembled a giant human iris. And most dismal of all, he wore a glass top hat which was a barber's shop pole, its red and white turn spiralling ever upward. The assembly roared with impatience.

'Structure applause around my temporary stance, everyone!' Karloff cried. 'I bring to you all the disadvantages of bloody mayhem! Parlour tricks which have escaped my control! Shabby secrets ejected and at large! Ballerinas to shock and appall you! Scalped clowns dipped in dove paint! Resentful rarees and pointless oddities! Barbaric skull percussionists and bandaged fire bugs! "I'm leaving here and don't care," you may tell yourself, but you crackers and yokels will experience the spectacle of hectic endeavour! We dangle into your landscape, as if asked! We're desperate men! There - I've said it! Old capers turn me on! In fact everything else is just pants! I realise that my constant proximity to such events may make it difficult for you to have any confidence in what I have to say. So feast your eyes. In fact I insist on it!'

Along the twisted rack of trailers carved with sigils and baffle-like creeper fluting, boilerplate doors flew off and a platoon of clowns surged into the square, bearing all the paraphernalia of their foul calling. Among them were freaks, tumblers, crumblers and flamers. The crowd screamed in disappointment. 'You expected dogs - now you understand!' cried Karloff Velocet. 'See the Killer Midgets, formerly known as the Terror Midgets! The Evolutionist, the Liquid Acrobat, Big Bumperton the Hornblower, the Caged Angel, Manticore Terry, the Fatal Rhino, Sue Egypt, the Ermine Fraud, the Beast Man and Blitzer Twill! Ben Panthera, falcon-headed problem that won't go away! Jeffrey Jamar - answerable to no-one! Nick Genie, speechless with drink! Mr Lipid, full of malice and anger - what a guy! Felix Kyro, who has killed until killing can reward him no longer! See the unexpected gasp for breath amid precious stones! The Operating Theatre of Flowers! The Tunnel of Hounds! The Cordial Perilous! The Hall of Mirrors - all flat and normal, for you are grotesque enough! And it's all nice and legal! Bring your gilly children and hear them scream as though snagged in a combine! Down with coincidence! Fugitive from the slowly converging bicycles of the dull - The Circus of the Heart's Shell! Check it out!'

'What's all this crap?' asked Barny, kicking a clown away.

'Karloff's stupid Circus,' said Edgy, his tufted head bobbing above the crowd. There prevails an unbroken harmony among those who enjoy strangling clowns. It is not merely the matter of remaining at large after the act, but the brotherhood created in the subtle comparison of pressure, bonecrush and pop-eyed expression. Edgy restricted the larynx of one now as he elaborated. 'You rescued the lion from them, remember?'

Barny remembered, and wheeled the cow slowly around to see Karloff entering the Mayoral palace.

'Look at that cute little bug-eyed pig standing on its back trotters,' cooed the Mayor.

'That's a mirror, sir,' Dietrich pointed out.

Rudloe was shaken. 'That's it,' he said with dignity. 'The next happy smile will be a guest here.' From his high office like a birdcage he gazed down on the square, alerted by calliope music. 'There's a procession of two-ton carny trucks all joined up like an accordion down there. And a load of clowns wearing fright fatigues. That music! Ears are the window to the brain, they say. Horrible, horrible.' He sat at his desk and cradled his primary chin. Recently the Mayor had fractured his jaw while attempting a cocksure expression and he was determined not to over-exert it today. 'Don't like Velocet. Always jumping to the right conclusions.'

The demon Dietrich, who had defected from hell to listen to this bullshit, nodded his anvil head. 'What I admire in a politician like yourself is not the intelligence you boast but the stupidity you hide beneath a bushel, Mr Mayor. As the philosopher Violaine said, "Blame an ant if you desire no repercussions".'

'You know who commissioned Violaine's statue? Violaine, a year before he died. He even specified the rock which was to be used. At this rate all I'll be leaving is the snot ejected by my final gasp.'

Karloff Velocet strode in unannounced, his hat spiralling and all. 'Don't kiss me, I've got a cold.'

'Very funny - Dietrich, this boiled twist of evil and chaos is Fall Marshall of the carny down there. Karloff, this totem of winged armour is Dietrich Hammerwire, my new campaign advisor.'

'A paravamp.' Karloff spun an imitation emerald cane topped by the shrunken head of a tailor. 'I forgot what a hub Accomplice is for transient demons. Attracted by the stink of failure - and prayer.'

'That's a lazy analysis,' said Dietrich.

'Why duplicate effort? Between demons and people, I'll curse people. Nothing's harder to exude than respect, eh Dietrich? Tends to come across as constipation. How do you pay it, Mayor? Him I mean. Mind if I sit down?'

'Dietrich eats the floor lobsters hereabouts. There's a knack. Tail first.'

'Convenient,' said Karloff, seating himself. 'I see you've added another floor to that multistorey chin of yours. Still in competition with doomed Eddie Gallo?'

'Yes. The brain nature provided him remains unclaimed in his skull. I doubt he knows of its existence. He's trying to rebuild the flyover with some sticks. Got a sliced turnip on his campaign posters. Not much of an enemy.'

'Yes, I think we can assume that the most exciting incidents in life occur *outside* a turnip. You know, Mayor, we're similar in many ways. Neither of us suffer fools gladly, and we both consider eachother fools. I have pondered the matter and decided that you and I shall be friends.'

'And when will this feeling grip me? I have a busy schedule.'

'Oh?'

'I accept your tantalizing until twelve-thirty. Then - slam in the face. That loco vimana you arrived in is clearly creepchannel-shielded, a scarship. You issued from a labyrinth - not an auspicious beginning. Then you come in here wearing those mad, mad trousers and commence tugging my chops as if there were no tomorrow.'

'I'm sure I'd select a more fulfilling way to pass my final hours than tugging your chops, Mayor.'

'That's as may be. But the fact is every time you visit, all hell rips loose.'

'Then why invite me.'

'My ex-advisor Max Gaffer invited you as a kiss-off when he quit - the chain of office sinks me in betrayal. Accomplice will have my guts.'

'Accomplice doesn't even know when or where it is. A locked peninsula, the Island of the Strong Door. Exactly how normal do you think *this* is?' Karloff gestured negligently back at the towering Dietrich, whose wings shivered in irritation.

The Mayor could see shadows moving beneath the question. 'One thing at a time.'

Karloff widened his eyes in mock outrage. 'Blasphemy.' He stood to leave. 'Come to our opening performance.' And he waved a hand at Dietrich. 'You must be at least this evil to enter.'

When he was gone, Dietrich suggested that Mayor Rudloe might want to 'get involved' in a folksy way. 'Hold the hankie in some dismal magic trick. Rescue a rodent from a hat. You'll be heaped with so much admiration your ribs'll stack down on eachother, trapping nerves and so on. Your corrupt and bloated administration will continue apace.'

The Mayor let out a sigh. 'Why appease the millstone of my constituents when I could so easily remove it. I've improved conditions quite a bit around here. Heads on an old wall, that soon changed. Surgical insect heaven - banned. But the moss'll be growing in my name before I'm appreciated. What's it all about, Dieter?'

'Greed, Mayor. In this sublunary world of yours, chaos is static or centrifugal. With this carny of Karloff's, better to be the centre of the storm.'

'I'm not sure I can recommend your audacious plan to the Conglomerate.'

'You could pass a town ordinance that what I say doesn't really matter.'

'That'd take the sting out of it certainly. And if anything goes wrong, I'll say to them, "The fault lies not in your stars but yourselves". The phrase'll put some mysterious starry influence in the place of us, as the manipulating force. It's a classic two-choice limitation statement, neither option being the accurate one. Pure distraction, beautiful. D'you know what happened when Violaine was taken to court?'

'The judge told him "Life isn't fair."'

'And Violaine pointed out that in the current context the judge was in a position to make it so.'

'A comment instantly stricken from the record.'

'Power's a funny thing.'

2

MEEOW

Government is like domestic abuse -
it manages to make the victim feel guilty

The demon Rammstein, a serrated lord with a head like a horseshoe, dragged a wooden crate through blasts of cold electricity. Entering Sweeney's hangar-sized cavern, he stood to attention in a black swallowtail coat.

The tyrannical mantis leaned its white glass head out of the mist. 'Bit nippy isn't it? Put on a radiator, there's a love. This the crate? It'll need some refinement, but there we are. The problem remains I eat souls, Rammy. How to get more of them into my domain? How to make it attractive?'

'You could get someone to denounce it.'

'People don't pay much attention to that sort of thing these days - if you weren't a preening cock-of-the-walk demon, you'd know that. As Violaine said, "Any rate of resentment lags behind the situation".'

'I am surprised to hear you quote your vanquished enemy, Majesty.'

'Violaine's still here, Rammy. Hearing us, noting us down. The fix is in, I'm sure of it. It hasn't been the same down here since Dietrich hung up his spikes.'

'Dietrich - a vulturine demon isn't he?'

'Paravamp. Draco class. He won't get much joy up there with the 3Ds, I assure you. Too much prejudice. Body's no place for a soul. And that lawyer - Max Gaffer.' Sweeney gave a bark of sour laughter which darkened the yellow air. 'Crawled in here clutching hell by the hems, all missed beats and status anxiety. It made for a heavy satisfaction to have him fail like a mime in a blackout.'

'Where is he now, Majesty?'

'Off on some compensatory bender I assume, with his tie in his pocket. I miscalculated sending old Rakeman above. Let's face it, he was just a bit of cold, bandaged stalk lightning. We need brute force, something that'll ignore whatever sorcery Juno throws at it.'

'You are still determined to destroy Barny Juno.'

'Ofcourse. Revenge is more acceptable when completed than when left ragged and undone - until it's finished people feel edgy. And old Violaine prophecied Juno was my nemesis. I think I'll send the demon Trubshaw to take care of him.'

Rammstein jerked a stare at his ratcheting emperor. 'Isn't Trubshaw some kind of pack beast, merely?'

'Yes, a slob demon. Mud-encrusted dorsal studs in the old screw-in style. Forehead of Portland stone. That's the stuff. You Sawvillian fiends are good for the scary chat but for unthinking action, give me a dunce demon every time. The closest I got to Juno was by working two angles at once. Now I'm trying three - sending Trubshaw across, priming my inside man to act on his revenge premise, and something else.'

'Max Gaffer?'

'Gaffer's sawn through the brake cables of his luck. No. It's myself I refer to. The future will arrive when everyone has forgotten about it. What do you say to that, Rammstein?'

Rammstein bowed. 'Joyous blood flows through all the links in my chain, Majesty.'

Barny and the others were in the low-ceilinged cellar in which they grappled with the destitute oblivion of their employment. Some days the sorting office was a crust theatre of boredom and Edgy was free to elaborate on his latest cash cow as everyone else just sat there. 'So that's the plan, Bubba. I dress up in clown duds, stand around near some crates and get people to hand over everything of value. Oh, I might have to give them a soda or something, but basically, yeah, it's a lock.'

'It's screaming bloody *death* for everyone,' said BB Henrietta, and slammed a knife through a jiffy bag, pinning it to the sorting table.

'Well that's putting it a bit strong. Admittedly it won't work. What's the time?'

Barny shrugged. 'Five to eight, twenty to three ...'

They stared a while at the Drop, an open corner into which they dumped most of the stuff which arrived here. It was basically a bottomless blank and wouldn't clog unless you threw too much in at once.

'I could dress myself up as a dog and threaten them. As Violaine said, "The human brain's a source of horror - there are reasons it's covered by a tarp."'

'Get some tips from Fang,' said Barny, 'he's a dog man.'

'He's a *bog* man,' Edgy told him, and gave a small gasp of exasperation. 'Barny, how many times do I need to explain about Fang being a zombie? He's one of the undead, Bubba, the *undead!*'

'I like him.'

'I love him, so what? Everything about him. Why are we here? I don't know what I'm saying any more!' And Edgy broke raggedly into coughing tears.

'Here he is,' Barny hailed as Fang wobbled down the steps.

The shambling cadaver wore boxing gloves for reasons he never discussed. He tilted toward the table and thudded down into a chair, a piece of his face shaking loose. 'My eyes have turned to mustard, lads.'

'Now that we're all here,' said BB Henrietta, 'except Gregor and Sags, and when Barny can stop looking at that stamped fly which looks like an asterix, he has something to tell us which he claims is important.'

'I'm glad you asked,' Barny told her. 'Yes, as you all know, I live to care for the winged and stepping animals of the earth, and Karloff's stupid Circus is packed to the rafters with, Christ - beefy elephants, horses, marmosets, ostriches, belly dancers, rhinoceri, cats, and a snake called Magic Onion. It's Magic Onion I want to focus on first.' Barny told them about Mahru the Snake Charmer, who always became angry at the snake's slow emergence and picked up the bucket, hurling the viper into the audience with a roar. Barny had tried before to catch the beautiful creature and take it to safety, but there was never any telling which part of the crowd would be blessed with its sudden arrival. 'We have to position ourselves at points around the circle and be ready,' he told Edgy, Fang and BB Henrietta.

'Ready for a deadly snake to fly towards us,' said BB in a flat tone.

'And don't just sit there eating a ham sandwich or something,' Barny said vaguely.

'You subnormal,' BB shrieked. 'Karloff wouldn't think twice about lining us up on the ground and beckoning an elephant carefully forward.'

Barny disagreed, opening a colourful book about wild animals. 'This says, "Being large enough to live unchallenged, the elephant elects to do so at its own pace, while spurting people with water." God, I love animals.'

'Why?'

'Well, they don't ponce about. Except cats ofcourse. And they've got swivelling ears, so that makes up for everything.'

Edgy wiped his eyes. 'Everything eh. Even laying around like a croissant? I don't think so.'

'Well I think it's a grand idea,' said Fang. 'And I for one will bake my own arse if it'll help.'

'It wouldn't really,' said Barny. 'But we need someone to work from the inside if I'm going to rescue any more lovely critters from the circus. Karloff wouldn't suspect if you returned to your brothers' trapeze act.'

Hunched under a low bare lightbulb, Fang was a sad figure of sinew and custard. He looked at his gloved hands where they rested on the table. For a while a rind of skin hanging from his forehead was the only part of him that moved. Then he said 'Does anyone here mind if I ...' and his head fell from his shoulders, banging loudly to the table like a rock.

Trubshaw stomped from a creepchannel exit, his heavy legs sloshing through gems and sleeping pills. He was basically a living spit-roast covered in armour plating. His mouth and neck were one and the same, his cranium ringed with ears like a crown. Raisin eyes surveyed the flaking car shells tilted in fields, the raggedy palm trees like exploded flags, the heat-white buildings in the distance. The whole day seemed exaggerated. He walked around the bleached and shattered bones of a Steinway spider and lumbered toward the town.

The carny was taking over the town square, acrobatic midgets pouncing across the rooftops to secure guy lines for the top canvas. These roustabouts shrieked constantly of 'the hell to come' and bit at eachother, ullulating strangely. The train had been cut up like a worm and Karloff's red-and-white-striped wagon stood near the entrance to Yodel Erratum Street. He was making up at a lightbulb shrine spread with a chaos of fabulation powders, pinecones painted gold, funfair drugs, etheric ordnance and apples of black glass, when someone ducked in through the ladybug beads. 'One of the infernally modified,' said Karloff, finishing up, then turned in his chair and directed a chin like a gondola at Max Gaffer. 'And once a lawyer.'

'How do you know?'

'You lack the watermark of a soul.'

Gaffer tripped on a mash hammer as he advanced into the trailer, his sword-crowned head tangling with a sigil mobile. While in the service of Sweeney he had been placed in an editing bay and customized with a system of barbs and coldwater piping, leaving him with a body so absurd everyone was surprised he still felt able to put his name to it. He coughed in smuts of blusher. 'You've heard of Sweeney?'

Karloff avoided his eye. 'Some kind of overfed mosquito isn't he?'

'Hardly. He's quite the king demon down there, oh yes - and I'm his right hand man. I've made a lotta changes across there, put hell on the map, brought it up to date with modern marketing. And I could do the same thing for your operation.'

Karloff had taken up a clockwork violin and was leaning into it with a frown. A complex of agonies wove through the air. 'This place has become hag-ridden with demons. Apparently two of them got married the other day and released a load of balloons.'

Gaffer was having to raise his voice. 'Too much for you to handle eh?'

'If you're really apprised of both situations, you'll know you demoted yourself when you went below.'

'Eh? Will you stop playing that thing?'

Karloff placed the instrument into its case and closed the lid, muffling the sound. He turned his grapewhite face upon Gaffer. 'Bewilderment, the great leveller. Man lets himself be momentarily enchanted by what is strange and expensive, yet as beyond his control as all else in his life. Here in the Circus of the Heart's Shell we love sawdust because it's the telltale sign of a wasted afternoon.'

'So what's the attraction?'

'The spectacle with its lights and colours, the capering animals, the clowns plying their bloody trade, all this transports man from the mundane.'

'Mundane? If people want to see shrieking clowns they watch the Mayor give a speech. They want to see capering animals they go within a few yards of Barny Juno's house and in seconds their world is framed by the lion's jaws.'

'The lion - indeed. *My* lion, stolen from me by Juno. What's Juno doing these days?'

'Oh, that one,' said Gaffer, sitting down stiffly on a wooden chair. 'Claims his life has been bailed out by badgers. Kissed the snout of a hedgehog and smiled. Has eight hundred eels in his garden. Chose a point halfway through a funeral to abandon his trousers as a bad bet. Got a job as an exterminator and showed up at people's homes to polish the roaches and wash the gunk out of the flies' compound eyes.'

'So he's unrepentant.'

'I don't really know what that means. Something to do with curtain rails?' Gaffer picked up a framed poster printed in red, blue and brown ink. It portrayed confusion by the book, sprung from a carnival coffin - carrion clowns squabbling over the prey, elephants wearing stockings and suspenders, and Karloff himself with ears like shark fins, fanning razorblades like playing cards, his spiral hat towering and strange sprites capering in clouds about his shoulders. Gaffer squinted at one of these haunts - was that a fanciful rendering of Skittermite whispering into Karloff's ear? Did the Fall Marshall have some connection with Sweeney? YOU WILL BE INJURED, the ad promised.

'I don't suppose you can box?' Karloff was saying. 'No? Shame - we've got a little fight setup on the side. Well, apparently your life counts as much as theatre smoke. There's only one way I can think of that you could possibly help me. I need a gun. Should have brought my own, forgot about the paucity here. We were kicking through guns where we stopped last. When the scarship emerged into the square I heard the exit victim say something about a "Wesley Kern gun". What is that?'

'Part of our history,' Gaffer told him in a thoughtful tone. 'A man used the weapon to attack a bunch of people from the Tower. As it happens, I do know where you can find that item.'

'Brief Cheney when he returns from his chores, then we can discuss your employment.' He called after Max as the lawyer was leaving. 'Don't get in the way of the canvas crew! Or the animals! And don't belittle them by saying "roar" or "chirp" - my animals are screaming in distress!'

Alone, Karloff looked out at a bunch of Cannon Church protesters shouting against the sacrilege of using a cannon in a secular strongman act. The window stained the people like wine, made them look like an ancient photograph. 'A thing is deemed sacred,' he thought, 'when there's reason to keep us from dusting for fingerprints.' Karloff picked up a copy of *The Blank Stare* which Cheney had dropped by earlier. The front page described the circus's arrival beneath the headline NO 'HORSE SENSE' WITH THESE BASTARDS and a photo of eleven clowns bidding to snog the same mare. Further down the page was a story about a man in trouble: 'Known to all as "Round One" and seemingly rambunctious, this fellow provoked a disturbance and smashed a restaurant window with his hips before shuddering at such speed the number of foamy flecks flying from his mouth surpassed an amount countable by this correspondent.'

'Round *One*?' Karloff mused.

Leapfrogging the burst sidewalks, a silver-painted midget with a set of useless wire wings and a head like a monkey-fist approached Del's Fright Foundry. The yard was filled with cans of lead, glass skulls and slot machines. 'Del?' Cheney called, entering the old garage to be confronted by a beetle like a giant black padlock rashed with rust.

Other massive sitch bugs filled the chamber, splayed legs snicking at every angle, and there in the corner of the nightmare was Del, satisfied, drinking a tinny. 'So you are back again, little man. I expected you when I went to the town centre for some paint and damned clowns were peering from every cranny. What's that stuff they're spreading on the front of the buildings?'

'Body fat,' said Cheney. 'Lard, to you.'

'Lard to me, eh? Is that so. And which of my things do you want this time?'

Cheney skirted the chubb beetle, patting its pelt of crumbled leather. The peeling gates of its wings flew open, startling him. 'Er ... well, this hook masterpiece waving at me, for a start.' He looked around at the anthem statues and freaked exhibits which Del insisted on dragging through from another realm. 'You crave regular intimacy with a plane of bloody posts, Del, no reason why you shouldn't profit from it.'

'Just make your choice and leave.'

Here were anatomies like trash-and-wire sculptures, a sweating stone wrapped in rope, a totem pole with eyes of lye velvet and a heavy tar sentry. 'Well, I'll hire this little beauty, and mini-head here, this peppery shell, that one with drillbit antennae, and that huge bit of stinking bacon. Not too venomous?'

'How much is too much,' Del grunted.

'Exactly. I'll send some clowns round to collect them. A few saddles and hawsers and we're laughing. Why struggle for horror when you can pay a small charge?'

That was the dodgem cars sorted. Cheney capered across town to the Church of Automata, slipping in through a window. The Grand Dollimo was standing on a platform above the slurry floor of the doll forge, reading a hinged mechanical book. Cheney walked along the scaffold toward him. 'You sir - I have something to say.'

'What could possibly atone for your face?'

'Never mind all that - the Fall Marshall secured an arrangement with you when we were last in town.'

The Dollimo thumped the book closed, locking it. He regarded Cheney through a smoked glass mask. 'Work with him do you. What do you do all day?'

'Mostly it has to do with frogs,' said Cheney diffidently.

'You study them?'

Cheney looked surprised. 'I *avoid* them.'

'You spend all day avoiding frogs.'

'Wouldn't you, if you could?'

'I am not in the business of mucking about. If this is all you learn, you won't have wasted your time.'

'Perhaps.'

'Not perhaps - my exalted frequency bars me from such horrors. Now, flesh into this room.' The Dollimo opened a bible door in the metal wall and ushered Cheney through. 'As Violaine said, "Research can be neither successful nor unsuccessful unless a particular conclusion is required." See how elegantly it works?'

In the dim vault two large Steinway Spiders were crouched, black as old cola. One reared a little, showing a gob like a Pontiac grill.

'That's the one we call Sterling, the other is Dragbelly. They've been in here for three years, living on dustcakes and abducted children. Their articulation is rare but sudden.' The Dollimo noticed Cheney's deflated meakness before these hulking mechanisms. 'Not like the scalped piano in the museum are they?'

'I ... I don't think I know what you mean. I'm going now. I'll send some hoosiers to pick them up.'

'Tell Karloff to be careful. Give these the wrong pecking orders and you'll end up quiet in the grave, your brain turning to marmite in your mouth.'

3

AS EELS GO

When someone starts saying 'vestibule',
you know you're in the wrong place

Stealing down crystal streets of ground glitter, past tough crocodilian trees and car metal too hot to touch, Karloff neared the chaos of decks and gangways which was Barny's house. Barny was standing outside, feeding a piglet with an eye-dropper. 'Hello Karloff,' he called to the Fall Marshall. 'The sun rose this morning and light started ricocheting around inside the marmalade.'

Karloff smiled winterly. 'I hate what I see - you live here?'

'Yes, ma'am.'

'I hear you've got hundreds of eels back there somewhere. But why am I surprised by anything you do?' He spotted a spaniel which nipped out through a catflap. 'A dog with merry eyes and shaved legs eh? Just look at the beast turn its own left ear inside-out. And to think that this is you at the top of your game.'

Barny put the piglet down. 'Off you go, Mister Bond. Want some lemonade, Karloff?'

'I'm afraid it's not that simple. What you pulled last time I was in town. It wasn't polite. Fences, cages - they didn't last long. Not with you putting ideas in those animals' heads. You could almost mistake it for a plan. Species galore becoming interested in freedom, brows creasing, the elephants talking about it openly. Bears looking at eachother. Biology darting forwards, doors torn from their hinges in a whoosh of escape, throats black with blood. A dozen blindworms lost into the swamps. The pain and swelling was incredible. And then, the lion you stole, as pointless as a crop avenger. As Violaine said, "It's difficult to forgive someone for something if they still treasure their reasons for having done it."'

'Sling me that bit of gore will you?'

'Gore? Sling? Have you heard a bloody word I've said?'

At this point the lion skipped out through a busted gap in the house's wooden wall.

'So there he is,' nodded Karloff, 'raw in the universe.'

'Mister Braintree's one of my best friends. His one-inch claws are retractable and he has thirty teeth -'

'I know how many teeth he's got!' Karloff barked. 'Didn't I spend two years getting used to them before you stole the bastard?'

The lion had stopped, staring at Karloff with hard eyes. The Fall Marshall was about to sneer something like 'You've fallen arse backwards into flowers for the last time' when all at once he realised his danger, and froze. For some reason he noticed a bug tickling across the path like a living doll shoe. 'Well,' he said quietly. 'I intended to arrive and I did. A whisper means the same as a declaration.' And he backed very slowly out of his hazard.

As the zombie Fang approached the town square it became clear to him that Karloff would be using Grapefruit Integrity Swoon Street as the circus midway, filling it with stalls and sideshows. Between the circus wagons he walked into the odor of sawdust and all the cacophony of varicoloured idiots shouting the gibberish of their profession. He passed amid novelty morons and bollock-naked murderers, clowns throwing roses onto bonfires and siamese twins joined at the eyelashes. The trick-riders spinning plate fungus seemed in his dead eyes to be freaky-assed and curious, throwing balls and rings into the air and catching them when they returned, only to throw them upward again as though nothing had been learnt by the previous experiment. He had been away a long time.

A pinhead in a jagged red suit hailed Fang from a half-built stall. 'Fang - still playing the decomposition card. You crawling back to your job?'

'That's right Panatella,' said Fang, going over. He looked at the principles in pickle jars and shit-scary notices like WARNING: THE DEAD CUT THE LIVING'S STRINGS. 'My left shoulder is completely rotten. I'm pretty well patched up with gaffa tape, as you can see.'

Panatella sipped some acorn coffee. 'Well, you're dead and that's what's important. It's good to see you again.' He pulled something from the trash. 'Interested in this?'

'The shape is very puzzling, like a trumpet.'

'It's a trumpet, that's why.'

'No thanks, Boney, I better go find the troupe.'

Panatella pointed the way, his drumstick head swivelling to look.

As Fang walked on he was greeted by hoosiers, fire-drivers, some kind of human/chef hybrid, a sawback manticore and another creature that was half dogboy, half pot-roast. 'Why keep lustrous innards hidden?' asked old Shockheed Martin, whose transparent skin revealed his knotty plumbing. Everywhere wandered clowns tooled up with precision blades and bladders ripped out to dry before the pigs' dying eyes. A family of fire turkeys squabbled under a jacked-up truck.

'What are eyes?' came a woman's voice.

'Tears minus a wife,' Fang sniggered by rote, and went over to join the fortune-teller Sue Egypt, who sat on the chariot step of a black-and-red enamelled wagon.

'So here he is - Fang Palaton in pants so worn I can see my face in 'em.'

Fang laughed. 'Sue Egypt - she has attracted all the curses of the Pharoahs and none of the mystery.' He sat down beside her. 'And as Violaine said, "Trousers are temporary, a bungled alliance."' They watched some seventh-circle clowns chase eachother around. 'Just look at those mothers give eachother a good kick in the pants. You can't beat originality. And who's that now?' He gestured to a passing hulk of muscle which had been topped with a head as an afterthought. The hairs on his arms were like spider legs and he was covered in iron jewellery. But the expression on his face was mild.

'Dugway Thrax, the Beast Man. He's our latest strong guy, does the cannon act. He's double-hearted, doesn't like it here.'

'In Accomplice?'

'The Circus, darling. Wants to settle down, become a townie. The way it is, he settles for five minutes, then gets shot into another postal district.'

'Another what? Well anyway, round here people only get shot out a cannon when they're dead, that's what those priests are protesting about.' They watched the slow passing of a stilt monk with a business card for a mouth. 'So how's Karloff?'

She lit a small cigar. 'Oh, that one. He's almost come to believe his own tailor. Watch what he's got us about now.' She gestured to the rehearsing Floor Lobster Parade. Several were treadling by on miniature bikes. 'They've taught those nightmare vermin to do tricks.'

Fang gasped, his appalled face following the antics of a bug which turned to him with epoxy eyes. 'What else?' he asked her.

'You know the old pitbull spiders? He's using pianos now.'

'You don't mean -?'

'I mean it like it is, like it sounds. Steinway rumbles.' She plucked a rose out of thin air. 'You never know what's going to happen in the future, and when it does, it's best ignored. Locked in this rose is my one doubt. Time will release it.'

'He must know what he's doing. Horror wouldn't survive if it wasn't selling something somebody wanted.'

'Tell it to a tornado. Horror doesn't need to sell - it has power, does what it wants, takes what it wants, doesn't negotiate or ask permission. We don't buy a tornado - it drops down when it feels like it.'

'Okay, enough with the tornado. Where are my brothers? I'm as fit as a chimp, look at me.'

'You're a mess, honey.'

'So regret me.'

He followed her directions to a few practice bars set up in the dust yard. On the way he saw a sort of lard ghoul stomping north, its face the colour of dead chewing gum, its head crested with ear coral. Flesh bulged between its armour plating like wall insulation overflow. *Accidents with accompaniment*, thought Fang, *that's us.*

When he found his brother Squill, this tall tilt of sinew was hammering a hitching bar. His entire back was a furrow of green mud, but Fang recognised at once the glint of the wishbone at the nape of his neck. When the zombie sibling turned, he looked like he had inhaled his own face. The yellow jawbone worked. 'So, dirty eyes regard my efforts.'

'Hello, brother. Like all great men, I suffer the stigma of being timely.'

'You were never reckless enough for this troupe, Fangy. Or putrescent enough, even now - are you using boot polish on that skin of yours?'

'I sleep in a tar pit.'

'There - ashamed to show your true lividity. Ladaat here lost both his eyes to decay years ago. His failures as a catcher have made our shows notorious since your departure. Eh Ladaat?'

'I'm a catcher?' asked a bewildered corpse propped among some crates.

'Ladaat, my brother,' Fang hailed him. 'You have no arms.'

'And no way of telling,' laughed Ladaat toothlessly, his face covered in aphids.

'Good grief, he's not up to a show,' Fang whispered to Squill. 'He's no more than an inky post.'

'The people expect him - look at this review: "A thousand people died in the accident, which has been voted worst in the nation's memory." And your brother Enrico is still angry at your leaving. He will never allow you to rejoin. As the late great Bingo Violaine told it, "History is buried alive."'

'Ah, here he is,' came a voice, and Fang turned to confront a lurch of meat with a purple-black head massively swollen on one side. A dried eruption of brain matter tufted out like stuffing. 'Shiny as a cheat conker. In death as in life eh?'

'He's been sitting in tar,' said brother Squill.

'Tar now, is it,' rattled Enrico. 'And boxing gloves. Ashamed of your catching claws eh? Didn't want to be reminded? Go to Karloff with your gloves, he's looking for fighters - you're not welcome among us.'

'Cut them off,' Fang instructed him.

Enrico looked skeptical, but reached for some shears. He snipped at the bindings, unwinding them and pulling the gloves off - they leaked embalming fluid. He cast them away into the dust.

'I didn't wear them for shame,' Fang told him, raising a set of leathery talons. 'But for preservation.'

Skirting around a cold troika sphinx from Del's collection deemed unfit for the dodgems, the demon Trubshaw passed a clown trailer on which the words

A clot of clowns will stop your heart
And you will die just so.
That's art.

were unreadable by the monster dullard. His attention was trans-fixed by two scarlet valentine hearts which lay in the dust. Picking them up by the vein-strings, he peered inside the cavities. Heart gloves?

Four corpses assembled at the door to Karloff's candy-coloured wagon. The Fall Marshall scrutinised Fang through a pair of stained-glass spectacles. 'I know these other cadavers are viable - but you, Fangy? That duct tape around your neck? Your head's been off recently.'

'So?' piped up brother Enrico. 'That's what you want in a zombie isn't it? A man so putrefied you could behead him as easy as a pint.'

'So whatever, I don't mind - if he can still do the job.'

'Nothing wasted there,' brother Squill chipped in. 'Hair over bone.'

'Get off your sky-high horse and give him another chance,' croaked Ladaat, staring through Karloff with empty sockets like large auxiliary nostrils.

Karloff gave something between a shrug and a nod. 'The path of circumstance runs infinite in all directions. We're a roomy canvas for death, lads - all of us.' And he gave a laugh hollow enough to shelter a fugitive.

4

TO HERE KNOWS WHEN

Death is never at stake

The sky over the tent was unfocused. Barny and Gregor walked through the stench of sulphur and melon slices, punching away clowns and others acting goofy for cash, looking for the tall figure of Edgy in the bustling midway. They passed caramelised diplomats and frilled foetuses in limbo water. Kids were challenged to read a page in a leopard's cage, though none would successfully see the words 'I have relieved you of minutes of the most powerless period of your life - the leopard could relieve you of more.' Here were blood-cough artists and lifelong eyeblink morsemen, their message ignored. Ince Elfshot was dealing out fish-head cards which disintegrated before they reached the table. Mr Macabre was displaying his insouciant control of a few daggers which he threw at and around a bikini-clad woman. Taken by surprise, she stood rigidly still in the act of buying an ice cream.

'Bits of my house are disappearing,' Barny complained to Gregor as they moved through the sideshows, chewing black wine gums with an aftertaste of turps. 'Whole lumps of the wall. I came back from staring at Chloe this morning and there were woolly monkeys all over the garden.'

'Well, I guess you know a thing's become a problem when the woolly monkeys start assembling.'

'Their vaulting-ladders have disappeared,' Barny explained. 'There was almost no way for them to spin upside down and engage in arse-display. Which is their main motive for waking up in the morning.'

'And mine. But I bet it only started happening since the circus came to town, right? I'll bet Karloff's behind it. How did the staring go, by the way? Chloe want you back yet?'

'Chloe wouldn't lie about something like that, and she's not crazy, so she must have meant it. I still need to see her though. This time I had to submerge myself near the Juice Museum sea-doors and watch her when she came down to hang up some parchments for drying.'

'So you're spying on her, like a sick man.'

'With the help of some tubular bracken, yes. I nearly drowned. Heaven begins at her feet, Round One, I can't help it.'

'And they call me perverted, for having sex with my reflection in a shop window.'

'Yes,' said Barny, 'they do.'

Barny detected Edgy's voice above the neon-skeleton melodies of the calliope. The tuft-headed one was done up like some jester or spicy fool, baying rubbish at a medicine stall and apparently cashing in on the fad for cheaply made aztec hope. 'And what in the name of boiling hell is this, you may ask? Temper temper. From the land of bolted windows, air mothers and endless rain, I offer a connoisseur's grief. Agony Eight Hundred! Must you live? Do you think the womb is that personalised? Choose my teeth for your neck, ladies, I implore you! My merits warrant awe!'

'I don't understand what he's saying,' Barny murmured.

Gregor rushed up to Edgy's stall, aghast, and called back to Barny. 'I'll start interrupting him now.' Then he strained his face toward Edgy. 'What the hell d'you think you're doing, Edge? Take off those funny duds, the clowning union'll piss all over you. Agony Eight Hundred - what is it?'

Plantin Edge grinned wickedly. 'Don't worry, Round One. I stole some Cordial Perilous and mixed it down.'

'Cordial Perilous is half venom. It's a demon dare drink. What did you mix it with?'

'Venom.'

'Run for your life, Edgy.'

'Nonsense - I have to stick around to help with the snake abduction later on, don't I? But I'll enter the tent only when it's necessary. Clowns are in there by the million. They're killers, Round One. Running, bouncing, distributing deadly curses. By the time one of those bastards pops the wheels off his little car you might as well forget it.'

A jar of hazelworms clinked with wriggling.

'What if someone chokes on this stuff?'

'I'll address the complainer in barely audible tones, into his forehead, describing patiently my favourite furniture.'

'That's your answer to everything,' said Gregor, and walked back through the crowd to Barny. 'He'll wait for the signal.'

A silver-painted midget was yelling as they approached the giant tent-flap at the end of the street. 'Step right up if you consider it's any of your business. Entry is simplicity itself - step and step and step this way, and be prepared for feats of strength and agility which will explode your eyes! Our clowns are donning their battle pants even now, think of it! Trials of mesmerism, conjuring, legerdemain and related larking about. By god, we'll test your patience! And no respite from boisterous diabolo jugglers whose expressions make clear to one and all that they are savages at heart! You want disaster? We think of little else! You want silverfish? Dozens pulse up the walls! I remember a lad all happy and aglow when he entered - his head exists on top of a staff now, unable to beat off the flies! That's right, in you go, my lovelies! Yellow moments remain unreclaimed - forever!'

Barny and Gregor passed near the vinyl smile of Cheney, then the flap had slapped closed behind them.

They had stepped into a chaos of swooping spotlights. The entire round of the town square had been roofed with a canopy, turning the centre of town into one giant big top. Grandstand seats were built against the surrounding buildings, the balcony of Rudloe Manor forming a royal box. Rudloe's face hung gormless in its frame.

The square was rammed. Barny didn't feel like he was in Accomplice town as he and Gregor found their seats and cold blue air flashed around them. Whips, capes and parasols hung from the statue of Bingo Violaine, making it a prop-rack for the Fall Marshall. Kerosene was burning in raised pan lamps. Concession barkers saddened kids in the audience by throwing gold ingots disguised as candy bars, cracking them upside the head, and then the disappointment. Through the swerving searchlights and blaring horns, Barny spotted BB Henrietta on the opposite side, fast asleep, and across the way sat Sags Dumbar, whose aqueous bag of a head could mean only failure. 'Keep your eyes peeled for Magic Onion,' Barny hushed aside to Gregor.

The square was plunged into silent darkness.

A sparkling infection of green metallic curtain bloomed with a spotlight, then parted. A banana-moon face leered under a tall humbug hat. 'Here I am, first poisoned and last dead! Just as god, under the most costly of canopies, rigs agonies for its dulled curiosity, we operate in infamy, trading in transgressions beyond number, accidents beyond definition, and all the awfuls of nightmare. We stoop to intervene in your drab affairs! I'm sorry to say some of you will be destroyed, for that is part of delivering more than mere pleasure and fancy! Come among you via the chill wonders of the Trans-Reptilian Express ... The Circus of the Heart's Shell, one immense indiscretion!'

An explosion went off and a storm of waivers fluttered down on the audience.

Karloff now hung off Violaine's statue at a jaunty angle, gesturing about the ring with a red cane of spine diamond. 'Big-name attractions crash to earth! Quick nannies sharpen their knives! See our clowns, empty flesh fetches who simply won't keep their private hell to themselves!'

The calliope struck up a reverse dirge as a colour flurry of clowns with crayola claws spread on to the hippodrome track, spinning paraphernalia gemmed and striped, their opaque eyes revealing nothing. Tumbling in attack jackets and zigzag pantaloons coordinated to some polychrome hierarchy of recent invention, they enraged all by throwing walnuts into the audience.

'Daring us all to smash their porcelain heads - but could we bear to touch? And if silence wore a beard, its name would be Mr Macabre. His magic is so modest in astonishment it must compensate in disgrace. Yes, a shiny foreigner is standing without shame, conjuring brains from your bonces - which surely were not there when he reached out his hand? His last performance ended in a chaos of industrial glass, shattered sawblades and gashed volunteers! Observe!'

A fragile girl in dragonfly coveralls assisted as Mr Macabre, a square yellow man with eyes like joy-buzzers, rolled a black box into the ring. A sheet-blade projected above it. It was made up to look like an old cabinet radio, a coffin for electricity, the blade its aerial. 'There are many ways to irritate,' the magician shouted. 'Whistle "thankyou" instead of saying it. When asked for directions, point the way with your tongue. And best of all, bisection with a saw, oh yes. Quickly you applaud, though clueless. You disgust me.' He climbed into the box, laying back and closing the two half-lids. 'Would someone of such skill as I spend time constructing an object without purpose? An old radio made of skin, it makes a sound like storms. Its inner workings are jet black, packed so dense with ants their blackness has given up and turned inside like a migraine. And don't your desperate eyes quicken and become rivetted as I tell you that to prove that the blade is real, I'll test it on my own body rather than standing within reach of the trapdoor release button. Oh god -'

The girl was drizzled with blood as the blade shunted down. Clowns capered over, running the box out of sight as Karloff watched.

'Damn it all, he deserved better. A lot better. And here, because I take an interest in you for which you should be grateful - Gemini Dog! By-blow of the frenzied union of a realtor and a human being. If his face offends you, all complaints here, in the fire. Fire is born old, ladies and gentlemen. Whisper it.' A piece of folded meat wobbled across the flashing plain on a tripwire tricycle lethal to anyone as Karloff raved on and the ring increased in resolution. Macabre's shaken assistant was being taunted and attacked. 'The Killer Midgets! There's a bounty on their heads! Staggering Joe Almighty - there's more to his antics than meets the eye! Kevin, he of the Smashed Face and Drinking Habit! Ten Beans Stapled to a Stupid Sod, ladies and gentlemen! My Mother, everyone! And here is Kaspar Blenny, a man made entirely of ear tissue!' A bloke bent over in a bow, and flipped quickly up again. 'Now you will see a creature as rare as a fish with shoulders, ladies and gentlemen - A Fish With Shoulders!' A fish with shoulders was wheeled on in a pram. 'Even the most learned conversation yields to a warning of fire - and the Trauma Clown imbibes to be ablaze and a lesson to us all! Winner of the Clown d'Or, it's like he's in the room!'

A death-headed harlequin stalked into view, antics galore about him, and an oiled hoop was set alight.

'The burning hoop, ladies and gentlemen, symbol of life - one big flaming zero! How long will it take for the maestro to eat it? Yet in this way he will challenge the world!'

The etiolated jester neared the hoop, his white face glistening like a soft boiled egg. His entire head had been dipped in grease-paint. As he flapped his mouth open and brought it to the flames, fire flashed across and ignited his cosmetic skull. He was a shrieking scarecrow, standing in place like a thing planted, the Killer Midgets dancing around him.

'So many questions, so little time! Longer backs are all the rage, baby - observe as Bibi Mahru Blitz deploys the biggest armoury of charms since the serpent prompted Eve! The viper Magic Onion resides in that urn - watch Bibi Mahru's efforts!'

The audience were by now weeping with disappointment. As Mahru sat cross-legged before the urn and began parping on some sort of bugle, Barny leaned over to Gregor. 'There he is - get ready.' Gregor lit the end of an arrow and fired it into the tent wall near the entrance.

'The Beast Man - rubbish, albeit I have tremendous respect for his physical strength! See him climb into the cannon and leave it at a blur! No homoerotic vision has been so bluntly metaphorical since the days of Sparta! Beware, the Beast Man!'

The grim and muscular Dugway Thrax flexed his arms redundantly and then clambered into a cannon which was immediately fired off by a few clowns. There was a hell of a lot of smoke, out of which his body flew and zoomed through the balcony window of the Mayoral Palace, the Mayor himself flinching like a failure. Cannonites roared their disapproval, waving banners which stated ELAPSED GHOULS SHOULD CLEAR THE WAY.

A rhino was lumbered across the showground. 'The Indian army would train rhinos to ride at the head of battle,' shouted Karloff, 'scattering the enemy! But for our purposes, the Fatal Rhino merely trots like a mule, an insult to his heritage! And look there - a pig with a nose like a punctured tankard!'

A pig skittered in, disappearing into the chaos somewhere.

'And no good can come of these aerial cadavers - look above, in bird light heights - the Flying Dead Brothers! Limbs busted aside, skin shredded like rind, spraying blood and gutwater where they go, they really are brothers, ladies and gentlemen!'

High in the rigging, Fang and his brothers began the gymnastics of entropy. These reaching armatures of tendon and catgut screamed quite audibly that 'This'll never work' as they flailed past the tarp lights. Coffin dust sprinkled the audience.

'There on the hanging rings it's quite dicey! Eternally famished, they gnash at the air, gnash at the air, gnash at the terrible air! And above all, see our new addition, a freak of purity, a bandaged lamb, captive in a barcode!' The spotlights converged upon a large cage which hung from the distant ceiling. It contained a winged angel, glowing white as though over-exposed. 'The Caged Angel, Evangelica of Rust, Eden Vulture in its own light. It's the oldest story in the world!'

'That's Mike Abblatia,' said Gregor, squinting up, 'the car sales-man. I'd always thought he was more sensible.'

Squill and Ladaat collided in mid-air, smashing like kites. Pieces of them fell, spinning around a central tangled mass. 'Acrobats often tire of audacity and catch the idea of landing in the stalls, bless 'em,' laughed Karloff as the twisted gristle hit the crowd.

Alerted by the spreading conflagration near the entrance, Edgy ran into the big top to do his part in the snake-rescue just as Mahru lost his patience. After resorting to the shout of 'Emerge, emerge!' and repeated shaking of the tub, the snake-charmer finally took it up and with a cry of 'I said you'd show yourself, Magic Onion, and - !' swung the container, ejecting the snake into the air. Edgy took it right in the eye and fell in the path of circling animals and bounding clowns. He lay amid the danger like a used firework, elephant legs stamping past him.

'Edgy, stop saving your energies and grab the beautiful serpent!' Barny yelled, finally turning aside to find that Gregor had disap-peared. The crowd were panicking due to the quickly spreading fire and Barny shoved through people and smoke toward the ring, where Edgy seemed to be groggily awaking.

'That boil-in-the-bag fakir has lost all self-control,' Karloff pro-claimed. 'And what's this? The lads are surprising me with new busi-ness! A clown in the melancholy vagabond style. Tolerate his ancient buffoonery if you can! See the other clowns chase him as he tries to steal Magic Onion! Check out the hairstyle like an exploded cheroot. To the extent that he waves his arms at us all he seems friendly and energetic. As Violaine said, "A good leg will know when to kick, know when to run, and handle the transition quickly."'

Bent sparks quicked past Edgy's screams as he rampaged away from the clowns, holding the viper Magic Onion away from himself. Behind him a new spurt of clowns roared into frenzy, baying through acrylic faces. Spotting Barny, he threw the snake to him just as a clown with a kitchen haircut and carnation barred his way. The clown's face darkened like a lightbulb when Edgy ploughed him to the ground, sand spraying like pepper.

Above the scene, blood hanging out of him, Fang swung at ease on the showboat bar. The top of his head had been exploded into tatters, which flapped glamorously as he waved to the swarming crowd.

'Join us again for our full performance,' Karloff proclaimed as blown sparks flurried around him. 'Watch when it profits you, ignore when it profits you, deplore when it profits you, war when it profits you.'

Barny ran into the flames.

Gregor wandered through the sideshows, ignoring the potato hospital and the Staring Cannibal booth. He had long ago visited a 'Trouble Me Not' tent full of witheringly sarcastic mirrors which corrected people's grammar and told them to stop giggling like tarts. That garish enterprise, set up in the pennygrounds by Prancer Diego for no apparent reason, was destroyed by a posse of fire-wielding townsfolk. The chaos of burning mirrors had called ironic abuse to the onlookers as the glass warped and burst in, impressing no-one.

But Gregor had never visited a real Hall of Mirrors, and now he found one. The steps had surfaces red as a heart and an arched sign over the entrance said 'Doubts tangle inside a stack of doors. Shall you enter?' The door handle was a shock, apparently made of nuts. Strange devices infected the architecture in the entrance hall and a tailor's dummy, symbol of hellish intoxication, hung suspended from the encrusted blue sky of the domed ceiling. Striped walls messed with Gregor's perspective. For a quick-assembly gig it was impressive.

He advanced into the dark mirror hall, eyes readjusting as his own chubby image stepped into view. He had to admit it, he was a lovely sight. Rather than being simply reflected, his image seemed to disturb some sort of molecularity on the surface, which curled into place after his movements. The very darkness swirled with brownian particles. This mirror flowed into the next, decanting him like wine. The frames were bottle-green and each was crested with a stupid slogan:

Can't sleep? Stick head in mill.
Lack imagination? Why not be a lackey?
Gore in the attic? Keep embroidering.

He looked at the hall as a whole. In each glass his own face spectated, a row of vacancies. He moved and looked, his limbs stopping in the distance. He shook his head and it dribbled along the wall like a stain. He was everywhere, a god in invincible trousers. The lights started frazzling, spatting on and off and burning the air. He was too much for them, even in the midst of this cheap, sinister hoax. His image bulged through everything, intrinsic as love.

Laughter burst from his face and was instantly blocked off as a cold hand discovered his mouth. 'Poison can appear precious,' said the voice of Karloff Velocet close by his ear. 'Maggots tickle the ears of the dead. The only puzzle worth doing is one which notices when it's solved - something is activated.'

Gregor's senses exploded in an opulent apocalypse and he stormed into darkness.

In fact Karloff had heard a bit of a commotion while passing the Hall of Mirrors and popped in to check it out. There he found a ridiculous gutbucket smashing seven shades of glass out of the mirrors by rushing upon them with his groin. By the time Karloff had recovered from walking in on this wall-to-wall incompetence, the strange fellow was having a convulsive fit on the floor, folded up like a discarded clay figure. Karloff did not in fact mutter in Gregor's ear and he didn't say anything clever or enigmatic. But he did recognise this as the man in the news report, the roaring boy known as - what was it - 'Round One' or 'First Round'? Here was someone he could use.

5

THE BIG HUGE

Always pick up a fish by the ears

His boots munching across the sand, EH Hunt carried a load of wood past a dissolved causeway to his construction area beside the gulping sea. He dumped it next to the hammered frame of spars and, gasping, addressed the Announcement Horse. 'This beard of mine conceals the fact that my chin was eaten off by a giant bass. Years ago.'

No-one had ever pronounced with certainty upon the Announcement Horse's species. It seemed unacceptable that it was simply a heavy iron horse which made an occasional declaration and never moved a muscle. 'What did I tell you,' boomed the sepulchral steed, 'about your chin and beard's equal unimportance.'

Hunt sat on the wooden travelling chest he took with him everywhere. 'I had trouble interpreting the notes of your speech so I concentrated on the words, which were all about death and strength and gate posts pushed two ways at once by a titan - the bloody fool need only push gently and hey presto, ah we're none of us perfect.'

'I stated that "Infinity has so much structure, it has no structure". Thus evil's limbs may believe themselves the heart. There is no heart.'

'I knew a fella,' said Hunt, 'who carved gargoyles out of pear wood so that with the rain and all they got smoother and younger as the years passed. Finally they were like babies. Well, I liked the idea so I carved a figurehead like an old woman. What with the surf and spume she got younger and younger, a beautiful babe, then more like an actual baby, then a smooth skull, and finally a sort of doorknob. Ah, I should have thought it through. The Skipper stabbed me in the abs for that little bit of mischief.' Hunt glanced at his sleeve capstan and said 'The show'll be winding down. Maybe that's enough timber for the hull.'

Barny and the bag-headed Sags Dumbar carried Edgy between them like a piece of frayed rope. 'Fang should eat more,' Barny said. 'He's skin and bone.'

'He's meant to be,' Edgy moaned. 'He's a zombie.'

As Ladderland came into view, Barny saw that the ground floor wall was missing. He thought at first that it must have been Karloff's doing but the lion loped on to the porch, untroubled.

They dumped Edgy on a sofa. 'I can't feel my arse,' he moaned.

'That's no great loss,' said Barny, and took Magic Onion from around his neck. 'Where's my house disappearing to?'

'I'll have the roast beef platter,' said Sags Dumbar.

Barny wandered across town to the canyon where doomed Eddie Gallo was said to be rebuilding the flyover. Sure enough, there were planks galore piled ready. Surprised at doomed Eddie Gallo's gall, Barny set about taking the wood back before Gallo should return. As Violaine said, 'The holder of stolen goods must have the patience and serenity of an oak.'

Dozens of punters surrounded an earth clearing in a small side-tent. Karloff pushed Gregor through the crowd. 'Watch closely, First Round. Our roasted champion the Trauma Clown is facing a new challenger there, the one with the crown of ears - he showed up with some old found gloves and a clueless expression.'

Gregor stared at the mayhem on the dirt-floor boxing ring - a sort of living practice bull was taking the Trauma Clown apart with ease. Flents of skin flew off as though from a circular saw.

'Full of belligerence and moxie, that one, eh Fall Marshall?' commented the midget Cheney.

'If that fella punches your face, your head snaps back,' Karloff agreed. 'He's going postal.'

'Going what?' asked Gregor.

'He'll smash your pegs down your throat.'

The Trauma Clown shattered as though its skull was fragile as a papadum. Cheney was already in there, sweeping away blank laminated puzzle pieces as a knocked lightbulb swung to illuminate and darken a red scrawl on the canvas wall: DROWN THE KNIGHT AND ARMOUR IS UNLOCKED BY WATER AND WORMS.

'I'm reluctant to characterise it as a fight at all,' remarked Karloff. 'It was more like a sort of decision against the other fellow's existence. Did you get a name from this roly-poly monster, Cheney?'

'Calls himself Trubshaw.'

'Then so shall we. Prepare yourself, First Round. In two days you will fight our new champ to a standstill.'

'I don't know how to fight this thing,' Gregor whined. 'What's wrong with its legs? It's probably some sort of demon or a thing grown from evil dough. It's wearing armour. D'you expect me to just dance around wearing two giant cherries on the end of my arms until I die?'

'You'll see no signs saying not. Put him through his paces, Cheney.'

As Karloff left the game tent and crossed the circus back yard, he saw Barny passing by with a few planks. 'Barny Juno!' he hailed him.

Barny looked over. 'Yes ma'am?'

Karloff gasped in exasperation but reset his features. 'Come here, Nature Boy, we've business to discuss.'

Barny wandered after Karloff toward his trailer. As Barny passed, a barrel monkey in a velvet jacket and cap immediately tore off its clothes and followed him. Barny leant the planks against Karloff's wagon and stepped up into the gemlike gloom. Karloff was brewing chain tea and sorting a few bugs. 'How did you enjoy the show?'

'By setting myself a distracting task,' said Barny. He was looking at a poster portraying carnival pathologies in reverse colours. In small type at the foot of the turmoil were the words 'No attraction dies nameless.' Chittering, the organ chimp jumped on to his shoulder.

'Your open face blasphemes the struggles of man,' Karloff observed.

'Why isn't the Caged Angel on this poster?'

'That flying flesh crucifix is a very recent addition.'

'His name's Mike Abblatia. He's a grease monkey from Spacey's Gas Station.'

'Perhaps he was. We acquire curiosities where we go. Freaks and novelties. The chefs are missing their horrific cupboard lord and we have a new exhibit - The Famine Siren, a mermaid of bones. Why, I've a little item here you may recognise.' Karloff brought a lobster trap from beneath his makeup table - it contained a dog-sized bug with many pale legs. 'Here in the wicker cage, this came from your friend Sags's head, yes? It's a Varney bug. Your friend had a bad idea, the worst. When involuntary truths volley from the face they can do alot of damage on the way out.'

'You've been in the sorting office.'

'Cheney has - he's paying several visits about town. This is a fertile recruiting ground for abductees. But perhaps we can come to an arrangement. You return the lion, the snake you just stole and certain other animals by way of compound interest and I return your angelic friend to you. The perfect sacrifice meets the perfect fool.'

'And I suppose you don't want me to tell anyone that the fab new zombie you announced is just an old one that had quit and returned.'

'A trifle.'

'I won't be bought that easily!' Barny shouted, kicking the dish aside and standing. 'And as for giving you any animals ...' And he held the poster in front of his face, pushing his whole head through the tearing paper and screaming in a surprising way, his tongue extended.

When Barny was gone, Karloff wandered over to Rudloe Manor to chat to the Mayor.

The Mayor was sitting there like a paperweight and talking on the phone as the huge armoured bat Dietrich Hammerwire perched on a sideboard, gnawing through the shelled back of a floor lobster.

'Ah, the left and its right hand,' said Karloff, 'the right and its left.'

'Crunches the undersecretary under slowly lowering ceiling, you say? I don't know, Verbal - sounds expensive. I'll have to call back, I have a visitor. Goodbye.' Mayor Rudloe replaced the receiver and turned his attention to Karloff as the Fall Marshall sat opposite. 'Karloff. When I offered space to your shortcomings it wasn't my understanding that you'd plunge the square into darkness and fill it with bone-shivering mutants. Our municipal fittings have become silted up with dead clownflesh and cancer confetti.'

'Your mouth's off-kilter, Mayor - have you recently suffered catastrophic chin failure, by any chance? And why have you got a picture of brutal damnation hanging behind you?'

'The world's come to a pretty pass when a ringmaster can't tell the difference between a portrait of me and a picture of brutal damnation.'

'You might consider that for a campaign slogan.'

'I believe doomed Eddie Gallo is already using it. Have a look at this. I've underlined the relevant passages.'

'None of it's underlined.'

'None of it's relevant. Drop it in the bin there. That document was doomed Eddie Gallo's latest manifesto, *Will I Ever Learn?* The clueless muppet proposed some sort of scheme for growing corn-on-the-cob in his eyesockets. His timid and compromised antics will ram him headfirst into hell.'

'Nothing to worry about then eh?'

'Isn't there. Have you noticed the cornice damage from that meathead you fired in here? And I've been looking at this skit you gave me to memorize. It's bloody death and bursting stomach-walls for everyone. Do I really have to swap jokes and drolleries with you in the full gape of public scrutiny?'

'It must be seen and heard if it's to work as entertainment. It's similar to the shrillness principle. Even Violaine said: "For propaganda to resist erosion, calm voices must be seen as more absurd than hysterical ones." What's the problem?'

'Well, this sort of thing. "I say I say I say, what do you get if you cross a barber with a camel?"/"I don't know, what do you get if you cross a barber with a camel?"/"An abomination." I mean, it's appalling. And this bit where I "pull out a fireman's hose and take ten years off the audience's life." The list goes on. The safety culture of endless curtailment depends on respect for my authority, especially with the blood levy coming up.'

'Pardon, Mayor,' the demon Dietrich chipped in, 'but the image is one of folksy participation. All in it together. A leech only works up close, after all.'

'Your hood ornament's right, Mayor - public opinion's an unending race for mutual peer approval. That and fear's why they bleed once a year. We've all heard about the levy skeletons buried behind the shed.' Karloff jerked a thumb in the direction of the blood clock. 'That bit of gruesome chronometry justifies nothing, as you know.'

Rudloe uttered a wordless grumble. 'In the final analysis I serve an implacable mass of lard with an insatiable lust for blood. Unfortunate, but there we are. When you're in a position where you must make unpopular, indeed disastrous, decisions every day, before you know it you've got chops like these ...' He pulled his cheeks out like empty pockets, then released them, giving up.

'You could escape.'

'Outside, you mean, through that icy razorbahn? I've heard enough about the world out there to know I've a good thing.'

'That's not quite what I meant - have you considered soul-secretion?'

'I've heard of the practice. Certain lawyers have attempted it.'

'My own assistant Cheney put his into the head of a sweetpea, a particularly short-lived flower.'

'An annual.'

'Indeed. When it rotted down, Cheney's soul was released and probably resides in several worm families today.'

'Now, now,' Rudloe chided. 'There are worse places to reside than in worm families.'

'If you say so old boy,' frowned Karloff. 'Now, it's not generally known that every one of my clowns is soulless. They're a handful of functions, merely - where their make-up ends their bones begin. The souls are stored in a cold grey stone buried deep in a fallow field. It's my belief that Bingo Violaine did something similar.' He produced a rusty star-shaped box from beneath his jacket. 'I can offer you this in return for a simple service.'

'That's a Steeping Template,' said the demon Dietrich with sudden curiosity. 'Or cannari cage. Avatar-made for soul storage.'

'A handy bolt-hole for the day your enemies come for you,' Karloff continued, nodding. 'Or put half in there and the rest reels in at death.'

'Dietrich, leave us,' said Rudloe, with a flick of his hand. Dietrich bowed his clawhammer head and stepped out. 'What do I do in return.'

'I've proposed a trade of talent with Barny Juno.'

'That subnormal? He once came in here and threw a rock-hard cooker apple at my eyes.'

'He's to hand over his beasts and I'll hand over an angel which I've discovered to be of rather callow vintage.'

'He's agreed to this?'

'He led me to understand he needed twelve hours to decide. But he'll do it, I'm sure. When the magical exchange takes place at the end of our final performance, I require it to be witnessed by representatives of each facet of this community - you, Mayor, plus doomed Eddie Gallo, Dietrich, a few industrialists like King Verbal, Beltane Carom the ordered arcane, the Grand Dollimo, Del, and Prancer Diego the stupid bastard who mucks about. All must witness that the lion has been returned voluntarily.'

'The shaman too? Oak law and hedge saints, that's all I need.

Why do you have to make a spectacle out of everything?'

'I've got detail all over my face,' said Karloff. 'I can do anything I like.'

The Mayor's face cleared like he was feeling strange and weightless. He shook his senses. 'That's the most marginal definition of freedom I've ever heard.'

'Freedom must needs be marginal and so my particularly marginal definition of it affected you unusually -'

'Oh, shut up. What are you doing *now*?'

'Pissing off the balcony,' Karloff called back. 'I suppose I might see my way to going on the rampage later, if I find a window.'

'Your circus is a contaminant, Karloff,' shouted the Mayor.

'We are chaos.'

'So are we - but yours is different from ours.'

Chloe sat in the bone room with her father, an old man with a soul as real as a cat's torn ear. 'I told him he should be more giving, think more about what other people need.'

Gully sipped tea from a tarot cup. 'And what did he say.'

'Something about feasting harmlessly and hot upon me like a lion. A lion won't stop at looking, he said.'

Gully Low gave a tired smile, his face as grey as a dead feather. 'He dotes on you like a sucker dart.'

'If he understood people as well as he understands animals ... '

'He'd give them all room in that decked hill station of his. I remember the days it began to get hot around here. It changed everything. Instead of being broken up in sharpness and rain, the land became heated like one large room. Tropicalia was a fashion for a while, then people had to deal with it for real. The chill was an old excuse for separation. And so a thousand new excuses were found. I get the feeling Juno doesn't have that fear - he's just a little distracted.'

'Did you hear the seadoors just now?' Chloe frowned. She stalked carefully out of the little room and peered through her lopsided hair at the sloping rock corridors of the Juice Museum.

'This sign looks pretty easy to read,' came a voice. 'Let's take a look at it.'

Chloe ducked back into the bone room. 'Father, someone's broken in!' But Gully Low was drowsing, a headache flower blooming in silence at his shoulder. His tea genie began seeping into view, fringed in shrivelling air.

She returned to the corridors, searching through silence. Mackaw wood, Sahara bibles, the Cyril Manifesto, DG Croley, boxes of crystal teeth. Everything seemed forgotten in place.

But down in the grotto, on the narrow ledge toward the low cave mouth, cotton candy shreds blew caught in the fencewire.

6

HELTERPOLITIK

When all history's lessons have been given, it begins to cycle

Barny entered the lambent green of the walled garden. The shaman sat at the centre of involutes of truth, consulting a nerve almanac.

'I need your advice, Beltane Carom. Something practical, though. That Power Shout you taught me was the crappiest thing I ever did.'

'Once again you interrupt my meditation with trifles.'

'How did you know about that? I refused it.' Barny sat down on the hot patterned flagstones. 'The deal was, I return the lion and he returns the angel.'

'How did you leave it?'

'I led him to understand I needed twelve hours to decide.'

'Pushed your head through a poster eh? Well, I'm sure your lion could find his way home. And if not, you could always follow Karloff's scarship into the creepchannel, with a suitably shielded car. Mike Abblatia could fit one up after you've sprung him perhaps.'

'But why does the ringmaster hate me so much? One lion I stole, and before that a camel, old Mister Bailey. And this time a snake. But why all the bile?'

'Probably it's demon-spun.'

'That's what you always say.'

'Truth isn't a bee, Juno - it doesn't die after it's stung you. Even you can't have failed to notice you attract hellfire like an intake fan.'

'These demons, where do they live?'

'In the brief darkness hidden in the middle of summer.'

'That's where they hide?'

'They don't need to hide. Neither does good need to hide. Wholeness is not purity. Wholeness is life, the lot.'

'I don't get it.'

Carom thought about it. 'Put it this way. That colossal demon, Sweeney, the acid one who dislikes you. It nestles there in ashspace thinking it's king shit. But it's not the source of anything.'

'I still don't understand.'

'Well. An octopus has many arms, yes? And every bit of every arm is octopus, every inch. It's not bird or dog, right? Evil's the same. There's no real king or centre to it.'

'What's an octopus?'

Carom had a kitchen scales the bowls of which were concave mirrors - these could weigh the despair of any face reflected there. He peered into this now and the bowl crashed to earth. But it seemed it was freighted with more than mere exasperation at his guest's stupidity. Carom looked up as Barny stood to leave. 'Juno. Insanity happens when all your adjustments to the world meet up by accident. You don't have any adjustments. I hope you never do.'

Barny left the garden and was about to head off to Karloff when the stringy Planti-n Edge lurched up with his arse in a sling.

'Hello Edgy - has your arse healed enough to give you any pleasure?'

'There's more to pleasure than a healthy arse, my friend.'

'Where's Gregor?'

'Shaped like a pear.'

'Where, I asked.'

'Oh - well, sleeping with his lack of money, probably. Or trying to sell the new line of Condemnation Cards they've got at Stampede.'

'That stall of yours was rubbish, by the way.'

'I suppose it didn't help that I advertised the fruit as "Treetop bounty, dispossessed and huddling in our bowl". I'm going to open a chain of dry cleaners called "Ruination" instead. Yeah we're all in it together, that's the idea. You been consulting the guru?'

'Karloff's proposed a trade - the Abblatia angel for my lion. I was asking the shaman for advice.'

'No need, Bubba. I've just been chatting to a fella with bacon hair over at the midway. Tipped me off on a dirtfight in a side-tent in the circus yard. Called the Tar Baby Concerns. There's a fighter called the Masked Inconvenience who was in absolute cracking form at the trials apparently. Got YOUR FACE HERE tattooed on his fists. That's the kind of brutal moron we need.'

'I haven't got the readies.'

'Listen to me Bubba, it's a sure thing. You bet on him and winner takes all - propose that to Karloff. The MI isn't a gumshield with gossamer wings like some of the fellas I've recommended in the past.'

'You're dreaming.'

'You are super-wrong, my friend. Each finger as heavy as a marble egg, that's the form. The Masked Inconvenience - there's power in mystery. It's a lock.'

Barny thought about it. 'I suppose it could save a lotta trouble. You know more about this stuff than me.'

'Great,' said Edgy, walking on, and called back over his shoulder. 'Apparently he's up against some amateur called Trubshaw.'

As Barny continued toward the town centre, listening with a smile to some low-key barking off a distant dog, he nearly collided with Chloe Low, her face milk-pale, her eyes like liquorice, her cherub gob working like a hypnotist's spiral. 'Barny,' she breathed. 'I think someone stole the Wesley Kern gun - it's all that's missing. Remember the story I told you? Kern made the gun in a dental forge with boneseed and headwater. Then he went up the Tower of Nowt and shot at the Mayoral Palace. They made it seem afterward that he'd fired on innocents.'

He remembered - Kern had tried a sort of shooting and screaming gambit before Barny or Chloe were born.

But Barny could only stare up and down her as though at a golden ladder. The heaven he lived in her minutes felt like contraband now.

She nodded forlornly. 'I sense something. Tragedy's at hand.'

'I love you.'

'This isn't about you, Barny.'

'I know.'

'Or your animals. People first, Barny. It's your civic duty.'

Without understanding why, Barny felt disappointed in her. He put the feeling away.

'I have to get back to the Juice. Beware the clowns.' She walked away. Barny watched a rust-coloured insect land on the white landscape of his hand.

The daredevil Beast Man, Dugway Thrax, dared to dream of an edible meal, but despite the new boxer Gregor's warnings, he visited the Ultimatum Restaurant and dragged the challenger with him. Intent over the table they kept an eye on the menu, a translation of which they listened to in a spirit of horror and fright. 'What's deathhead chowder?' Thrax asked the waiter.

'Gulch bulbs in blue ink, throats leaking old rain, disarmingly poisonous eye-roots and a tangle of stinking weeds. With french fries.'

'Well, fries at least. We'll have it.'

'You're making an error,' said Gregor with finality as the waiter departed. 'You don't know how things work here.'

'Oh, don't exaggerate,' said Thrax. 'I ate fire for a living once. And I mean once.'

An odd hour was passed like a coded message as they learnt their worth in the eyes of the staff. Gregor was already in a semi-trance. He had slipped up somewhere. Society had finally caught up with him and thus he was condemned to be destroyed by a sort of hairless ape with a multitude of ears. He had expected it to happen eventually in one form or another - only the precise circumstances were a surprise.

'What's this crap I keep hearing about you thrusting your hips at a mirror?' the Beast Man asked him, trying to maintain the outward semblance of easy freedom in this oppressive place.

'I'm in love with myself, it's true.'

'Yourself.'

'Isn't that meant to be healthy? I've thrown away all my dummy cosmetics and dinosaur porn.'

When the meal arrived, it was a pig which seemed to have come to grief in a malarial swamp. Trailing from it was a padlock of fat, flash-fried in the cold sweat of years. A paper flag pronged into its hide warned: 'Those who free me never escape.'

'What's this?' asked the Beast Man.

'Something brought too soon from the incubator, by the look of it.'

'This is a meal?'

'Very much so. And a surprisingly expensive one.'

'Where are all the waiters?'

'Hiding. I *told* you how it would be.'

Looking at these seared relics, they devised a plan. Working as a team they could use the scalpel to hatch a few preliminary wounds and maybe scoop out the slime with apostle spoons. Then they would push the rest off the table and run.

But as they breached the torso they found that the entire thing was constructed of bucket pasta, painted with gravy. This was the last straw for the Beast Man. He found a waiter crouched behind the counter, sniggering into his hand. 'Get me the manager,' he told the startled employee, and the owner and master chef, Quandia Lucent, came out from the kitchen. Thrax gestured at the embryonic pasta hog. 'This meal is an obvious subterfuge - when's the real food coming?'

Perfectly composed, the chef raised an eyebrow. 'This is pasta, sir - consensus chow.'

'This is a joke, right?'

'Perhaps sir is a philistine,' Lucent responded dryly. 'With a glass tongue. One cannot put a price on pasta.'

'You do, every day.'

'I am initiated into the mysteries. "Without feast, no cruelty" is the chefs' credo. Food poisoning is the one constant throughout history. Is this round friend of yours the gentleman who smashed our front window with his hips, by any chance?'

'Don't try to change the subject to that unfortunate reality.'

'If sir is blind to the charms of slimy flour, perhaps sir would prefer the Carcinia Platelet, a medley of mushrooms in -'

'*Damn* your mushroom medley - such plunder and invention, yet no custard? We're getting out of here before our gorges rise and storm the freezer.'

Gregor followed Thrax out of the Restaurant, leaving behind the dead and others who weren't so lucky. 'I told you, a cabinet fiend advises the chefs,' he reminded the Beast Man as they emerged into the Square. 'Let's go to the cakeworks over there.' As they wandered over, he asked the Beast Man about the metal cross which hung about his neck. 'What is it? A key to something?'

'I think it used to be, but it's been copied and re-copied so many times, a copy of a copy and so on, a million times, I suspect it's changed too much to open anything now.'

They entered the bakers and the proprietor asked after Gregor's wellbeing.

'Quickly my stomach increases, the trial of doctors,' said Gregor lustily, then asked for jackal cake.

The proprietor shook his head sadly. 'No demand, senor. Which is a shame, because people come in here and ask for it all the time.'

'Exactly, and it's advertised everywhere.'

'Propaganda is buried in the greatest desirability, senor,' said the drooping baker. 'Look at the crazy new gears on this fondant creation.'

'Controls on a bun?' the Beast Man queried.

'Young people don't care, senor,' sighed the baker. 'They live for craziness.'

'Well, as Bingo Violaine said,' the Beast Man smiled, '"Man's arse is a despised necessity."'

'Come on out, Beast Man!' came a voice from outside. Looking through the display window, Thrax and Gregor saw five Followers of the Cannon in the street, flexing their gobs to emit sounds. 'Come out of that cake shop and face your crimes against the one true religion!'

'Isn't chomping a religion?'

'Chomping? Are you alright, Beast Man?'

'I'm on top of the world. And chomping, yes, I'm sure of it. Chomp, chomp, I'm a better man. Oh the beauty's almost unbearable.'

'You transgress against the holy cannon by your secular antics! Is it not enough that we cannot find our murdered master's remains to fire unto the heavens? While your new friend Gregor acts like he's got a playground in his pocket?'

The baker opened a panel in the side wall and urged Gregor through it. 'Fools mean trouble senor - heart pounding, blown up lungbags, not good for man or beast.'

Gregor found himself in the darkness of Donna Greeley's furniture store. All the furniture here was joined up into one big unweildy piece which no-one could move or afford - it had never been sold and the store had fallen into disuse. Greeley herself had died and dried out long ago, and Gregor felt leery of the dim carcass propped in the shadows. The Beast Man crawled in after him just before the front door burst open and the cannonites entered.

One of the benefits of having a heart like an ancient boiled sweet, Karloff reflected as he strolled under the sparred sky of the town square, is that when you see a strongman and a prizefighter being dragged out of a furniture shop and beaten up by a handful of priests, you don't react rashly. Enjoying a small cigar, Karloff watched the fight with interest.

He looked on till Cheney appeared beside him. 'What's the score, boss?'

'Examine well this boneless striver, Cheney. Our new boxer, I mean. Compound extremists came out in a rush, months away from satisfaction. Religion is not candid. Smug dozens don't see both ways. Yet he looked at the anger and bungled his response. Tried a begging gambit.'

'Begging.'

'And weeping. The Beast Man also.'

'A weeping gambit's good for embarrassing the opponent.'

'Well it didn't this time. The Fuseheads just stood there. First Round realised after a while his attackers had selected a basic staring gambit, so he stopped. Then the priests attacked them both anew.'

'How'd the victims respond?'

'With a bleeding and blacking-out gambit - and that's where you came in. Our so-called "Masked Inconvenience" has been unconscious in the dust for ten minutes now. I think I see how the land lies with that one.'

'I got the gun,' said Cheney.

'Ah,' sighed the Fall Marshall. 'As Violaine said, "Even an illusion is made from the real". I should get some practice in.'

*

Mayor Rudloe pushed back the hood of his containment suit, removed his Jonathan glasses and looked nervously about the striped operating tent. Against a tragedy-stained backdrop stood the Fall Marshall, the red stripes of his glass hat corkscrewing ever to the sky. Behind angled aluminum bars paced a tiger striped like a zebra, its movement creating moray patterns. 'Ah, this is what it's all about eh?' asked Rudloe uncertainly.

Dietrich ducked in behind the Mayor.

'You can tell the wingding to get lost,' said Karloff.

'Who?'

'The paravamp. Ave tyrannis.'

Dietrich raised the crust of an eyebrow. 'You seem to know a lot about it.' The he turned and went out.

'Never mind that method-acting demon of yours,' said Karloff, messing with some equipment. 'We are an itinerant collective and in this world that means swift travel via other realms - our arrivals are unwelcome enough without our trailing clouds of poison effluvia from the mainlands. So the creepchannel is convenient, but I rarely pause to have dealings with demons.'

'A rather lengthy denial about something I don't remotely understand. And what's this?' The Mayor picked something off the ground.

'The Chestnut of Death.'

'*God* Almighty!' Rudloe threw the nut away in a puff of goofer dust. 'I've serious reservations about this three-ring circus you call a ... circus.'

'You upper classes - so at home in a vacuum you can find three syllables in it. Bite into doubt, you'll find good reason. You'll end undone and sliding down bathmirror condenstation, Mayor.'

'Well, it's true that being petitioned by ghastly scum is not all it's cracked up to be. The hairpin turns of m'policies have left my mind scratched to oblivion, really. No thought can travel smoothly across it anymore. Maybe you've got the right idea, living out of your hat. Midden freaks and no traceable premises - that's probably the stuff.'

'Yes, my pleasure in gain displayed as entertainment, for a hefty charge - immaculate profit, I think you'll agree.' Karloff took what looked like a length of twisted bone from a carved wooden box. 'Do you know what this is?'

'A measure of your desperation?'

A middle-of-the-range clown entered in funny duds and makeup.

'The recent unpleasantness of our performance is to be repeated,' the Fall Marshall continued. 'And since Chance Macabre now has a pressing engagement with some maggots, I must take up his act.

Just as the illusionist relies on misdirection, living the clown's life is a simple thing if you exaggerate your legs and cover your face in shame. This bright-eyed, saucy little gun is a product of the white heat of technology. When I fire, Brit Hume here will catch the bullet in his teeth.'

'The white heat of my arse more like! That's the Wesley Kern Gun!'

Karloff aimed the gun at the glum smile of Hume, and fired. The head of mushroom flesh exploded, the clown dropping like a sack of worms. Rudloe rushed up and stared aghast at the corpse as Karloff briskly wiped the pistol.

'I thought you said he'd catch the bullet in his teeth.'

'He did - as you can plainly see.'

'I suppose I misunderstood your claim.'

'Once again,' said Karloff, replacing the gun in the ornate case. 'Misdirection. No real loss - dualistic thought's been cranking out clowns for centuries. Now let's see if we can't rehearse a similar act with you, Mr Mayor.'

'I'll battle it all the way to the wire,' gasped Rudloe.

'But your stone bald misrule requires such occasional charm offensives.'

'On condition I survive!' shouted Rudloe.

A silver-painted midget with eyes like seeds entered the tent, skidding in slurry and quickly righting himself.

'This is my assistant, Mayor – HH Cheney.'

'The one who put his soul into a worm family?'

The midget ignored him. 'Message from the target, Mr Velocet. He's putting the entire crap axis on the Masked Inconvenience. Winner takes all, angel and animals.'

'You're joking.'

'I'm telling you what he said.'

Karloff gave a delighted, astonished bark of laughter. 'Tell him I accept.'

'And that new zombie's scaring the riggers.'

'Excellent. Did you see how Fang threw himself into it? A putrescent streak a mile wide, that one. Skeleton makes good. Those demised daredevils were incomplete without him. I heard there was an incident with one of the Iscariot beetles you got from Del.'

'One of the saddles slid and a kid became entangled in some legs like black scissors. Oh, and that shyster mug wants to see you.'

Max Gaffer stormed into the tent, his head-swords slashing slits in the canopy.

'I thought you were dead,' said the Mayor.

'Sure, dead like a *fox*!'

'Metal visor nailed directly into your face eh? Can't say I'm entirely surprised. And those swords look awkward.'

'They are.'

'You know this hen-in-waiting too, Karloff?' Mayor Rudloe asked the Fall Marshall.

'Who better to liaise with criminals than a bungling brimstone-bandit?' And Karloff turned to the lawyer to bark, 'Well, what is it? Speak up man!'

'I delivered - it's your turn.'

'My heart falls open like a pocketwatch, Gaffer, and gives you a few minutes. What a pity that isn't enough. I'm dangling my gratitude your way - in the form of some liver, look.' Karloff pulled some meat from his coat and flung it at the lawyer's feet.

'Liver? I did what I promised. Two positives can't make a negative.'

'Yeah, right. I promised that the consequences would be aimed at someone else and so they will. That's politics after all, eh?'

Gaffer pounded his forehead with the heels of his palms, spluttering as his hands were lacerated. 'What - what's ...?'

'You take yourself too seriously, Maximillion. More seriously than I take you, or the Mayor here. That set chin and gleaming eyes of yours won't make any difference I'm afraid - they're rubbish to me. You see, even among clowns there's a limit. Your rotted-out motivations appall everybody. You've made a pig's ear of this, haven't you? As above, so below.'

'You know about that?'

'Your position with Sweeney? That you're the office plunger? I have absolute confidence your every ambition will end at the base of a cliff. Cheney, take it outside.'

The midget plunged his head into Gaffer's belly, pedalling his legs so that the demidemon was forced backward out of the tent, tears like worms dangling from its eyes.

'Now,' resumed Karloff, 'where were we - ah yes, calamitous mayhem and insane megalomania.'

But before they could continue, the Beast Man entered, looking roughed-up and apologetic. 'I've come to tender my resignation, Mr Velocet.'

'Oh really? Well that's an awful shame.'

'It's the pure evil, Mr Velocet - it's just not me. I hope this won't inconvenience you.'

'I always knew you'd become a townie, Dugway,' laughed Karloff good-naturedly. 'Go off with you, and no hard feelings eh?'

'Thankyou Mr Velocet.' And the Beast Man ducked out.

'Shame about old Dugway, he's a sweet man despite his Popeye arms. Wears that carmencross because it's an infinity compass containing every detail. You can bet a reindeer doesn't know *that*. Not really surprised he threw in the sponge.'

'I don't want to hear about this bizarre world of sponges, liver and reindeer knowledge you inhabit!' shouted the Mayor. 'What's this nonsense about shooting me in the face?'

'Oh, no need for that now - you'll be replacing the Beast Man.'

'Being shot out of a cannon?'

'It doesn't often happen the other way around, and what if it did. It's like a man swallowing fire - evens the score.'

'What's this crazy talk?'

'Minutes black as ants as you wait for the blast. When midday hurtles at you for the first time, you'll love it.'

'What then?'

'You'll be found months later, fool's-parsley growing through your ribcage.'

By the time the Mayor returned to his office he felt inchoate, all volition gone, like a man plucked this way and that by a tailor. He fell into his seat with a gasp and sat resembling almost exactly the portrait behind him, in which he looked like a lump of scorched dough. He was about to clang his eyelids when Max Gaffer flung into the room, followed by an apologetic Dietrich. 'I grabbed hold of him, sir, but he's so slimy ...'

'I know - what do you want, Gaffer?'

'Is that all you have to say?'

'No, I'd like to thank you - your troubles are an ore-body I mine for glee. Your downfall's been a marvel to watch. Has a mistake ever been so precise at such a speed? I'd like to shake your hand and stop awkwardly for a photo.'

'Don't be absurd.'

'So you tried a task in your exile - was the result of any worth? Your head's ribbed and flavoured, are you satisfied?'

'No,' said Max Gaffer, exhaling his anger and sitting down miserably. 'I'm treated like a makeweight down there ... over there. Cold hell. Sweeney regards m'lying skills as rudimentary at best.'

'The world of grief is not always one of participation,' the demon Dietrich chipped in.

'What does that mean.'

'I mean it's inescapable. Grief is.'

Gaffer looked at Dietrich with slow scorn. 'You demons. It's just hog heaven for you round here isn't it.'

'You're a demon yourself, Max,' Rudloe pointed out. 'What are those pulsing lugs in your throat?'

'Shrike-filters.'

'Well there you go, a demon. So what do you want?'

'Treason is pliant. I want you to take me back.'

'Are you hearing this, Dieter? He wants to come back. Used to walk around with ears instead of warrants.'

'And now I've got warrants for ears, so what?'

'Does all shame cease under the Planck length?'

'Bet your life it does. It's unbeatable.'

'Stop saying that, Max.'

'What?'

'"Unbeatable". That privilege is no longer yours. I refuse to take your request seriously. Dietrich here barely knows what human beings are and even he's better liked than you - people wave at him in the street, throw babies at him, everything.'

'Flowers,' Dietrich added.

'Give him flowers and so on. You? Obsessed with your underwear, your time in this office was a monsoon of unparalleled depravity. Unprecedented criticism was voiced of your buttocks, both separately and together. You're not telling me such flak was unfounded. So here you are finally, toppled and confessed. Even that ringmaster won't have you.'

'He's a fool - thinks he can teach tricks to a Steinway Spider.'

'Eh? Steinways you say?'

'With whip and piano stool.'

'I don't believe you - you'll say anything at this point. Maybe you should go see doomed Eddie Gallo. Squeaking of rights and freedoms, he snips his scissors at the rain. You and he deserve eachother.'

Gaffer stood abruptly, knocking his chair over backwards. 'My performance in vice is unassailable, punctuated as it is by regular betrayal. But you? You're a limb on the Conglomerate. As Violaine said: "Cheap harm lasts just as long."'

And he stormed out of the room, his head-swords slashing chips from the doorframe.

'Send out the Brigade,' the Mayor told Dietrich, 'to keep the clowns in line. And I don't like this notion of rogue pianos.'

Never one to waste a bit of rotting meat, Karloff took the liver into his wagon and slapped it on to the table, closing the door and sitting down. From a drawer he took a thin black spine resembling barbed wire and pushed it into the glossy congestion so that it stood like an antenna. Rewiring mercy nerves in the face of this hepatic conduit, he recited a credo which ended with the words 'Reform changes the shape of injustice.' The searing grey drone of creepchannel flux leaked sour light from the forensic transmitter. Migraine bile scrambled up the trailer walls as Karloff was filled with a dirty vacuum.

'Quit griping or whatever that noise is,' said the demon Sweeney, its voice fluttering against the crackle of the underworld. 'I need hardly remind you that I purchased your rapacious handiwork for fifty large and an agreement not to snip your nose off - tee hee! How's Accomplice?'

'Species of bark are given names. Bugs cross the face of a barn in less than an hour - fact. And the front of the heads have eyes now.'

'They have had for a long time haven't they?'

Karloff thought about it. 'Yes, I suppose they have. And their customs, compared to elsewhere ... one more bit of etiquette and I swear the dead will return in exasperation.'

'Yes, "manners" - two laws look at eachother. Press on anyway, eh? What was that?'

'Nothing, I was nodding in agreement.'

'Knobbing?'

'Nodding, I said. And watching a fist-sized tarantula going past.'

'Ah, that thick spindle of fear, the tarantula - I wish I was there to see it with you. If there was any animal I could fold up and put in my mouth I'd select the good old tarantula. Eating well?'

'Apple fritters.'

'Playing it safe eh. Good. Is the massacre prepared?'

'Can't you tell?'

'I know only a centre of it, never all the details.'

'Well, I test-fired the gun and it's a peach. I have a false crisis planned for the purpose of subsequent complacency. And my cover is perfect. In the ring I load standard wonders into their vacant faces. I float by my comrades as ever, dispensing aspersions like an acclesiast. Horror is expected, and horror it shall be.'

'I told you the possession of their cultural icons would give you even greater hypnotic power. I await the influx of graves. Enough jawing.'

'OK. Here I go.'

Karloff unpicked the radio, kicked open the wagon door and threw it to a dog.

7

OCTOPUS

Damnation - it takes as long as it takes

The Flying Dead Brothers ascended the Tower of Nowt in broad daylight, pieces of their skin dropping on to passersby. Fang was stressed. 'Are you sure we're authorised to clamber up here?'

'Doctors are mermaids in their imagination,' called Squill.

'That's not what I asked. And wouldn't it be better to do this at night?'

'I'm laughing.'

'No you're not.'

'I would be if I weren't busy climbing. Hoop-la!' Squill swung on a dead flagpole through an upper window. He stuck his head out of the window again to shout 'And put your weight behind it!' but his head fell away through space, smashing in the road.

The brain-hung Enrico muscled swiftly upward, hauling himself inside. When Fang joined him in the upper chamber, carrying the badly-rotted Ladaat, the tower guard Murdster was stood there fully alert to their intrusion. He held a machete the colour of tar.

The hefty Enrico gaped in sick dismay, but Fang placed Ladaat carefully down and turned his custard head and canary-yellow eyes upon the sentinel. 'What course of exhaustion d'you favour, friend?'

'I pretend to be alert.'

'Where?'

'Here.'

'What do they pay a guard these days?'

'With carefully contrived documents of a threatening nature, bills of lading, and a shout upside the face.'

'I'm surprised. Nine french-fries are usually adequate.'

With a yell, Murdster swung the blade and slashed Fang's arm from his shoulder.

Fang awaited some follow-up remark from the sentinel and, receiving none, gestured to his stump and asked 'Well? Whattya mean?'

'Fang, the Rotten Star!' bellowed Enrico and when Murdster turned to look at him, Fang kicked Ladaat from the floor - the torso hit Murdster full in the nose, knocking him backward over the headless Squill and through an opposite window.

'Is this it?' asked Fang, inspecting the length of fake-looking ham stretched between two pegs on a pedestal. 'The Moral Fibre?'

Enrico shook his head slowly and fiercely. 'I don't know, Fangy my brother. I just don't know.'

Ladaat piped up from the floor. 'Remember what the Fall Marshall said - "Bring back that little beauty from the Tor Magdala or you'll never fly again."'

Fang frowned. 'And what Bingo Violaine said. "Consensus is reality with the crusts cut off."'

The lawyer Max Gaffer wandered over to the canyon edge where doomed Eddie Gallo was crouching quietly on the stumped flyover with a hammer and a length of wood.

Doomed Eddie Gallo looked up slowly and carefully. His cardigan flapped and cracked in the wind. 'Hello, Max Gaffer,' he whispered. 'These are planks newly sawn from the Awkward Forest. Boy, the trouble I had. They've got keys to the trees round there. And I suspect they are constantly stealing the wood back.' A sloth appeared from behind a buckled nugget of concrete and began creeping slowly toward him. He regarded the sloth sadly. 'I'd like to sit on those things. But I daren't.'

The sloth exploded suddenly, knocking doomed Eddie Gallo backward into a hedge on terra firma. He seemed to be laughing.

This is what I've come to, thought Gaffer.

Wise old heifers gazed at the scene, and then at eachother.

Gaffer went over and helped the mayoral candidate out of the bushes. 'How goes the mayoral campaign, doomed Eddie Gallo?'

'I carve lovely hearts from bits of turnip and throw them out the window of a car,' whispered doomed Eddie Gallo. 'One hit an old gran in the eye and she sued me to within an inch of my life, screeching and pointing all the time. That got me a lot of press, as you can imagine.'

Gaffer wasn't surprised. This idiot had once made a miniature sculpture of his own head and shoulders from white bread. 'Why are you whispering, doomed Eddie Gallo?'

'Am I? I can't hear a thing. Too many sloth explosions. I mainly look these days. Yesterday my attention was captured by a high thing which moved in air-knocking motion.'

Gaffer smacked dust from doomed Eddie Gallo's clothes and yelled in his ear. 'You mean you saw a *bird!*'

'Bird? I suppose it was. Something different about you, Max Gaffer. A haircut?'

'I've been modified into a sort of semi-demon, doomed Eddie Gallo! Look at me!'

'Eh?'

'Demon, I said! Swords in my head! See?'

'Ah!'

'Swords! And the Church of Automata hammered this bridle into my cheeks!'

'Bridle? Ah, I see, a sort of metal mask. The day has left your trouble swollen, eh?'

'Yes!'

They sat down among duct stones, ear weeds and cactus skeletons.

'I'd like to help with your mayoral campaign, doomed Eddie Gallo! I of course put Rudloe where he is today!'

'Oh? I heard you were running on fumes.'

'Wha -? Well that's as may be, but I can give you a fair shake at it! For instance, how many rich tea biscuits have you eaten today?'

'No more than two or three thousand.'

'That's what I'm talking about! Look at the politics, doomed Eddie Gallo, what it's all about! King Verbal could boneseed a bridge here with ease - but would he personally see that as progress? He's got himself quite a set-up, after all!'

Gallo's face lit up, then became puzzled. 'Yes, I suppose he could. These are our tall poppy days, our salad days - ever put tall poppies in a salad? The stalks push your cheeks out like a tent.'

'Don't zone out on me, doomed Eddie Gallo! I think you're on to something with this canyon crossing stunt! But you have to be practical! And "Bless the ultimate strangeness" is not a campaign slogan!'

'Oh I've a back-up plan, Max Gaffer, never fear - look. Gull glue, from the Shop of a Thousand Spiders. Found it between the blood glass and the cannibal cigarettes. My tin friend Maquette is working there with that scary boy. With this application, I won't have to hammer and disturb those sloths.'

Gaffer looked at the tube of glue which doomed Eddie Gallo had handed him:

Ingredients: rogue lard; negative flake (2%); some kind of stringy ectoplasmic snot from the muzzle of a jagged old crone whose better days exist only in her mind; aqua; colouring (mole-pearl, E171); tears; vulture shadow; daisies (95%); modified starch; carnauba wax.

As the lawyer finished the list, someone kicked into his ribs, falling on top of him. The trickster Prancer Diego could never work out how to slow up before he reached people. 'An unfortunate incident, happily in the past,' Prancer chortled, thrashing among them. 'The problem is: *aaaaaaaaah!*'

'What's the matter with you?' Gaffer choked.

'I'm growing ten individual species of nostril lizards.'

'Nostril lizards?'

Doomed Eddie Gallo laughed fit to burst. 'Ho ho! This fellow Prancer - a lot of gumption, eh Max Gaffer?'

Closing his eyes, Max Gaffer finally shrugged off the encumbrance of hope.

Seeing everything through the added context of time, the Abblatia angel saw his cage as a tiny barcode, a barely noticeable detail amid green battlements sparkling in rain, orchards cut and bleeding summer into coffee earth, branches underground laden with coral rinds and deep-packed stairs of old empire. Light, flowers and immense material, a realm of zooming fire. The cage was in fact only five days wide, and elsewhere Abblatia visited Spacey's Gas Station to find Barny Juno looking at a car covered in radiator backblow and semiobliterated decals.

'Hello Mike Abblatia,' Barny said. 'This thing needs plugging with muscle junk and etheric shielding. Penny rhino on the dash and spoiler adornments like sovereign rings. Couldn't wake Dot.'

Abblatia gladly worked with Barny on the car a while, fitting it with a narrow goofer tank, a soapstone dashboard and an old carpet which had absorbed creepchannel leakage from a previous roof and was sprouting tough mushrooms. They were just callibrating new palladium valves to the suicide clutch when Chloe Low walked by and Barny asked her if she'd seen the fight.

'There you go again,' Chloe sighed. 'With your animals.'

'Not just that - my house is disappearing.'

Doctor Perfect hove up in front of Abblatia, his long spatulate fingers spindling like a spider. 'Gold bones? How did he arrive at this condition?'

Karloff Velocet was stood with the Doctor atop a scaffold, looking through Abblatia's cage bars. 'Some sort of progress glowing beyond its size.'

'Change without needles - that's objectionable.'

'So is anything without profit, surely, for a corpse artisan?'

'I won't deny it. Well, I don't see what you want me to do here. I suspect it's simply been re-forgotten so many times it's fallen into its own sidespace.'

'I was just curious. You're available for the fight tonight?'

'Ofcourse. Doctors do not want for purpose - they want for one they can achieve. I'll bring some of my famous knives.'

The Doctor lived in stethoscope darkness, ignoring the condition of his cigarette heart.

*

Brimming in the poison yolk of his throne, Sweeney called down the Ruby Aspict as creatures of blown ghost sifted in and out of the walls, reciting laws and raising their eyebrows ironically. The Sawvillian protocol demon Rammstein kicked through some black ice buds which had been born dead to the yellowed frost of hell. Every atom here had jaws, gnawing at life's feeble push. The biomechanical king demon peered down from its leathery halfshell. 'I'm checking up on old Trouble Trubshaw, Rammy. He should be well into mischief by now. Let's take a peek into this harebrained scheme they call the miracle of creation.'

Everything would be seen in red, a fever window. The fleshy gemstone turned, a dented heaven dark in its depths. Then appeared broken-down gardens, cored cars, slang vines and Vonn Stropp crows. 'Well we know he's in the right place, at least.'

But the scene which next appeared showed Trubshaw belting away at a heavy punch-bag, sweat flying off him. At his back Karloff Velocet shouted 'Carry on that slow you'll become a byword for soil, boy!'

'So regret me,' Trubshaw growled.

'What did he say?' Sweeney asked.

Rammstein was embarrassed. 'It's in an unfamiliar dialect, your majesty.'

'That big lug of a demon, what's he doing?'

'Nothing useful, that's for sure. Genius is like a pause - transplant it and it loses meaning.'

'Trubshaw's not a genius, he's just a bastard, a thug.'

'Then perhaps he's in the right place after all.'

'What's he punching? Barny Juno better be in that bag.'

But Trubshaw was now snoozing peacefully in the shade of bitter apples.

'What's Juno doing?'

The Aspict switched to a view of Barny leaning on a lion's head and looking at his partly-disassembled house.

'What about that frayed exclamation mark, what's his name: Edge. Plantin Edge - show him!'

A ripple passed through the Aspict, revealing a tree the living green of lizards. Beneath it, standing in tropical cotton and car-tyre sandals, Edgy was slowly moving a placid hen through the air as if it flew. A fierce woman snapped at him. 'You only just woke up?'

'For my part, new days are nothing - I always crouch in my shirt. Don't try to change me baby.'

The girl stood staring point-blank into Edgy's face. 'Don't make me come over there, Palatino.'

'What about the hen?'

'Get rid of it!' snapped the demon Sweeney.

'He can't hear you, Lord,' said Rammstein.

'I was dismissing the Aspict!' Sweeney roared as the Ruby cleared. He sat back, fulminating. 'It's like a recurring dream which I can't effect. Why was Karloff urging Trubshaw to punch some sort of huge sausage?'

'A mere formality, perhaps.'

'In any case, Plan A and B have collided. I can no longer depend on the efficiency of either.' Sweeney leaned forward and, bracing his many legs, began to tear himself from his throne. Sinews stretched, gas exploding from fluke-holes as Sweeney exposed a spine made of black gemstone. Torn rags leaked yellow acid. It was like a monstrous lobster wrenching itself from a trapped and useless tail. Muscles shut behind him, sealing, and he stood free in the freezing electric air. 'The life photo uncorks and I'm with them, my sharp chin in their shoulder. The implications are bleak, eh? Above I go! Ha ha! If there could have been more moments like this!'

Passing walls like a scald, Sweeney heaved from the cavern and the beating of his coldwater heart faded away.

As Rammstein stood bathed in the rubine saturation of the blanked Aspict, he gazed toward the towering bloody socket of the Emperor's throne.

8

IT'S YOUR FUNERAL

Fear is not a real baby

Mayor Rudloe walked across the soft collagen floor of the extraction shed's basement. He was thankful for his containment suit. Bloody ropes and knots of greed hung from the ceiling and cancer curds like rotting fruit marshed the walls around Old Gory. The Conglomerate, a biocracy of sloshing bodies joined in an alimentary morass, whispered among themselves. 'Remember poor old option twenty.'

Rudloe coughed to gain their attention and a few turret mouths projected from the mass. 'Mr Rudloe,' said one. 'How goes the long con.'

'M'jurisdiction is shimmering before me. And I've a new campaign slogan - "My Pelvis is Grand".'

'It's rubbish.'

Rudloe grimaced. 'I know.'

'Anything else?'

'I found some snot on the stair rail. Oh, and someone stole the Moral Fibre again, the new rubber version. I think this time I'll use some sort of hard plastic, so long as it looks right. A cheap pink shoe-horn or something, I think I've got one in the drawer.'

One slubby mouth asked another. 'This antique shock regarding the Fibre - does it really operate?'

'No,' its neighbour responded, 'it's just traditional. Its function is primarily to distract and waste time, like the circus. Speaking of which - how's that going, Rudloe?'

'Eh?' Rudloe had been stepping carefully around some intestinal links. 'Oh, it's all anyone can talk about. And dogs, ofcourse.'

'Dogs are talking about the Circus?'

'People are talking about dogs.'

Another mouth piped up. 'The citizenry certainly know how to have a good time. We trust that your token show of mayhem in the ring will not imply you've anything but sham originality at your disposal.'

'I guarantee you that all will attend the levy. That my show of being folksy is understood by everyone to be mere pretense. I met a farmer the other day and tried to convince him I was a fine fella. He wasn't having any of it.'

'How are you sure?'

'How? His disbelief was expressed facially, if you really want to know. All right? His features could barely keep up with eachother in the stampede toward incredulity. In fact you'll be pleased to hear that acts of complete disregard have reached record figures. They understand that there is a threat to them, behind our blithe shite. You know, I suspect I could tell them the whole truth? And nothing would happen.'

'They already know it - and either pretend otherwise or that they approve. That's what participation is, and why you can't truly call them victims. D'you think anyone's really dumb enough not to know?'

'I suppose not.'

'Ructions occur only at a transition - if everyone already knows they are powerless, what's to adjust to? We expect a fine extraction this year.'

*

The demons Dietrich and Gettysburg had a room in the observatory. Their window was an auxiliary observation blister facing the sea. 'Is that a new house out there?' asked Gettysburg, peering out with strange pearlite eyes. 'Near the Announcement Horse?'

'Can't be - it would have to be in the sea.'

'This is Accomplice - they'd build houses in their ears if they thought it would help them avoid some sort of blame.'

Dietrich shook his heavy head. 'There's still so much I don't know.' He turned away from the domed window and sat in a bone-seed armchair. 'I mean, I've settled in all right. I've got a black breastplate, a head like an anchor - what's not to love?'

The white and winged Getty stood against the blaze of the window, a silhouette with lazer eyes. 'I agree, obviously.'

'But I think they assume I'm so fascinated by human beings that if certain laws were repealed I'd immediately start killing one. Well I don't mind. If necessary I'll forgive them by brute force. There's no place for me below anymore, even if I wanted it - you know Sweeney's promoted Rammy to my station?'

'The Ponce? He's not captain material.'

'I know.' Dietrich looked through several walls at the old astronomer who sat in the central chamber. Then he turned back to the dazzling demon. 'How was it when you defected anyway?'

'I sprung out all aglee, and banged against a hell hound - not what I wanted.'

'I can imagine.'

'I didn't really know what to do, once I got here. I decided to cackle in slants of illuminated dust. Old habits die hard.'

'Well, the hordes of Satan need something to do,' Dietrich conceded encouragingly. 'It's been a tough stretch for the hordes.'

'Anyway, in the end I had to remind myself what brought me here.' Getty gestured to Bingo Violaine's lower jaw which was fixed to a wooden plaque on the wall.

Dietrich sat forward. 'You too? You never told me that.'

'Yes. So I plunged finally inside the minutes. What did Violaine say? "A virtuous path in the world doesn't cease to function, it's just obscured."'

'Yeah, but a path obscured ceases to function.'

'Hmm ... you're right. That's what I love - between scorn and dry laughter, you really mean it.'

'You remember what he said in *The Hive of Heaven*? "Nature is not murdered without a consequent haunting. A lesson may be learned. Yet some bodies take medicine as a reproach."'

Some sort of gilled carrot with big eyes crawled across the outside of the window, claiming their attention briefly.

'Anyway, Violaine may be the best of them,' Dietrich continued. 'But we still disagree on this - you think these people are angels; I came here because humanity's way more evil than anything below, our vaudeville villainy.' Dietrich scratched the rust on his chin, looking aside. 'At least, the manipulators are.'

Gettysburg was suddenly alert. 'A little more than you realised,' he said. 'And monotonous. Unimaginative.'

'Yes,' said Dietrich, shifting a little uncomfortably. 'At close quarters, I find myself accessory to worse evils than any Sweeney asked of me. I confess the un-officed characters around here are more interesting, though they're collaborators.'

Gettysburg could hardly believe it. He frowned, happy. 'You're going to quit.'

'Maybe I am.'

Dietrich stood and deployed the window, his leather wings stretching open, and soon two demons were in full sail, miles high and ducking clouds.

The Brigade entered the forest, the Sarge's uptilted face immediately cooled by dappled leafshade. It was still hot, though late afternoon. 'Ah, lads, it gave me a fine and special feeling when I went before the disciplinary committee. Very quickly they had had a bellyful. "Give me ten half-decent soldiers," I told them, "and I'll give you five decent ones. I have glue." Ha, ha - that's the stuff to give 'em. And now duty forces us to intrude into the Awkward Forest, a lot of which seems to have been sawn down by clowns.'

'I saw a cartoon of clowns sawing at trees, sarge. Years ago. They did the same movement over and over, all quivery and with big eyes. I was really scared.'

'Scared of an old cartoon, Gibbs? What's that paper, what are you about now?'

'Translating poetry, sarge - *Four Sky Code*, from the Kraut. And Perkins here is illustrating it with pictures of birds in their glory.'

'I can draw birds,' said the cadet, showing the sarge a sketch of a frog.

'That's not a bird, Perkins - it's a canyon tree frog. It's good though. Doesn't he look as if he existed in that crevice? That's because his rough skin provides a bark-like camouflage.' He indicated the foliage detail. 'The main virtue of these flowers is that they are not and never will be our last resort in battle.' The Sarge chuckled to himself. 'Imagine that, though. Flowers.' Chuffed, he turned to his deputy, who brandished a dish.

'Snail, sarge?'

'Don't mind if I do. What are they?'

'Snails sarge.'

'Snails. Don't mind if I do.'

'Get your face round that then.'

'What is it.'

'A snail, sarge.'

'Snail. Alright then. Eat it do I?'

'Eat it sarge, that's right.'

'What is it.'

'Snail - a snail, sarge.'

'Snail.'

'A snail, sarge. See? It's a snail.'

'Snail is it. Well now.'

'Snail.'

'Snail, eh. Well, don't mind if I do.'

'Good on yuh.'

'Right.'

'You eatin' it then?'

'Eh?'

'You eatin' that?'

'What is it.'

Before the deputy could reply, the Sarge fell into a ditch. 'On the face of it, I was careless. But only if you misunderstand what I intended to achieve. I managed to disturb a crow, which went whacking off into the upper canopy. There's a lesson in that, eh Perkins?'

'I understand, sarge.'

The rest of the troops jumped into the ditch, disturbing dozens of crows.

9

HOW SOME PEOPLE ADJUST

When every channel shows the same picture,
you know it's something you should ignore

On the way into the fight tent, Barny asked BB Henrietta if she'd seen Gregor anywhere: 'I went to his basement. Pillow sprats and dust monkeys, that's all I found.' Dust monkeys were formed when corner dust became so dense it began to develop a limb structure and efforted to caper awkwardly about.

'Playing pocket billiards in a vat of dough, for all I care,' BB replied, and they joined Edgy in the wooden seats around the ring. There was a stall crowded with dried clenched fists and false animals made of greasy wrought iron for kids to hug and cherish. Stampede Door-to-Door had paid for ad space around the ring, with shouts for products such as Exploding Bridal Gowns, Dismle (the Dismal Trifle), Stern Greeting Cards, Edible Embers and Britch Biscuits - 'just pop 'em in the washing machine and in no time at all your clothes will disintegrate'. In a corner of the ring, the withered corpse of an old lady was propped in a wicker chair.

Disguised in the audience, the Mayor and Dietrich Hammerwire conferred. 'Makes a change from crab races,' muttered the Mayor.

'And headless darts.'

'Headless you say?' the Mayor replied with fulsome disinterest, frowning past the ring.

On the other side a media commotion was headed by Douglas Bar of the Douglas Bar Show, whose oily mouth was saying 'Where's my undying driver' and 'Tonight defies observation or analysis, I'll need mints' and 'Shove my broadcast on the air, my mirth is priceless, last night I taught nobody, tonight I'll offer independence.' Then he shoved a microphone at Karloff Velocet, who sat in the front row. 'Mr Velocet, tell me about yourself.'

'Which appalling legend do you want to hear?'

'It's said that you had to be coaxed and persuaded to put on such a savage fight.'

'I was approached three times. First time I indicated a banana, second time I indicated a river.'

'Was this intended as a negative.'

'No, I like both those things and I wanted them combined together at last.'

'And here comes the Masked Inconvenience. This balloon, as it seems easiest to term him, wears a black woollen mask yet seems to flinch whenever anyone approaches him.' Bar pushed through the crowd to the masked Gregor. 'Mr Inconvenience, how do you feel about your chances?'

'Life hasn't been kind to me. Dogged by bad luck, I'm also an idiot.'

'And how have you spent the crucial twelve hours before the fight?'

'I decided to pet a cat and the animal looked reconciled to the prospect, so we embarked upon that ordeal together.'

Frowning, Karloff Velocet snipped a zippo at the underside of a plastic tulip. 'Shall we get on?'

Bar took his place at the commentator's table with the hated Rooster as Gregor crawled through the ropes and stood droopy in the spotlight. Rooster bent to the mike. 'Hello and welcome to the Tar Baby Concerns - we're here at the fight of the year, something I haven't really got a clue about, I freely admit. Time me, Jim, as I look from one end of the ring to the other.'

'That took four seconds, Rooster, the way you did it. And my name's not Jim. It's Douglas Bar speaking, with the hated Rooster as we attempt to remain civilised before an audience of raging primitives. The champion Trubshaw versus the Masked Inconvenience. Put on your Jonathan glasses, everyone - this'll be a blinder, sponsored as it is by Stampede Products, "The firm that flirts with danger". And here's the Fall Marshall to announce the losers.'

Karloff Velocet took to the ring and hailed the participants. 'In the red corner, stern and showing it, that mountain of muscle and infernodyne innards, a head with its own microclimate and a pluck of hair like the true bastard - a man who pronounces "stegosaurus" as a single syllable word - Trubshaw!'

The demon Trubshaw lumbered out of the shadows, its ears cleaned and armour buffed to high polish. Its face was way, way smaller than its head, as though rubber-stamped on the front of it. Gregor began sobbing as the crowd cheered.

'And in the blue corner, weighing more than anyone should, breathing beyond his means, sobbing like a child and already shaky on his pins - the challenger, the Masked Inconvenience!'

The crowd threw dried clenched fists and false animals made of greasy wrought iron at Gregor.

'It's fish against fowl,' cried Karloff, 'a war as groundless and profitable as ever there were. To your corners!'

Karloff vacated the ring and Gregor staggered to his corner, where his cornerman Thrax tried to wring tears from the woolly mask without revealing Gregor's identity.

Douglas Bar and Rooster were drawing excitement from empty air. 'Rumour has it,' stated Rooster, 'that the Masked Inconvenience has made little effort to research his opponent's strategy and exercised not at all.'

'If so, this young man is about to reap the whirlwind of his lethargy. Unless he takes the precaution of smashing his legs in the opening minutes of the fight -'

'His own legs, Jim?'

'Any two of the six legs out there, if broken, would make a differ-ence to this battle. Both fighters are fairly shapeless and we must assume they know it. This masked fellow, after his own fashion, is a human being. His opponent, by contrast, looks slightly demonic, what with the claws and many ears.'

'Could be trained in the supernatural assault tradition, Jim. He lives from the fist outward. It's said he refuses to remove his gum shield during conversation.'

'I heard he was born with one already in place. One thing's for sure - it won't be any dance around the maypole for the Mask. As our great philosopher said, "Real suffering is not a spectacle for philoso-phers - too messy."'

'He also said "Only a spectator may inherit the riches of war - participants merely pick over the lessons." I don't understand either quote and the subject bores me. The ref tonight is the dead Donna Greeley of Greeley's furniture store, and there's the bell.'

Gregor cringed across the tattooed floor toward the glittering monster. Trubshaw was instantly lamping him one around the belly.

'A right hook to the belly,' shouted Bar, 'knocking it aside. But the rest of the masked man's body structure remains in place and Trubshaw can only stand and wait while the belly decelerates and re-settles into place. We're waiting too. Trubshaw's gloves are in flamin-go leather, by the way. And the masked man's gloves are giraffe vel-vet. Well, the belly has stopped and the Masked Inconvenience is drooping forward like a flower. He looks pale, like a mime hit by light-ning. And Trubshaw delivers a deadly uppercut to his primary chin and the challenger's head snaps back, sending twenty-seven beads of sweat into the air. He staggers backward, crossing the floor with what reason insists must be his legs.'

'My skeleton! My skeleton!' screamed Gregor.

'And the masked man is screaming about his skeleton, it seems he's having trouble with it. He shields his forehead and thinks he's hidden. But the beefy Trubshaw can see the stout and fretful figure well enough. Mr Inconvenience chooses to slump in the rigging with arms hung quivering in the breach, I kid you not, just flapping in the breeze. As Trubshaw approaches with only one decision to make: whether to punch his lights out or measure him up for a nightgown. And there's the bell - I could barely hear it above another rending, wailing shriek from the challenger.'

The fighters returned to their corners under the cavernous stare of Donna Greeley.

'Well, that was tragic and lopsided,' declared Douglas Bar. 'This oval young man seems to be banking on Trubshaw getting bored looking at his face. I hear tell it's a face remarkably lacking in detail, but he'll develop a few worry lines tonight. If he lives, which now seems unlikely.'

'Thanks, Jim - funny, funny stuff,' Rooster cut in. 'Mind you, there's death and then there's death.'

'True enough, Rooster. Hear about Rohm Crosslin? Tusked by an elephant. That's class.'

'And it's only going to get worse,' Rooster laughed.

In the blue corner, Gregor sat like a mashed potato. The Beast Man was yelling 'Doesn't courage at least have rarity value in your world?' into his ear when Doctor Perfect, the match medic, stumped up with his knife bag.

'Are you going to introduce me to this mound of jelly which appears to function as a human being?' he asked the Beast Man.

'Never mind all that - patch him up!'

Doctor Perfect leaned down at the man on the stool, his permed brain threatening to unravel on to the patient. 'What's up, laddie? Tell the whole dreadful tale.'

Gregor roused a little, tilting. 'Punch,' he slurred, and 'death.'

'Punch death,' the doctor repeated as though enunciating to a simple child. 'My prognosis too, laddie. Manage to snort?'

'Once.'

'Enough to establish your feelings about it, then. Not that it matters. He'll be stepping over your legs before this is over.'

'Don't you have any liniment?' shouted the Beast Man.

Perfect flipped a catch and opened his case. 'I have ten paintings of medicine, and a terrible creature which is mainly chin. See?' He removed a strange, furless guinea pig from the case.

'What the hell's *that*?'

The bell rang - Thrax hustled Gregor to his feet as Doctor Perfect ducked out. Gregor walked into a punch which turned his face to red lace.

'The multi-eared champ ploughs in,' announced Douglas Bar, 'with a series of jabs, hooks and eye-fluttering blandishments which leave the challenger dizzy and slow. The Masked Inconvenience is slobbing around in the corner. He doesn't know or care where he is. Even his stumbling and lolling is far below the standard of a competent boxer. Yet the organisers have been putting it about that this masked man frequently disposes of his opponents in Round One. I watched a witch-burning once and the bonfire mother spoke a language to watch - signalling and mouthing to the crowd through the flames as though possessed of new and urgent knowledge. The Masked Inconvenience is making similar motions now to anyone who can bear to look. I'm surprised Trubshaw hasn't knocked him out yet.'

'Knock him out?' Rooster commented. 'That's pushing at an open door isn't it?'

'The Masked Inconvenience is flailing round and round the outside of the ring, his cries volleying into that crown of ears from many directions and confusing the champ. Now Trubshaw's caught on and belted him to a standstill, and there's a shot under the heart - that punch disturbed his full content, I'm sure. Trubshaw is inflicting a diverse medley of wounds upon his opponent, always advancing. We're seeing a man who doesn't know how to back away.'

'Against a man who doesn't know how to fight,' Rooster chipped in.

'Your evaluation is spot-on, Rooster, though I hate you with the fire of a million suns.'

Gregor yelled and accidentally punched Trubshaw's face as he failed to complete a flinching maneouvre.

'The Masked Inconvenience has scuffed the polished forehead of Trubshaw. It's the first punch he's thrown since this ambush began. Can those inchoate arms encourage Trubshaw to kiss the canvas here today? A body shot has little hope of penetrating that armour. And I thought the omni-furious Trubshaw couldn't get any more upset - look at him now, pounding the masked man with overhand rights. The challenger is twitching as though hurt at the nerve's core. I heard his skull's ceramic.'

'You just can't help these people, Jim,' said Rooster.

'True enough for our purposes, Rooster. For years to come, these will be the benchmark for terrified screams in the boxing ring. And there's the bell - at which the challenger crawls toward his stool like a first-year drama student.'

The Mayor and the demon Dietrich sat in the shadows. 'It's not very restful is it?' the Mayor remarked, watching Trubshaw. Between rounds the armoured slob took out his eyeballs, dropping them in grape alcohol solution.

'I suppose you're running a side book on the fight?' Dietrich asked mildly.

'Yes indeed. Trubshaw's a lock and a lovely boy. He's probably part-mechanical or something.'

'Want to know what I really think, Mayor?'

'If expressed by signs, and uncertain.'

'You're a complete bastard. Well don't look offended - this can hardly be new information. I've seen some horrors since I came here. To discover pedestrians was dismal enough - but you, and this ...'

'It's an encounter stuffed with combat, that's all. What's the matter with you?'

'You remember that Violaine thing: "The potent theatre of lies and ignorance - this is the value of Parliament." But it's more boring than anything. The fact is, there's a limit for things like me. I think you need a human.'

Dietrich stood and started walking away sideways along the row.

Mayor Rudloe was spluttering, taken utterly by surprise. 'You'll get yours in hell, Dietrich!'

'I already did, Mayor. But thanks.'

Gregor sat in his corner, all ragged-edged wounds and split meat. He couldn't remember how he'd been roped into this barn dance. His brain had burned out until it was a turkey skeleton with a weak drift of smoke in the cavity. Beast Man Thrax was yelling in his ear 'The theory of the situation is that you have a mind of your own! That's the theory! And god forgive me for believing it!'

Dr Perfect was prancing gleefully about in front of him saying 'The heart is a terrible loop' or something like that, and waving a bit of hose. Gregor wanted to give him a choice kick in the bollocks and then, why not, he did it. Gregor was so exhausted he didn't stop feeling grouchy when the doctor fell howling. But he knew he'd remember the moment with affection later on.

When the bell rang, Gregor unbent and toppled into the ring, missing Trubshaw altogether and crashing into the carcass of the lady ref. Her neck buckled and the head took a dive in back of the shoulders. Gregor was getting squirly, his senses slow - he saw the head setting like a sun behind the grey torso. Boxing gloves veered across his eyes like inflatable valentines. He was tumbling at Trubshaw, flailing weakly at the tough tortoiseshell skull. A punch landed in the slob demon's face, which squelched like a bath mat. A chorus of recriminations burst from the crowd. Gregor bit into one of Trubshaw's ears, clamping on like a child. *No-one can blame me for acting like this*, he thought with complete assurance. Trubshaw squealed and spun until Gregor was lifted off the ground, attached by the teeth, his legs flying. *No-one can blame me for acting like this*, Gregor thought again, comforted more by the notion than any before. And to think that these were the precise circumstances required to generate it. Life was too specific for generalised wisdom.

The ear came away and Gregor shot into the ropes, tangling there. Trubshaw approached with his right cocked. Gregor received a smack in the mouth - the accident rattled his bones, his gumshield firing upward behind his mask and becoming lodged in his left eye. As he staggered backward he stomped a foot into Donna Greeley's head so that he was wearing it like a boot.

And he saw a phantom in the panels of Trubshaw's armour. It was the image of desire he had pursued into the window of the Ultimatum Restaurant and the Hall of Mirrors - himself. Here was his heaven, his window of escape. Gathering the dregs of his strength, he dived into that pool of loveliness.

Douglas Bar watched as Trubshaw fell like an extinguished fountain. When the slob elected to remain unconscious, Bar slammed words into the mike. 'Trubshaw is down for the count. He looked to be on top in the third until, through a blend of fistic absurdity and happy coincidence, the challenger flew at his gut with both fists. The Masked Inconvenience also knocked out the ref and the match surgeon. Everyone thought we'd be latching his skull to a beam over the local bar, but this twitching lunatic has stirred up a hill of beans. The Masked Inconvenience is the new champ. Though what a reindeer would make of any of this, I don't know.'

'The everyday has bruised alright,' said Rooster. 'You can cook a surprise that big over a slow fire and live off it a week.'

'The ring is swarming with dissatisfied gamblers. I do declare I'm trying to push through the crowd to get at the new champ for a few simple-minded words. Excuse me, ladies and gentlemen. Here he is - Mr Inconvenience, what was your strategy for the fight?'

'I hoped to allow the ground under me by moving it with these legs, but ...'

'Dick, get in there and stop it!' Karloff Velocet was heard to shout, at which a silver midget jackflipped over the ropes and tackled Bar by the waist.

In a corner of the chaos, Karloff handed over the Abblatia Angel to Barny, who was chuffed. 'Laugh while you can, monkey-boy,' said Karloff. 'I'll see you and your friends at the main presentation. I will hurt your feelings by ... look out!'

Gregor's mask had been torn away and he was running from an angry mob, each member of which had quickly committed to breaking a different and distinct bone in his body.

The next edition of *The Blank Stare* would bear the headline FIGHT PROVES USELESS AS ENTERTAINMENT and a subheading OR ANYTHING ELSE.

A picture of Gregor looking shagged out accompanied the caption: 'Mutant blames nobody but himself for pitiful display. Lives in charnel house and is fascinated by pain.'

Ladderland was being stripped down, the clockworks of its decks and gangways exposed. Animals had begun to wander, pestering neighbours with their inscrutable expressions and suddenly clamping jaws. A banished tailor who had wandered back into town was clawed into a bush by Mister Braintree. An old gran glimpsed a spaniel outside her kitchen window but when she looked again, only a vivid smudge of lipstick remained. Gangs of monkeys pounced through town waving useless plastic scissors at disinterested shoppers.

Mister Braintree loped along the beach, strips of gabardine hanging from his mouth. EH Hunt admired the lion but pushed his luck, even going so far as to claim that there was such a thing as a 'sea lion'. The sailor now sat on his storage trunk and poked a fire of seacoral, watching the animal and commenting to the Announcement Horse, 'Continents consorted to exile me before my arrival, Nonny. But by god, after a shaky start I was accepted here.' Hunt had tried making a living as a tattoo artist, but he only did pictures of oatmeal and prawns, often on people who did not want a tattoo. He had finally settled into the role of a wily captain who was not believed. He'd shrivelled down like a burger. 'The eyeball is a knot for holding beauty. I've seen a bunch. Dead metals in India, dirty ziggurats in the soaked jungle, deserts of lion-coloured sand.'

'Blindness began underwater,' chimed the rigid Announcement Horse, an ebony totem in ebony sand.

'Here's a riddle for you: I am not mad - nor do I possess reason. I whisk bones and bodies in the chill. A modest cash subsidy will not deter me. I may wear a hat for a short time. I retreat, leaving clammy horrors. What am I?'

'A chef.'

'The sea, you moron, the *sea!*'

'That again.'

'Listen to the distance, Nonny,' the old captain advised the horse. 'Do you know what piranha music is?'

'Prahna music ...'

'Piranha. It can only be heard by placing both ears into the water - your whole head, in other words. So nobody has ever returned in a fit state to describe it, a perpetual mystery. What's out there will always be a mystery to you, Nonny, because it's piranha music, all of it. Even if I told you about it, you wouldn't understand - it's something you have to experience for yourself.'

'I weigh one-and-a-half tons,' the Horse pronounced without inflection.

Hunt's white-haired leonine head bounced as he chuckled. 'I'll think on the problem. The shore I'll be moving with this boat is not so strong really - land becomes a mere shade.'

'No, the land is strong. It keeps to itself. Do you intend to complete your vessel standing on that half-submerged platform of rock?'

'You have to take your half-submerged platforms of rock where you can at my age.' And Hunt took out a harmonica, tapping the sand out of it to begin playing "Wedding Veil Jellyfish".

The lion sat staring out at the ship as its spars and decks grew taller.

10

THIS IS YESTERDAY

By the time you've been judged guilty,
you've learnt enough about the system to take the moral sting out of it

Barny lifted the hood like a scab and stared at a coalface engine. He hadn't a clue how to rig this car for creeptravel and was glad when the Abblatia Angel showed up, its wings like a couple of white shirts hung in the sun.

'Hello Mike Abblatia,' Barny said. 'This thing needs plugging with muscle junk and etheric shielding. Penny rhino on the dash and spoiler adornments like sovereign rings. Couldn't wake Dot.'

They worked on the valves and servitors until Chloe Low walked by the gas station.

'You see the fight, Chloe?' Barny asked her. 'They were shouting, lashing out, everything.'

'There you go again,' Chloe sighed, walking slowly over the hot forecourt. 'With your animals.'

'Not just that - my house is disappearing.'

Mike Abblatia seemed to fold himself out of the moment, stepping behind the air, then flickered back into solidity.

'The animals are wandering about confused,' Barny continued. 'I'm having to steal the timber back from doomed Eddie Gallo.'

'Have you asked him about it?'

'I suppose I could. "I am searching, I am searching." How does that sound?'

'Like the selfish ravings of a madman. You should think about other people. Why don't you think about how to contribute, Barny?'

'You never used to say so,' said the angel, its voice light as light.

Chloe was about to go when Dugway Thrax the Beast Man wandered by, looking lost and desolate. Barny called him. 'Help us to lift this deathtrap, Mr Beast Man.'

The Beast Man lumbered over and lifted the car one-handed. Barny wheeled a dead mime artist out of the garage on a low trolley, sliding it under the axel. 'Lower away,' he said.

The Beast Man did so, moving against a honey-blond sunset. Chloe was impressed.

Doomed Eddie Gallo was wearing a paper cone on the front of his face when Barny approached him at the Canyon edge the next morning. 'What's that on your face, doomed Eddie Gallo?'

'Some sort of paper beak,' whispered doomed Eddie Gallo. 'That funny lawyer gave me the idea, with his harness. You'll have to shout, Barny - one of those sloths went off right next to my eager expression.'

'I wanted to ask you point-blank about this wood!'

'Ah, Barny - I'm finished with wood. But I knew I needed something like wood, in any way at all. And here it is.' He gestured to several hundred packs of rich tea biscuits. 'Bog-standard crackers of the kind I eat every day. And they will take us to a lovely place perhaps.'

'How will you hold all these biscuits together, doomed Eddie Gallo!'

'Using gull glue,' he said, showing Barny a flattened tube of the stuff. Conceived when King Verbal, attacked by seven doves, stamped on one and noticed that a fluid like glue emerged from the bird's mouth, gull glue was at first advertised as 'a thinly disguised attempt to bring in democracy by the back door'. When this didn't work, the manufacturers decided to advertise it as 'glue' and sales soared. It was years before Verbal realised he had mis-identified his attackers. 'I've realised the contents of this head of mine are the booby prize in some cerebral lottery,' Gallo continued. 'But I decided long ago that one should live as one's disastrous self, on the grounds of honesty.'

'What if Mayor Rudloe attacks you with a stone?'

'I could use this beak of mine. I might snip a hole in his chin; anything.'

'Will you?'

'Probably not, but you never know. The mood might suddenly overtake me - don't you have unexpected urges like that?'

'I grabbed a fern once when I was walking past, and mashed it.'

'Well ...' Gallo frowned into the middle distance.

*

Beltane Carom stood at the centre of his pattern yard, muttering to himself. 'My entire body's a Judas window here. Nothing behind my ribs but pollen. A quick-change to one or the other is easy, but both of us at the same time?' He looked about at the mossed frog-stands and ferned fountains, and finally at his own shadow before him on the heat-white flagstones. 'So much information stored there. Oh, why not. Fire in the hole.'

He sucked in his breath, and his shadow started to shorten toward him. The light began to flush, reversing its colours. Beltane was shaking as vision wedges opened around him, raking out blood. His shadow was crawling like oil. It retreated beneath him, sucking up through his soles. He darkened, his eyes black.

An air split descended, creasing his brow and proceeding down-ward. He was dividing like a cell. The process spat off energy which burnt holes in the garden, stirring daygreen sounds from the true mouths of flowers and the moving heads of statuary standing in the soil years. Supporting eachother, the two halves of the split began to digress in character, one becoming multicoloured and stupid. Soon a rag-and-bone jester stood next to Beltane Carom.

Prancer Diego started poncing about like a bastard. 'This violence means more visiting afterwards of churches, to laugh or cry!'

'Shut up!' said Beltane. 'This sudden-death absurdity of yours -'

'Start in panic and there's somewhere to go - begin tired, and we lose. Trumpet that, I reckon!' Prancer wrenched a daffodil from the ground and started playing it like a horn.

The shaman tore the flower from him. 'Karloff demanded we both appear at the ceremony. In matters of ceremony concerning Juno, all patterns must be adhered to - there's probably a reason we don't see yet.'

'Don't spill the pudding on my battleshield Mary!'

'Don't call me Mary. I face you for the first time and -'

'I've a cheese stick for a brain!'

'Damn right you have,' yelled Beltane savagely. 'You'll end up in a cuddle-coat you bastard -'

'I will die chuckling at something no-one else thinks is funny!'

'This rather athletic sarcasm of yours, it's just rubbish and has no place in our ... get *off!*'

1 1

LET'S ROCK

Pity the spectators of revolution ...
its success is not their success, and nor is its failure

The Mayor entered a circus back yard full of panic artists, fetches, gut crew and the bustle of preparation. In powder thick enough to hide a snake, the Fall Marshall stood idly playing a veda lute among discarded liquorice paper tickets and drums of goofer fuel. 'Hello, Mayor - you look well.'

'Then the illusion is complete.'

'Cool piglet vest.'

'A bit more austerity would suit this circus of yours.'

'Austerity, you plank? A prefab opulence richer than gold, that's the stuff. Our second-rate mayhem's lovely, admit it.'

'I refuse to understand you.'

Fang trotted past stretching his perished face. 'Karloff, your dwarves were meant to wash the previous gore off the rigging.'

'I can do without the undead getting stroppy, thankyou!'

'These meat puppets you glory in,' Rudloe asked the Fall Marshall as Fang departed, 'all hang and hamstring - what are they about?'

'Zombies are ideal for acrobatics - they flop about up there like fish on a line, why not. Circular energy - while I take the profits. There's beauty.'

'Why did you join the circus?'

'An alibi might as well drip colour.'

'What about family entertainment?'

'The family's finished - it's been replaced by mere relatives.'

A girl pure as snake oil walked past, tattooed around every inch with curlicue-cyphers: 'I will organise my faults so that I resemble a public servant' disappeared into her cleavage and emerged 'proud to death' across her belly.

The Mayor was shaking his head in reproach as Cheney scampered over. 'The Vanishing Vorporal has vanished, Karloff.'

'Maybe you should take his name off the posters,' Rudloe suggested.

'Nonsense, he's the most dependable act on the bill,' said Karloff. 'Delivers exactly what he claims, every time. What's the crowd like, Cheney?'

'Alive, for now.' The silver midget strutted away.

The nightmare calliope echoed from the showgrounds. Karloff placed his lute upon a barrel. 'The magic starts in three minutes. The alternative to that arrangement is to release twelve donkeys.'

'Why?' Rudloe asked.

'They're very frightening.'

'Can't you keep your malice under control?'

'Control,' Karloff repeated blankly. 'And where's your demon?'

'A horse in a cardigan eh?' said the Mayor, trying to change the subject as one passed.

'Now,' called Karloff suddenly, 'our masked company are assembled! The day's gaudy extravagances ready for release! Facial stains established! Abandon shrines! Priorities, people - Brian, put a skirt on! Places!'

And he marched past Rudloe, casting the tentflap aside and storming into the big top.

'Perhaps a volcano will erupt,' hoped the Mayor dismally. 'Spewing slag onto the town.'

'Why are we here?' Edgy asked as he and Barny took their seats. Dark colours blew through calliope tunes like confetti. 'So I can be ripped open by a bloodthirsty mob again? Those mothers punched me in the belly fifteen times. I counted.' His injuries were a mixed lot. After a day using a hernia for a hammock on Barny's porch and another trying to convince a placid hen it could fly, he felt stiff, his skin like burnt paper over his bones.

'I need you to keep an eye out for Karloff's cheating and betrayal,' Barny told him, looking at the safety net which was suspended above the hippodrome like a giant cobweb. 'Working as a team, we could stab eachother awake in front of this rubbish. I can't rely on Gregor now that he's one round bruise. You're my friend.'

'Well, it's true. Oh by the way, me and the Round One are going in together. Those "ceiling toilets" of his are a complete loss. We're opening my beach bar from scratch.'

'What do you mean, from scratch?'

'We're setting up a still by the sea. Sort of stuff turns your face to jelly.'

'Good idea.'

'Thanks. I picked it up in one of those slot machines with the claw.'

Karloff Velocet burst into the round and began grandstanding, shot-voiced and spotlit. 'Karloff Velocet, talky goon and more! I need a second bed for my mouth, that's how smart I am! Wader of sawdust, knot captain of the free, I bring the language of games, dance and artistic performance; all for you, an audience of sleepy cattle! Eruption in each eye guaranteed! You will feel astonishment! We will drive it into you like a nail! There is no escape for you, ultimately!' Briefly the showman blocked his mouth with a rat, then cast it away and proceeded with the announcements. 'We are honoured to perform on Exaction Day - the law taketh away, and the law taketh away. You are the fox doornailed and jerking, his own dreams on his muzzle!'

A bunch of ghoul-clowns exploded into the arena and seemed to be indulging in some sort of all-out tag match - one so dismal as to set half the audience to the activity of idly sketching flowers and birds, which they compared among themselves with raised eyebrows of appraisal.

'Is the Theatre of Misrule a disruptive influence on the universe,' boomed the Fall Marshall, 'or are we just a small part of it? The clown - emblem of suffering and pain. Nothing gets newer, ladies and gentlemen. Their barely-choreographed thuggery makes them the greatest rabble of killers and unhappy madmen ever assembled in one place! They thrive stinking on nasty mysteries and incredulations. Would that I could put a stop to it. Their dayglo irresponsibility sickens me. See them come on like sugar-rot and beware of harmful emissions!'

A clown with cartoon bones tripped on a bucket, breaking his neck.

Karloff used a green glass cane to point out a clown which turned out to have a concave face like the old optical illusion. 'Nothing's the way it seems when it comes to Energy Hog. And "Good grief, what the hell's that?" you may ask. An emu-like bird with a brittle eggshell head - it struts around in a seeming dare to one and all. Crunch me, crunch me! Or do you refer to Boney Panatella, who bears more than a passing resemblance to a wooden spoon? Or Manticore Terry?'

Out pounced a creature with the head of a lion, clawed feet, a barbed scorpion tail, and the face of a failure. The Killer Midgets ran around him, trying to ride on his back.

'He's a sawback manticore. Hire a swan if you want - I prefer our Terry. And the Killer Midgets can't keep away - Donald Kagan, Gary Schmitt and Thomas Donnelly there, making his life hell. While Roy Bullock is having such an intricate tantrum you'll have to film it and run the footage at an eighth of the speed to know his concerns. Foon and his Vengeful Autopsy! And notice I'm at great pains to point out the Praline Lad!' A dismay artist maneouvred his ill-arranged body. 'He has a mango where others have their common sense. Here we observe Tam Sidethroat, long travelled from beyond the soda moat you call death, worked on forever by a wild pain and decay, bitten by a scary goose, the list goes on. I beg you - have nothing to do with this man. Glaring Ben, the tetchy bear! Lon Horiuchi looks a right charlie as he proves to be a slaughtering psychopath! And here's the Talent Phantom - he will dance for you, not well, but without screaming.'

A man all in black moved tentatively on the sawdust. It was like watching a stone grow. Then he started screaming as though trapped.

Barny leaned toward Plantin Edge. 'He said he wasn't going to scream.'

'You know how fashions change.'

'Mystifying John Hull - come among us to give something which no-one could possibly mistake for a performance!' Karloff sounded vexed, watching John. 'Yes, he has possibilities, and nothing but! And here's Ken the Murky Colossus, and his friend Brad! They've enough indecision to kill a horse. Archer Midland, an archer probably! Mr Patchcoat, who is here to avoid the bother of official investigation! See the sheer wanton damage he can do when challenged! I will repeatedly refer to his activities as "a necessary correction" in order to trivialise the whole matter. Watch!'

Mr Patchcoat pranced round the hippodrome in a shellsuit, foam flying from his mouth as he screamed a paeon to relentless hate. Several chimps avoided him, scrambling like living mud over the statue of Violaine and on across the ring to dart among the slow legs of an elephant.

'A necessary correction there, ladies and gentlemen, you'll agree. Perhaps more disturbingly Hatfill Weberman offers us the chance to sublimate our sexual tensions. He can dislocate all his limbs from their sockets!'

'So can I,' Barny hissed to Edgy.

'I think he means Weberman can then put them back again.'

More thoughtful, Barny continued to watch.

'If everything we've been told about him is true, this pickled-onion-flavour savage and self-styled "bouncy bastard" regularly whips himself into a fever. While Ludlow Belcher Belk wishes to be made a part-time member of staff!'

A man ran across the ring pursued by a snorting rhino.

'And this fellow may attack you with a machete! Look out! Hello, Frank! That bastard's a social plague in his own right. Cally the Mess. Sweet is she? Nine hundred packs of sugar can be a heavy burden! Howe Halabja, playing a waterphone - it's been that kind of a day. Now look above - swapping angles and blocking my vision, yes, it's those demised daredevils, those semi-perished flyers, those liquefaction lads - approve if you can the putrescent stylings of ... the Flying Dead Brothers!'

Upon the showboat bar the four revenants waved shredded limbs. 'Buckets of charm!' they chorused and then began the real donkey work of dangling about.

'I'm bored,' Barny whispered to Plantin Edge, who nodded. They wandered outside and the circus seemed a world away, the concession stands mostly abandoned. Wandering west toward the Furfur district, they passed through some deal trees and entered the scrub around the pennyground.

Edgy kicked at dry cortex cacti. 'What are your thoughts, Barny?'

Barny knelt on the ground, tilling over fluff and feathers snarled up with stones. 'I wonder if I do the right things. Chloe makes me wonder.'

'She's just trying to get at you. Now that you've split up she'll travel miles to pump poison gasses into your mental atmosphere.'

'I don't care. I could use those gasses. Look at me, I'm a nervous wreck.'

'Well,' said Edgy uncertainly, scrutinising his placid friend. 'Maybe you could vent your lusts with some o' them magazines you turn sideways.'

'*Snake Keepers Weekly*?'

'You and your critters. I hear Mister Braintree's been scudding about, nipping the legs of one and all.'

'Yeah I hear he got a tailor who dared come back into town.' Barny related how the man's yells provoked the laughter of passers-by. The tailor had begged a Gubba Man for help and the silent sentry held him in place while the lion dined upon his ravelled innards. If you've ever meddled with a four-hundred-pound cat, you'll know this is the last thing you need. 'Meanwhile my house is being gradually stolen - the winged and stepping animals of the earth have only half a home to go back to.'

Edgy suggested that they walk back to town for the animal presentation ceremony. 'Those tigers are probably creaming themselves in anticipation.'

Meanwhile in the top, Karloff gestured up at the zooming cadaverines. 'The Flying Dead Brothers there, real card-carrying revenants, leaving one and all bewildered and probably damned. And now, to interrupt your enjoyment of the meat and potatoes of the show, your own Mayor appears upon his expensive balcony above.'

In the bowed mouth of Rudloe Manor's balcony, the Mayor was laying half-in half-out of a cannon barrel. He could see the hippo-drome and the central showground through the high web of the safe-ty net. With a numb, hammy hand he wiped his brow. A chalky corpse swung by at eye-level.

'The Mayor is unteachable. His brain seems to be a ball of tinfoil. My words vibrate it merely. He is not equipped to solve the sad mys-tery of his appointment to office. Even his attempts to stifle innova-tion have failed. Now he has contracted to fire himself from a can-non. A foolhardy stunt, Mayor. You were mad to suggest it.'

'Me?' squawked Rudloe, and was shoved into darkness by a sud-den clown with a plush head and a gob like a rubber rainbow.

'Delicious concrete awaits you, m'Lord. As your local philosopher once said, "I have never seen a scorpion shrug - I have never seen a government err to the good. I've seen monsters being born in newsprint. Corruption is only self-vanquished - thus corruption is not vanquished. I am certain of nothing but trouble." I hope you're wear-ing your flame-retardant underwear - dynamite doesn't mess around.'

Filling with nausea, Rudloe felt a surge of black heat as reversed-acid colours sucked toward him.

He smashed faultlessly through the swinging zombies and caused one of Fang's legs to boomerang into the screaming audience.

Then he was snagged in the safety net amid assorted rotten limbs. Karloff was dancing by below him. The audience's response to his splashdown, if any less impassioned, would have been unde-tectable.

Then a roar went up. At first Rudloe assumed it was his dismal electorate's usual delayed reaction. But the shout was one of alarm. As he twisted about, Rudloe saw a massive black construction toil-ing and barging toward him across the net. 'Steinway!' he screamed, struggling.

'Merriment concluding!' Karloff cried. 'Piano joy beginning!'

'So Max was right - you've been keeping these black-lacquered bastards for your own ends.'

'Never fear,' the Fall Marshall assured him in a confidential tone. 'That tragic creature works by a series of reducing gear ratios.' Then he raised his voice for the audience. 'In the spirit of fair play I just told him he was safe, but in truth this net's purpose is anything but safety. Would it surprise you, Mayor, to hear the safety net's made of nerves?'

'Nerves? You usually use a few old veins.'

'True, but these nerves are all the better to alert the Steinway Spiders to the presence of prey.'

Hearing the plural, Rudloe wrenched around to see a second piano surging forward from the other direction. The crowd began to panic, climbing over eachother to get out of the tent.

'Metal springs - man's oldest foe! And their turning arc's a killer I'm afraid. You may run but you cannot escape the ebony racket of these legendary automata - Sterling and Dragbelly!'

The nearest Steinway slammed its lid on the zombie Ladaat, scarfing him back with discordant chimes and then continuing toward Rudloe, pistoning its eight black enamel legs.

'Isn't there a danger someone could get hurt?' someone stopped to posit from the fleeing audience, and was shoved aside by citizens galore.

'I wish pleasures were quieter,' another commented, and was punched to the floor.

Rudloe watched the populace run. Whimpering his weight, a scream of retreat was his only strength. 'Help! I'm a rookie at this sort of thing!'

Sterling fiddled massively closer, the heavy contraption bowing a deep dent in the net. Fang's head rolled downhill.

It was these dull circumstances which conspired to free me from my earthly tether. As I once said, 'It's an illusion to believe you're not ruled, unless you do what you're forbidden to do.'

Something was wobbling through the sky like a bat. Was one of the Brothers still aloft? The object was joined by another and they swooped in a flash of thin-skinned wings. The two defector demons Dietrich and Gettysburg, scabbed with scales and silver with blades, blurred above the crowds and phased in and out of the local band-width. Dietrich seemed to be eating a chocolate egg and Getty was wearing some sort of car coat - it was as if they had dropped by casually between other activities.

Veins showed in the back-illuminated wings as they descended upon Sterling. The Mayor's eager, upturned face didn't change at all as they clamped on to the piano and hauled the machine aloft, beating hard. Loose hammers chimed at the wires as they lifted it across. Its black legs were clawing at air. Then the Steinway fell from their grasp and slammed upon the Violaine statue like a judge's gavel upon the rights of man.

My monument shattered like plaster as the other Steinway fled the scene and the safety net collapsed. The etheric leash unravelled and I bloomed out invisible, free as disease. Air surrounded klieg lights which swept past my escape - I blurred over this vale of entrances and tropic-slow angels stirring like heat. Momentary people stood undoing bundles of air. They were already perfection, merely folded and complicated into disguise. By virtue of being a ghost on the way out, I was feeling soft. Here were wide pathless times and simple breath. I slowed to look back on curiosity, nothing left now but to watch the end. No longer hooked upon the sky, I slipped between gaps in the colour with a victim's success. Me, you bastards - Bingo Violaine.

12

HE DO THE POLICE IN DIFFERENT VOICES

Language will die of slow starvation

The troops normally refused camouflage because it bored them to tears but today they tried some of that bark-effect stuff the sarge had told them the frogs wore. Within minutes of donning the things they had forgotten about its glories. A Steinway piano was amok in the Coum district and when they arrived, Dragbelly popped and clattered, whipping strings at prim madams and necklacing blood over pale faces - all inside of a minute. A Gubba Man was smashed aside and burst open against a streetlamp, a body without organs.

The Sarge gestured the entire length of the suburbs. 'Terminate these lights - I'll watch.'

'It's done, sarge,' Perkins said, presenting the illustrated *Four Sky Code* with a shy glee.

'Done, Perkins?' the Sarge rumbled. 'We'll see.' And he frowned down at the translation with a judicious eye. Then his large face brightened. 'Good work, Gibbs. A bit blocky but you've caught the subtleties. And these birds, Perkins - beautiful.'

'It'll help tame and impound this leggy bastard,' shouted Gibbs, pointing at the specialty behemoth.

'Be rational, boy. And by "rational" I mean the condition which will exist when we're finished here and have all calmed down.'

Up the driveway the piano dragged its stomach, its lid slamming open and closed with a sheen like black glass. The Sarge glimpsed sinews of octavial wires as he approached. 'Resistance harvests excitement from the dynamic tension, lads,' he said. 'And it builds up the balls.'

'Really, sarge?'

'That's right, Ripper.' The Sarge vaulted over the creature's legs and hit the flatbed of its back. 'Tilted marvels viewed on the level, they are marvels still!'

The hulking beast began to balk.

Waste messes up your life, the Sarge was thinking, quite placidly. *Action. Remember it. Remember.*

More troops scurried up and put the boot in as the Sarge continued to rodeo. 'I attack,' said Gibbs. 'Barracks twinkle with apprehension.'

This retinue of jellyheads could be strangled by joined-up writing, thought the Sarge in the calm oasis of his head. *But a statement can be a set of triangulation coordinates. It won't necessarily make sense where you are - it points to the place where it'll line up perfect and ring like a bell. Those places are usually quite interesting. Ofcourse, this is a luxury and of no use if you're hungry or in danger. Yes, I'm really a fortunate man.*

And suddenly the beast went still beneath him, all becalmed. The lads stepped back as their leader climbed down from the creature's back and drew up an empty crate, sitting before the keyboard. The spider sat low as though dead and dry, its legs clawed in underneath. 'Here we go, Gibbs,' said the Sarge, and began to play, singing the difficult translation of *Four Sky Code*:

> *every time we stride*
> *our many legs collide*
> *look to science*
> *to exterminate us and our kind*
> *Three hundred puppets with one voice!*
> *There's an endorsement*
>
> *and fear may stop for breath*
> *but I'll continue biting your face*
> *for I am the law*
> *clamping hard to my wages.*
> *You will solve all my problems.*
> *Three hundred puppets with one voice!*
> *I must claim they are different*
>
> *my face is too close*
> *for you to remain undiseased.*
> *You will solve my dilemma.*
> *Take this terrible duty from me*
> *I will pay you a small stipend.*

Three hundred puppets with one voice!
Report it as their victory

'Oh yes,' he said, concluding with relish. 'Heaven grills a ladybug
- top of the summer!'

'We love you, sarge. Hooray for the sarge: a geezer!'

Under a sickly, forensic sky, riggers were already striking the big
tent. A ramped stage had been set up before the frontage of Rudloe
Manor. Barny and the Mayor stood upon it, crowded by some stinking orchid arrangements. The populace, tempted by the false promise of 'dogs with merry eyes and ears of velvet, and the quiet and pri-
vacy to enjoy such charms', was already growing suspicious and
restless. Beltane Carom had a venomous yellow headache. It had
been exhausting, sucking up the shadow where the other man was
stored, and then the split. Now both Beltane and Prancer stood
drained and quavery, spectating from opposite sides of the stage.
Neither cast a shadow.

Karloff mounted the stage in a cloth-of-gold robe and arcane
cuffs for effect. His wraparound hat revolved ever upward. Rudloe
immediately snapped at him. 'You've got some explaining to do!'

'How do you feel?' asked Karloff, bland and affable.

'Like a fried maggot, if you must know. The worse for having to
contain m'sizzling rage.'

'Why are you in a bad temper, Nelly?'

'Your diverse cavorts and bagatelles damn near ripped my head
off! And don't call me Nelly!'

'You wouldn't even begin to understand the real reason we do
these things. But even you knew it was an imprudent challenge.'

'Imprudent? It was hell! Everyone here saw it and some were taking detailed notes!'

'Carnival critics. Their praise has paralysed my work. But I suppose you call that democracy.'

'Democracy is the whisper of a near-dead clown trapped beneath
a street grating, heard for one uncertain second and dismissed as a
laughable irrelevance.'

'Can I quote you on that, Mayor?'

'You bloody crook. You'll understand the sky between bars.'

'Shall we get on with this ridiculous ceremony?'

'Yes!' the Mayor agreed bitterly.

But before they could get started they had to watch a display of
Rooster's hydraulic pants - these he inflated with an industrial-
strength bellows and feed-pipe which he attached to his dungarees.

Both Rudloe and Karloff became increasingly impatient, and Rooster himself was clearly baffled. He gave a running commentary during the demonstration, the last few minutes of which was inaudible. Though the audible parts were rammed with contradictions and vagueries, most of the onlookers were too drunk to consider it a bad omen.

The Mayor bellied forward before he had decided which expression to wear, and the result was a sort of sweaty blank. 'Rooster there, going straight to the heart of things as usual. Farewell Rooster, you back out dressed brutally, Well, we've endured some corny routines over the last few days, and some of us have come to grief. I thank the Circus of the Heart's Shell for providing the public with another distracting consolation. Later on today, you will salute the needs of your leaders. And just as we provide a tent for your subsequent recovery, relationships too must be healed, which is what this ceremony is all about. You all know about the feud between Barny Juno here and the Fall Marshall, regarding the freedom of the winged and stepping animals of the earth, most of them quite lethal. The signs are that they have reached an agreement. Karloff Velocet will address you now, with his stark malevolence.'

'Thank you Mayor. Given the limitations of this wrecked parish our travelling company have provided you all a fine entertainment, if a little bit chancey.'

Ninety eyes locked closed against the speaker's bragging.

'Consider, I beg of you - you failures who thrive in this hotbed of lethargy and torpor - the mirths and upheavals we have shown you. The clown, his acrylic gob bending glumly downward. The spitter of fire and his threatening behaviour, his implied demand that you be impressed. The dead man drooping from bits of string. Those heroes have to live by clear practical rules, not by blear generalisations like you bastards. Or like Mayor Rudloe, who apparently feels he can zoom out of a cannon without any special effort.'

Rudloe butted in with a forced smile. 'I believed him in the crowd - I mistrusted him when his features advanced.'

'Your Mayor,' Karloff continued, waving what seemed to be a piece of rubbery ham for emphasis, 'having loused it up in grand style, blames me for his recent failure. Our contradictions annoy the tidy-minded. From worm one we have been ominous and said as much. We are the golden shame. Nothing must be left to chance.'

Behind Karloff, Barny tried to spot Chloe in the crowd. There was just the dog Help and a mass of folk standing idle. Edgy was there too, dressed in a sheet - he never missed a chance to see the Mayor talking gibberish. A few clowns were leading the Fatal Rhino up the ramp toward the podium.

On opposite sides of the stage, both Beltane Carom and Prancer Diego were shaking, the air around them fluttering with instability. Beltane realised the separation was feebly anchored. He couldn't keep it down. He and Prancer started to distort weirdly toward the stage, blots of flame flaring behind their teeth.

'I concede defeat,' Karloff was reciting, 'and honour my agreement with the halfwit Juno. My animals are his, and by ceremonially snogging the Fatal Rhino, he inherits ownership of them all. I have enjoyed inconveniencing you with my antics. I have often been called an idealist. In fact I am a killer and a criminal. As Violaine said, "muscle across rooms, through leagues of rage, veins full of grey wind, 'til murder is reached." Greatness is all.' He threw down the Moral Fibre with studied nonchalance, believing that the crowd knew and cared what it was. 'And many die as supposed greatness's lesser, fading echo.'

As Barny stepped forward to snog the rhino, Karloff reached the Wesley Kern Gun from under his golden robe and swept it at him.

On either side of the stage, Beltane and Prancer were stretching and multiplying toward eachother like soap bubbles - two distorting images trying to merge.

'From Sweeney,' Karloff said, finding the trigger. 'And from me.' Then a fleshy conflagration flooded in at him from two directions, trapping him like a bug in gum. Karloff's hat exploded, scattering glass and some brain matter over the assembly. The air was tainted with a plasma spritz and the stench of ozone. He was a standing, moaning mass of limbs and merged faces, his own stirred in with that of Beltane and Prancer. Two spines were visible, twisted around eachother like a giant DNA strand. The Wesley Kern gun was pushed through the arrangement like a sausage stick.

Beltane was alarmed. 'Flypaper!'

'Trapped like kings!' Prancer cried, laughing.

'Who'll protect Juno?'

The Karloff face was screaming. Barny stood by in mild confusion. The audience was surprised enough to applaud.

'Well,' Rudloe told them, hiding his slight bewilderment, 'that concludes the ceremony. Pick up any rubbish as you leave, please.'

Barny gave the rhino a quick peck on the cheek as Help skittered up and ate the Moral Fibre.

Like a funeral reversed in the sun's saturation, a curlicued and feathered procession tumbled through town with Barny at its head. Here was the simpleton whose garden was home to eight hundred eels, who flew upon a swan, whose trousers were alchemised to fallen trousers as he spoke words of sorcery, now proving tidiness an absurd and unnecessary myth. His core audience of affronted bastards found their eyes pinned open by a sort of vivid delirium of forms. A tiger the size of a car, a rhino like a tusken boulder, an elephant like walking drought earth, a panther as sleek as a seal and black as a beetle, a crocodile with teeth the size of Brazil nuts, cow-print zebras and paper-headed birds like rod-puppets, a living tumble of fur and biology. Crowded species were flowing together, mates and foes mixed as though crayoned by a kid, wed in tooth and claw like saints beyond nameable colour.

Outnumbered by undulating detail, Barny drew to a halt at the gate to his house. Nothing remained but the gate, some rubble and a burst sofa on which Gregor lay, bruised and bandaged and covered in leeches.

Barny's bland countenance drained out. 'Is that all there is?' he said. 'Gregor?'

'Except these slugs ... oh, my lovers!'

'Gregor, what's the matter with you - slugs?'

'They applied themselves to my wounds and now I adore them.'

'Oh,' Barny said, already distracted. He was wax-pale against the golden coat of new lions.

'Bubba?' Gregor was calling as Barny wandered away. The animals, not knowing where to go, gathered amiably around the couch, where Gregor was sitting up in gradual anxiety.

13

ROLL AWAY THE STONE

Lucifer is a black glove we wear to hide our own fingerprints

Hearing about the public appearance of the Wesley Kern Gun, Chloe Low went to ask Karloff about it. What she found at the centre of the circus turmoil was a clumsy, tilting amalgam of Beltane Carom, Prancer Diego and the ringmaster. 'We're upping sticks, missy. Clearing out. Karloff's idea - my idea. It's his idea, Miss Low, he's got stuff to hide. Rather ironic, really. Then some meat was eaten by Help and fell under his fatal spell. Our flesh and blood is in debt to mother. Prancer, just shut up.'

'What happened to you, Beltane?'

'Me and Prancer couldn't stay divided long and good old Karloff here got in the middle. He was about to shoot Barny and everyone else, as far as we could tell. As many people as I could, anyway.' This last was added by Karloff himself, his head melded with that of Prancer. At the joining point was an eye with a twin pupil like a black double egg. 'Life is never the whole story. We're sorry we can't give you back the gun but as you see ...' The triple man gestured to the rigidly impaled rifle.

The carriages of the loco vimana had been re-coupled and loading was almost complete. A withered clown stumbled over holding a wooden frame stretched with skin. Stitched into the centre of this contraption were some bone fragments and teeth.

'Is Barny all right?' Chloe asked.

'He went off with the animals,' said Karloff, and wheeled the whole body about to view the exit frame. 'That'll do. Put it over there. All aboard!' Beltane turned the body to Chloe. 'Goodbye, Miss Low. You'll have to take care of your Juno now, if you can. Most pupils teach the same thing back, eager to please, but not him. In this age, an honest man is like a grenade thrown into a crowd.'

Fang took a last look and boarded the creep train with his brothers. Clowns, tumblers, huxters and hoosiers leapt aboard, including several local mimes desperate to escape persecution. These were shoved out as Karloff-Beltane-Prancer stepped up to the head engine and activated the massive rack of spectral palladium valves. The train shunted off with the pale stares of geeks at the windows, accelerating toward Grapefruit Integrity Swoon Street and the framed fragments of Rod Jayrod's head. The hull of black and gold was already blurring as the engine hit the exit frame and the scarship streamed behind a hole in the air, disappearing in a blast of goofer exhaust.

Chloe went to Barny's house and found only a dusty lot, a smashed sofa and the bug-eyed Golden Sid sort of casting about amid the trash in bent spectacles, his gob a howling hole already emptied of sense. Sid had worked for Barny for years taking care of the animals and now seemed lost. He pointed to the southwest, sobbing.

'This car is some sort of passenger thing.'

'That's what I've been *telling* you, doomed Eddie Gallo.'

'Those head swords of yours are dripping vinegar everywhere.'

'Pay *attention*, doomed Eddie Gallo. Unclip the jump cables. *God Almighty!*' Inside Gaffer's steepled head was a mind like a dead tooth. He tried to rub some vitality into the emptiness as doomed Eddie

Gallo stood vacantly with the jump clips hanging from his hand like dead snakes.

The muscle car they were fussing around in the garage bay was painted fire-apple red and had a hood ornament like a syringe. Max Gaffer was already in the passenger seat when the Abblatia angel appeared in the inner office doorway, its half-open wings skimming the frame. 'Every forty minutes I shock it off a stainless steel donut coil.'

'Eh?' Gaffer snapped, taken by surprise. 'Er, well why?'

'It would seem appropriate that I do so.'

'Appropriate.' Gaffer chuckled, relaxing a little at the angel's ineffectiveness. 'There's what you get from dying on a budget, eh, doomed Eddie Gallo?'

Gallo waved amiably at the angel. 'Hello Mike Abblatia.'

'Hello doomed Eddie Gallo. An artist pulls love from chaos.'

'I hear you, my friend. Max Gaffer here is full of ideas.'

'Get in the car, doomed Eddie Gallo,' the demon lawyer told him, leaning under the dash and sparking the hotwires.

'Right-o,' said Gallo, getting into the passenger seat all jolly as the engine fired up.

'Are you stealing this vehicle, then?' asked the angel calmly.

'It's not all bottled endings and laughter, Abblatia,' shouted Max Gaffer above the roar. 'That's a pigment of your imagination. Go to hell.' And whooping, he swerved the car across the forecourt and into the street, driving away.

Gaffer steered with one hand and raised a megaphone with the other, blaring. 'Doomed Eddie Gallo. His philosophy is reputed to have marvellously restorative powers when ignored. Get down honkies.' He turned to Gallo without lowering the megaphone and blasted. 'That'll hook those bastards and their rotted-out principles.' Sticking his head out the window, he told the town that 'Gallo will now jump the canyon in the most daring venture to oh I can't be bothered.' He threw the hailer aside as they arrived at the fragile ramp of rich tea biscuits.

The only onlookers were two children - one made of tin, one made of gilled meat. 'I got my invite,' Maquette called, waving.

Gaffer, becoming only vaguely aware that some of the gears were off at odd angles, backed up a way, lining up on the ramp. They sat there, the engine turning over. 'Well, doomed Eddie Gallo?'

Gaffer was feeling the floor. 'This picture carpet is full of ink.'

'Shall we go, Gallo?'

Gallo looked ahead at the twisted ramp. 'It's what I've worked towards, I suppose. Alright. Push the button, Max.'

With the hum of servitors and meat valves firing, the view accelerated into stretched geography. The car surged forward, dragging lightning behind it.

As the kids watched, it balked on to the ramp, rocketed above the abyss, convulsed and disappeared in mid-air.

The car was bouncing through billowing twists of pain and cold entropy, an icily transparent universe of sickly nerves. The vehicle they had stolen was a scarcar with pig-trotter indicators and a baffler stuffed with discredited passes. They were firing down the etheric creep lanes, flashing past dead dimensional port authorities of necrotic grey. White razorbahns tumbled toward the windshield and fluxions beat the panelling. Swelling into view ahead and to the right was Karloff's vimana train, the hull's gold running to liquid.

'I didn't bring any biscuits,' said doomed Eddie Gallo.

'What?' shouted the lawyer, his form a silhouette as fizzing incineration lashed past the window. He had never been this far out before. 'Are you aware of our situation, doomed Eddie Gallo?'

The shrinking locomotive powered out of their lane's bandwidth, venting goofer fuel and sending a chilling wallop through their skulls. They began to fluoresce. Barbed ropes glowed amid them. These were delirium organs, ghostly until required, exclusively toxic. Now they glittered into solidity, corrosive absence gone rampant. 'Er, wait a minute for really strident strategy yelling,' Gallo cautioned the blurring labyrinth, holding up a momentary hand and clearing his throat. Then he hollered '*Help me!*', his mouth tromboning like an old cartoon. Shrivelled highways clobbered up over the hood, exploding both windshields.

'It's too late for all that,' snapped the lawyer, blue ice flames tearing across his metal faceplate. Max Gaffer had taken his bearings by a constellation of crappy ideas and now rushed pell-mell to a bog-standard doom. 'Sorry, Gallo,' he said, and his head blew apart, scattering through the empty rear window.

Gallo looked aside at the headless driver. Part of the smile bridle hung on, flapping like a tow bar.

The vehicle was calming a little, the channel walls becoming visible. Doomed Eddie Gallo saw nested bones, demons up on blocks and the hanging threads of civilization, then the car coughed into open space, dirty oxygen flying beside the door. With a jarring smash, the car was scudding to a halt in a slash of white dust.

Shaken, doomed Eddie Gallo climbed out of the scarcar into a wasteland of dry riverbed diagrams. Golf balls and pebbles cracked in the desert. A parched feral scream cut through the poison air from nearby. It was the sound of bandages over bones, a shelled species of raw survival.

On some scrubby desolation a little way east of the boneseed factory, the blood shed was doing strong business. It was a corrugated structure covered in pepperbird droppings and painted-over Cyrilist slogans. Only a metal chimney against a bush suggested that anything lay underground.

The Mayor passed the line of citizens who were queuing to give, ignored the levy pumps and slipped through a hidden door, entering the antique elevator. Underground, he walked down the silverine hallway and entered the chamber of the Conglomerate. The intake pumps were jumping with each pulse of fluid, feeding the flushed biomass which filled the room. 'Ah, extraction day. It's a very good year, Mayor.' Several other voiced agreed, chuckling glutinously.

'I want to penalise the Church of Automata for hiring out those mechanical spiders.'

'The Church of Automata? A production line built from human bones? I doubt they'll feel much abashed. And the community's always seen the Spiders as an outside threat. Distraction's good for them and good for us. Not one brown penny will be spent on their longterm happiness.'

'Events themselves sit on the fence,' said another mouth amid the bulging biology. 'We need an occasional occasion. Don't you think?'

'Yes, yes, no, you're right, yes. What about Karloff?'

'Recent evil is fickle. Evil grown from infant depths has a stronger foundation. How did you react to his antics?'

'I cared steadily, my reaction arranged beforehand.'

Rudloe glanced around at the palpitating walls and perspiring pipes. Everything was stained red.

'And did you enjoy the show, Mayor?'

Rudloe laughed uneasily. 'I'm not a common citizen.'

'Your duty - as a citizen - is to help us pretend we're not the bad guys. That you are not taxed under threat. That all are created equal. That our office is earned. That there is no luck or privilege. That there is justice. And this you have done as an example to all.'

'I may yet tell all,' said Rudloe quietly.

'Oh dear,' gurgled another voice. 'He was doing so well.'

'I will,' said Rudloe, attempting truculence. 'I'll walk over there like nothing you've ever seen, and tell them where the blood goes.'

'See what it changes, when you tell the truth to cowards. We've been gnawing the meat from the floating rib of this province for years. Today, if I'm not mistaken, you flicked away your last vestige of dignity like a bit of rolled snot. You are ready to join us.'

The Mayor sensed a trap. 'Join you.'

'Now now, don't thank us - you've earned it.'

The Mayor stared at the steaming elite in stricken silence. Faced with the prospect of being incorporated into a multi-slob of farting blebs and stinking ligaments, his mind's grasp was slippery. The translucent wall of a large stomach displayed a slosh of red liquid. The Conglomerate always joked about 'transparent government' - here it was. The pumps were hammering.

'Advance, Rudloe,' the voices chorused, and one added: 'Let's meet in the morgue and pull out all the stops. Whattya say?'

'You're raving.' Rudloe's voice trembled.

'Grow up, Mayor - leave deniability behind. Know the truth, freeing the relief and tragedy at once.'

Rudloe took a step forward. 'Is a thing freed by knowing it?'

'It helps one's strategy to know the truth of a situation. Gallo or someone can take over, so long as the machinery's the same. He's a useful idiot, a fully paid-up moron. Even by the smart an accurate conclusion may always be adroitly avoided.'

Rudloe slipped in gore, yelping. He lunged for a handhold, his arm plunging into jellied meat. Then he felt it being sucked in solid until he was up to the elbow. His face began to push into the flubbering guts. 'You're nothing but gall and greed!' he blurted in a rush of candour, just before his mouth filled with blood and transparent fat.

'Just keep telling yourself that, Mayor. Structure is imposed. There is no centre - it needn't hold. We make our own centre. We take.'

Rudloe lay suspended in the slicks, veins threading through him, sumps bypassing his alimentary system. He screamed into meat.

Maybe Chloe was right, Barny had thought - he should do some of these things that people seemed to want, that normal people took for granted. He would do his social duty and then drop by the recovery tent.

He felt strange as he waited in line. There didn't seem to be any animals around here; no birds sang. Hammering machinery sounded from the metal shed. Barny noticed that BB Henrietta was in line in front of him. 'Hello BB.'

'Barny. I heard you stood up in the town square and shrieked racial abuse till the cows came home.'

'Did I?'

'Yes.'

'Oh.'

'Not a good idea, Boo. You'll find that strangers, up close, become more craggy, but remain strangers.'

Pale, shaky people wandered out and past them. The line shuffled forwards and he and BB were inside.

'Best avoided then? Strangers?'

'Yes.' She saw a cubicle vacate and grimaced nervously. 'Oh, this is me. See you later.' She went into a pump booth and closed the door.

Barny felt lonely. He found himself wishing Mr Low, Chloe's father, were here to talk to.

A booth was vacated and Barny went over, feeling strange. He closed the door behind him and lay back on the oblique-angled surgical table. Relationships too must be healed, he remembered from somewhere. A glass ribcage closed upon him, two racks of spikes piercing his body. Barny was surprised at how much it hurt. The glass turned dark red as blood began to exit.

Barny was seeing warm smoke moving through his head. He thought of the hot fur of bears in the sun. He was feeling unfocussed, couldn't pin any information down. It was like his mind had disappeared, leaving closed eyes and a body. He wandered over thoughts of his animals, Help's lipsticked face, Gregor resting finally on the lion's head and the leopard raking open Edgy's cheek at a jaunty angle. Edgy laughing fit to burst, Dumbar's placental head, Fang snogging bat after bat in the sorting office, Beltane Carom in his garden, a current of slow liquid flowing from one to the other of his raised hands. Mister Braintree yawning like an adder. Maquette and Spooky Staring Boy among the dreamspores and activans of the Shop. The Mayor, growing redder and fatter than the town. Mr Low, he could see him clearly - an old man pure as old water, his corrugated forehead, the stitching of wrinkles around his eyes, teeth like sunflower seeds and a parchment voice. 'A riot of nature is the definition of a riot.' Chloe's perfectly pale face moving with a smile. Everything moved slowly, strange tastes staining space, clouds fighting over the sky, fogs rolling the land in darkness, numbness among nothing else.

Barny's own face was sucking in, ageing as tissues imploded. No overlevy warning sounded, because it never did. Only a clean-up crew was alerted.

A vermilion rain was falling in the gutty cellar. The huge coral abdomen heaved. Rudloe's thick tongue caught ruby drips from above and retracted into the mass. 'So regret me.'

'What, you don't like it?'

'No, I like it, I like it ...'

'There are no secrets between us anymore, I hope.'

'How can there be?' laughed Rudloe, a smear in the bloodshot anatomy. 'And why do the work of hiding? That's the point.'

'The point,' jabbered the other voices, echoing in a flurry of corpuscles. 'He has one, after all.'

'That a lie will find itself surrounded by competition. Maybe that's not the business to be in. Point taken.'

A ripple passed through the Conglomerate, rubbery guts flubbering. It reared, weak veils of pink membrane tearing. The mass stretched toward the north wall and surged through the entrance to the ancient pipe which long ago donated a miniscule token of the levy to the blood clock.

Dry dirt spuffed up in a trail passing Spacey's Gas Station, Del's Fright Foundry and a goat waiting for a taxi. The Conglomerate passed under the town square and ascended into Rudloe Manor, infecting the architecture and blotting every room with a shrieking hurricane of blood. Pouring down the pipes and gutters of the blood clock, the crimson committee burst from the eaves, clotting across the palace facade like knotty red gargoyles. A dozen sticky meat faces stretched and mouthed from the stonework. 'Why hide? Let our citizens do the pretending. It's what they want.'

Chloe met Edgy in Butane Reply Street. He was pushing a cart bearing Gregor and a metal keg. 'Hello Chloe,' said Edgy. 'Can you spot the relief in my face? I've given up on society at last and am pushing Gregor around in a cart.'

'Where's Barny?'

'He left Gregor surrounded by woolly monsters. Gregor ran as fast as his arms and legs could take him. Baying pursuers have always been the key to staying slim.'

'Except in my case,' Gregor said. 'I weigh more and believe less.'

'Your final state may be that of a dead whale,' Chloe observed.

'I'd like that.'

'Which way did Barny go?'

'He went all embryo on me. Followed the crowd toward the Blood Shed. Maybe he was going to pay.'

Chloe followed the violet grey of the sky toward the milking shed. When she reached the building the line had been exhausted. Only a couple of cubicles were occupied, and these occupants wilted out, leaving the building and heading for the recovery tent. Going outside into strange silence, Chloe stumbled across broken black tarmac hairy with weeds. She circled the tin building. Overgrown behind the shed lay broken bricks, rotten car tyres and dead sump equipment.

Two or three dry husks also lay here, like bundles of dark red sticks. These were levy skeletons, lives discarded in favour of the mechanism. Conceding to what was expected, Barny had died out of hand.

14

THE VIGIL (THE SEA)

Justice knows when it's not wanted

'Barny says you want a job here,' BB Henrietta nodded darkly. She bumped four closets closed and started pointing out features of interest in the dungeonlike basement of the sorting office. She gestured to the sweating walls. 'These barnacles - don't be tempted to prize them off the walls, they've been here for years and the meat is way tough and tastes bitter. That bracket fungus over there has a mouth containing a set of gnashers, you can feed it raisins if you like.' Flipping a hand at some black bats in the eaves, she gave a withering look. 'Those are wall-warmers, smackerbats. To keep you from getting lonely, if you know what I mean. The thermostat is a marshmallow, that should give you an idea of the way we do things down here. Oh these dangling soft bladders are just for show.' She pointed at Dumbar, who sat in a dim corner, his placental head sagging aside. 'Mr Airbag Head over there - his head's full of rain, so what? Aren't you even remotely interested in the particulars of the job?'

'Yes, I am,' the Beast Man assured her quickly.

'Stuff comes down the delivery chute on to the long sorting table here. You take a hold of the stuff, and depending on the size and shape, get rid of it one way or another. If you don't know what to do, if you're not sure about anything, say "Lizards crowd the censor". That's code for us to start ignoring you, or keep ignoring you if we are already. Say it enough and you may not even get paid. Our boss is the Captain. Bloody cheek treating us with such understanding. Enthusiasm's at a premium round here. Think coldly about this place and all your memories, and you'll be respectable enough.'

Dugway Thrax looked at the watercooler - three pale scorpions scuttled at the bottom of the tank. 'How do we get rid of the ... "stuff"?'

'Oh, burn it, eat it, drive it over a cliff in a dodgy Anglia, whatever you can think of, really. The best way is the Drop over here - a sort of vacuum vortex.' She pointed at a large open corner of pinwheeling darkness. 'Sometimes you need to soften stuff up before you chuck it in there. And this is Gregor's oven, from when he used to work here. Around noon the boiler flames red.'

'Does that matter?'

'Not really. Trip on the secret slices if you want to fall. Sorry if I'm going over stuff you already know or what's obvious.'

'Thanks, Miss Henrietta,' Thrax said with a shapeless apprehension.

Several boxes and bundles pushed through some bacon hangings and slid down the delivery chute, barging onto the sorting table. 'Grab the big one!' BB shouted, and began stoking up the furnace. 'Into the Drop!'

Thrax looked at the wooden crate. 'There's Barny Juno's name written on here. And "Ladderland", isn't that where he lives?'

'Never mind what's written on it, get rid of the damn thing and quick about it!' she shouted, cranking a black handle in blasts of steam. 'Yours not to reason why! Where's the sense in crowing about detail and duty! Just do it!'

'Eh?'

'Soften it up with a few kicks, then into the Drop! And the rest of that stuff!'

The Beast Man booted the crate a few times without inspiration, denting it in, then kicked it skidding into the Drop. It fell out of sight.

So this is the white-collar world, he thought, and remembered a saying of Violaine: 'Work keeps you occupied during the period of your life when you might be achieving something.'

Sweeney was folded and compressed like a bloom packed in a bud. But now he found himself weightless and without direction, feeling something new which aged instantly. As he extended his many legs into a ghostburnt vacuum, the crate fragments floating away from him, he looked into blasts of detergent like a recurring white sunset. Opinions, crumbs and insignificance slashed past his skull-cowling in a grey blizzard. He'd got off at the wrong end of the universe. This was a realm of results and grievances, gritty smithereens, the essence of the human world. Their vacuum was far superior to his, receding past zero into the negative. What he was feeling was boredom. 'We're downright colourful by comparison. At least we've got a sense of theatre.' He suddenly saw the answer with absolute clarity. 'We got it wrong ... we're not the enemy. We just gathered another centre to ourselves.' He tried to breathe, falling away into the scratch and glint of empty commotion.

The epicine demon Rammstein fretted in the cavern, pacing like a parrot. Sweeney had been gone too long and a stumped throne was wrong, wrong - something had thinned and broken.

The light changed, flensing his shadow into flickering feathers. He knelt, drained and feeble.

The colossal bleeding throne began to pulse, sprouting a set of massive blades. Spinning like a top, it unfolded a body of recurrences, snipping barbs and gripping hooks, spraying sizzling blood like a catherine wheel. It slowed, hissing, limbs still agitated, a morass of agonies heaving at its heart. Eyes slammed open in the black hull.

EH Hunt watched a jellyfish full of broken veins swim off into the chilling, darkening sea. Stars like thorns pushed through above as he prepared to cast off. But the crowd of animals which had joined Mister Braintree was no longer content to watch from the dissolving seawalls and had begun wandering aboard, settling in as though at home. 'This leopard is seemingly intent on carrying my trousers to the top of the sterncastle,' screamed Hunt to the Announcement Horse.

'Understandable,' chimed the iron steed, whose talent for inanimate pride now found full expression as the ship's figurehead. 'Since by your systematic theft you have created a floating replica of Ladderland.'

'Eh?'

'Where are you going, EH Hunt?' called Plantin Edge from the beach. He and Gregor had trolled up with some kind of battered whiskey still.

'How obvious must something be before one's mother doesn't say it?'

'Beyond.'

'You have your answer. I hunt big berths and terminal risks, strange stronger places and perhaps a whale with teeth as tall and hairy as a man. When they find recordings of my navigation sobs, they'll see the harrowing side. Did you ever think it'd be like this? Keep those bloody animals away from here!'

Another gaggle of wildlife was trailing toward the ramp. They were the circus animals, following their instinct for inconvenience. They tramped on-deck and began scrapping with the others.

Hunt hauled on mast ropes and the sails opened, dislodging several chimps. Midnight faces covered the mainsail. 'Obviously drawn in a studio,' Edgy remarked.

'What?' Hunt called, exasperated, and cast off. A panther leapt on to his back, clinging on until the Fatal Rhino hooked it away with a snorting toss of its horn. The ramp fell into the surf as the tall boat moved. Hunt didn't have any buoys so he used orange spacehoppers, guylines tied to their antlers. The ship hauled out between these, the hull passing through the sky of an urchin sleeping transparent in coral. 'All these winged and stepping animals that have suddenly become a part of my life - the vessel won't take the weight!' And he dragged his treasure chest across the deck to the rail, unlatching the lid and tipping it over - a gush of sea water poured out, joining the ocean. Hunt was screaming, demented, phlegm dripping from his beard as the ship moved off, its equine figurehead prowing into the spray.

The vessel was a tower of tumbling biology. As its caterwauling noise receded into the dark, Edgy and Gregor watched from the shore. 'So all was justly appointed and no-one was hurt,' said Edgy with satisfaction.

'How are we going to distribute these?' asked Gregor, holding a wadge of leaflets which proclaimed EDGY'S STILL BY THE SEA. HE WAITS ON YOU WITH HOT LUBRICATION.

'By hand, I suppose,' Edgy muttered. 'Through people's doors? There's no other system. We'll get Barny to help us. A week to worry, another to pine, a third to know we've wasted our time.'

On the bluff behind them an angel landed, fragile as a feather made of bone. Under a sky deep as grief it closed its silent white wings.

Edgy turned. 'Mike?'

The angel blinked its black eyes. 'I like it here. As Violaine said: "Paradise is individually reflexive -"'

- otherwise it might not be to everyone's taste. I had once pulled up the truth-sentence like a buried rope from the sand, hadn't I? But interrupting favoured myths is a hazardous undertaking. The sidelines swallow honest men, removing all but their eyes.

Watching the tall man, the round man, the angel, I decide I've been witness to enough. Now I cast my own ashes over my shoulder and try my luck in the sky.

A patch of dark in the night, the place dwindles. Insane at last, blood flowing from a dream. Taking my every effort in a ghost of a head, I shoot the works. My mind melts into tears, and I can't remember the first line.

THE BLANK ST.

IDIOT DROPS PANTS AT FUNEI

DANGEROUS simpleton Barny Juno bust out of all moral constraints yesterday by dropping his trousers during a traditional funeral ceremony. Juno was reading a eulogy for a dead lizard when the pants descended, smashing our society.

The lizard, a pet known as 'Mister Spiderman', was said by Barny Juno to be 'going to heaven'. As he said the words, his trousers fell as though freighted with the lad's evil.

Juno (pictured here with acquaintance GI Bill last year) has been responsible for a string of alarming incidents in Accomplice town and environs, including the recent 'rock-band frozen hen on the path' debacle in Court. Yesterday's funeral is merely the latest and most reckless of his stunts.

Several members of the Cannon Sect were present to protest at the sacrilege of burying the dead in the ground, and were among the spectators appalled and damaged by Juno's fantastic behaviour. "We all know Barny Juno as a sort of seacow, but there is a limit to the horrors we can allow just because he pitches up with a pig on a lead or something. I saw him rotating a flower and smiling with such glee I was sick

TEN CLUES

1. Covert agencies speak of a "useful idiot". Could they be talking about Rudloe or doomed Eddie Gallo - or both or neither?
2. Notice how Accomplice is described (or not) by people who have been outside it.
3. What links the contents of the chest, Sweeney's throne, the Mayorship and the Conglomerate? Where is the centre?
4. Notice how Accomplice is described by people who are old.
5. "... on the way to people's breakdowns" - how's Barny?
6. Listen to Dietrich Hammerwire.
7. Who or what does the shaman help?
8. Hypocrisy is always harmful in Accomplice. Watch out for those close to Barny.
9. Violaine refers to "a black glove" and Gettysburg talks about "what brought me here" - do demons exist?
10. How many times is Barny seen after the levy in Book 4?

Dactylian mischief fiend.

nought will change - all is inward sprung.

27

The presence at caring is stand retrospectively & safely when nought can be done and the once distressed are dead.

The Errorverse

28

a costly disaster.

Your king is not a king to all living things.

The skittering mite -
Kemmat - Kimmit - Kermit

Poison is yet honest.

STEVE AYLETT IS ALSO THE AUTHOR OF LINT, SLAUGHTERMATIC, SHAMANSPACE, THE INFLATABLE VOLUNTEER, AND YOUR POINT IS?, ATOM, REBEL AT THE END OF TIME, FAIN THE SORCERER, THE CRIME STUDIO, TOXICOLOGY, NOVAHEAD and BIGOT HALL.

WWW.STEVEAYLETT.COM

"If you're going to make something light, be sure it contains the important parts of something heavy."

Bingo Violaine